Phantastes
and
Lilith

Phantastes
and
Lilith

by

George MacDonald

with an Introduction by

C. S. LEWIS

WM. B. EERDMANS PUBLISHING COMPANY
Grand Rapids, Michigan

PHANTASTES, first published, 1858

LILITH, first published, 1895

INTRODUCTION BY C. S. LEWIS*

All that I know of George MacDonald I have learned either from his own books or from the biography (*George MacDonald and his Wife*) which his son, Dr. Greville MacDonald, published in 1924; nor have I ever, but once, talked of him to anyone who had met him. For the very few facts which I am going to mention I am therefore entirely dependent on Dr. MacDonald.

We have learned from Freud and others about those distortions in character and errors in thought which result from a man's early conflicts with his father. Far the most important thing that we can know about George MacDonald is that his whole life illustrates the opposite process. An almost perfect relationship with his father was the earthly root of all his wisdom. From his own father, he said, he first learned that Fatherhood must be at the core of the universe. He was thus prepared in an unusual way to teach that religion in which the relation of Father and Son is of all relations the most central.

His father appears to have been a remarkable man — a man hard and tender and humorous all at once, in the old fashion of Scotch Christianity. He had had his leg cut off above the knee in the days before chloroform, refusing the customary dose of preliminary whiskey, and 'only for one moment, when the knife first transfixed the flesh, did he turn his face away and ejaculate a faint, sibilant *whiff*.' He had quelled with a fantastic joke at his own expense an ugly riot in which he was being burned in effigy. He forbade his son to touch a saddle until he had learned to ride well without one. He advised him

* This is a slightly abbreviated version of Dr. Lewis's Preface to *George MacDonald: an Anthology,* published by Geoffrey Bles in 1946. It is reproduced here by kind permission of Dr. Lewis and Messrs. Bles.

'to give over the fruitless game of poetry.' He asked from him, and obtained, a promise to renounce tobacco at the age of twenty-three. On the other hand he objected to grouse shooting on the score of cruelty and had in general a tenderness for animals not very usual among farmers more than a hundred years ago; and his son reports that he never, as boy or man, asked him for anything without getting what he asked. Doubtless this tells us as much about the son's character as the father's. ' He who seeks the Father more than anything he can give, is likely to have what he asks, for he is not likely to ask amiss.' The theological maxim is rooted in the experiences of the author's childhood. This is what may be called the 'anti-Freudian predicament' in operation.

George MacDonald's family (though hardly his father) were of course Calvinists. On the intellectual side his history is largely a history of escape from the theology in which he had been brought up. Stories of such emancipation are common in the Nineteenth Century; but George MacDonald's story belongs to this familiar pattern only with a difference. In most such stories the emancipated person, not content with repudiating the doctrines, comes also to hate the persons of his forebears, and even the whole culture and way of life with which they are associated. Thus books like *The Way of All Flesh* come to be written; and later generations, if they do not swallow the satire wholesale as history, at least excuse the author for a one-sidedness which a man in his circumstances could hardly have been expected to avoid. Of such personal resentment I find no trace in MacDonald. It is not we who have to find extenuating circumstances for his point of view. On the contrary, it is he himself, in the very midst of his intellectual revolt, who forces us, whether we will or no, to see elements of real and perhaps irreplaceable worth in the thing from which he is revolting.

All his life he continued to love the rock from which he had been hewn. All that is best in his novels carries us back to that 'kaleyard' world of granite and heather, of bleaching greens beside burns that look as if they flowed not with water but with stout, to the thudding of wooden machinery, the oatcakes, the fresh milk, the pride, the poverty, and the passionate love of hard-won learning. His best characters are those which reveal how much real charity and spiritual wisdom can co-exist with the profession of a theology that seems to encourage neither. His own grandmother, a truly terrible old woman who had burnt his uncle's fiddle as a Satanic snare, might well have appeared to him as what is now (inaccurately) called 'a mere sadist.' Yet when something very like her is delineated in *Robert Falconer* and again in *What's Mine's Mine,* we are compelled to look deeper — to see, inside the repellent crust something that we can whole-heartedly pity and even, with reservations, respect. In this way MacDonald illustrates, not the doubtful maxim that to know all is to forgive all, but the unshakeable truth that to forgive is to know. He who loves, sees.

He was born in 1824 at Huntly in Aberdeenshire and entered King's College at Aberdeen in 1840. In 1842 he spent some months in the North of Scotland cataloguing the library of a great house which has never been identified. I mention the fact because it made a life-long impression on MacDonald. The image of a great house seen principally from the library and always through the eyes of a stranger or a dependent (even Mr. Vane in *Lilith* never seems at home in the library which is called his) haunts his books to the end. It is therefore reasonable to suppose that the 'great house in the North' was the scene of some important crisis or development in his life. Perhaps it was here that he first came under the influence of German Romanticism.

In 1850 he received what is technically known as a 'Call' to become the Minister of a dissenting chapel in Arundel. By 1852 he was in trouble with the 'deacons' for heresy, the charges being that he had expressed belief in a future state of probation for heathens and that he was tainted with German theology. The deacons took a roundabout method to be rid of him, by lowering his salary — it had been £150 a year and he was now married — in the hope that this would induce him to resign. But they had misjudged their man. MacDonald merely replied that this was bad enough news for him but that he supposed he must try to live on less. And for some time he continued to do so, often helped by the offerings of his poorest parishioners who did not share the views of the more prosperous Deacons. In 1853, however, the situation became impossible. He resigned and embarked on the career of lecturing, tutoring, occasional preaching, writing, and 'odd jobs' which was his lot almost to the end. He died in 1905.

His lungs were diseased and his poverty was very great. Literal starvation was sometimes averted only by those last moment deliverances which agnostics attribute to chance and Christians to Providence. It is against this background of reiterated failure and incessant peril that some of his writing can be most profitably read. His resolute condemnations of anxiety come from one who has a right to speak; nor does their tone encourage the theory that they owe anything to the pathological wishful thinking — the *spes phthisica* — of the consumptive. None of the evidence suggests such a character. His peace of mind came not from building on the future but resting in what he called 'the holy Present.' His resignation to poverty was at the opposite pole from that of the stoic. He appears to have been a sunny, playful man, deeply appreciative of all really beautiful and delicious things that money can buy, and no less deeply content to do without them. It is perhaps significant — it is certainly touching — that his chief recorded weakness was a Highland love of finery; and he was all his life hospitable as only the poor can be.

If we define Literature as an art whose medium is words, then certainly MacDonald has no place in its first rank — perhaps not even in its second. There are indeed passages where the wisdom and (I would dare to call it) the holiness that are in him triumph over and even burn away the baser elements in his style: the expression becomes precise, weighty, economic; acquires a cutting edge. But he does not maintain this level for long. The texture of his writing as a whole is undistinguished, at times fumbling. Bad pulpit traditions cling to it; there is sometimes a nonconformist verbosity, sometimes an old Scotch weakness for florid ornament (it runs right through them from Dunbar to the Waverley Novels), sometimes an over-sweetness picked up from Novalis. But this does not quite dispose of him even for the literary critic. What he does best is fantasy — fantasy that hovers between the allegorical and the mythopoeic. And this, in my opinion, he does better than any man. The critical problem with which we are confronted is whether this art — the art of myth-making — is a species of the literary art. The objection to so classifying it is that the Myth does not essentially exist in *words* at all. We all agree that the story of Balder is a great myth, a thing of inexhaustible value. But of whose version — whose *words* — are we thinking when we say this?

For my own part, the answer is that I am not thinking of any one's words. No poet, as far as I know or can remember, has told this story supremely well. I am not thinking of any particular version of it. If the story is anywhere embodied in words, that is almost an accident. What really delights and nourishes me is a particular pattern of events, which would equally delight and nourish if it had reached me by some medium which involved no words at all — a mime or silent film. And I find this to be true of all such stories. When I think of the story of the Argonauts and praise it I am not praising Apollonius Rhodius (whom I never finished) nor Kingsley (whom I have forgotten) nor even Morris, though I consider his version a very pleasant poem. In this respect stories of the mythical type are at the opposite pole from lyrical poetry. If you try to take the 'theme' of Keats' *Nightingale* apart from the very words in which he has embodied it, you find that you are talking about almost nothing. Form and content can there be separated only by a false abstraction. But in a myth — in a story where the mere pattern of events is all that matters — this is not so. Any means of communication whatever which succeeds in lodging those events in our imagination has, as we say, 'done the trick.' After that you can throw the means of communication away. To be sure, if the means of communication are words, it is desirable that they should be well chosen: just as it is desirable that a letter which brings you important news should be fairly written. But this is only a minor convenience; for the letter will, in any case, go into the waste paper basket as soon as you have mastered its contents, and the words (those of Lemprière would have done) are going to be forgotten as soon as you have mastered the Myth. In poetry the words are the body and the 'theme' or 'content' is the soul. But in myth the imagined events are the body and something inexpressible is the soul: the words, or mime, or film, or pictorial series are not even clothes — they are not much more than a telephone. Of this I had evidence some years ago when I first heard the story of Kafka's *Castle* related in conversation and afterwards read the book for myself. The reading added nothing. I had already received the myth, which was all that mattered.

Most myths were made in prehistoric times, and, I suppose, not consciously made by individuals at all. But every now and then there occurs in the modern world a genius — a Kafka or a Novalis — who can make such a story. MacDonald is the greatest genius of this kind whom I know. But I do not know how to classify such genius. To call it literary genius seems unsatisfactory since it can co-exist with great inferiority in the art of words — nay, since its connection with words at all turns out to be merely external and, in a sense, accidental. Nor can it be fitted into any of the other arts. It begins to look as if there were an art, or a gift, which criticism has largely ignored. It may even be one of the greatest arts; for it produces works which give us (at the first meeting) as much delight and (on prolonged acquaintance) as much wisdom and strength as the works of the greatest poets. It is in some ways more akin to music than to poetry or at least to most poetry. It goes beyond the expression of things we have already felt. It arouses in us sensations we have never had before, never anticipated having, as though we had broken out of our normal mode of consciousness and 'possessed joys not promised to our birth.' It gets under our skin, hits us at a level deeper than our thoughts or even our passions, troubles oldest certainties till all questions are re-opened, and in general shocks us more fully awake than we are for most of our lives.

It was in this mythopoeic art that MacDonald excelled. And from this it follows that his best art is least represented in the Anthology I prepared in 1946.* The great works are *Phantastes,* the *Curdie* bcoks, *The Golden Key, The Wise Woman,* and *Lilith.*

It must be more than thirty years ago that I bought — almost unwillingly, for I had looked at the volume on that bookstall and rejected it on a dozen previous occasions — the Everyman edition of *Phantastes.* A few hours later I knew that I had crossed a great frontier. I had already been waist deep in Romanticism; and likely enough, at any moment, to flounder into its darker and more evil forms, slithering down the steep descent that leads from the love of strangeness to that of eccentricity and thence to that of perversity. Now *Phantastes* was romantic enough in all conscience; but there was a difference. Nothing was at that time further from my thoughts than Christianity and I therefore had no notion what this difference really was. I was only aware that if this new world was strange, it was also homely and humble; that if this was a dream, it was a dream in which one at least felt strangely vigilant; that the whole book had about it a sort of cool, morning innocence, and also, quite unmistakably, a certain quality of Death, *good* Death. What it actually did to me was to convert, even to baptise (that was where the Death came in) my imagination. It did nothing to my intellect nor (at that time) to my conscience. Their turn came far later and with the help of many other books and men. But when the process was complete — by which, of course, I mean 'when it had *really* begun' — I found that I was still with MacDonald and that he had accompanied me all the way and that I was now at last ready to hear from him much that he could not have told me at that first meeting. But in a sense, what he was now telling me was the very same that he had told me from the beginning. There was no question of getting through to the kernel and throwing

* *George MacDonald: an Anthology* (Geoffrey Bles.)

away the shell: no question of a gilded pill. The pill was gold all through. The quality which had enchanted me in his imaginative works turned out to be the quality of the real universe, the divine, magical, terrifying and ecstatic reality in which we all live. I should have been shocked in my 'teens if anyone had told me that what I learned to love in *Phantastes* was goodness. But now that I know, I see there was no deception. The deception is all the other way round — in that prosaic moralism which confines goodness to the region of Law and Duty, which never lets us feel in our face the sweet air blowing from 'the land of righteousness,' never reveals that elusive Form which if once seen must inevitably be desired with all but sensuous desire — the thing (in Sappho's phrase) 'more gold than gold.'

C. S. LEWIS

PHANTASTES

A FAERIE ROMANCE

"Phantastes from 'their fount' all shapes deriving,
In new habiliments can quickly dight."
FLETCHER's *Purple Island.*

"Es lassen sich Erzählungen ohne Zusammenhang, jedoch mit Association, wie Träume, denken; Gedichte, die bloss wohlklingend und voll schöner Worte sind, aber auch ohne allen Sinn und Zusammenhang, höchstens einzelne Strophen verständlich, wie Bruchstücke aus den verschiedenartigsten Dingen. Diese wahre Poesie kann höchstens einen allegorischen Sinn im Grossen, und eine indirecte Wirkung, wie Musik haben. Darum ist die Natur so rein poetisch, wie die Stube eines Zauberers, eines Physikers, eine Kinderstube, eine Polterund Vorrathskammer....

"Ein Mährchen ist wie ein Traumbild ohne Zusammenhang. Ein Ensemble wunderbarer Dinge und Begebenheiten, z. B. eine Musikalische Phantasie, die harmonischen Folgen einer Aeolsharfe, die Natur selbst.

. . . .

"In einem echten Mährchen muss alles wunderbar, geheimnissvoll und zusammenhängend sein; alles belebt, jeder auf eine andere Art. Die ganze Natur muss wunderlich mit der ganzen Geisterwelt gemischt sein; hier tritt die Zeit der Anarchie, der Gesetzlosigkeit, Freiheit, der Naturstand der Natur, die Zeit vor der Welt ein. . . . Die Welt des Mährchens ist die, der Welt der Wahrheit durchaus entgegengesetzte, und eben darum ihr so durchaus ähnlich, wie das Chaos der vollendeten Schöpfung ähnlich ist."—NOVALIS.

CHAPTER I

"A spirit . . . .

.   .   .   .   .

> The undulating woods, and silent well,
> And rippling rivulet, and evening gloom,
> Now deepening the dark shades, for speech assuming,
> Held commune with him; as if he and it
> Were all that was."—SHELLEY's *Alastor*.

I AWOKE ONE MORNING with the usual perplexity of mind
which accompanies the return of consciousness. As I lay and
looked through the eastern window of my room, a faint streak
of peach-colour, dividing a cloud that just rose above the low
swell of the horizon, announced the approach of the sun. As
my thoughts, which a deep and apparently dreamless sleep had
dissolved, began again to assume crystalline forms, the strange
events of the foregoing night presented themselves anew to my
wondering consciousness. The day before had been my one-and-
twentieth birthday. Among other ceremonies investing me with
my legal rights, the keys of an old secretary, in which my father
had kept his private papers, had been delivered up to me. As
soon as I was left alone, I ordered lights in the chamber where
the secretary stood, the first lights that had been there for many
a year; for, since my father's death, the room had been left undisturbed. But, as if the darkness had been too long an inmate to
be easily expelled, and had dyed with blackness the walls to
which, bat-like, it had clung, these tapers served but ill to light
up the gloomy hangings, and seemed to throw yet darker
shadows into the hollows of the deep-wrought cornice. All the
further portions of the room lay shrouded in a mystery whose
deepest folds were gathered around the dark oak cabinet which
I now approached with a strange mingling of reverence and

curiosity. Perhaps, like a geologist, I was about to turn up to the light some of the buried strata of the human world, with its fossil remains charred by passion and petrified by tears. Perhaps I was to learn how my father, whose personal history was unknown to me, had woven his web of story; how he had found the world, and how the world had left him. Perhaps I was to find only the records of lands and moneys, how gotten and how secured; coming down from strange men, and through troublous times, to me, who knew little or nothing of them all.

To solve my speculations, and to dispel the awe which was fast gathering around me as if the dead were drawing near, I approached the secretary; and having found the key that fitted the upper portion, I opened it with some difficulty, drew near it a heavy high-backed chair, and sat down before a multitude of little drawers and slides and pigeon-holes. But the door of a little cupboard in the centre especially attracted my interest, as if there lay the secret of this long-hidden world. Its key I found. One of the rusty hinges cracked and broke as I opened the door : it revealed a number of small pigeon-holes. These, however, being but shallow compared with the depth of those around the little cupboard, the outer ones reaching to the back of the desk, I concluded that there must be some accessible space behind; and found, indeed, that they were formed in a separate framework, which admitted of the whole being pulled out in one piece. Behind, I found a sort of flexible portcullis of small bars of wood laid close together horizontally. After long search, and trying many ways to move it, I discovered at last a scarcely projecting point of steel on one side. I pressed this repeatedly and hard with the point of an old tool that was lying near, till at length it yielded inwards; and the little slide, flying up suddenly, disclosed a chamber—empty, except that in one corner lay a little heap of withered rose-leaves, whose long-lived scent had long since departed; and, in another, a small packet of papers, tied with a bit of ribbon, whose colour had gone with the rose-scent. Almost fearing to touch them, they witnessed so mutely to the law of oblivion, I leaned back in my chair, and regarded them for a moment; when suddenly there stood on the threshold of the little chamber, as though she had just emerged from its depth, a tiny woman-form, as perfect in shape as if she had been a small Greek statuette roused to life and motion. Her dress was of a kind that

could never grow old-fashioned, because it was simply natural :
a robe plaited in a band around the neck, and confined by a belt
about the waist, descended to her feet. It was only afterwards,
however, that I took notice of her dress, although my surprise
was by no means of so overpowering a degree as such an apparition might naturally be expected to excite. Seeing, however, as I
suppose, some astonishment in my countenance, she came forward within a yard of me, and said, in a voice that strangely
recalled a sensation of twilight, and reedy river banks, and a low
wind, even in this deathly room—

"Anodos, you never saw such a little creature before, did
you?"

"No," said I; "and indeed I hardly believe I do now."

"Ah! that is always the way with you men; you believe
nothing the first time; and it is foolish enough to let mere
repetition convince you of what you consider in itself unbeliev-
able. I am not going to argue with you, however, but to grant
you a wish."

Here I could not help interrupting her with the foolish speech,
of which, however, I had no cause to repent—

"How can such a very little creature as you grant or refuse
anything?"

"Is that all the philosophy you have gained in one-and-twenty
years?" said she. "Form is much, but size is nothing. It is a mere
matter of relation. I suppose your six-foot lordship does not feel
altogether insignificant, though to others you do look small beside
your old Uncle Ralph, who rises above you a great half-foot at
least. But size is of so little consequence with me, that I may as
well accommodate myself to your foolish prejudices."

So saying, she leapt from the desk upon the floor, where she
stood a tall, gracious lady, with pale face and large blue eyes.
Her dark hair flowed behind, wavy but uncurled, down to her
waist, and against it her form stood clear in its robe of white.

"Now," said she, "you will believe me."

Overcome with the presence of a beauty which I could now
perceive, and drawn towards her by an attraction irresistible as
incomprehensible, I suppose I stretched out my arms towards
her, for she drew back a step or two, and said—

"Foolish boy, if you could touch me, I should hurt you.
Besides, I was two hundred and thirty-seven years old, last

Midsummer eve; and a man must not fall in love with his grandmother, you know."

"But you are not my grandmother," said I.

"How do you know that?" she retorted. "I dare say you know something of your great-grandfathers a good deal further back than that; but you know very little about your great-grandmothers on either side. Now, to the point. Your little sister was reading a fairy-tale to you last night."

"She was."

"When she had finished, she said, as she closed the book, 'Is there a fairy-country, brother?' You replied with a sigh, 'I suppose there is, if one could find the way into it.'"

"I did; but I meant something quite different from what you seem to think."

"Never mind what I seem to think. You shall find the way into Fairy Land to-morrow. Now look in my eyes."

Eagerly I did so. They filled me with an unknown longing. I remembered somehow that my mother died when I was a baby. I looked deeper and deeper, till they spread around me like seas, and I sank in their waters. I forgot all the rest, till I found myself at the window, whose gloomy curtains were withdrawn, and where I stood gazing on a whole heaven of stars, small and sparkling in the moonlight. Below lay a sea, still as death and hoary in the moon, sweeping into bays and around capes and islands, away, away, I knew not whither. Alas! it was no sea, but a low fog burnished by the moon. "Surely there is such a sea somewhere!" said I to myself. A low sweet voice beside me replied—

"In Fairy Land, Anodos."

I turned, but saw no one. I closed the secretary, and went to my own room, and to bed.

All this I recalled as I lay with half-closed eyes. I was soon to find the truth of the lady's promise, that this day I should discover the road into Fairy Land.

CHAPTER II

" 'Wo ist der Strom?' rief er mit Thränen. 'Siehst du nicht seine blauen Wellen über uns?' Er sah hinauf, und der blaue Strom floss leise über ihrem Haupte."—Novalis, *Heinrich von Ofterdingen*.

" 'Where is the stream?' cried he, with tears. 'Seest thou not its blue waves above us?' He looked up, and lo! the blue stream was flowing gently over their heads."

WHILE THESE STRANGE events were passing through my mind, I suddenly, as one awakes to the consciousness that the sea has been moaning by him for hours, or that the storm has been howling about his window all night, became aware of the sound of running water near me; and looking out of bed, I saw that a large green marble basin, in which I was wont to wash, and which stood on a low pedestal of the same material in a corner of my room, was overflowing like a spring; and that a stream of clear water was running over the carpet, all the length of the room, finding its outlet I knew not where. And, stranger still, where this carpet, which I had myself designed to imitate a field of grass and daisies, bordered the course of the little stream, the grass-blades and daisies seemed to wave in a tiny breeze that followed the water's flow; while under the rivulet they bent and swayed with every motion of the changeful current, as if they were about to dissolve with it, and, forsaking their fixed form, become fluent as the waters.

My dressing-table was an old-fashioned piece of furniture of black oak, with drawers all down the front. These were elaborately carved in foliage, of which ivy formed the chief part. The nearer end of this table remained just as it had been, but on the further end a singular change had commenced. I happened to fix my eye on a little cluster of ivy-leaves. The first of these was evidently the work of the carver; the next looked curious; the third was unmistakably ivy; and just beyond it a tendril of clematis had twined itself about the gilt handle of one of the drawers. Hearing next a slight motion above me, I looked up, and saw that the branches and leaves designed upon the curtains of my bed were slightly in motion. Not knowing what change

might follow next, I thought it high time to get up; and, springing from the bed, my bare feet alighted upon a cool green sward;
and although I dressed in all haste, I found myself completing
my toilet under the boughs of a great tree, whose top waved in
the golden stream of the sunrise with many interchanging lights,
and with shadows of leaf and branch gliding over leaf and
branch, as the cool morning wind swung it to and fro, like a
sinking sea-wave.

After washing as well as I could in the clear stream, I rose and
looked around me. The tree under which I seemed to have lain
all night, was one of the advanced guard of a dense forest,
towards which the rivulet ran. Faint traces of a footpath, much
overgrown with grass and moss, and with here and there a
pimpernel even, were discernible along the right bank. "This,"
thought I, "must surely be the path into Fairy Land, which the
lady of last night promised I should so soon find." I crossed the
rivulet, and accompanied it, keeping the footpath on its right
bank, until it led me, as I expected, into the wood. Here I left it,
without any good reason, and with a vague feeling that I ought
to have followed its course : I took a more southerly direction.

CHAPTER III

"Man doth usurp all space,
  Stares thee, in rock, bush, river, in the face.
  Never yet thine eyes behold a tree;
  'Tis no sea thou seést in the sea,
  'Tis but a disguised humanity.
  To avoid thy fellow, vain thy plan;
  All that interests a man, is man."—HENRY SUTTON.

THE TREES, WHICH were far apart where I entered, giving
free passage to the level rays of the sun, closed rapidly as I
advanced, so that ere long their crowded stems barred the sunlight out, forming as it were a thick grating between me and the
East. I seemed to be advancing towards a second midnight. In
the midst of the intervening twilight, however, before I entered
what appeared to be the darkest portion of the forest, I saw a
country maiden coming towards me from its very depths. She did

not seem to observe me, for she was apparently intent upon a bunch of wild flowers which she carried in her hand. I could hardly see her face; for, though she came right towards me, she never looked up. But when we met, instead of passing, she turned and walked alongside of me for a few yards, still keeping her face downwards, and busied with her flowers. She spoke rapidly, however, all the time, in a low tone, as if talking to herself, but evidently addressing the purport of her words to me. She seemed afraid of being observed by some lurking foe. "Trust the Oak," said she; "trust the Oak, and the Elm, and the great Beech. Take care of the Birch, for though she is honest, she is too young not to be changeable. But shun the Ash and the Alder; for the Ash is an ogre—you will know him by his thick fingers; and the Alder will smother you with her web of hair, if you let her near you at night." All this was uttered without pause or alteration of tone. Then she turned suddenly and left me, walking still with the same unchanging gait. I could not conjecture what she meant, but satisfied myself with thinking that it would be time enough to find out her meaning when there was need to make use of her warning, and that the occasion would reveal the admonition. I concluded from the flowers that she carried, that the forest could not be everywhere so dense as it appeared from where I was now walking; and I was right in this conclusion. For soon I came to a more open part, and by-and-by crossed a wide grassy glade, on which were several circles of brighter green. But even here I was struck with the utter stillness. No bird sang. No insect hummed. Not a living creature crossed my way. Yet somehow the whole environment seemed only asleep, and to wear even in sleep an air of expectation. The trees seemed all to have an expression of conscious mystery, as if they said to themselves, "We could, an' if we would." They had all a meaning look about them. Then I remembered that night is the fairies' day, and the moon their sun; and I thought—Everything sleeps and dreams now : when the night comes, it will be different. At the same time I, being a man and a child of the day, felt some anxiety as to how I should fare among the elves and other children of the night who wake when mortals dream, and find their common life in those wondrous hours that flow noiselessly over the moveless death-like forms of men and women and children, lying strewn and parted beneath the weight of the heavy waves of night, which flow on and beat them down, and hold them drowned and senseless, until the ebb-tide comes, and the waves sink away, back into the ocean of the dark. But I took courage and went on. Soon, however, I became again anxious, though from another cause. I had eaten nothing that day, and for an hour past had been feeling the want of food. So I grew afraid lest I should find nothing to meet my human necessities in this strange place; but once more I comforted myself with hope and went on.

Before noon, I fancied I saw a thin blue smoke rising amongst the stems of larger trees in front of me; and soon I came to an open spot of ground in which stood a little cottage, so built that the stems of four great trees formed its corners, while their branches met and intertwined over its roof, heaping a great cloud of leaves over it, up towards the heavens. I wondered at finding a human dwelling in this neighbourhood; and yet it did not look altogether human, though sufficiently so to encourage me to expect some sort of food. Seeing no door, I went round to the other side, and there I found one, wide open. A woman sat beside it, preparing some vegetables for dinner. This was homely and comforting. As I came near, she looked up, and seeing me, showed no surprise, but bent her head again over her work, and said in a low tone—

"Did you see my daughter?"

"I believe I did," said I. "Can you give me something to eat, for I am very hungry?"

"With pleasure," she replied, in the same tone; "but do not say anything more, till you come into the house, for the Ash is watching us."

Having said this, she rose and led the way into the cottage; which, I now saw, was built of the stems of small trees set closely together, and was furnished with rough chairs and tables, from which even the bark had not been removed. As soon as she had shut the door and set a chair—

"You have fairy blood in you," said she, looking hard at me.

"How do you know that?"

"You could not have got so far into this wood if it were not so; and I am trying to find out some trace of it in your countenance. I think I see it."

"What do you see?"

"Oh, never mind : I may be mistaken in that."

"But how then do you come to live here?"

"Because I too have fairy blood in me."

Here I, in my turn, looked hard at her, and thought I could perceive, notwithstanding the coarseness of her features, and especially the heaviness of her eyebrows, a something unusual—I could hardly call it grace, and yet it was an expression that strangely contrasted with the form of her features. I noticed too that her hands were delicately formed, though brown with work and exposure.

"I should be ill," she continued, "if I did not live on the borders of the fairies' country, and now and then eat of their food. And I see by your eyes that you are not quite free of the same need; though, from your education and the activity of your mind, you have felt it less than I. You may be further removed too from the fairy race."

I remembered what the lady had said about my grandmothers.

Here she placed some bread and some milk before me, with a kindly apology for the homeliness of the fare, with which, however, I was in no humour to quarrel. I now thought it time to try to get some explanation of the strange words both of her daughter and herself.

"What did you mean by speaking so about the Ash?"

She rose and looked out of the little window. My eyes followed her; but as the window was too small to allow anything to be seen from where I was sitting, I rose and looked over her shoulder. I had just time to see, across the open space, on the edge of the denser forest, a single large ash-tree, whose foliage showed bluish, amidst the truer green of the other trees around it; when she pushed me back with an expression of impatience and terror, and then almost shut out the light from the window by setting up a large old book in it.

"In general," said she, recovering her composure, "there is no danger in the daytime, for then he is sound asleep; but there is something unusual going on in the woods; there must be some solemnity among the fairies to-night, for all the trees are restless, and although they cannot come awake, they see and hear in their sleep."

"But what danger is to be dreaded from him?"

Instead of answering the question, she went again to the window and looked out, saying she feared the fairies would be interrupted by foul weather, for a storm was brewing in the west.

"And the sooner it grows dark, the sooner the Ash will be awake," added she.

I asked her how she knew that there was any unusual excitement in the woods. She replied—

"Besides the look of the trees, the dog there is unhappy; and the eyes and ears of the white rabbit are redder than usual, and he frisks about as if he expected some fun. If the cat were at home, she would have her back up; for the young fairies pull the sparks out of her tail with bramble thorns, and she knows when they are coming. So do I, in another way."

At this instant, a gray cat rushed in like a demon, and disappeared in a hole in the wall.

"There, I told you!" said the woman.

"But what of the ash-tree?" said I, returning once more to the subject. Here, however, the young woman, whom I had met in the morning, entered. A smile passed between the mother and daughter; and then the latter began to help her mother in little household duties.

"I should like to stay here till the evening," I said; "and then go on my journey, if you will allow me."

"You are welcome to do as you please; only it might be better to stay all night, than risk the dangers of the wood then. Where are you going?"

"Nay, that I do not now," I replied; "but I wish to see all that is to be seen, and therefore I should like to start just at sundown."

"You are a bold youth, if you have any idea of what you are daring; but a rash one, if you know nothing about it; and, excuse me, you do not seem very well informed about the country and its manners. However, no one comes here but for some reason, either known to himself or to those who have charge of him; so you shall do just as you wish."

Accordingly I sat down, and feeling rather tired, and disinclined for further talk, I asked leave to look at the old book which still screened the window. The woman brought it to me directly, but not before taking another look towards the forest, and then drawing a white blind over the window. I sat down opposite to it by the table, on which I laid the great old volume,

and read. It contained many wondrous tales of Fairy Land, and
olden times, and the Knights of King Arthur's table. I read on
and on, till the shades of the afternoon began to deepen; for in
the midst of the forest it gloomed earlier than in the open
country. At length I came to this passage :—

"Here it chaunced, that upon their quest, Sir Galahad and
Sir Percivale rencountered in the depths of a great forest. Now,
Sir Galahad was dight all in harness of silver, clear and shining;
the which is a delight to look upon, but full hasty to tarnish, and
withouten the labour of a ready squire, uneath to be kept fair
and clean. And yet withouten squire or page, Sir Galahad's
armour shone like the moon. And he rode a great white mare,
whose bases and other housings were black, but all besprent with
fair lilys of silver sheen. Whereas Sir Percivale bestrode a red
horse, with a tawny mane and tail; whose trappings were all to-
smirched with mud and mire; and his armour was wondrous
rosty to behold, ne could he by any art furbish it again; so that
as the sun in his going down shone twixt the bare trunks of the
trees, full upon the knights twain, the one did seem all shining
with light, and the other all to glow with ruddy fire. Now it came
about in this wise. For Sir Percivale, after his escape from the
demon lady, whenas the cross on the handle of his sword smote
him to the heart, and he rove himself through the thigh, and
escaped away, he came to a great wood; and, in nowise cured
of his fault, yet bemoaning the same, the damosel of the alder-
tree encountered him, right fair to see; and with her fair words
and false countenance she comforted him and beguiled him,
until he followed her where she led him to a——"

Here a low hurried cry from my hostess caused me to look up
from the book, and I read no more.

"Look there!" she said. "Look at his fingers!"

Just as I had been reading in the book, the setting sun was
shining through a cleft in the clouds piled up in the west; and a
shadow as of a large distorted hand, with thick knobs and humps
on the fingers, so that it was much wider across the fingers than
across the undivided part of the hand, passed slowly over the
little blind, and then as slowly returned in the opposite direction.

"He is almost awake, mother; and greedier than usual
to-night."

"Hush, child; you need not make him more angry with us than

he is; for you do not know how soon something may happen to oblige us to be in the forest after nightfall."

"But you are in the forest," said I; "how is it that you are safe here?"

"He dares not come nearer than he is now," she replied; "for any of those four oaks, at the corners of our cottage, would tear him to pieces; they are our friends. But he stands there and makes awful faces at us sometimes, and stretches out his long arms and fingers, and tries to kill us with fright; for, indeed, that is his favourite way of doing. Pray, keep out of his way to-night."

"Shall I be able to see these beings?" said I.

"That I cannot tell yet, not knowing how much of the fairy nature there is in you. But we shall soon see whether you can discern the fairies in my little garden, and that will be some guide to us."

"Are the trees fairies too, as well as the flowers?" I asked.

"They are of the same race," she replied; "though those you call fairies in your country are chiefly the young children of the flower fairies. They are very fond of having fun with the thick people, as they call you; for, like most children, they like fun better than anything else."

"Why do you have flowers so near you then? Do they not annoy you?"

"Oh, no, they are very amusing, with their mimicries of grown people, and mock solemnities. Sometimes they will act a whole play through before my eyes, with perfect composure and assurance, for they are not afraid of me. Only, as soon as they have done, they burst into peals of tiny laughter, as if it was such a joke to have been serious over anything. These I speak of, however, are the fairies of the garden. They are more staid and educated than those of the fields and woods. Of course they have near relations amongst the wild flowers, but they patronise them, and treat them as country cousins, who know nothing of life, and very little of manners. Now and then, however, they are compelled to envy the grace and simplicity of the natural flowers."

"Do they live *in* the flowers?" I said.

"I cannot tell," she replied. "There is something in it I do not understand. Sometimes they disappear altogether, even from me, though I know they are near. They seem to die always with the flowers they resemble, and by whose names they are called; but whether they return to life with the fresh flowers, or, whether it be new flowers, new fairies, I cannot tell. They have as many sorts of dispositions as men and women, while their moods are yet more variable; twenty different expressions will cross their little faces in half-a-minute. I often amuse myself with watching them, but I have never been able to make personal acquaintance with any of them. If I speak to one, he or she looks up in my face, as if I were not worth heeding, gives a little laugh, and runs away." Here the woman started, as if suddenly recollecting herself, and said in a low voice to her daughter, "Make haste—go and watch him, and see in what direction he goes."

I may as well mention here, that the conclusion I arrived at from the observations I was afterwards able to make, was, that the flowers die because the fairies go away; not that the fairies disappear because the flowers die. The flowers seem a sort of house, for them, or outer bodies, which they can put on or off when they please. Just as you could form some idea of the nature of a man from the kind of house he built, if he followed his own taste, so you could, without seeing the fairies, tell what any one of them is like, by looking at the flower till you feel that you understand it. For just what the flower says to you, would the face and form of the fairy say; only so much more plainly as a face and human figure can express more than a flower. For the house or the clothes, though like the inhabitant or the wearer, cannot be wrought into an equal power of utterance. Yet you would see a strange resemblance, almost oneness, between the flower and the fairy, which you could not describe, but which described itself to you. Whether all the flowers have fairies, I cannot determine, any more than I can be sure whether all men and women have souls.

The woman and I continued the conversation for a few minutes longer. I was much interested by the information she gave me, and astonished at the language in which she was able to convey it. It seemed that intercourse with the fairies was no bad education in itself. But now the daughter returned with the news that the Ash had just gone away in a south-westerly direction; and, as my course seemed to lie eastward, she hoped I should be in no danger of meeting him if I departed at once. I looked out of the little window, and there stood the ash-tree, to my eyes the same as before; but I believed that they knew better than I did, and prepared to go. I pulled out my purse, but to my dismay there was nothing in it. The woman with a smile begged me not to trouble myself, for money was not of the slightest use there; and as I might meet with people in my journeys whom I could not recognise to be fairies, it was well I had no money to offer, for nothing offended them so much.

"They would think," she added, "that you were making game of them; and that is their peculiar privilege with regard to us." So we went together into the little garden which sloped down towards a lower part of the wood.

Here, to my great pleasure, all was life and bustle. There was still light enough from the day to see a little; and the pale half-moon, half-way to the zenith, was reviving every moment. The whole garden was like a carnival, with tiny, gaily decorated forms, in groups, assemblies, processions, pairs or trios, moving stately on, running about wildly, or sauntering hither and thither. From the cups or bells of tall flowers, as from balconies, some looked down on the masses below, now bursting with laughter, now grave as owls; but even in their deepest solemnity, seeming only to be waiting for the arrival of the next laugh. Some were launched on a little marshy stream at the bottom, in boats chosen from the heaps of last year's leaves that lay about, curled and withered. These soon sank with them; whereupon they swam ashore and got others. Those who took fresh rose-leaves for their boats floated the longest; but for these they had to fight; for the fairy of the rose-tree complained bitterly that they were stealing her clothes, and defended her property bravely.

"You can't wear half you've got," said some.

"Never you mind; I don't choose you to have them : they are my property."

"All for the good of the community !" said one, and ran off with a great hollow leaf. But the rose-fairy sprang after him (what a beauty she was; only too like a drawing-room young lady), knocked him heels-over-head as he ran, and recovered her great red leaf. But in the meantime twenty had hurried off in different directions with others just as good; and the little creature sat down and cried, and then, in a pet, sent a perfect pink snowstorm of petals from her tree, leaping from branch to branch, and stamping and shaking and pulling. At last, after

another good cry, she chose the biggest she could find, and ran
away laughing, to launch her boat amongst the rest.

But my attention was first and chiefly attracted by a group of
fairies near the cottage, who were talking together around what
seemed a last dying primrose. They talked singing, and their talk
made a song, something like this :

> "Sister Snowdrop died
>   Before we were born."
> "She came like a bride
>   In a snowy morn."
> "What's a bride?"
>   "What is snow?"
> "Never tried."
>   "Do not know."
>
> "Who told you about her?"
>   "Little Primrose there
> Cannot do without her."
>   "Oh, so sweetly fair!"
> "Never fear,
>   She will come,
> Primrose dear."
>   "Is she dumb?"
>
> "She'll come by-and-by."
>   "You will never see her."
> "She went home to die,
>   Till the new year."
> "Snowdrop!" " 'Tis no good
>   To invite her."
> "Primrose is very rude,
>   I will bite her."
>
> "Oh, you naughty Pocket!
>   Look, she drops her head."
> "She deserved it, Rocket,
>   And she was nearly dead."
> "To your hammock—off with you!"
>   "And swing alone."
> "No one will laugh with you."
>   "No, not one."
>
> "Now let us moan."
>   "And cover her o'er."

"Primrose is gone."
    "All but the flower."
"Here is a leaf."
    "Lay her upon it."
"Follow in grief."
    "Pocket has done it."

"Deeper, poor creature!
    Winter may come."
"He cannot reach her—
    That is a hum."
"She is buried, the beauty!"
    "Now she is done."
"That was the duty."
    "Now for the fun."

And with a wild laugh they sprang away, most of them towards the cottage. During the latter part of the song-talk, they had formed themselves into a funeral procession, two of them bearing poor Primrose, whose death Pocket had hastened by biting her stalk, upon one of her own great leaves. They bore her solemnly along some distance, and then buried her under a tree. Although I say *her*, I saw nothing but the withered primrose-flower on its long stalk. Pocket, who had been expelled from the company by common consent, went sulkily away towards her hammock, for she was the fairy of the calceolaria, and looked rather wicked. When she reached its stem, she stopped and looked round. I could not help speaking to her, for I stood near her. I said, "Pocket, how could you be so naughty?"

"I am never naughty," she said, half-crossly, half-defiantly; "only if you come near my hammock, I will bite you, and then you will go away."

"Why did you bite poor Primrose?"

"Because she said we should never see Snowdrop; as if we were not good enough to look at her, and she was, the proud thing!—served her right!"

"Oh, Pocket, Pocket," said I; but by this time the party which had gone towards the house, rushed out again, shouting and screaming with laughter. Half of them were on the cat's back, and half held on by her fur and tail, or ran beside her; till, more coming to their help, the furious cat was held fast; and they proceeded to pick the sparks out of her with thorns and pins, which they handled like harpoons. Indeed, there were more instruments at work about her than there could have been sparks in her. One little fellow who held on hard by the tip of the tail, with his feet planted on the ground at an angle of forty-five degrees, helping to keep her fast, administered a continuous flow of admonitions to Pussy.

"Now, Pussy, be patient. You know quite well it is all for your good. You cannot be comfortable with all those sparks in you; and, indeed, I am charitably disposed to believe" (here he became very pompous) "that they are the cause of all your bad temper; so we must have them all out, every one; else we shall be reduced to the painful necessity of cutting your claws, and pulling out your eye-teeth. Quiet! Pussy, quiet!"

But with a perfect hurricane of feline curses, the poor animal broke loose, and dashed across the garden and through the hedge, faster than even the fairies could follow. "Never mind, never mind, we shall find her again; and by that time she will have laid in a fresh stock of sparks. Hooray!" And off they set, after some new mischief.

But I will not linger to enlarge on the amusing displays of these frolicsome creatures. Their manners and habits are now so well known to the world, having been so often described by eye-witnesses, that it would be only indulging self-conceit, to add my account in full to the rest. I cannot help wishing, however, that my readers could see them for themselves. Especially do I desire that they should see the fairy of the daisy; a little, chubby, round-eyed child, with such innocent trust in his look! Even the most mischievous of the fairies would not tease him, although he did not belong to their set at all, but was quite a little country bumpkin. He wandered about alone, and looked at everything, with his hands in his little pockets, and a white night-cap on, the darling! He was not so beautiful as many other wild flowers I saw afterwards, but so dear and loving in his looks and little confident ways.

CHAPTER IV

"When bale is att hyest, boote is nyest."
                    Ballad of Sir Aldingar.

B Y THIS TIME, my hostess was quite anxious that I should be gone. So, with warm thanks for their hospitality, I took my leave, and went my way through the little garden towards the forest. Some of the garden flowers had wandered into the wood, and were growing here and there along the path, but the trees soon became too thick and shadowy for them. I particularly noticed some tall lilies, which grew on both sides of the way, with large dazzlingly white flowers, set off by the universal green. It was now dark enough for me to see that every flower was shining with a light of its own. Indeed it was by this light that I saw them, an internal, peculiar light, proceeding from each, and not reflected from a common source of light as in the daytime. This light sufficed only for the plant itself, and was not strong enough to cast any but the faintest shadows around it, or to illuminate any of the neighbouring objects with other than the faintest tinge of its own individual hue. From the lilies above mentioned, from the campanulas, from the foxgloves, and every bell-shaped flower, curious little figures shot up their heads, peeped at me, and drew back. They seemed to inhabit them, as snails their shells; but I was sure some of them were intruders, and belonged to the gnomes or goblin-fairies, who inhabit the ground and earthy creeping plants. From the cups of Arum lilies, creatures with great heads and grotesque faces shot up like Jack-in-the-box, and made grimaces at me; or rose slowly and slily over the edge of the cup, and spouted water at me, slipping suddenly back, like those little soldier-crabs that inhabit the shells of sea-snails. Passing a row of tall thistles, I saw them crowded with little faces, which peeped every one from behind its flower, and drew back as quickly; and I heard them saying to each other, evidently intending me to hear, but the speaker always hiding behind his tuft, when I looked in his direction, "Look at him!

Look at him! He has begun a story without a beginning, and it
will never have any end. He! he! he! Look at him!"

But as I went further into the wood, these sights and sounds
became fewer, giving way to others of a different character. A
little forest of wild hyacinths was alive with exquisite creatures,
who stood nearly motionless, with drooping necks, holding each
by the stem of her flower, and swaying gently with it, whenever
a low breath of wind swung the crowded floral belfry. In like
manner, though differing of course in form and meaning, stood
a group of harebells, like little angels waiting, ready, till they
were wanted to go on some yet unknown message. In darker
nooks, by the mossy roots of the trees, or in little tufts of grass,
each dwelling in a globe of its own green light, weaving a network of grass and its shadows, glowed the glowworms. They
were just like the glowworms of our own land, for they are fairies
everywhere; worms in the day, and glowworms at night, when
their own can appear, and they can be themselves to others as
well as themselves. But they had their enemies here. For I saw
great strong-armed beetles, hurrying about with most unwieldy
haste, awkward as elephant-calves, looking apparently for glowworms; for the moment a beetle espied one, through what to it
was a forest of grass, or an underwood of moss, it pounced upon
it, and bore it way, in spite of its feeble resistance. Wondering
what their object could be, I watched one of the beetles, and
then I discovered a thing I could not account for. But it is no
use trying to account for things in Fairy Land; and one who
travels there soon learns to forget the very idea of doing so, and
takes everything as it comes; like a child, who, being in a chronic
condition of wonder, is surprised at nothing. What I saw was
this. Everywhere, here and there over the ground, lay little, dark-
looking lumps of something more like earth than anything else,
and about the size of a chestnut. The beetles hunted in couples
for these; and having found one, one of them stayed to watch it,
while the other hurried to find a glowworm. By signals, I presume, between them, the latter soon found his companion again :
they then took the glowworm and held its luminous tail to the
dark earthy pellet; when lo, it shot up into the air like a sky-
rocket, seldom, however, reaching the height of the highest tree.
Just like a rocket too, it burst in the air, and fell in a shower of
the most gorgeously coloured sparks of every variety of hue;

golden and red, and purple and green, and blue and rosy fires
crossed and intercrossed each other, beneath the shadowy heads,
and between the columnar stems of the forest trees. They never
used the same glowworm twice, I observed; but let him go,
apparently uninjured by the use they had made of him.

In other parts, the whole of the immediately surrounding
foliage was illuminated by the interwoven dances in the air of
splendidly coloured fire-flies, which sped hither and thither,
turned, twisted, crossed, and recrossed, entwining every com-
plexity of intervolved motion. Here and there, whole mighty
trees glowed with an emitted phosphorescent light. You could
trace the very course of the great roots in the earth by the faint
light that came through; and every twig, and every vein on
every leaf was a streak of pale fire.

All this time, as I went on through the wood, I was haunted
with the feeling that other shapes, more like my own in size and
mien, were moving about at a little distance on all sides of me.
But as yet I could discern none of them, although the moon was
high enough to send a great many of her rays down between the
trees, and these rays were unusually bright, and sight-giving, notwithstanding she was only a half-moon. I constantly imagined,
however, that forms were visible in all directions except that to
which my gaze was turned; and that they only became invisible,
or resolved themselves into other woodland shapes, the moment
my looks were directed towards them. However this may have
been, except for this feeling of presence, the woods seemed
utterly bare of anything like human companionship, although
my glance often fell on some object which I fancied to be a
human form; for I soon found that I was quite deceived; as, the
moment I fixed my regard on it, it showed plainly that it was a
bush, or a tree, or a rock.

Soon a vague sense of discomfort possessed me. With variations
of relief, this gradually increased; as if some evil thing were
wandering about in my neighbourhood, sometimes nearer and
sometimes further off, but still approaching. The feeling continued and deepened, until all my pleasure in the shows of
various kinds that everywhere betokened the presence of the
merry fairies vanished by degrees, and left me full of anxiety and
fear, which I was unable to associate with any definite object
whatever. At length the thought crossed my mind with horror :

"Can it be possible that the Ash is looking for me? or that, in his nightly wanderings, his path is gradually verging towards mine?" I comforted myself, however, by remembering that he had started quite in another direction; one that would lead him, if he kept it, far apart from me; especially as, for the last two or three hours, I had been diligently journeying eastward. I kept on my way, therefore, striving by direct effort of the will against the encroaching fear; and to this end occupying my mind, as much as I could, with other thoughts. I was so far successful that, although I was conscious, if I yielded for a moment, I should be almost overwhelmed with horror, I was yet able to walk right on for an hour or more. What I feared I could not tell. Indeed, I was left in a state of the vaguest uncertainty as regarded the nature of my enemy, and knew not the mode or object of his attacks; for, somehow or other, none of my questions had succeeded in drawing a definite answer from the dame in the cottage. How then to defend myself I knew not; nor even by what sign I might with certainty recognise the presence of my foe; for as yet this vague though powerful fear was all the indication of danger I had. To add to my distress, the clouds in the west had risen nearly to the top of the skies, and they and the moon were travelling slowly towards each other. Indeed, some of their advanced guard had already met her, and she had begun to wade through a filmy vapour that gradually deepened. At length she was for a moment almost entirely obscured. When she shone out again, with a brilliancy increased by the contrast, I saw plainly on the path before me—from around which at this spot the trees receded, leaving a small space of green sward— the shadow of a large hand, with knotty joints and protuberances here and there. Especially I remarked, even in the midst of my fear, the bulbous points of the fingers. I looked hurriedly all round, but could see nothing from which such a shadow should fall. Now, however, that I had a direction, however undeter- mined, in which to project my apprehension, the very sense of danger and need of action overcame the stifling which is the worst property of fear. I reflected in a moment, that if this were indeed a shadow, it was useless to look for the object that cast it in any other direction than between the shadow and the moon. I looked, and peered, and intensified my vision, all to no purpose. I could see nothing of that kind, not even an ash-tree in the neighbourhood. Still the shadow remained; not steady, but moving to and fro, and once I saw the fingers close, and grind themselves close, like the claws of a wild animal, as if in uncontrollable longing for some anticipated prey. There seemed but one mode left of discovering the substance of this shadow. I went forward boldly, though with an inward shudder which I would not heed, to the spot where the shadow lay, threw myself on the ground, laid my head within the form of the hand, and turned my eyes towards the moon. Good heavens! what did I see? I wonder that ever I arose, and that the very shadow of the hand did not hold me where I lay until fear had frozen my brain. I saw the strangest figure; vague, shadowy, almost transparent, in the central parts, and gradually deepening in substance towards the outside, until it ended in extremities capable of casting such a shadow as fell from the hand, through the awful fingers of which I now saw the moon. The hand was uplifted in the attitude of a paw about to strike its prey. But the face, which throbbed with fluctuating and pulsatory visibility—not from changes in the light it reflected, but from changes in its own conditions of reflecting power, the alterations being from within, not from without—it was horrible. I do not know how to describe it. It caused a new sensation. Just as one cannot translate a horrible odour, or a ghastly pain, or a fearful sound, into words, so I cannot describe this new form of awful hideousness. I can only try to describe something that is not it, but seems somewhat parallel to it; or at least is suggested by it. It reminded me of what I had heard of vampires; for the face resembled that of a corpse more than anything else I can think of; especially when I can conceive such a face in motion, but not suggesting any life as the source of the motion. The features were rather handsome than otherwise, except the mouth, which had scarcely a curve in it. The lips were of equal thickness; but the thickness was not at all remarkable, even although they looked slightly swollen. They seemed fixedly open, but were not wide apart. Of course I did not *remark* these lineaments at the time: I was too horrified for that. I noted them afterwards, when the form returned on my inward sight with a vividness too intense to admit of my doubting the accuracy of the reflex. But the most awful of the features were the eyes. These were alive, yet not with life. They seemed lighted up with an infinite greed. A gnawing voracity, which devoured the devourer, seemed to be the indwelling and propelling power of the whole ghastly apparition. I lay for a few moments simply imbruted with terror; when another cloud, obscuring the moon, delivered me from the immediately paralysing effects of the presence to the vision of the object of horror, while it added the force of imagination to the power of fear within me; inasmuch as, knowing far worse cause for apprehension than before, I remained equally ignorant from what I had to defend myself, or how to take any precautions : he might be upon me in the darkness any moment. I sprang to my feet, and sped I knew not whither, only away from the spectre. I thought no longer of the path, and often narrowly escaped dashing myself against a tree, in my headlong flight of fear.

Great drops of rain began to patter on the leaves. Thunder began to mutter, then growl in the distance. I ran on. The rain fell heavier. At length the thick leaves could hold it up no longer; and, like a second firmament, they poured their torrents on the earth. I was soon drenched, but that was nothing. I came to a small swollen stream that rushed through the woods. I had a vague hope that if I crossed this stream, I should be in safety from my pursuer; but I soon found that my hope was as false as it was vague. I dashed across the stream, ascended a rising ground, and reached a more open space, where stood only great trees. Through them I directed my way, holding eastward as nearly as I could guess, but not at all certain that I was not moving in an opposite direction. My mind was just reviving a little from its extreme terror, when, suddenly, a flash of lightning, or rather a cataract of successive flashes, behind me, seemed to throw on the ground in front of me, but far more faintly than before, from the extent of the source of the light, the shadow of the same horrible hand. I sprang forward, stung to yet wilder speed; but had not run many steps before my foot slipped, and, vainly attempting to recover myself, I fell at the foot of one of the large trees. Half-stunned, I yet raised myself, and almost involuntarily looked back. All I saw was the hand within three feet of my face. But, at the same moment, I felt two large soft arms thrown round me from behind; and a voice like a woman's said : "Do not fear the goblin; he dares not hurt you now." With that, the hand was suddenly withdrawn as from a fire, and disappeared in the darkness and the rain. Overcome with the mingling of terror and joy, I lay for some time almost insensible. The first thing I remember is the sound of a voice above me, full and low, and strangely reminding me of the sound of a gentle wind amidst the leaves of a great tree. It murmured over and over again : "I may love him, I may love him; for he is a man, and I am only a beech-tree." I found I was seated on the ground, leaning against a human form, and supported still by the arms around me, which I knew to be those of a woman who must be rather above the human size, and largely proportioned. I turned my head, but without moving otherwise, for I feared lest the arms should untwine themselves; and clear, somewhat mournful eyes met mine. At least that is how they impressed me; but I could see very little of colour or outline as we sat in the dark and rainy shadow of the tree. The face seemed very lovely, and solemn from its stillness; with the aspect of one who is quite content, but waiting for something. I saw my conjecture from her arms was correct : she was above the human scale throughout, but not greatly.

"Why do you call yourself a beech-tree?" I said.

"Because I am one," she replied, in the same low, musical, murmuring voice.

"You are a woman," I returned.

"Do you think so? Am I very like a woman then?"

"You are a very beautiful woman. Is it possible you should not know it?"

"I am very glad you think so. I fancy I feel like a woman sometimes. I do so to-night—and always when the rain drips from my hair. For there is an old prophecy in our woods that one day we shall all be men and women like you. Do you know anything about it in your region? Shall I be very happy when I am a woman? I fear not; for it is always in nights like these that I feel like one. But I long to be a woman for all that."

I had let her talk on, for her voice was like a solution of all musical sounds. I now told her that I could hardly say whether women were happy or not. I knew one who had not been happy; and for my part, I had often longed for Fairy Land, as she now longed for the world of men. But then neither of us had lived long, and perhaps people grew happier as they grew older. Only I doubted it. I could not help sighing. She felt the sigh, for her arms were still round me. She asked me how old I was.

"Twenty-one," said I.

"Why, you baby!" said she, and kissed me with the sweetest kiss of winds and odours. There was a cool faithfulness in the kiss that revived my heart wonderfully. I felt that I feared the dreadful Ash no more.

"What did the horrible Ash want with me?" I said.

"I am not quite sure, but I think he wants to bury you at the foot of his tree. But he shall not touch you, my child."

"Are all the ash-trees as dreadful as he?"

"Oh, no. They are all disagreeable selfish creatures—(what horrid men they will make, if it be true!) but this one has a hole in his heart that nobody knows of but one or two; and he is always trying to fill it up, but he cannot. That must be what he wanted you for. I wonder if he will ever be a man. If he is, I hope they will kill him."

"How kind of you to save me from him!"

"I will take care that he shall not come near you again. But there are some in the wood more like me, from whom, alas! I cannot protect you. Only if you see any of them very beautiful, try to walk round them."

"What, then?"

"I cannot tell you more. But now I must tie some of my hair about you, and then the Ash will not touch you. Here, cut some off. You men have strange cutting things about you."

She shook her long hair loose over me, never moving her arms.

"I cannot cut your beautiful hair. It would be a shame."

"Not cut my hair! It will have grown long enough before any is wanted again in this wild forest. Perhaps it may never be of any use again—not till I am a woman." And she sighed.

As gently as I could, I cut with a knife a long tress of flowing, dark hair, she hanging her beautiful head over me. When I had finished, she shuddered and breathed deep, as one does when an acute pain, steadfastly endured without sign of suffering, is at length relaxed. She then took the hair and tied it round me, singing a strange sweet song, which I could not understand, but which left in me a feeling like this—

> "I saw thee ne'er before;
> I see thee never more;
> But love, and help, and pain, beautiful one,
> Have made thee mine, till all my years are done."

I cannot put more of it into words. She closed her arms about me again, and went on singing. The rain in the leaves, and a light wind that had arisen, kept her song company. I was wrapt in a trance of still delight. It told me the secret of the woods, and the flowers, and the birds. At one time I felt as if I was wandering in childhood through sunny spring forests, over carpets of primroses, anemones, and little white starry things—I had almost said, creatures, and finding new wonderful flowers at every turn. At another, I lay half dreaming in the hot summer noon, with a book of old tales beside me, beneath a great beech; or, in autumn, grew sad because I trod on the leaves that had sheltered me, and received their last blessing in the sweet odours of decay; or, in a winter evening, frozen still, looked up, as I went home to a warm fireside, through the netted boughs and twigs to the cold, snowy moon, with her opal zone around her. At last I had fallen asleep; for I know nothing more that passed, till I found myself lying under a superb beech-tree, in the clear light of the morning, just before sunrise. Around me was a girdle of fresh beech-leaves. Alas! I brought nothing with me out of Fairy Land, but memories—memories. The great boughs of the beech hung drooping around me. At my head rose its smooth stem, with its great sweeps of curving surface that swelled like undeveloped limbs. The leaves and branches above kept on the song which had sung me asleep; only now, to my mind, it sounded like a farewell and a speedwell. I sat a long time, unwilling to go; but my unfinished story urged me on. I must act and wander. With the sun well risen, I rose, and put my arms as far as they would reach around the beech-tree, and kissed it, and said good-bye. A trembling went through the leaves; a few of the last drops of the night's rain fell from off them at my feet; and as I walked slowly away, I seemed to hear in a whisper once more the words : "I may love him, I may love him; for he is a man, and I am only a beech-tree."

CHAPTER V

"And she was smooth and full, as if one gush
Of life had washed her, or as if a sleep
Lay on her eyelid, easier to sweep
Than bee from daisy."—BEDDOES' *Pygmalion*.

"Sche was as whyt as lylye yn May.
Or snow that sneweth yn wynterys day."
Romance of Sir Launfal.

I WALKED ON, IN the fresh morning air, as if new-born. The
only thing that damped my pleasure was a cloud of something
between sorrow and delight, that crossed my mind with the
frequently returning thought of my last night's hostess. "But
then," thought I, "if she is sorry, I could not help it; and she has
all the pleasures she ever had. Such a day as this is surely a joy
to her, as much at least as to me. And her life will perhaps be
the richer, for holding now within it the memory of what came,
but could not stay. And if ever she is a woman, who knows but
we may meet somewhere? there is plenty of room for meeting
in the universe." Comforting myself thus, yet with a vague com-
punction, as if I ought not to have left her, I went on. There
was little to distinguish the woods to-day from those of my own
land; except that all the wild things, rabbits, birds, squirrels,
mice, and the numberless other inhabitants, were very tame;
that is, they did not run away from me, but gazed at me as I
passed, frequently coming nearer, as if to examine me more
closely. Whether this came from utter ignorance, or from fam-
iliarity with the human appearance of beings who never hurt
them, I could not tell. As I stood once, looking up to the splendid
flower of a parasite, which hung from the branch of a tree over
my head, a large white rabbit cantered slowly up, put one of its
little feet on one of mine, and looked up at me with its red eyes,
just as I had been looking up at the flower above me. I stooped
and stroked it; but when I attempted to lift it, it banged the
ground with its hind feet, and scampered off at a great rate,
turning, however, to look at me, several times before I lost sight

of it. Now and then, too, a dim human figure would appear and
disappear, at some distance, amongst the trees, moving like a
sleep-walker. But no one ever came near me.

This day I found plenty of food in the forest—strange nuts
and fruits I had never seen before. I hesitated to eat them; but
argued that, if I could live on the air of Fairy Land, I could live
on its food also. I found my reasoning correct, and the result
was better than I had hoped; for it not only satisfied my hunger,
but operated in such a way upon my senses, that I was brought
into far more complete relationship with the things around me.
The human forms appeared much more dense and defined; more
tangibly visible, if I may say so. I seemed to know better which
direction to choose when any doubt arose. I began to feel in
some degree what the birds meant in their songs, though I could
not express it in words, any more than you can some landscapes.
At times, to my surprise, I found myself listening attentively, and
as if it were no unusual thing with me, to a conversation between
two squirrels or monkeys. The subjects were not very interesting,
except as associated with the individual life and necessities of
the little creatures : where the best nuts were to be found in the
neighbourhood, and who could crack them best, or who had most
laid up for the winter, and such like; only they never said
where the store was. There was no great difference in kind
between their talk and our ordinary human conversation. Some
of the creatures I never heard speak at all, and believe they
never do so, except under the impulse of some great excitement.
The mice talked; but the hedgehogs seemed very phlegmatic;
and though I met a couple of moles above ground several times,
they never said a word to each other in my hearing. There were
no wild beasts in the forest; at least, I did not see one larger than
a wild cat. There were plenty of snakes, however, and I do not
think they were all harmless; but none ever bit me.

Soon after mid-day I arrived at a bare rocky hill, of no great
size, but very steep; and, having no trees—scarcely even a bush
—upon it, entirely exposed to the heat of the sun. Over this my
way seemed to lie, and I immediately began the ascent. On
reaching the top, hot and weary, I looked around me, and saw
that the forest still stretched as far as the sight could reach on
every side of me. I observed that the trees, in the direction in
which I was about to descend, did not come so near the foot of

the hill as on the other side, and was especially regretting the unexpected postponement of shelter, because this side of the hill seemed more difficult to descend than the other had been to climb, when my eye caught the appearance of a natural path, winding down through broken rocks and along the course of a tiny stream, which I hoped would lead me more easily to the foot. I tried it, and found the descent not at all laborious; nevertheless, when I reached the bottom, I was very tired, and exhausted with the heat. But just where the path seemed to end, rose a great rock, quite overgrown with shrubs and creeping plants, some of them in full and splendid blossom : these almost concealed an opening in the rock, into which the path appeared to lead. I entered, thirsting for the shade which it promised. What was my delight to find a rocky cell, all the angles rounded away with rich moss, and every ledge and projection crowded with lovely ferns, the variety of whose forms, and groupings, and shades wrought in me like a poem; for such a harmony could not exist, except they all consented to some one end! A little well of the clearest water filled a mossy hollow in one corner. I drank, and felt as if I knew what the elixir of life must be; then threw myself on a mossy mound that lay like a couch along the inner end. Here I lay in a delicious reverie for some time; during which all lovely forms, and colours, and sounds seemed to use my brain as a common hall, where they could come and go, unbidden and unexcused. I had never imagined that such capacity for simple happiness lay in me, as was now awakened by this assembly of forms and spiritual sensations, which yet were far too vague to admit of being translated into any shape common to my own and another mind. I had lain for an hour, I should suppose, though it may have been far longer, when, the harmonious tumult in my mind having somewhat relaxed, I became aware that my eyes were fixed on a strange, time-worn bas-relief on the rock opposite to me. This, after some pondering, I concluded to represent Pygmalion, as he awaited the quickening of his statue. The sculptor sat more rigid than the figure to which his eyes were turned. That seemed about to step from its pedestal and embrace the man, who waited rather than expected.

"A lovely story," I said to myself. "This cave, now, with the bushes cut away from the entrance to let the light in, might be such a place as he would choose, withdrawn from the notice of

men, to set up his block of marble, and mould into a visible
body the thought already clothed with form in the unseen hall
of the sculptor's brain. And, indeed, if I mistake not," I said,
starting up, as a sudden ray of light arrived at that moment
through a crevice in the roof, and lighted up a small portion of
the rock, bare of vegetation, "this very rock is marble, white
enough and delicate enough for any statue, even if destined to
become an ideal woman in the arms of the sculptor."

I took my knife and removed the moss from a part of the
block on which I had been lying; when, to my surprise, I found
it more like alabaster than ordinary marble, and soft to the edge
of the knife. In fact, it was alabaster. By an inexplicable, though
by no means unusual kind of impulse, I went on removing the
moss from the surface of the stone; and soon saw that it was
polished, or at least smooth, throughout. I continued my labour;
and after clearing a space of about a couple of square feet, I
observed what caused me to prosecute the work with more
interest and care than before. For the ray of sunlight had now
reached the spot I had cleared, and under its lustre the alabaster
revealed its usual slight transparency when polished, except
where my knife had scratched the surface; and I observed that
the transparency seemed to have a definite limit, and to end
upon an opaque body like the more solid, white marble. I was
careful to scratch no more. And first, a vague anticipation gave
way to a startling sense of possibility; then, as I proceeded, one
revelation after another produced the entrancing conviction, that
under the crust of alabaster, lay a dimly visible form in marble,
but whether of man or woman I could not yet tell. I worked on
as rapidly as the necessary care would permit; and when I had
uncovered the whole mass, and rising from my knees, had
retreated a little way, so that the effect of the whole might fall
on me, I saw before me with sufficient plainness—though at
the same time with considerable indistinctness, arising from the
limited amount of light the place admitted, as well as from the
nature of the object itself—a block of pure alabaster enclosing
the form, apparently in marble, of a reposing woman. She lay
on one side, with her hand under her cheek, and her face
towards me; but her hair had fallen partly over her face, so
that I could not see the expression of the whole. What I did see
appeared to me perfectly lovely; more near the face that had

been born with me in my soul, than anything I had seen before in nature or art. The actual outlines of the rest of the form were so indistinct, that the more than semi-opacity of the alabaster seemed insufficient to account for the fact; and I conjectured that a light robe added its obscurity. Numberless histories passed through my mind of change of substance from enchantment and other causes, and of imprisonments such as this before me. I thought of the Prince of the Enchanted City, half marble and half a living man; of Ariel; of Niobe; of the Sleeping Beauty in the Wood; of the bleeding trees; and many other histories. Even my adventure of the preceding evening with the lady of the beech-tree contributed to arouse the wild hope, that by some means life might be given to this form also, and that, breaking from her alabaster tomb, she might glorify my eyes with her presence. "For," I argued, "who can tell but this cave may be the home of Marble, and this, essential Marble—that spirit of marble which, present throughout, makes it capable of being moulded into any form? Then if she should awake! But how to awake her? A kiss awoke the Sleeping Beauty! a kiss cannot reach her through the incrusting alabaster." I kneeled, however, and kissed the pale coffin; but she slept on. I bethought me of Orpheus, and the following stones;—that trees should follow his music seemed nothing surprising now. Might not a song awake this form, that the glory of motion might for a time displace the loveliness of rest? Sweet sounds can go where kisses may not enter. I sat and thought.

Now, although always delighting in music, I had never been gifted with the power of song, until I entered the fairy forest. I had a voice, and I had a true sense of sound; but when I tried to sing, the one would not content the other, and so I remained silent. This morning, however, I had found myself, ere I was aware, rejoicing in a song; but whether it was before or after I had eaten of the fruits of the forest, I could not satisfy myself. I concluded it was after, however; and that the increased impulse to sing I now felt, was in part owing to having drunk of the little well, which shone like a brilliant eye in a corner of the cave. I sat down on the ground by the "antenatal tomb," leaned upon it with my face towards the head of the figure within, and sang—the words and tones coming together, and inseparably connected, as if word and tone formed one thing; or, as if each word could be uttered only in that tone, and was incapable of distinction from it, except in idea, by an acute analysis. I sang something like this : but the words are only a dull representation of a state whose very elevation precluded the possibility of remembrance; and in which I presume the words really employed were as far above these, as that state transcended this wherein I recall it :

> "Marble woman, vainly sleeping
> In the very death of dreams!
> Wilt thou—slumber from thee sweeping,
> All but what with vision teems—
> Hear my voice come through the golden
> Mist of memory and hope;
> And with shadowy smile embolden
> Me with primal Death to cope?
>
> "Thee the sculptors all pursuing,
> Have embodied but their own;
> Round their visions, form enduing,
> Marble vestments thou hast thrown;
> But thyself, in silence winding,
> Thou hast kept eternally;
> Thee they found not, many finding—
> I have found thee: wake for me."

As I sang, I looked earnestly at the face so vaguely revealed before me. I fancied, yet believed it to be but fancy, that through the dim veil of the alabaster, I saw a motion of the head as if caused by a sinking sigh. I gazed more earnestly, and concluded that it was but fancy. Nevertheless I could not help singing again—

> "Rest is now filled full of beauty,
> And can give thee up, I ween;
> Come thou forth, for other duty
> Motion pineth for her queen.
>
> "Or, if needing years to wake thee
> From thy slumbrous solitudes,
> Come, sleep-walking, and betake thee
> To the friendly, sleeping woods.

"Sweeter dreams are in the forest,
    Round thee storms would never rave;
And when need of rest is sorest,
    Glide thou then into thy cave.

"Or, if still thou choosest rather
    Marble, be its spell on me;
Let thy slumber round me gather,
    Let another dream with thee!"

Again I paused, and gazed through the stony shroud, as if, by very force of penetrative sight, I would clear every lineament of the lovely face. And now I thought the hand that had lain under the cheek, had slipped a little downward. But then I could not be sure that I had at first observed its position accurately. So I sang again; for the longing had grown into a passionate need of seeing her alive—

"Or art thou Death, O woman? for since I
    Have set me singing by thy side,
Life hath forsook the upper sky,
    And all the outer world hath died.

"Yea, I am dead; for thou hast drawn
    My life all downward unto thee.
Dead moon of love! let twilight dawn:
    Awake! and let the darkness flee.

"Cold lady of the lovely stone!
    Awake! or I shall perish here;
And thou be never more alone,
    My form and I for ages near.

"But words are vain; reject them all—
    They utter but a feeble part:
Hear thou the depths from which they call,
    The voiceless longing of my heart."

There arose a slightly crashing sound. Like a sudden apparition that comes and is gone, a white form, veiled in a light robe of whiteness, burst upwards from the stone, stood, glided forth, and gleamed away towards the woods. For I followed to the mouth of the cave, as soon as the amazement and concentration of delight permitted the nerves of motion again to act; and saw the white form amidst the trees, as it crossed a little glade on the edge of the forest where the sunlight fell full, seeming to gather with intenser radiance on the one object that floated rather than flitted through its lake of beams. I gazed after her in a kind of despair; found, freed, lost! It seemed useless to follow, yet follow I must. I marked the direction she took; and without once looking round to the forsaken cave, I hastened towards the forest.

CHAPTER VI

"Ach, hüte sich doch ein Mensch, wenn seine erfüllten Wünsche auf ihn herad regnen, und er so über alle Maase fröhlich ist!"—FOUQUÉ: *Der Zauberring.*

"Ah, let a man beware, when his wishes, fulfilled, rain down upon him, and his happiness is unbounded."

"Thy red lips, like worms,
Travel over my cheek."—MOTHERWELL.

BUT AS I CROSSED the space between the foot of the hill and the forest, a vision of another kind delayed my steps. Through an opening to the westward flowed, like a stream, the rays of the setting sun, and overflowed with a ruddy splendour the open place where I was. And riding as it were down this stream towards me, came a horseman in what appeared red armour. From frontlet to tail, the horse likewise shone red in the sunset. I felt as if I must have seen the knight before; but as he drew near, I could recall no feature of his countenance. Ere he came up to me, however, I remembered the legend of Sir Percival in the rusty armour, which I had left unfinished in the old book in the cottage : it was of Sir Percival that he reminded me. And no wonder; for when he came close up to me, I saw that, from crest to heel, the whole surface of his armour was covered with a light rust. The golden spurs shone, but the iron greaves glowed in the sunlight. The *morning star*, which hung from his wrist, glittered and glowed with its silver and bronze. His whole appearance was terrible; but his face did not answer to this appearance. It was sad, even to gloominess; and something of shame seemed to cover it. Yet it was noble and high, though thus beclouded; and the form looked lofty, although the head drooped, and the whole frame was bowed as with an inward grief. The horse seemed to share in his master's dejection, and walked spiritless and slow. I noticed, too, that the white plume on his helmet was discoloured and drooping. "He has fallen in a joust with spears," I said to myself; "yet it becomes not a noble knight to be conquered in spirit because his body hath fallen." He appeared not to observe me, for he was riding past without looking up, and started into a warlike attitude the moment the first sound of my voice reached him. Then a flush, as of shame, covered all of his face that the lifted beaver disclosed. He returned my greeting with distant courtesy, and passed on. But suddenly, he reined up, sat a moment still, and then turning his horse, rode back to where I stood looking after him.

"I am ashamed," he said, "to appear a knight, and in such a guise; but it behoves me to tell you to take warning from me, lest the same evil, in his kind, overtake the singer that has befallen the knight. Hast thou ever read the story of Sir Percival and the" (here he shuddered, that his armour rang)—"Maiden of the Alder-tree?"

"In part, I have," said I; "for yesterday, at the entrance of this forest, I found in a cottage the volume wherein it is recorded."

"Then take heed," he rejoined; "for, see my armour;—I put it off; and as it befell to him, so has it befallen to me. I that was proud am humble now. Yet is she terribly beautiful—beware. Never," he added, raising his head, "shall this armour be furbished, but by the blows of knightly encounter, until the last speck has disappeared from every spot where the battle-axe and sword of evil-doers, or noble foes, might fall; when I shall again lift my head, and say to my squire, 'Do thy duty once more, and make this armour shine.'"

Before I could inquire further, he had struck spurs into his horse and galloped away, shrouded from my voice in the noise of his armour. For I called after him, anxious to know more about this fearful enchantress; but in vain—he heard me not. "Yet," I said to myself, "I have now been often warned; surely I shall be well on my guard; and I am fully resolved I shall not be ensnared by any beauty, however beautiful. Doubtless, some one man may escape, and I shall be he." So I went on into the wood, still hoping to find, in some one of its mysterious recesses, my lost lady of the marble. The sunny afternoon died into the loveliest twilight. Great bats began to flit about with their own noiseless flight, seemingly purposeless, because its objects are unseen. The monotonous music of the owl issued from all un-expected quarters in the half-darkness around me. The glow-worm was alight here and there, burning out into the great universe. The night-hawk heightened all the harmony and still-ness with his oft-recurring, discordant jar. Numberless unknown sounds came out of the unknown dusk; but all were of twilight-kind, oppressing the heart as with a condensed atmosphere of dreamy undefined love and longing. The odours of night arose, and bathed me in that luxurious mournfulness peculiar to them, as if the plants whence they floated had been watered with bygone tears. Earth drew me towards her bosom; I felt as if I could fall down and kiss her. I forgot I was in Fairy Land, and seemed to be walking in a perfect night of our own old nursing earth. Great stems rose about me, uplifting a thick multitudinous roof above me of branches, and twigs, and leaves—the bird and insect world uplifted over mine, with its own landscapes, its own thickets, and paths, and glades, and dwellings; its own bird-ways and insect-delights. Great boughs crossed my path; great roots based the tree-columns, and mightily clasped the earth, strong to lift and strong to uphold. It seemed an old, old forest, perfect in forest ways and pleasure. And when, in the midst of this ecstasy, I remembered that under some close canopy of leaves, by some giant stem, or in some mossy cave, or beside some leafy well, sat the lady of the marble, whom my songs had called forth into the outer world, waiting (might it not be?) to meet and thank her deliverer in a twilight which would veil her confusion, the whole night became one dream-realm of joy, the central form of which was everywhere present, although unbeheld. Then, re-membering how my songs seemed to have called her from the marble, piercing through the pearly shroud of alabaster— "Why," thought I, "should not my voice reach her now, through the ebon night that inwraps her." My voice burst into song so spontaneously that it seemed involuntarily.

> "Not a sound
> But, echoing in me,
> Vibrates all around

With a blind delight,
Till it breaks on thee,
Queen of Night!

"Every tree,
O'ershadowing with gloom,
Seems to cover thee
Secret, dark, love-still'd,
In a holy room
Silence-filled.

"Let no moon
Creep up the heaven to-night;
I in darksome noon
Walking hopefully,
Seek my shrouded light—
Grope for thee!

"Darker grow
The borders of the dark!
Through the branches glow,
From the roof above,
Star and diamond-spark,
Light for love."

Scarcely had the last sounds floated away from the hearing of my own ears, when I heard instead a low delicious laugh near me. It was not the laugh of one who would not be heard, but the laugh of one who has just received something long and patiently desired—a laugh that ends in a low musical moan. I started, and, turning sideways, saw a dim white figure seated beside an intertwining thicket of smaller trees and underwood.

"It is my white lady!" I said, and flung myself on the ground beside her; striving, through the gathering darkness, to get a glimpse of the form which had broken its marble prison at my call.

"It is your white lady," said the sweetest voice, in reply, sending a thrill of speechless delight through a heart which all the love charms of the preceding day and evening had been tempering for this culminating hour. Yet, if I would have confessed it, there was something either in the sound of the voice, although it seemed sweetness itself, or else in this yielding which awaited no gradation of gentle approaches, that did not vibrate harmoniously with the beat of my inward music. And likewise, when, taking her hand in mine, I drew closer to her, looking for the beauty of her face, which, indeed, I found too plenteously, a cold shiver ran through me; but "it is the marble," I said to myself, and heeded it not.

She withdrew her hand from mine, and after that would scarce allow me to touch her. It seemed strange, after the fulness of her first greeting, that she could not trust me to come close to her. Though her words were those of a lover, she kept herself withdrawn as if a mile of space interposed between us.

"Why did you run away from me when you woke in the cave?" I said.

"Did I?" she returned. "That was very unkind of me; but I did not know better."

"I wish I could see you. The night is very dark."

"So it is. Come to my grotto. There is light there."

"Have you another cave, then?"

"Come and see."

But she did not move until I rose first, and then she was on her feet before I could offer my hand to help her. She came close to my side, and conducted me through the wood. But once or twice, when, involuntarily almost, I was about to put my arm around her as we walked on through the warm gloom, she sprang away several paces, always keeping her face full towards me, and then stood looking at me, slightly stooping, in the attitude of one who fears some half-seen enemy. It was too dark to discern the expression of her face. Then she would return and walk close beside me again, as if nothing had happened. I thought this strange; but, besides that I had almost, as I said before, given up the attempt to account for appearances in Fairy Land, I judged that it would be very unfair to expect from one who had slept so long and had been so suddenly awakened, a behaviour correspondent to what I might unreflectingly look for. I knew not what she might have been dreaming about. Besides, it was possible that, while her words were free, her sense of touch might be exquisitely delicate.

At length, after walking a long way in the woods, we arrived at another thicket, through the intertexture of which was glimmering a pale rosy light.

"Push aside the branches," she said, "and make room for us to enter."

I did as she told me.

"Go in," she said; "I will follow you."

I did as she desired, and found myself in a little cave, not very unlike the marble cave. It was festooned and draperied with all kinds of green that cling to shady rocks. In the furthest corner, half-hidden in leaves, through which it glowed, mingling lovely shadows between them, burned a bright rosy flame on a little earthen lamp. The lady glided round by the wall from behind me, still keeping her face towards me, and seated herself in the furthest corner, with her back to the lamp, which she hid completely from my view. I then saw indeed a form of perfect loveliness before me. Almost it seemed as if the light of the rose-lamp shone through her (for it could not be reflected from her); such a delicate shade of pink seemed to shadow what in itself must be a marbly whiteness of hue. I discovered afterwards, however, that there was one thing in it I did not like; which was, that the white part of the eye was tinged with the same slight roseate hue as the rest of the form. It is strange that I cannot recall her features; but they, as well as her somewhat girlish figure, left on me simply and only the impression of intense loveliness. I lay down at her feet, and gazed up into her face as I lay.

She began, and told me a strange tale, which, likewise, I cannot recollect; but which, at every turn and every pause, somehow or other fixed my eyes and thoughts upon her extreme beauty; seeming always to culminate in something that had a relation, revealed or hidden, but always operative, with her own loveliness. I lay entranced. It was a tale which brings back a feeling as of snows and tempests; torrents and water-sprites; lovers parted for long, and meeting at last; with a gorgeous summer night to close up the whole. I listened till she and I were blended with the tale; till she and I were the whole history. And we had met at last in this same cave of greenery, while the summer night hung round us heavy with love, and the odours that crept through the silence from the sleeping woods were the only signs of an outer world that invaded our solitude. What followed I cannot clearly remember. The succeeding horror almost obliterated it. I woke as a grey dawn stole into the cave. The damsel had disappeared; but in the shrubbery, at the mouth of the cave, stood a strange horrible object. It looked like an open coffin set up on one end; only that the part for the head and neck was defined from the shoulder-part. In fact, it was a rough representation of the human frame, only hollow, as if made of decaying bark torn from a tree. It had arms, which were only slightly seamed, down from the shoulder-blade by the elbow, as if the bark had healed again from the cut of a knife. But the arms moved, and the hands and fingers were tearing asunder a long silky tress of hair. The thing turned round—it had for a face and front those of my enchantress, but now of a pale greenish hue in the light of the morning, and with dead lustreless eyes. In the horror of the moment, another fear invaded me. I put my hand to my waist, and found indeed that my girdle of beech-leaves was gone. Hair again in her hands, she was tearing it fiercely. Once more, as she turned, she laughed a low laugh, but now full of scorn and derision; and then she said, as if to a companion with whom she had been talking while I slept, "There he is; you can take him now." I lay still, petrified with dismay and fear; for I now saw another figure beside her, which, although vague and indistinct, I yet recognised but too well. It was the Ash-tree. My beauty was the Maid of the Alder! and she was giving me, spoiled of my only availing defence, into the hands of my awful foe. The Ash bent his Gorgon-head, and entered the cave. I could not stir. He drew near me. His ghoul-eyes and his ghastly face fascinated me. He came stooping, with the hideous hand outstretched, like a beast of prey. I had given myself up to a death of unfathomable horror, when, suddenly, and just as he was on the point of seizing me, the dull, heavy blow of an axe echoed through the wood, followed by others in quick repetition. The Ash shuddered and groaned, withdrew the outstretched hand, retreated backwards to the mouth of the cave, then turned and disappeared amongst the trees. The other walking Death looked at me once, with a careless dislike on her beautifully moulded features; then, heedless any more to conceal her hollow deformity, turned her frightful back and likewise vanished amid the green obscurity without. I lay and wept. The Maid of the Alder-tree had befooled me—nearly slain me—in spite of all the warnings I had received from those who knew my danger.

CHAPTER VII

"Fight on, my men, Sir Andrew sayes,
  A little Ime hurt, but yett not slaine;
Ile but lye downe and bleede awhile,
  And then Ile rise and fight againe."
                    Ballad of Sir Andrew Barton.

BUT I COULD NOT remain where I was any longer, though
the daylight was hateful to me, and the thought of the great,
innocent, bold sunrise unendurable. Here there was no well to
cool my face, smarting with the bitterness of my own tears. Nor
would I have washed in the well of that grotto, had it flowed
clear as the rivers of Paradise. I rose, and feebly left the
sepulchral cave. I took my way I knew not whither, but still
towards the sunrise. The birds were singing; but not for me. All
the creatures spoke a language of their own, with which I had
nothing to do, and to which I cared not to find the key any
more. I walked listlessly along. What distressed me most—more
even than my own folly—was the perplexing question—How
can beauty and ugliness dwell so near? Even with her altered
complexion and her face of dislike; disenchanted of the belief
that clung around her; known for a living, walking sepulchre,
faithless, deluding, traitorous; I felt, notwithstanding all this,
that she was beautiful. Upon this I pondered with undiminished
perplexity, though not without some gain. Then I began to
make surmises as to the mode of my deliverance; and concluded
that some hero, wandering in search of adventure, had heard
how the forest was infested; and, knowing it was useless to
attack the evil thing in person, had assailed with his battle-axe
the body in which he dwelt, and on which he was dependent for
his power of mischief in the wood. "Very likely," I thought, "the
repentant knight, who warned me of the evil which has befallen
me, was busy retrieving his lost honour, while I was sinking into
the same sorrow with himself; and, hearing of the dangerous and
mysterious being, arrived at his tree in time to save me from
being dragged to its roots, and buried like carrion, to nourish
him for yet deeper insatiableness." I found afterwards that my

conjecture was correct. I wondered how he had fared when his blows recalled the Ash himself, and that too I learned afterwards.

I walked on the whole day, with intervals of rest, but without food; for I could not have eaten, had any been offered me; till, in the afternoon, I seemed to approach the outskirts of the forest, and at length arrived at a farm-house. An unspeakable joy arose in my heart at beholding an abode of human beings once more, and I hastened up to the door, and knocked. A kind-looking, matronly woman, still handsome, made her appearance; who, as soon as she saw me, said kindly, "Ah, my poor boy, you have come from the wood! Were you in it last night?"

I should have ill endured, the day before, to be called *boy*; but now the motherly kindness of the word went to my heart; and, like a boy indeed, I burst into tears. She soothed me right gently; and, leading me into a room, made me lie down on a settle, while she went to find me some refreshment. She soon returned with food, but I could not eat. She almost compelled me to swallow some wine, when I revived sufficiently to be able to answer some of her questions. I told her the whole story.

"It is just as I feared," she said; "but you are now for the night beyond the reach of any of these dreadful creatures. It is no wonder they could delude a child like you. But I must beg you, when my husband comes in, not to say a word about these things; for he thinks me even half crazy for believing anything of the sort. But I must believe my senses, as he cannot believe beyond his, which give him no intimations of this kind. I think he could spend the whole of Midsummer-eve in the wood and come back with the report that he saw nothing worse than himself. Indeed, good man, he would hardly find anything better than himself, if he had seven more senses given him."

"But tell me how it is that she could be so beautiful without any heart at all—without any place even for a heart to live in."

"I cannot quite tell," she said; "but I am sure she would not look so beautiful if she did not take means to make herself look more beautiful than she is. And then, you know, you began by being in love with her before you saw her beauty, mistaking her for the lady of the marble—another kind altogether, I should think. But the chief thing that makes her beautiful is this: that, although she loves no man, she loves the love of any man; and when she finds one in her power, her desire to bewitch him and gain his love (not for the sake of his love either, but that she may be conscious anew of her own beauty, through the admiration he manifests), makes her very lovely—with a self-destructive beauty, though; for it is that which is constantly wearing her away within, till, at last, the decay will reach her face, and her whole front, when all the lovely mask of nothing will fall to pieces, and she be vanished for ever. So a wise man, whom she met in the wood some years ago, and who, I think, for all his wisdom, fared no better than you, told me, when, like you, he spent the next night here, and recounted to me his adventures."

I thanked her very warmly for her solution, though it was but partial; wondering much that in her, as in the woman I met on my first entering the forest, there should be such superiority to her apparent condition. Here she left me to take some rest; though, indeed, I was too much agitated to rest in any other way than by simply ceasing to move.

In half an hour, I heard a heavy step approach and enter the house. A jolly voice, whose slight huskiness appeared to proceed from overmuch laughter, called out : "Betsy, the pigs' trough is quite empty, and that is a pity. Let them swill, lass! They're of no use but to get fat. Ha! ha! ha! Gluttony is not forbidden in their commandments. Ha! ha! ha!" The very voice, kind and jovial, seemed to disrobe the room of the strange look which all new places wear—to disenchant it out of the realm of the ideal into that of the actual. It began to look as if I had known every corner of it for twenty years; and when, soon after, the dame came and fetched me to partake of their early supper, the grasp of his great hand, and the harvest-moon of his benevolent face, which was needed to light up the rotundity of the globe beneath it, produced such a reaction in me, that, for a moment, I could hardly believe that there was a Fairy Land; and that all I had passed through since I left home, had not been the wandering dream of a diseased imagination, operating on a too mobile frame, not merely causing me indeed to travel, but peopling for me with vague phantoms the regions through which my actual steps had led me. But the next moment my eye fell upon a little girl who was sitting in the chimney-corner, with a little book open on her knee, from which she had apparently just looked up to fix great inquiring eyes upon me. I believed in Fairy Land again. She went on with her reading, as soon as she saw that I observed her looking at me. I went near, and peeping over her shoulder, saw that she was reading *The History of Graciosa and Percinet.*

"Very improving book, sir," remarked the old farmer, with a good-humoured laugh. "We are in the very hottest corner of Fairy Land here. Ha! ha! Stormy night, last night, sir."

"Was it, indeed?" I rejoined. "It was not so with me. A lovelier night I never saw."

"Indeed! Where were you last night?"

"I spent it in the forest. I had lost my way."

"Ah! then, perhaps, you will be able to convince my good woman, that there is nothing very remarkable about the forest; for, to tell the truth, it bears but a bad name in these parts. I dare say you saw nothing worse than yourself there?"

"I hope I did," was my inward reply; but, for an audible one, I contented myself with saying, "Why, I certainly did see some appearances I could hardly account for; but that is nothing to be wondered at in an unknown wild forest, and with the uncertain light of the moon alone to go by."

"Very true! you speak like a sensible man, sir. We have but few sensible folks round about us. Now, you would hardly credit it, but my wife believes every fairy-tale that ever was written. I cannot account for it. She is a most sensible woman in everything else."

"But should not that make you treat her belief with something of respect, though you cannot share in it yourself?"

"Yes, that is all very well in theory; but when you come to live every day in the midst of absurdity, it is far less easy to behave respectfully to it. Why, my wife actually believes the story of the 'White Cat.' You know it, I dare say."

"I read all these tales when a child, and know that one especially well."

"But, father," interposed the little girl in the chimney-corner, "you know quite well that mother is descended from that very princess who was changed by the wicked fairy into a white cat. Mother has told me so a many times, and you ought to believe everything she says."

"I can easily believe that," rejoined the farmer, with another fit of laughter; "for, the other night, a mouse came gnawing and scratching beneath the floor, and would not let us go to sleep. Your mother sprang out of bed, and going as near it as she could, mewed so infernally like a great cat, that the noise

ceased instantly. I believe the poor mouse died of the fright, for
we have never heard it again. Ha! ha! ha!"

The son, an ill-looking youth, who had entered during the
conversation, joined in his father's laugh; but his laugh was very
different from the old man's: it was polluted with a sneer. I
watched him, and saw that, as soon as it was over, he looked
scared, as if he dreaded some evil consequences to follow his
presumption. The woman stood near, waiting till we should seat
ourselves at the table, and listening to it all with an amused air,
which had something in it of the look with which one listens to
the sententious remarks of a pompous child. We sat down to
supper, and I ate heartily. My bygone distresses began already
to look far off.

"In what direction are you going?" asked the old man.

"Eastward," I replied; nor could I have given a more definite
answer. "Does the forest extend much further in that direction?"

"Oh! for miles and miles; I do not know how far. For
although I have lived on the borders of it all my life, I have
been too busy to make journeys of discovery into it. Nor do I see
what I could discover. It is only trees and trees, till one is sick of
them. By the way, if you follow the eastward track from here,
you will pass close to what the children say is the very house of
the ogre that Hop-o'-my-Thumb visited, and ate his little
daughters with the crowns of gold."

"Oh, father! ate his little daughters! No; he only changed
their gold crowns for nightcaps; and the great long-toothed ogre
killed them in mistake; but I do not think even he ate them, for
you know they were his own little ogresses."

"Well, well, child; you know all about it a great deal better
than I do. However, the house has, of course, in such a foolish
neighbourhood as this, a bad enough name; and I must confess
there is a woman living in it, with teeth long enough, and white
enough too, for the lineal descendant of the greatest ogre that
ever was made. I think you had better not go near her."

In such talk as this the night wore on. When supper was
finished, which lasted some time, my hostess conducted me to
my chamber.

"If you had not had enough of it already," she said, "I would
have put you in another room, which looks towards the forest;
and where you would most likely have seen something more of

its inhabitants. For they frequently pass the window, and even enter the room sometimes. Strange creatures spend whole nights in it, at certain seasons of the year. I am used to it, and do not mind it. No more does my little girl, who sleeps in it always. But this room looks southward towards the open country, and they never show themselves here; at least I never saw any."

I was somewhat sorry not to gather any experience that I might have, of the inhabitants of Fairy Land; but the effect of the farmer's company, and of my own later adventures, was such, that I chose rather an undisturbed night in my more human quarters; which, with their clean white curtains and white linen, were very inviting to my weariness.

In the morning I awoke refreshed, after a profound and dreamless sleep. The sun was high, when I looked out of the window, shining over a wide, undulating, cultivated country. Various garden-vegetables were growing beneath my window. Everything was radiant with clear sunlight. The dew-drops were sparkling their busiest; the cows in a near-by field were eating as if they had not been at it all day yesterday; the maids were singing at their work as they passed to and fro between the out-houses : I did not believe in Fairy Land. I went down, and found the family already at breakfast. But before I entered the room where they sat, the little girl came to me, and looked up in my face, as though she wanted to say something to me. I stooped towards her; she put her arms round my neck, and her mouth to my ear, and whispered—

"A white lady has been flitting about the house all night."

"No whispering behind doors!" cried the farmer; and we entered together. "Well, how have you slept? No bogies, eh?"

"Not one, thank you; I slept uncommonly well."

"I am glad to hear it. Come and breakfast."

After breakfast, the farmer and his son went out; and I was left alone with the mother and daughter.

"When I looked out of the window this morning," I said, "I felt almost certain that Fairy Land was all a delusion of my brain; but whenever I come near you or your little daughter, I feel differently. Yet I could persuade myself, after my last adventures, to go back, and have nothing more to do with such strange beings."

"How will you go back?" said the woman.

"Nay, that I do not know."

"Because I have heard, that, for those who enter Fairy Land, there is no way of going back. They must go on, and go through it. How, I do not in the least know."

"That is quite the impression on my own mind. Something compels me to go on, as if my only path was onward, but I feel less inclined this morning to continue my adventures."

"Will you come and see my little child's room? She sleeps in the one I told you of, looking towards the forest."

"Willingly," I said.

So we went together, the little girl running before to open the door for us. It was a large room, full of old-fashioned furniture, that seemed to have once belonged to some great house. The window was built with a low arch, and filled with lozenge-shaped panes. The wall was very thick, and built of solid stone. I could see that part of the house had been erected against the remains of some old castle or abbey, or other great building; the fallen stones of which had probably served to complete it. But as soon as I looked out of the window, a gush of wonderment and longing flowed over my soul like the tide of a great sea. Fairy Land lay before me, and drew me towards it with an irresistible attraction. The trees bathed their great heads in the waves of the morning, while their roots were planted deep in gloom; save where on the borders the sunshine broke against their stems, or swept in long streams through their avenues, washing with brighter hue all the leaves over which it flowed; revealing the rich brown of the decayed leaves and fallen pine-cones, and the delicate greens of the long grasses and tiny forests of moss that covered the channel over which it passed in motion-less rivers of light. I turned hurriedly to bid my hostess farewell without further delay. She smiled at my haste, but with an anxious look.

"You had better not go near the house of the ogre, I think. My son will show you into another path, which will join the first beyond it."

Not wishing to be headstrong or too confident any more, I agreed; and having taken leave of my kind entertainers, went into the wood, accompanied by the youth. He scarcely spoke as we went along; but he led me through the trees till we struck upon a path. He told me to follow it, and, with a muttered "good morning," left me.

CHAPTER VIII

"Ich bin ein Theil des Theils, der anfangs alles war."
GOETHE.—*Mephistopheles* in *Faust*.

"I am a part of the part, which at first was the whole."

M Y SPIRITS ROSE as I went deeper into the forest; but I could not regain my former elasticity of mind. I found cheerfulness to be like life itself—not to be created by any argument. Afterwards I learned, that the best way to manage some kinds of painful thoughts, is to dare them to do their worst; to let them lie and gnaw at your heart till they are tired; and you find you still have a residue of life they cannot kill. So, better and worse, I went on, till I came to a little clearing in the forest. In the middle of this clearing stood a long, low hut, built with one end against a single tall cypress, which rose like a spire to the building. A vague misgiving crossed my mind when I saw it; but I must needs go closer, and look through a little half-open door, near the opposite end from the cypress. Window I saw none. On peeping in, and looking towards the further end, I saw a lamp burning, with a dim, reddish flame, and the head of a woman, bent downwards, as if reading by its light. I could see nothing more for a few moments. At length, as my eyes got used to the dimness of the place, I saw that the part of the rude building near me was used for household purposes; for several rough utensils lay here and there, and a bed stood in the corner. An irresistible attraction caused me to enter. The woman never raised her face, the upper part of which alone I could see distinctly; but, as soon as I stepped within the threshold, she began to read aloud, in a low and not altogether unpleasing voice, from an ancient little volume which she held open with one hand on the table upon which stood the lamp. What she read was something like this :

"So, then, as darkness had no beginning, neither will it ever have an end. So, then, is it eternal. The negation of aught else, is its affirmation. Where the light cannot come, there abideth the darkness. The light doth but hollow a mine out of the infinite extension of the darkness. And ever upon the steps of the light treadeth the darkness; yea, springeth in fountains and wells amidst it, from the secret channels of its mighty sea. Truly, man is but a passing flame, moving unquietly amid the surrounding rest of night; without which he yet could not be, and whereof he is in part compounded."

As I drew nearer, and she read on, she moved a little to turn a leaf of the dark old volume, and I saw that her face was sallow and slightly forbidding. Her forehead was high, and her black eyes repressedly quiet. But she took no notice of me. This end of the cottage, if cottage it could be called, was destitute of furniture, except the table with the lamp, and the chair on which the woman sat. In one corner was a door, apparently of a cupboard in the wall, but which might lead to a room beyond. Still the irresistible desire which had made me enter the building, urged me : I must open that door, and see what was beyond it. I approached, and laid my hand on the rude latch. Then the woman spoke, but without lifting her head or looking at me : "You had better not open that door." This was uttered quite quietly; and she went on with her reading, partly in silence, partly aloud; but both modes seemed equally intended for herself alone. The prohibition, however, only increased my desire to see; and as she took no further notice, I gently opened the door to its full width, and looked in. At first, I saw nothing worthy of attention. It seemed a common closet, with shelves on each hand, on which stood various little necessaries for the humble uses of a cottage. In one corner stood one or two brooms, in another a hatchet and other common tools; showing that it was in use every hour of the day for household purposes. But, as I looked, I saw that there were no shelves at the back, and that an empty space went in further; its termination appearing to be a faintly glimmering wall or curtain, somewhat less, however, than the width and height of the doorway where I stood. But, as I continued looking, for a few seconds, towards this faintly-luminous limit, my eyes came into true relation with their object. All at once, with such a shiver as when one is suddenly conscious of the presence of another in a room where he has, for hours, considered himself alone, I saw that the seemingly luminous extremity was a sky, as of night, beheld through the long perspective of a narrow, dark passage, through what, or built of what, I could not tell. As I gazed, I clearly discerned two or three stars glimmering faintly in the distant blue. But, suddenly, and as if it had been running fast from a far distance for this very point, and had turned the corner without abating its swiftness, a dark figure sped into and along the passage from the blue opening at the remote end. I started back and shuddered, but kept looking, for I could not help it. On and on it came, with a speedy approach but delayed arrival; till, at last, through the many gradations of approach, it seemed to come within the sphere of myself, rushed up to me, and passed me into the cottage. All I could tell of its appearance was, that it seemed to be a dark human figure. Its motion was entirely noiseless, and might be called a gliding, were it not that it appeared that of a runner, but with ghostly feet. I had moved back yet a little to let him pass me, and looked round after him instantly. I could not see him.

"Where is he?" I said, in some alarm, to the woman, who still sat reading.

"There, on the floor, behind you," she said, pointing with her arm half-outstretched, but not lifting her eyes. I turned and looked, but saw nothing. Then with a feeling that there was yet something behind me, I looked round over my shoulder; and there, on the ground, lay a black shadow, the size of a man. It was so dark, that I could see it in the dim light of the lamp, which shone full upon it, apparently without thinning at all the intensity of its hue.

"I told you," said the woman, "you had better not look into that closet."

"What is it?" I said, with a growing sense of horror.

"It is only your shadow that has found you," she replied. "Everybody's shadow is ranging up and down looking for him. I believe you call it by a different name in your world : yours has found you, as every person's is almost certain to do who looks into that closet, especially after meeting one in the forest, whom I dare say you have met."

Here, for the first time, she lifted her head, and looked full at me : her mouth was full of long, white, shining teeth; and I knew that I was in the house of the ogre. I could not speak, but turned and left the house, with the shadow at my heels. "A nice sort of valet to have," I said to myself bitterly, as I stepped into

the sunshine, and, looking over my shoulder, saw that it lay
yet blacker in the full blaze of the sunlight. Indeed, only when
I stood between it and the sun, was the blackness at all diminished. I was so bewildered—stunned—both by the event itself
and its suddenness, that I could not at all realise to myself what
it would be to have such a constant and strange attendance; but
with a dim conviction that my present dislike would soon grow
to loathing, I took my dreary way through the wood.

CHAPTER IX

"O Lady! we receive but what we give,
And in our life alone does nature live:
Ours is her wedding garment, ours her shroud!

.   .   .   .   .   .

Ah! from the soul itself must issue forth,
A light, a glory, a fair luminous cloud,
    Enveloping the Earth—
And from the soul itself must there be sent
    A sweet and potent voice, of its own birth,
Of all sweet sounds the life and element!"

COLERIDGE.

FROM THIS TIME, until I arrived at the palace of Fairy Land,
I can attempt no consecutive account of my wanderings and
adventures. Everything, henceforward, existed for me in its
relation to my attendant. What influence he exercised upon
everything into contact with which I was brought, may be
understood from a few detached instances. To begin with this
very day on which he first joined me : after I had walked heartlessly along for two or three hours, I was very weary, and lay
down to rest in a most delightful part of the forest, carpeted with
wild-flowers. I lay for half an hour in a dull repose, and then
got up to pursue my way. The flowers on the spot where I had
lain were crushed to the earth : but I saw that they would soon
lift their heads and rejoice again in the sun and air. Not so those
on which my shadow had lain. The very outline of it could be
traced in the withered lifeless grass, and the scorched and
shrivelled flowers which stood there, dead, and hopeless of any

resurrection. I shuddered, and hastened away with sad forebodings.

In a few days, I had reason to dread an extension of its baleful influences from the fact, that it was no longer confined to one position in regard to myself. Hitherto, when seized with an irresistible desire to look on my evil demon (which longing would unaccountably seize me at any moment, returning at longer or shorter intervals, sometimes every minute), I had to turn my head backwards, and look over my shoulder; in which position, as long as I could retain it, I was fascinated. But one day, having come out on a clear grassy hill, which commanded a glorious prospect, though of what I cannot now tell, my shadow moved round, and came in front of me. And, presently, a new manifestation increased my distress. For it began to coruscate, and shoot out on all sides a radiation of dim shadow. These rays of gloom issued from the central shadow as from a black sun, lengthening and shortening with continual change. But wherever a ray struck, that part of earth, or sea, or sky, became void, and desert, and sad to my heart. On this, the first development of its new power, one ray shot out beyond the rest, seeming to lengthen infinitely, until it smote the great sun on the face, which withered and darkened beneath the blow. I turned away and went on. The shadow retreated to its former position; and when I looked again, it had drawn in all its spears of darkness, and followed like a dog at my heels.

Once, as I passed by a cottage, there came out a lovely fairy child, with two wondrous toys, one in each hand. The one was the tube through which the fairy-gifted poet looks when he beholds the same thing everywhere; the other that through which he looks when he combines into new forms of loveliness those images of beauty which his own choice has gathered from all regions wherein he has travelled. Round the child's head was an aureole of emanating rays. As I looked at him in wonder and delight, round crept from behind me the something dark, and the child stood in my shadow. Straightway he was a commonplace boy, with a rough broad-brimmed straw hat, through which brim the sun shone from behind. The toys he carried were a multiplying glass and a kaleidoscope. I sighed and departed.

One evening, as a great silent flood of western gold flowed through an avenue in the woods, down the stream, just as when

I saw him first, came the sad knight, riding on his chestnut
steed. But his armour did not shine half so red as when I saw
him first. Many a blow of mighty sword and axe, turned aside
by the strength of his mail, and glancing adown the surface, had
swept from its path the fretted rust, and the glorious steel had
answered the kindly blow with the thanks of returning light.
These streaks and spots made his armour look like the floor of a
forest in the sunlight. His forehead was higher than before, for
the contracting wrinkles were nearly gone; and the sadness that
remained on his face was the sadness of a dewy summer twilight,
not that of a frosty autumn morn. He, too, had met the Alder-
maiden as I, but he had plunged into the torrent of mighty
deeds, and the stain was nearly washed away. No shadow
followed him. He had not entered the dark house; he had not
had time to open the closet door. "Will he ever look in?" I said
to myself. "*Must* his shadow find him some day?" But I could
not answer my own questions.

We travelled together for two days, and I began to love him. It
was plain that he suspected my story in some degree; and I saw
him once or twice looking curiously and anxiously at my attendant gloom, which all this time had remained very obsequiously
behind me; but I offered no explanation, and he asked none.
Shame at my neglect of his warning, and a horror which shrunk
from even alluding to its cause, kept me silent; till, on the
evening of the second day, some noble words from my companion roused all my heart; and I was at the point of falling on
his neck, and telling him the whole story; seeking, if not for
helpful advice, for of that I was hopeless, yet for the comfort of
sympathy—when round slid the shadow and inwrapt my friend;
and I could not trust him. The glory of his brow vanished; the
light of his eye grew cold; and I held my peace. The next
morning we parted.

But the most dreadful thing of all was, that I now began to
feel something like satisfaction in the presence of my shadow. I
began to be rather vain of my attendant, saying to myself, "In
a land like this, with so many illusions everywhere, I need his
aid to disenchant the things around me. He does away with all
appearances, and shows me things in their true colour and form.
And I am not one to be fooled with the vanities of the common
crowd. I will not see beauty where there is none. I will dare to

behold things as they are. And if I live in a waste instead of a paradise, I will live knowing where I live." But of this a certain exercise of his power which soon followed quite cured me, turning my feeling towards him once more into loathing and distrust. It was thus :—

One bright noon, a little maiden joined me, coming through the wood in a direction at right angles to my path. She came along singing and dancing, happy as a child, though she seemed almost a woman. In her hands—now in one, now in another—she carried a small globe, bright and clear as the purest crystal. This seemed at once her plaything and her greatest treasure. At one moment, you would have thought her utterly careless of it, and at another, overwhelmed with anxiety for its safety. But I believe she was taking care of it all the time, perhaps not least when least occupied with it. She stopped by me with a smile, and bade me good day with the sweetest voice. I felt a wonderful liking to the child—for she produced on me more the impression of a child, though my understanding told me differently. We talked a little, and then walked on together in the direction I had been pursuing. I asked her about the globe she carried, but getting no definite answer, I held out my hand to take it. She drew back, and said, but smiling almost invitingly the while, "You must not touch it;"—then, after a moment's pause—"Or if you do, it must be very gently." I touched it with a finger. A slight vibratory motion arose in it, accompanied, or perhaps manifested, by a faint sweet sound. I touched it again, and the sound increased. I touched it the third time : a tiny torrent of harmony rolled out of the little globe. She would not let me touch it any more.

We travelled on together all that day. She left me when twilight came on; but next day, at noon, she met me as before, and again we travelled till evening. The third day she came once more at noon, and we walked on together. Now, though we had talked about a great many things connected with Fairy Land, and the life she had led hitherto, I had never been able to learn anything about the globe. This day, however, as we went on, the shadow glided round and inwrapt the maiden. It could not change her. But my desire to know about the globe, which in his gloom began to waver as with an inward light, and to shoot out flashes of many-coloured flame, grew irresistible. I put out both my hands and laid hold of it. It began to sound as before. The sound rapidly increased, till it grew a low tempest of harmony, and the globe trembled, and quivered, and throbbed between my hands. I had not the heart to pull it away from the maiden, though I held it in spite of her attempts to take it from me; yes, I shame to say, in spite of her prayers, and, at last, her tears. The music went on growing in intensity and complication of tones, and the globe vibrated and heaved; till at last it burst in our hands, and a black vapour broke upwards from out of it; then turned, as if blown sideways, and enveloped the maiden, hiding even the shadow in its blackness. She held fast the fragments, which I abandoned, and fled from me into the forest in the direction whence she had come, wailing like a child, and crying, "You have broken my globe; my globe is broken—my globe is broken!" I followed her, in the hope of comforting her; but had not pursued her far, before a sudden cold gust of wind bowed the tree-tops above us, and swept through their stems around us; a great cloud overspread the day, and a fierce tempest came on, in which I lost sight of her. It lies heavy on my heart to this hour. At night, ere I fall asleep, often, whatever I may be thinking about, I suddenly hear her voice, crying out, "You have broken my globe; my globe is broken; ah, my globe!"

Here I will mention one more strange thing; but whether this peculiarity was owing to my shadow at all, I am not able to assure myself. I came to a village, the inhabitants of which could not at first sight be distinguished from the dwellers in our own land. They rather avoided than sought my company, though they were very pleasant when I addressed them. But at last I observed, that whenever I came within a certain distance of any one of them, which distance, however, varied with different individuals, the whole appearance of the person began to change; and this change increased in degree as I approached. When I receded to the former distance, the former appearance was restored. The nature of the change was grotesque, following no fixed rule. The nearest resemblance to it that I know, is the distortion produced in your countenance when you look at it as reflected in a concave or convex surface—say, either side of a bright spoon. Of this phenomenon I first became aware in rather a ludicrous way. My host's daughter was a very pleasant pretty girl, who made herself more agreeable to me than most of those about me. For some days my companion-shadow had been less obtrusive than usual; and such was the reaction of spirits occasioned by the simple mitigation of torment, that, although I had cause enough besides to be gloomy, I felt light and comparatively happy. My impression is, that she was quite aware of the law of appearances that existed between the people of the place and myself, and had resolved to amuse herself at my expense; for one evening, after some jesting and raillery, she, somehow or other, provoked me to attempt to kiss her. But she was well defended from any assault of the kind. Her countenance became, of a sudden, absurdly hideous; the pretty mouth was elongated and otherwise amplified sufficiently to have allowed of six simultaneous kisses. I started back in bewildered dismay; she burst into the merriest fit of laughter, and ran' from the room. I soon found that the same undefinable law of change operated between me and all the other villagers; and that, to feel I was in pleasant company, it was absolutely necessary for me to discover and observe the right focal distance between myself and each one with whom I had to do. This done, all went pleasantly enough. Whether, when I happened to neglect this precaution, I presented to them an equally ridiculous appearance, I did not ascertain; but I presume that the alteration was common to the approximating parties. I was likewise unable to determine whether I was a necessary party to the production of this strange transformation, or whether it took place as well, under the given circumstances, between the inhabitants themselves.

CHAPTER X

"From Eden's bowers the full-fed rivers flow,
  To guide the outcasts to the land of woe:
  Our Earth one little toiling streamlet yields,
  To guide the wanderers to the happy fields."

AFTER LEAVING THIS village, where I had rested for nearly a week, I travelled through a desert region of dry sand and glittering rocks, peopled principally by goblin-fairies. When I first entered their domains, and, indeed, whenever I fell in with another tribe of them, they began mocking me with offered handfuls of gold and jewels, making hideous grimaces at me, and performing the most antic homage, as if they thought I expected reverence, and meant to humour me like a maniac. But ever, as soon as one cast his eyes on the shadow behind me, he made a wry face, partly of pity, partly of contempt, and looked ashamed, as if he had been caught doing something inhuman; then, throwing down his handful of gold, and ceasing all his grimaces, he stood aside to let me pass in peace, and made signs to his companions to do the like. I had no inclination to observe them much, for the shadow was in my heart as well as at my heels. I walked listlessly and almost hopelessly along, till I arrived one day at a small spring; which, bursting cool from the heart of a sun-heated rock, flowed somewhat southwards from the direction I had been taking. I drank of this spring, and found myself wonderfully refreshed. A kind of love to the cheerful little stream arose in my heart. It was born in a desert; but it seemed to say to itself, "I will flow, and sing, and lave my banks, till I make my desert a paradise." I thought I could not do better than follow it, and see what it made of it. So down with the stream I went, over rocky lands, burning with sunbeams. But the rivulet flowed not far, before a few blades of grass appeared on its banks, and then, here and there, a stunted bush. Sometimes it disappeared altogether under ground; and after I had wandered some distance, as near as I could guess, in the direction it seemed to take, I would suddenly hear it again, singing, sometimes far away to my right or left, amongst new rocks, over which it made new cataracts of watery melodies. The verdure on its banks increased as it flowed; other streams joined it; and at last, after many days' travel, I found myself, one gorgeous summer evening, resting by the side of a broad river, with a glorious horse-chestnut tree towering above me, and dropping its blossoms, milk-white and rosy-red, all about me. As I sat, a gush of joy sprang forth in my heart, and overflowed at my eyes. Through my tears, the whole landscape glimmered in such bewitching loveliness, that I felt as if I were entering Fairy Land for the first time, and some loving hand were waiting to cool my head, and a loving word to warm my heart. Roses, wild roses, every-where! So plentiful were they, they not only perfumed the air, they seemed to dye it a faint rose-hue. The colour floated abroad with the scent, and clomb, and spread, until the whole west blushed and glowed with the gathered incense of roses. And my heart fainted with longing in my bosom. Could I but see the Spirit of the Earth, as I saw once the indwelling woman of the beech-tree, and my beauty of the pale marble, I should be content. Content!—Oh, how gladly would I die of the light of her eyes! Yea, I would cease to be, if that would bring me one word of love from the one mouth. The twilight sank around, and infolded me with sleep. I slept as I had not slept for months. I did not awake till late in the morning; when, refreshed in body and mind, I rose as from the death that wipes out the sadness of life, and then dies itself in the new morrow. Again I followed the stream; now climbing a steep rocky bank that hemmed it in; now wading through long grasses and wild flowers in its path; now through meadows; and anon through woods that crowded down to the very lip of the water.

At length, in a nook of the river, gloomy with the weight of overhanging foliage, and still and deep as a soul in which the torrent eddies of pain have hollowed a great gulf, and then, subsiding in violence, have left it full of a motionless, fathomless sorrow—I saw a little boat lying. So still was the water here, that the boat needed no fastening. It lay as if some one had just stepped ashore, and would in a moment return. But as there were no signs of presence, and no track through the thick bushes; and, moreover, as I was in Fairy Land, where one does very much as he pleases, I forced my way to the brink, stepped into the boat, pushed it, with the help of the tree-branches, out into the stream, lay down in the bottom, and let my boat and me float whither the stream would carry us. I seemed to lose myself in the great flow of sky above me, unbroken in its infinitude, except when, now and then, coming nearer the shore at a bend in the river, a tree would sweep its mighty head silently above mine, and glide away back into the past, never more to fling its shadow over me. I fell asleep in this cradle, in which mother Nature was rocking her weary child; and while I slept, the sun slept not, but went round his arched way. When I awoke, he slept in the waters, and I went on my silent path beneath a round silvery moon. And a pale moon looked up from the floor of the great blue cave that lay in the abysmal silence beneath.

Why are all reflections lovelier than what we call the reality?

—not so grand or so strong, it may be, but always lovelier? Fair as is the gliding sloop on the shining sea, the wavering, trembling, unresting sail below is fairer still. Yea, the reflecting ocean itself, reflected in the mirror, has a wondrousness about its waters that somewhat vanishes when I turn towards itself. All mirrors are magic mirrors. The commonest room is a room in a poem when I turn to the glass. (And this reminds me, while I write, of a strange story which I read in the fairy palace, and of which I will try to make a feeble memorial in its place.) In whatever way it may be accounted for, of one thing we may be sure, that this feeling is no cheat; for there is no cheating in nature and the simple unsought feelings of the soul. There must be a truth involved in it, though we may but in part lay hold of the meaning. Even the memories of past pain are beautiful; and past delights, though beheld only through clefts in the grey clouds of sorrow, are lovely as Fairy Land. But how have I wandered into the deeper fairyland of the soul, while as yet I only float towards the fairy palace of Fairy Land! The moon, which is the lovelier memory or reflex of the down-gone sun, the joyous day seen in the faint mirror of the brooding night, had rapt me away.

I sat up in the boat. Gigantic forest trees were about me; through which, like a silver snake, twisted and twined the great river. The little waves, when I moved in the boat, heaved and fell with a plash as of molten silver, breaking the image of the moon into a thousand morsels, fusing again into one, as the ripples of laughter die into the still face of joy. The sleeping woods, in undefined massiveness; the water that flowed in its sleep; and, above all, the enchantress moon, which had cast them all, with her pale eye, into the charmed slumber, sank into my soul, and I felt as if I had died in a dream, and should never more awake.

From this I was partly aroused by a glimmering of white, that, through the trees on the left, vaguely crossed my vision, as I gazed upwards. But the trees again hid the object; and at the moment, some strange melodious bird took up its song, and sang, not an ordinary bird-song, with constant repetitions of the same melody, but what sounded like a continuous strain, in which one thought was expressed, deepening in intensity as evolved in progress. It sounded like a welcome already overshadowed with the coming farewell. As in all sweetest music, a tinge of sadness was in every note. Nor do we know how much of the pleasures even of life we owe to the intermingled sorrows. Joy cannot unfold the deepest truths, although deepest truth must be deepest joy. Cometh white-robed Sorrow, stooping and wan, and flingeth wide the doors she may not enter. Almost we linger with Sorrow for very love.

As the song concluded, the stream bore my little boat with a gentle sweep round a bend of the river; and lo! on a broad lawn, which rose from the water's edge with a long green slope to a clear elevation from which the trees receded on all sides, stood a stately palace glimmering ghostly in the moonshine : it seemed to be built throughout of the whitest marble. There was no reflection of moonlight from windows—there seemed to be none; so there was no cold glitter; only, as I said, a ghostly shimmer. Numberless shadows tempered the shine, from column and balcony and tower. For everywhere galleries ran along the face of the buildings; wings were extended in many directions; and numberless openings, through which the moonbeams vanished into the interior, and which served both for doors and windows, had their separate balconies in front, communicating with a common gallery that rose on its own pillars. Of course, I did not discover all this from the river, and in the moonlight. But, though I was there for many days, I did not succeed in mastering the inner topography of the building, so extensive and complicated was it.

Here I wished to land, but the boat had no oars on board. However, I found that a plank, serving for a seat, was unfastened, and with that I brought the boat to the bank, and scrambled on shore. Deep soft turf sank beneath my feet, as I went up the ascent towards the palace. When I reached it, I saw that it stood on a great platform of marble, with an ascent, by broad stairs of the same, all round it. Arrived on the platform, I found there was an extensive outlook over the forest, which, however, was rather veiled than revealed by the moonlight. Entering by a wide gateway, but without gates, into an inner court, surrounded on all sides by great marble pillars supporting galleries above, I saw a large fountain of porphyry in the middle, throwing up a lofty column of water, which fell, with a noise as of the fusion of all sweet sounds, into a basin beneath; overflowing which, it ran in a single channel towards the interior of the building. Although the moon was by this time so low in the west, that not a ray of her light fell into the court, over the height of the surrounding buildings; yet was the court lighted by a second reflex from the sun of other lands. For the top of the column of water, just as it spread to fall, caught the moonbeams; and like a great pale lamp, hung high in the night air, threw a dim memory of light (as it were) over the court below. This court was paved in diamonds of white and red marble. According to my custom since I entered Fairy Land, of taking for a guide whatever I first found moving in any direction, I followed the stream from the basin of the fountain. It led me to a great open door, beneath the ascending steps of which it ran through a low arch, and disappeared. Entering here, I found myself in a great hall, surrounded with white pillars, and paved with black and white. This I could see by the moonlight, which, from the other side, streamed through open windows into the hall. Its height I could not distinctly see. As soon as I entered, I had the feeling so common to me in the woods, that there were others there besides myself, though I could see no one, and heard no sound to indicate a presence. Since my visit to the Church of Darkness, my power of seeing the fairies of the higher orders had gradually diminished, until it had almost ceased. But I could frequently believe in their presence while unable to see them. Still, although I had company, and doubtless of a safe kind, it seemed rather dreary to spend the night in an empty marble hall, however beautiful; especially as the moon was near the going down, and it would soon be dark. So I began at the place where I entered, and walked round the hall, looking for some door or passage that might lead me to a more hospitable chamber. As I walked, I was deliciously haunted with the feeling that behind some one of the seemingly innumerable pillars, one who loved me was waiting for me. Then I thought she was following me from pillar to pillar as I went along; but no arms came out of the faint moonlight, and no sigh assured me of her presence.

At length I came to an open corridor, into which I turned; notwithstanding that, in doing so, I left the light behind. Along this I walked with outstretched hands, groping my way; till, arriving at another corridor, which seemed to strike off at right angles to that in which I was, I saw at the end a faintly glimmering

light, too pale even for moonshine, resembling rather a stray
phosphorescence. However, where everything was white, a little
light went a great way. So I walked on to the end, and a long
corridor it was. When I came up to the light, I found that it
proceeded from what looked like silver letters upon a door of
ebony; and, to my surprise even in the home of wonder itself,
the letters formed the words, *The Chamber of Sir Anodos*.
Although I had as yet no right to the honours of a knight, I
ventured to conclude that the chamber was indeed intended
for me; and, opening the door without hesitation, I entered. Any
doubt as to whether I was right in so doing, was soon dispelled.
What to my dark eyes seemed a blaze of light, burst upon me.
A fire of large pieces of some sweet-scented wood, supported by
dogs of silver, was burning on the hearth, and a bright lamp
stood on a table, in the midst of a plentiful meal, apparently
awaiting my arrival. But what surprised me more than all, was,
that the room was in every respect a copy of my own room, the
room whence the little stream from my basin had led me into
Fairy Land. There was the very carpet of grass and moss and
daisies, which I had myself designed; the curtains of pale blue
silk, that fell like a cataract over the windows; the old-fashioned
bed, with the chintz furniture, on which I had slept from boyhood. "Now I shall sleep," I said to myself. "My shadow dares
not come here."

I sat down to the table, and began to help myself to the good
things before me with confidence. And now I found, as in many
instances before, how true the fairy tales are; for I was waited
on, all the time of my meal, by invisible hands. I had scarcely
to do more than look towards anything I wanted, when it was
brought me, just as if it had come to me of itself. My glass was
kept filled with the wine I had chosen, until I looked towards
another bottle or decanter; when a fresh glass was substituted,
and the other wine supplied. When I had eaten and drank more
heartily and joyfully than ever since I entered Fairy Land, the
whole was removed by several attendants, of whom some were
male and some female, as I thought I could distinguish from the
way the dishes were lifted from the table, and the motion with
which they were carried out of the room. As soon as they were
all taken away, I heard a sound as of the shutting of a door;
and knew that I was left alone. I sat long by the fire, meditating,

and wondering how it would all end; and when at length, wearied with thinking, I betook myself to my own old bed, it was half with a hope that, when I awoke in the morning, I should awake not only in my own room, but in my own castle also; and that I should walk out upon my own native soil; and find that Fairy Land was, after all, only a vision of the night. The sound of the falling waters of the fountain floated me into oblivion.

CHAPTER XI

"A wilderness of building, sinking far
 And self-withdrawn into a wondrous depth,
 Far sinking into splendour—without end :
 Fabric it seemed of diamond and of gold,
 With alabaster domes, and silver spires,
 And blazing terrace upon terrace, high
 Uplifted."

WORDSWORTH.

BUT WHEN, AFTER a sleep, which, although dreamless, yet left behind it a sense of past blessedness, I awoke in the full morning, I found, indeed, that the room was still my own; but that it looked abroad upon an unknown landscape of forest and hill and dale on the one side—and on the other, upon the marble court, with the great fountain, the crest of which now flashed glorious in the sun, and cast on the pavement beneath a shower of faint shadows from the waters that fell from it into the marble basin below.

Agreeably to all authentic accounts of the treatment of travellers in Fairy Land, I found by my bedside a complete suit of fresh clothing, just such as I was in the habit of wearing; for, though varied sufficiently from the one removed, it was yet in complete accordance with my tastes. I dressed myself in this, and went out. The whole palace shone like silver in the sun. The marble was partly dull and partly polished; and every pinnacle, dome, and turret ended in a ball, or cone, or cusp of silver. It was like frost-work, and too dazzling, in the sun, for earthly eyes like mine. I will not attempt to describe the environs, save by saying, that all the pleasures to be found in the most varied and artistic arrangement of wood and river, lawn and wild forest, garden and shrubbery, rocky hill and luxurious vale; in living creatures wild and tame, in gorgeous birds, scattered fountains, little streams, and reedy lakes—all were here. Some parts of the palace itself I shall have occasion to describe more minutely.

For this whole morning I never thought of my demon shadow; and not till the weariness which supervened on delight brought it again to my memory, did I look round to see if it was behind me : it was scarcely discernible. But its presence, however faintly revealed, sent a pang to my heart, for the pain of which, not all the beauties around me could compensate. It was followed, however, by the comforting reflection that, peradventure, I might here find the magic word of power to banish the demon and set me free, so that I should no longer be a man beside myself. The Queen of Fairy Land, thought I, must dwell here : surely she will put forth her power to deliver me, and send me singing through the further gates of her country back to my own land. "Shadow of me !" I said; "which art not me, but which representest thyself to me as me; here I may find a shadow of light which will devour thee, the shadow of darkness ! Here I may find a blessing which will fall on thee as a curse, and damn thee to the blackness whence thou hast emerged unbidden." I said this, stretched at length on the slope of the lawn above the river; and as the hope arose within me, the sun came forth from a light fleecy cloud that swept across his face; and hill and dale, and the great river winding on through the still mysterious forest, flashed back his rays as with a silent shout of joy; all nature lived and glowed; the very earth grew warm beneath me; a magnificent dragon-fly went past me like an arrow from a bow, and a whole concert of birds burst into choral song.

The heat of the sun soon became too intense even for passive support. I therefore rose, and sought the shelter of one of the arcades. Wandering along from one to another of these, wherever my heedless steps led me, and wondering everywhere at the simple magnificence of the building, I arrived at another hall, the roof of which was of a pale blue, spangled with constellations of silver stars, and supported by porphyry pillars of a paler red than ordinary.—In this house (I may remark in passing), silver seemed everywhere preferred to gold; and such was the purity of the air, that it showed nowhere signs of tarnishing.—The whole of the floor of this hall, except a narrow path behind the pillars, paved with black, was hollowed into a huge basin, many feet deep, and filled with the purest, most liquid and radiant water. The sides of the basin were white marble, and the bottom was paved with all kinds of refulgent stones, of every shape and hue. In their arrangement, you would have supposed, at first sight, that there was no design, for they seemed to lie as if cast there from careless and playful hands; but it was a most harmonious confusion; and as I looked at the play of their colours, especially when the waters were in motion, I came at last to feel as if not one little pebble could be displaced, without injuring the effect of the whole. Beneath this floor of the water, lay the reflection of the blue inverted roof, fretted with its silver stars, like a second deeper sea, clasping and upholding the first. This fairy bath was probably fed from the fountain in the court. Led by an irresistible desire, I undressed, and plunged into the water. It clothed me as with a new sense and its object both in one. The waters lay so close to me, they seemed to enter and revive my heart. I rose to the surface, shook the water from my hair, and swam as in a rainbow, amid the coruscations of the gems below seen through the agitation caused by my motion. Then, with open eyes, I dived, and swam beneath the surface. And here was a new wonder. For the basin, thus beheld, appeared to extend on all sides like a sea, with here and there groups as of ocean rocks, hollowed by ceaseless billows into wondrous caves and grotesque pinnacles. Around the caves grew sea-weeds of all hues, and the corals glowed between; while far off, I saw the glimmer of what seemed to be creatures of human form at home in the waters. I thought I had been enchanted; and that when I rose to the surface, I should find myself miles from land, swimming alone upon a heaving sea; but when my eyes emerged from the waters, I saw above me the blue spangled vault, and the red pillars around. I dived again, and found myself once more in the heart of a great sea. I then arose, and swam to the edge, where I got out easily, for the water reached the very brim, and, as I drew near washed in tiny waves over the black marble border. I dressed, and went out, deeply refreshed.

And now I began to discern faint, gracious forms, here and there throughout the building. Some walked together in earnest conversation. Others strayed alone. Some stood in groups, as if looking at and talking about a picture or a statue. None of them heeded me. Nor were they plainly visible to my eyes. Sometimes a group, or single individual, would fade entirely out of the realm of my vision as I gazed. When evening came, and the moon arose, clear as a round of a horizon-sea when the sun hangs over it in the west, I began to see them all more plainly; especially when they came between me and the moon; and yet more especially, when I myself was in the shade. But, even then, I sometimes saw only the passing wave of a white robe; or a lovely arm or neck gleamed by in the moonshine; or white feet went walking alone over the moony sward. Nor, I grieve to say, did I ever come much nearer to these glorious beings, or ever look upon the Queen of the Fairies herself. My destiny ordered otherwise.

In this palace of marble and silver, and fountains and moonshine, I spent many days; waited upon constantly in my own room with everything desirable, and bathing daily in the fairy bath. All this time I was little troubled with my demon shadow. I had a vague feeling that he was somewhere about the palace; but it seemed as if the hope that I should in this place be finally freed from his hated presence, had sufficed to banish him for a time. How and where I found him, I shall soon have to relate.

The third day after my arrival, I found the library of the palace; and here, all the time I remained, I spent most of the middle of the day. For it was, not to mention far greater attractions, a luxurious retreat from the noontide sun. During the mornings and afternoons, I wandered about the lovely neighbourhood, or lay, lost in delicious day-dreams, beneath some mighty tree on the open lawn. My evenings were by-and-by spent in a part of the palace, the account of which, and of my adventures in connection with it, I must yet postpone for a little.

The library was a mighty hall, lighted from the roof, which was formed of something like glass, vaulted over in a single piece, and stained throughout with a great mysterious picture in gorgeous colouring. The walls were lined from floor to roof with books and books : most of them in ancient bindings, but some in strange new fashions which I had never seen, and which, were I to make the attempt, I could ill describe. All around the walls, in front of the books, ran galleries in rows, communicating by stairs. These galleries were built of all kinds of coloured stones;

all sorts of marble and granite, with porphyry, jasper, lapis
lazuli, agate, and various others, were ranged in wonderful
melody of successive colours. Although the material, then, of
which these galleries and stairs were built, rendered necessary
a certain degree of massiveness in the construction, yet such was
the size of the place, that they seemed to run along the walls
like cords. Over some parts of the library, descended curtains of
silk of various dyes, none of which I ever saw lifted while I was
there; and I felt somehow that it would be presumptuous in me
to venture to look within them. But the use of the other books
seemed free; and day after day I came to the library, threw
myself on one of the many sumptuous eastern carpets, which lay
here and there on the floor, and read, and read, until weary; if
that can be designated as weariness, which was rather the faintness of rapturous delight; or until, sometimes, the failing of the
light invited me to go abroad, in the hope that a cool gentle
breeze might have arisen to bathe, with an airy invigorating
bath, the limbs which the glow of the burning spirit within had
withered no less than the glow of the blazing sun without.

One peculiarity of these books, or at least most of those I
looked into, I must make a somewhat vain attempt to describe.

If, for instance, it was a book of metaphysics I opened, I had
scarcely read two pages before I seemed to myself to be pondering over discovered truth, and constructing the intellectual
machine whereby to communicate the discovery to my fellow-
men. With some books, however, of this nature, it seemed rather
as if the process was removed yet a great way further back; and
I was trying to find the root of a manifestation, the spiritual
truth whence a material vision sprang; or to combine two
propositions, both apparently true, either at once or in different
remembered moods, and to find the point in which their in-
visibly converging lines would unite in one, revealing a truth
higher than either and differing from both; though so far from
being opposed to either, that it was that whence each derived its
life and power. Or if the book was one of travels, I found
myself the traveller. New lands, fresh experiences, novel customs,
rose around me. I walked, I discovered, I fought, I suffered, I
rejoiced in my success. Was it a history? I was the chief actor
therein. I suffered my own blame; I was glad in my own praise.
With a fiction it was the same. Mine was the whole story. For I

took the place of the character who was most like myself, and
his story was mine; until, grown weary with the life of years
condensed in an hour, or arrived at my deathbed, or the end of
the volume, I would awake, with a sudden bewilderment, to
the consciousness of my present life, recognising the walls and
roof around me, and finding I joyed or sorrowed only in a book.
If the book was a poem, the words disappeared, or took the
subordinate position of an accompaniment to the succession of
forms and images that rose and vanished with a soundless
rhythm, and a hidden rime.

In one, with a mystical title, which I cannot recall, I read of
a world that is not like ours. The wondrous account, in such a
feeble, fragmentary way as is possible to me, I would willingly
impart. Whether or not it was all a poem, I cannot tell; but,
from the impulse I felt, when I first contemplated writing it, to
break into rime, to which impulse I shall give way if it comes
upon me again, I think it must have been, partly at least, in
verse.

CHAPTER XII

"Chained is the Spring. The night-wind bold
    Blows over the hard earth;
Time is not more confused and cold,
    Nor keeps more wintry mirth.

"Yet blow and roll the world about;
    Blow, Time—blow, winter's Wind!
Through chinks of Time, heaven peepeth out,
    And Spring the frost behind."— G. E. M.

THEY WHO BELIEVE in the influences of the stars over the
fates of men, are, in feeling at least, nearer the truth than they
who regard the heavenly bodies as related to them merely by
a common obedience to an external law. All that man sees has
to do with man. Worlds cannot be without an intermundane
relationship. The community of the centre of all creation
suggests an interradiating connection and dependence of the
parts. Else a grander idea is conceivable than that which is
already imbodied. The blank, which is only a forgotten life,

lying behind the consciousness, and the misty splendour, which is an undeveloped life, lying before it, may be full of mysterious revelations of other connexions with the worlds around us, than those of science and poetry. No shining belt or gleaming moon, no red and green glory in a self-encircling twin-star, but has a relation with the hidden things of a man's soul, and, it may be, with the secret history of his body as well. They are portions of the living house wherein he abides.

Through the realms of the monarch Sun
Creeps a world, whose course had begun,
On a weary path with a weary pace,
Before the Earth sprang forth on her race:
But many a time the Earth had sped
Around the path she still must tread,
Ere the elder planet, on leaden wing,
Once circled the court of the planet's king.

There, in that lonely and distant star,
The seasons are not as our seasons are;
But many a year hath Autumn to dress
The trees in their matron loveliness;
As long hath old Winter in triumph to go
O'er beauties dead in his vaults below;
And many a year the Spring doth wear
Combing the icicles from her hair;
And Summer, dear Summer, hath years of June,
With large white clouds, and cool showers at noon:
And a beauty that grows to a weight like grief,
Till a burst of tears is the heart's relief.

Children, born when Winter is king,
May never rejoice in the hoping Spring;
Though their own heart-buds are bursting with joy,
And the child hath grown to the girl or boy;
But may die with cold and icy hours
Watching them ever in place of flowers.
And some who awake from their primal sleep,
When the sighs of Summer through forests creep,
Live, and love, and are loved again;
Seek for pleasure, and find its pain;
Sink to their last, their forsaken sleeping,
With the same sweet odours around them creeping.

Now the children, there, are not born as the children are born in worlds nearer to the sun. For they arrive no one knows how. A maiden, walking alone, hears a cry : for even there a cry is the first utterance; and searching about, she findeth, under an overhanging rock, or within a clump of bushes, or, it may be, betwixt gray stones on the side of a hill, or in any other sheltered and unexpected spot, a little child. This she taketh tenderly, and beareth home with joy, calling out, "Mother, mother"—if so be that her mother lives—"I have got a baby—I have found a child!" All the household gathers round to see;—"*Where is it? What is it like? Where did you find it?*" and such-like questions, abounding. And thereupon she relates the whole story of the discovery; for by the circumstances, such as season of the year, time of the day, condition of the air, and such like, and, especially, the peculiar and never-repeated aspect of the heavens and earth at the time, and the nature of the place of shelter wherein it is found, is determined, or at least indicated, the nature of the child thus discovered. Therefore, at certain seasons, and in certain states of the weather, according, in part, to their own fancy, the young women go out to look for children. They generally avoid seeking them, though they cannot help sometimes finding them, in places and with circumstances uncongenial to their peculiar likings. But no sooner is a child found, than its claim for protection and nurture obliterates all feeling of choice in the matter. Chiefly, however, in the season of summer, which lasts so long, coming as it does after such long intervals; and mostly in the warm evenings, about the middle of twilight; and principally in the woods and along the river banks, do the maidens go looking for children, just as children look for flowers. And ever as the child grows, yea, more and more as he advances in years, will his face indicate to those who understand the spirit of Nature, and her utterances in the face of the world, the nature of the place of his birth, and the other circumstances thereof; whether a clear morning sun guided his mother to the nook whence issued the boy's low cry; or at eve the lonely maiden (for the same woman never finds a second, at least while the first lives) discovers the girl by the glimmer of her white skin, lying in a nest like that of the lark, amid long encircling grasses, and the upward-gazing eyes of the lowly daisies; whether

the storm bowed the forest trees around, or the still frost fixed
in silence the else flowing and babbling stream.

After they grow up, the men and women are but little
together. There is this peculiar difference between them, which
likewise distinguishes the women from those of the earth. The
men alone have arms; the women have only wings. Resplendent
wings are they, wherein they can shroud themselves from head
to foot in a panoply of glistering glory. By these wings alone, it
may frequently be judged in what seasons, and under what
aspects, they were born. From those that came in winter, go
great white wings, white as snow; the edge of every feather
shining like the sheen of silver, so that they flash and glitter like
frost in the sun. But underneath, they are tinged with a faint
pink or rose-colour. Those born in spring have wings of a
brilliant green, green as grass; and towards the edges the feathers
are enamelled like the surface of the grass-blades. These again
are white within. Those that are born in summer have wings of
a deep rose-colour, lined with pale gold. And those born in
autumn have purple wings, with a rich brown on the inside. But
these colours are modified and altered in all varieties, corresponding to the mood of the day and hour, as well as the season
of the year; and sometimes I found the various colours so intermingled, that I could not determine even the season, though
doubtless the hieroglyphic could be deciphered by more
experienced eyes. One splendour, in particular, I remember—
wings of deep carmine, with an inner down of warm gray,
around a form of brilliant whiteness. She had been found as the
sun went down through a low sea-fog, casting crimson along a
broad sea-path into a little cave on the shore, where a bathing
maiden saw her lying.

But though I speak of sun and fog, and sea and shore, the
world there is in some respects very different from the earth
whereon men live. For instance, the waters reflect no forms. To
the unaccustomed eye they appear, if undisturbed, like the
surface of a dark metal, only that the latter would reflect indistinctly, whereas they reflect not at all, except light which falls
immediately upon them. This has a great effect in causing the
landscapes to differ from those on the earth. On the stillest
evening, no tall ship on the sea sends a long wavering reflection
almost to the feet of him on the shore; the face of no maiden

brightens at its own beauty in a still forest-well. The sun and moon alone make a glitter on the surface. The sea is like a sea of death, ready to ingulf and never to reveal : a visible shadow of oblivion. Yet the women sport in its waters like gorgeous sea-birds. The men more rarely enter them. But, on the contrary, the sky reflects everything beneath it, as if it were built of water like ours. Of course, from its concavity there is some distortion of the reflected objects; yet wondrous combinations of form are often to be seen in the overhanging depth. And then it is not shaped so much like a round dome as the sky of the earth, but, more of an egg-shape, rises to a great towering height in the middle, appearing far more lofty than the other. When the stars come out at night, it shows a mighty cupola, "fretted with golden fires," wherein there is room for all tempests to rush and rave.

One evening in early summer, I stood with a group of men and women on a steep rock that overhung the sea. They were all questioning me about my world and the ways thereof. In making reply to one of their questions, I was compelled to say that children are not born in the Earth as with them. Upon this I was assailed with a whole battery of inquiries, which at first I tried to avoid; but, at last, I was compelled, in the vaguest manner I could invent, to make some approach to the subject in question. Immediately a dim notion of what I meant, seemed to dawn in the minds of most of the women. Some of them folded their great wings all around them, as they generally do when in the least offended, and stood erect and motionless. One spread out her rosy pinions, and flashed from the promontory into the gulf at its foot. A great light shone in the eyes of one maiden, who turned and walked slowly away, with her purple and white wings half dispread behind her. She was found, the next morning, dead beneath a withered tree on a bare hill-side, some miles inland. They buried her where she lay, as is their custom; for, before they die, they instinctively search for a spot like the place of their birth, and having found one that satisfies them, they lie down, fold their wings around them, if they be women, or cross their arms over their breasts, if they are men, just as if they were going to sleep; and so sleep indeed. The sign or cause of coming death is an indescribable longing for something, they know not what, which seizes them, and drives them into solitude, consuming them within, till the body fails. When a youth and a maiden look too deep into each other's eyes, this longing seizes and possesses them; but instead of drawing nearer to each other, they wander away, each alone, into solitary places, and die of their desire. But it seems to me, that thereafter they are born babes upon our earth : where, if, when grown, they find each other, it goes well with them; if not, it will seem to go ill. But of this I know nothing. When I told them that the women on the Earth had not wings like them, but arms, they stared, and said how bold and masculine they must look; not knowing that their wings, glorious as they are, are but undeveloped arms.

But see the power of this book, that, while recounting what I can recall of its contents, I write as if myself had visited the far-off planet, learned its ways and appearances, and conversed with its men and women. And so, while writing, it seemed to me that I had.

The book goes on with the story of a maiden, who, born at the close of autumn, and living in a long, to her endless winter, set out at last to find the regions of spring; for, as in our earth, the seasons are divided over the globe. It begins something like this :

> She watched them dying for many a day,
> Dropping from off the old trees away,
> One by one; or else in a shower
> Crowding over the withered flower.
> For as if they had done some grievous wrong,
> The sun, that had nursed them and loved them so long,
> Grew weary of loving, and, turning back,
> Hastened away on his southern track;
> And helplessly hung each shrivelled leaf,
> Faded away with an idle grief.
> And the gusts of wind, sad Autumn's sighs,
> Mournfully swept through their families;
> Casting away with a helpless moan
> All that he yet might call his own,
> As the child, when his bird is gone for ever,
> Flingeth the cage on the wandering river.
> And the giant trees, as bare as Death,
> Slowly bowed to the great Wind's breath;
> And groaned with trying to keep from groaning
> Amidst the young trees bending and moaning.
> And the ancient planet's mighty sea

Was heaving and falling most restlessly,
And the tops of the waves were broken and white,
Tossing about to ease their might;
And the river was striving to reach the main,
And the ripple was hurrying back again.
Nature lived in sadness now;
Sadness lived on the maiden's brow,
As she watched, with a fixed, half-conscious eye,
One lonely leaf that trembled on high,
Till it dropped at last from the desolate bough—
Sorrow, oh, sorrow! 'tis winter now.
And her tears gushed forth, though it was but a leaf,
For little will loose the swollen fountain of grief:
When up to the lip the water goes,
It needs but a drop, and it overflows.

    Oh! many and many a dreary year
Must pass away ere the buds appear;
Many a night of darksome sorrow
Yield to the light of a joyless morrow,
Ere birds again, on the clothed trees,
Shall fill the branches with melodies.
She will dream of meadows with wakeful streams;
Of wavy grass in the sunny beams;
Of hidden wells that soundless spring,
Hoarding their joy as a holy thing;
Of founts that tell it all day long
To the listening woods, with exultant song;
She will dream of evenings that die into nights,
Where each sense is filled with its own delights,
And the soul is still as the vaulted sky,
Lulled with an inner harmony;
And the flowers give out to the dewy night,
Changed into perfume, the gathered light;
And the darkness sinks upon all their host,
Till the sun sail up on the eastern coast—
She will awake and see the branches bare,
Weaving a net in the frozen air.

The story goes on to tell how, at last, weary with wintriness, she travelled towards the southern regions of her globe, to meet the spring on its slow way northwards; and how, after many sad adventures, many disappointed hopes, and many tears, bitter and fruitless, she found at last, one stormy afternoon, in a leafless forest, a single snowdrop growing betwixt the borders of the winter and spring. She lay down beside it and died. I almost believe that a child, pale and peaceful as a snowdrop, was born in the Earth within a fixed season from that stormy afternoon.

CHAPTER XIII

"I saw a ship sailing upon the sea,
  Deeply laden as ship could be;
But not so deep as in love I am,
  For I care not whether I sink or swim."
Old Ballad.

"But Love is such a Mystery
  I cannot find it out:
For when I think I'm best resolv'd,
  I then am in most doubt."
Sir John Suckling.

ONE STORY I WILL try to reproduce. But, alas! it is like trying to reconstruct a forest out of broken branches and withered leaves. In the fairy book, everything was just as it should be, though whether in words or something else, I cannot tell. It glowed and flashed the thoughts upon the soul, with such a power that the medium disappeared from the consciousness, and it was occupied only with the things themselves. My representation of it must resemble a translation from a rich and powerful language, capable of embodying the thoughts of a splendidly developed people, into the meagre and half-articulate speech of a savage tribe. Of course, while I read it, I was Cosmo, and his history was mine. Yet, all the time, I seemed to have a kind of double consciousness, and the story a double meaning. Sometimes it seemed only to represent a simple story of ordinary life, perhaps almost of universal life; wherein two souls, loving each other and longing to come nearer, do, after all, but behold each other as in a glass darkly.

As through the hard rock go the branching silver veins; as into the solid land run the creeks and gulfs from the unresting sea; as the lights and influences of the upper worlds sink silently through the earth's atmosphere; so doth Faerie invade the world of men, and sometimes startle the common eye with an association as of cause and effect, when between the two no connecting links can be traced.

Cosmo von Wehrstahl was a student at the University of Prague. Though of a noble family, he was poor, and prided himself upon the independence that poverty gives; for what will not a man pride himself upon, when he cannot get rid of it? A favourite with his fellow-students, he yet had no companions; and none of them had ever crossed the threshold of his lodging in the top of one of the highest houses in the old town. Indeed, the secret of much of that complaisance which recommended him to his fellows, was the thought of his unknown retreat, whither in the evening he could betake himself and indulge undisturbed in his own studies and reveries. These studies, besides those subjects necessary to his course at the University, embraced some less commonly known and approved; for in a secret drawer lay the works of Albertus Magnus and Cornelius Agrippa, along with others less read and more abstruse. As yet, however, he had followed these researches only from curiosity, and had turned them to no practical purpose.

His lodging consisted of one large low-ceiled room, singularly bare of furniture; for besides a couple of wooden chairs, a couch which served for dreaming on both by day and night, and a great press of black oak, there was very little in the room that could be called furniture. But curious instruments were heaped in the corners; and in one stood a skeleton, half-leaning against the wall, half-supported by a string about its neck. One of its hands, all of fingers, rested on the heavy pommel of a great sword that stood beside it. Various weapons were scattered about over the floor. The walls were utterly bare of adornment; for the few strange things, such as a large dried bat with wings dispread, the skin of a porcupine, and a stuffed sea-mouse, could hardly be reckoned as such. But although his fancy delighted in vagaries like these, he indulged his imagination with far different fare. His mind had never yet been filled with an absorbing passion; but it lay like a still twilight open to any wind, whether the low breath that wafts but odours, or the storm that bows the great trees till they strain and creak. He saw everything as through a rose-coloured glass. When he looked from his window on the street below, not a maiden passed but she moved as in a story, and drew his thoughts after her till she disappeared in the vista. When he walked in the streets, he always felt as if reading a tale, into which he sought to weave every face of interest that went by; and every sweet voice swept his soul as with the wing of a passing angel. He was in fact a poet without words; the more absorbed and endangered, that the springing waters were dammed back into his soul, where, finding no utterance, they grew, and swelled, and undermined. He used to lie on his hard couch, and read a tale or a poem, till the book dropped from his hand; but he dreamed on, he knew not whether awake or asleep, until the opposite roof grew upon his sense, and turned golden in the sunrise. Then he arose too; and the impulses of vigorous youth kept him ever active, either in study or in sport, until again the close of the day left him free; and the world of night, which had lain drowned in the cataract of the day, rose up in his soul, with all its stars, and dim-seen phantom shapes. But this could hardly last long. Some one form must sooner or later step within the charmed circle, enter the house of life, and compel the bewildered magician to kneel and worship.

One afternoon, towards dusk, he was wandering dreamily in one of the principal streets, when a fellow-student roused him by a slap on the shoulder, and asked him to accompany him into a little back alley to look at some old armour which he had taken a fancy to possess. Cosmo was considered an authority in every matter pertaining to arms, ancient or modern. In the use of weapons, none of the students could come near him; and his practical acquaintance with some had principally contributed to establish his authority in reference to all. He accompanied him willingly. They entered a narrow alley, and thence a dirty little court, where a low arched door admitted them into a heterogeneous assemblage of everything musty, and dusty, and old, that could well be imagined. His verdict on the armour was satisfactory, and his companion at once concluded the purchase. As they were leaving the place, Cosmo's eye was attracted by an old mirror of an elliptical shape, which leaned against the wall, covered with dust. Around it was some curious carving, which he could see but very indistinctly by the glimmering light which the owner of the shop carried in his hand. It was this carving that attracted his attention; at least so it appeared to him. He

left the place, however, with his friend, taking no further notice
of it. They walked together to the main street, where they
parted and took opposite directions.

No sooner was Cosmo left alone, than the thought of the
curious old mirror returned to him. A strong desire to see it more
plainly arose within him, and he directed his steps once more
towards the shop. The owner opened the door when he knocked,
as if he had expected him. He was a little, old, withered man,
with a hooked nose, and burning eyes constantly in a slow restless motion, and looking here and there as if after something
that eluded them. Pretending to examine several other articles,
Cosmo at last approached the mirror, and requested to have it
taken down.

"Take it down yourself, master; I cannot reach it," said the
old man.

Cosmo took it down carefully, when he saw that the carving
was indeed delicate and costly, being both of admirable design
and execution; containing withal many devices which seemed
to embody some meaning to which he had no clue. This,
naturally, in one of his tastes and temperament, increased the
interest he felt in the old mirror; so much, indeed, that he now
longed to possess it, in order to study its frame at his leisure. He
pretended, however, to want it only for use; and saying he
feared the plate could be of little service, as it was rather old, he
brushed away a little of the dust from its face, expecting to see
a dull reflection within. His surprise was great when he found
the reflection brilliant, revealing a glass not only uninjured by
age, but wondrously clear and perfect (should the whole correspond to this part) even for one newly from the hands of the
maker. He asked carelessly what the owner wanted for the
thing. The old man replied by mentioning a sum of money far
beyond the reach of poor Cosmo, who proceeded to replace the
mirror where it had stood before.

"You think the price too high?" said the old man.

"I do not know that it is too much for you to ask," replied
Cosmo; "but it is far too much for me to give."

The old man held up his light towards Cosmo's face. "I like
your look," said he.

Cosmo could not return the compliment. In fact, now he
looked closely at him for the first time, he felt a kind of repug-

nance to him, mingled with a strange feeling of doubt whether a man or a woman stood before him.

"What is your name?" he continued.

"Cosmo von Wehrstahl."

"Ah, ah! I thought as much. I see your father in you. I knew your father very well, young sir. I dare say in some odd corners of my house, you might find some old things with his crest and cipher upon them still. Well, I like you: you shall have the mirror at the fourth part of what I asked for it; but upon one condition."

"What is that?" said Cosmo; for, although the price was still a great deal for him to give, he could just manage it; and the desire to possess the mirror had increased to an altogether unaccountable degree, since it had seemed beyond his reach.

"That if you should ever want to get rid of it again, you will let me have the first offer."

"Certainly," replied Cosmo, with a smile; adding, "a moderate condition indeed."

"On your honour?" insisted the seller.

"On my honour," said the buyer; and the bargain was concluded.

"I will carry it home for you," said the old man, as Cosmo took it in his hands.

"No, no; I will carry it myself," said he; for he had a peculiar dislike to revealing his residence to any one, and more especially to this person, to whom he felt every moment a greater antipathy.

"Just as you please," said the old creature, and muttered to himself as he held his light at the door to show him out of the court: "Sold for the sixth time! I wonder what will be the upshot of it this time. I should think my lady had enough of it by now!"

Cosmo carried his prize carefully home. But all the way he had an uncomfortable feeling that he was watched and dogged. Repeatedly he looked about, but saw nothing to justify his suspicions. Indeed, the streets were too crowded and too ill lighted to expose very readily a careful spy, if such there should be at his heels. He reached his lodging in safety, and leaned his purchase against the wall, rather relieved, strong as he was, to be rid of its weight; then, lighting his pipe, threw himself on the couch, and was soon lapt in the folds of one of his haunting dreams.

He returned home earlier than usual the next day, and fixed the mirror to the wall, over the hearth, at one end of his long room. He then carefully wiped away the dust from its face, and, clear as the water of a sunny spring, the mirror shone out from beneath the envious covering. But his interest was chiefly occupied with the curious carving of the frame. This he cleaned as well as he could with a brush; and then he proceeded to a minute examination of its various parts, in the hope of discovering some index to the intention of the carver. In this, however, he was unsuccessful; and, at length, pausing with some weariness and disappointment, he gazed vacantly for a few moments into the depth of the reflected room. But ere long he said, half aloud : "What a strange thing a mirror is ! and what a wondrous affinity exists between it and a man's imagination ! For this room of mine, as I behold it in the glass, is the same, and yet not the same. It is not the mere representation of the room I live in, but it looks just as if I were reading about it in a story I like. All its commonness has disappeared. The mirror has lifted it out of the region of fact into the realm of art; and the very representing of it to me has clothed with interest that which was otherwise hard and bare; just as one sees with delight upon the stage the representation of a character from which one would escape in life as from something unendurably wearisome. But is it not rather that art rescues nature from the weary and sated regards of our senses, and the degrading injustice of our anxious every-day life, and, appealing to the imagination, which dwells apart, reveals Nature in some degree as she really is, and as she represents herself to the eye of the child, whose every-day life, fearless and unambitious, meets the true import of the wonder-teeming world around him, and rejoices therein without questioning? That skeleton, now—I almost fear it, standing there so still, with eyes only for the unseen, like a watch-tower looking across all the waste of this busy world into the quiet regions of rest beyond. And yet I know every bone and every joint in it as well as my own fist. And that old battle-axe looks as if any moment it might be caught up by a mailed hand, and, borne forth by the mighty arm, go crashing through casque, and skull, and brain, invading the Unknown with yet another bewildered ghost. I should like to live in *that* room if I could only get into it."

Scarcely had the half-moulded words floated from him, as he

stood gazing into the mirror, when, striking him as with a flash of amazement that fixed him in his posture, noiseless and un-announced, glided suddenly through the door into the reflected room, with stately motion, yet reluctant and faltering step, the graceful form of a woman, clothed all in white. Her back only was visible as she walked slowly up to the couch in the further end of the room, on which she laid herself wearily, turning towards him a face of unutterable loveliness, in which suffering, and dislike, and a sense of compulsion, strangely mingled with the beauty. He stood without the power of motion for some moments, with his eyes irrecoverably fixed upon her; and even after he was conscious of the ability to move, he could not summon up courage to turn and look on her, face to face, in the veritable chamber in which he stood. At length, with a sudden effort, in which the exercise of the will was so pure, that it seemed involuntary, he turned his face to the couch. It was vacant. In bewilderment, mingled with terror, he turned again to the mirror : there, on the reflected couch, lay the exquisite lady-form. She lay with closed eyes, whence two large tears were just welling from beneath the veiling lids; still as death, save for the convulsive motion of her bosom.

Cosmo himself could not have described what he felt. His emotions were of a kind that destroyed consciousness, and could never be clearly recalled. He could not help standing yet by the mirror, and keeping his eyes fixed on the lady, though he was painfully aware of his rudeness, and feared every moment that she would open hers, and meet his fixed regard. But he was, ere long, a little relieved; for, after a while, her eyelids slowly rose, and her eyes remained uncovered, but unemployed for a time; and when, at length, they began to wander about the room, as if languidly seeking to make some acquaintance with her environment, they were never directed towards him : it seemed nothing but what was in the mirror could affect her vision; and, therefore, if she saw him at all, it could only be his back, which, of necessity, was turned towards her in the glass. The two figures in the mirror could not meet face to face, except he turned and looked at her, present in his room; and, as she was not there, he concluded that if he were to turn towards the part in his room corresponding to that in which she lay, his reflection would either be invisible to her altogether, or at least it must appear to her to gaze vacantly towards her, and no meeting of the eyes would produce the impression of spiritual proximity. By and by her eyes fell upon the skeleton, and he saw her shudder and close them. She did not open them again, but signs of repugnance continued evident on her countenance. Cosmo would have removed the obnoxious thing at once, but he feared to discompose her yet more by the assertion of his presence, which the act would involve. So he stood and watched her. The eyelids yet shrouded the eyes, as a costly case the jewels within; the troubled expression gradually faded from the countenance, leaving only a faint sorrow behind; the features settled into an unchanging expression of rest; and by these signs, and the slow regular motion of her breathing, Cosmo knew that she slept. He could now gaze on her without embarrassment. He saw that her figure, dressed in the simplest robe of white, was worthy of her face; and so harmonious, that either the delicately-moulded foot, or any finger of the equally delicate hand, was an index to the whole. As she lay, her whole form manifested the relaxation of perfect repose. He gazed till he was weary, and at last seated himself near the new-found shrine, and mechanically took up a book, like one who watches by a sick-bed. But his eyes gathered no thoughts from the page before him. His intellect had been stunned by the bold contradiction, to its face, of all its experience, and now lay passive, without assertion, or speculation, or even conscious astonishment; while his imagination sent one wild dream of blessedness after another coursing through his soul. How long he sat he knew not; but at length he roused himself, rose, and, trembling in every portion of his frame, looked again into the mirror. She was gone. The mirror reflected faithfully what his room presented, and nothing more. It stood there like a golden setting whence the central jewel has been stolen away; like a night-sky without the glory of its stars. She had carried with her all the strangeness of the reflected room. It had sunk to the level of the one without. But when the first pangs of his disappointment had passed, Cosmo began to comfort himself with the hope that she might return, perhaps the next evening, at the same hour. Resolving that if she did, she should not at least be scared by the hateful skeleton, he removed that and several other articles of questionable appearance into a recess by the side of the hearth, whence they could not possibly cast any reflection into the mirror; and having made his poor room as tidy as he could, sought the solace of the open sky and of a night wind that had begun to blow; for he could not rest where he was. When he returned, somewhat composed, he could hardly prevail with himself to lie down on his bed; for he could not help feeling as if she had lain upon it; and for him to lie there now would be something like sacrilege. However, weariness prevailed; and laying himself on the couch, dressed as he was, he slept till day.

With a beating heart, beating till he could hardly breathe, he stood in dumb hope before the mirror, on the following evening. Again the reflected room shone as through a purple vapour in the gathering twilight. Everything seemed waiting like himself for a coming splendour to glorify its poor earthliness with the presence of a heavenly joy. And just as the room vibrated with the strokes of the neighbouring church bell, announcing the hour of six, in glided the pale beauty, and again laid herself on the couch. Poor Cosmo nearly lost his senses with delight. She was there once more ! Her eyes sought the corner where the skeleton had stood, and a faint gleam of satisfaction crossed her face, apparently at seeing it empty. She looked suffering still, but there was less of discomfort expressed in her countenance than there had been the night before. She took more notice of the things about her, and seemed to gaze with some curiosity on the strange apparatus standing here and there in her room. At length, however, drowsiness seemed to overtake her, and again she fell asleep. Resolved not to lose sight of her this time, Cosmo watched the sleeping form. Her slumber was so deep and absorbing, that a fascinating repose seemed to pass contagiously from her to him, as he gazed upon her; and he started as if awaking from a dream, when the lady moved, and, without opening her eyes, rose, and passed from the room with the gait of a somnambulist.

Cosmo was now in a state of extravagant delight. Most men have a secret treasure somewhere. The miser has his golden hoard; the virtuoso his pet ring; the student his rare book; the poet his favourite haunt; the lover his secret drawer; but Cosmo had a mirror with a lovely lady in it. And now that he knew by the skeleton, that she was affected by the things around her, he had a new object in life : he would turn the bare chamber in the mirror into a room such as no lady need disdain to call her own. This he could effect only by furnishing and adorning his. And Cosmo was poor. Yet he possessed accomplishments that could be turned to account; although, hitherto, he had preferred living on his slender allowance, to increasing his means by what his pride considered unworthy of his rank. He was the best swordsman in the University; and now he offered to give lessons in fencing and similar exercises, to such as chose to pay him well for the trouble. His proposal was heard with surprise by the students; but it was eagerly accepted by many; and soon his instructions were not confined to the richer students, but were anxiously sought by many of the young nobility of Prague and its neighbourhood. So that very soon he had a good deal of money at his command. The first thing he did was to remove his apparatus and oddities into a closet in the room. Then he placed his bed and a few other necessaries on each side of the hearth, and parted them from the rest of the room by two screens of Indian fabric. Then he put an elegant couch for the lady to lie upon, in the corner where his bed had formerly stood; and, by degrees, every day adding some article of luxury, converted it, at length, into a rich boudoir.

Every night, about the same time, the lady entered. The first time she saw the new couch, she started with a half-smile; then her face grew very sad, the tears came to her eyes, and she laid herself upon the couch, and pressed her face into the silken cushions, as if to hide from everything. She took notice of each addition and each change as the work proceeded; and a look of acknowledgment, as if she knew that some one was ministering to her, and was grateful for it, mingled with the constant look of suffering. At length, after she had lain down as usual one evening, her eyes fell upon some paintings with which Cosmo had just finished adorning the walls. She rose, and to his great delight, walked across the room, and proceeded to examine them carefully, testifying much pleasure in her looks as she did so. But again the sorrowful, tearful expression returned, and again she buried her face in the pillows of her couch. Gradually, however, her countenance had grown more composed; much of the suffering manifest on her first appearance had vanished, and a kind of quiet, hopeful expression had taken its place; which, however, frequently gave way to an anxious, troubled look, mingled with something of sympathetic pity.

Meantime, how fared Cosmo? As might be expected in one of

his temperament, his interest had blossomed into love, and his love—shall I call it *ripened*, or—*withered* into passion? But, alas! he loved a shadow. He could not come near her, could not speak to her, could not hear a sound from those sweet lips, to which his longing eyes would cling like bees to their honey-founts. Ever and anon he sang to himself :

"I shall die for love of the maiden;"

and ever he looked again, and died not, though his heart seemed ready to break with intensity of life and longing. And the more he did for her, the more he loved her; and he hoped that, although she never appeared to see him, yet she was pleased to think that an unknown would give his life to her. He tried to comfort himself over his separation from her, by thinking that perhaps some day she would see him and make signs to him, and that would satisfy him; "for," thought he, "is not this all that a loving soul can do to enter into communion with another! Nay, how many who love never come nearer than to behold each other as in a mirror; seem to know and yet never know the inward life; never enter the other soul; and part at last, with but the vaguest notion of the universe on the borders of which they have been hovering for years? If I could but speak to her, and knew that she heard me, I should be satisfied." Once he contemplated painting a picture on the wall, which should, of necessity, convey to the lady a thought of himself; but, though he had some skill with the pencil, he found his hand tremble so much when he began the attempt, that he was forced to give it up.

.   .   .   .   .

"Who lives, he dies; who dies, he is alive."

One evening, as he stood gazing on his treasure, he thought he saw a faint expression of self-consciousness on her countenance, as if she surmised that passionate eyes were fixed upon her. This grew; till at last the red blood rose over her neck, and cheek, and brow. Cosmo's longing to approach her became almost delirious. This night she was dressed in an evening costume, resplendent with diamonds. This could add nothing to her beauty, but it presented it in a new aspect; enabled her loveliness to make a new manifestation of itself in a new embodiment. For essential beauty is infinite; and, as the soul of Nature needs an endless succession of varied forms to embody

her loveliness, countless faces of beauty springing forth, not any
two the same, at every one of her heart-throbs; so the individual
form needs an infinite change of its environments, to enable it
to uncover all the phases of its loveliness. Diamonds glittered
from amidst her hair, half-hidden in its luxuriance, like stars
through dark rain-clouds; and the bracelets on her white arms
flashed all the colours of a rainbow of lightnings, as she lifted
her snowy hands to cover her burning face. But her beauty
shone down all its adornment. "If I might have but one of her
feet to kiss," thought Cosmo, "I should be content." Alas! he
deceived himself, for passion is never content. Nor did he know
that there are *two* ways out of her enchanted house. But, suddenly, as if the pang had been driven into his heart from
without, revealing itself first in pain, and afterwards in definite
form, the thought darted into his mind, "She has a lover somewhere. Remembered words of his bring the colour on her face
now. I am nowhere to her. She lives in another world all day,
and all night, after she leaves me. Why does she come and make
me love her, till I, a strong man, am too faint to look upon her
more?" He looked again, and her face was pale as a lily. A
sorrowful compassion seemed to rebuke the glitter of the restless
jewels, and the slow tears rose in her eyes. She left her room
sooner this evening than was her wont. Cosmo remained alone,
with a feeling as if his bosom had been suddenly left empty and
hollow, and the weight of the whole world was crushing in its
walls. The next evening, for the first time since she began to
come, she came not.

And now Cosmo was in wretched plight. Since the thought of
a rival had occurred to him, he could not rest for a moment.
More than ever he longed to see the lady face to face. He
persuaded himself that if he but knew the worst he would be
satisfied; for then he could abandon Prague, and find that relief
in constant motion, which is the hope of all active minds when
invaded by distress. Meantime he waited with unspeakable
anxiety for the next night, hoping she would return : but she did
not appear. And now he fell really ill. Rallied by his fellow-
students on his wretched looks, he ceased to attend the lectures.
His engagements were neglected. He cared for nothing. The sky,
with the great sun in it, was to him a heartless, burning desert.
The men and women in the streets were mere puppets, without

motives in themselves, or interest to him. He saw them all as on the ever-changing field of a *camera obscura*. She—she alone and altogether—was his universe, his well of life, his incarnate good. For six evenings she came not. Let his absorbing passion, and the slow fever that was consuming his brain, be his excuse for the resolution which he had taken and begun to execute, before that time had expired.

Reasoning with himself, that it must be by some enchantment connected with the mirror, that the form of the lady was to be seen in it, he determined to attempt to turn to account what he had hitherto studied principally from curiosity. "For," said he to himself, "if a spell can force her presence in that glass (and she came unwillingly at first), may not a stronger spell, such as I know, especially with the aid of her half-presence in the mirror, if ever she appears again, compel her living form to come to me here? If I do her wrong, let love be my excuse. I want only to know my doom from her own lips." He never doubted, all the time, that she was a real earthly woman; or, rather, that there was a woman, who, somehow or other, threw this reflection of her form into the magic mirror.

He opened his secret drawer, took out his books of magic, lighted his lamp, and read and made notes from midnight till three in the morning, for three successive nights. Then he replaced his books; and the next night went out in quest of the materials necessary for the conjuration. These were not easy to find; for, in love-charms and all incantations of this nature, ingredients are employed scarcely fit to be mentioned, and for the thought even of which, in connection with her, he could only excuse himself on the score of his bitter need. At length he succeeded in procuring all he required; and on the seventh evening from that on which she had last appeared, he found himself prepared for the exercise of unlawful and tyrannical power.

He cleared the centre of the room; stooped and drew a circle of red on the floor, around the spot where he stood; wrote in the four quarters mystical signs, and numbers which were all powers of seven or nine; examined the whole ring carefully, to see that no smallest break had occurred in the circumference; and then rose from his bending posture. As he rose, the church clock struck seven; and, just as she had appeared the first time, reluctant, slow, and stately, glided in the lady. Cosmo trembled;

and when, turning, she revealed a countenance worn and wan, as with sickness or inward trouble, he grew faint, and felt as if he dared not proceed. But as he gazed on the face and form, which now possessed his whole soul, to the exclusion of all other joys and griefs, the longing to speak to her, to know that she heard him, to hear from her one word in return, became so unendurable, that he suddenly and hastily resumed his preparations. Stepping carefully from the circle, he put a small brazier into its centre. He then set fire to its contents of charcoal, and while it burned up, opened his window and seated himself, waiting, beside it.

It was a sultry evening. The air was full of thunder. A sense of luxurious depression filled the brain. The sky seemed to have grown heavy, and to compress the air beneath it. A kind of purplish tinge pervaded the atmosphere, and through the open window came the scents of the distant fields, which all the vapours of the city could not quench. Soon the charcoal glowed. Cosmo sprinkled upon it the incense and other substances which he had compounded, and, stepping within the circle, turned his face from the brazier and towards the mirror. Then, fixing his eyes upon the face of the lady, he began with a trembling voice to repeat a powerful incantation. He had not gone far, before the lady grew pale; and then, like a returning wave, the blood washed all its banks with its crimson tide, and she hid her face in her hands. Then he passed to a conjuration stronger yet. The lady rose and walked uneasily to and fro in her room. Another spell; and she seemed seeking with her eyes for some object on which they wished to rest. At length it seemed as if she suddenly espied him; for her eyes fixed themselves full and wide upon his, and she drew gradually, and somewhat unwillingly, close to her side of the mirror, just as if his eyes had fascinated her. Cosmo had never seen her so near before. Now at least, eyes met eyes; but he could not quite understand the expression of hers. They were full of tender entreaty, but there was something more that he could not interpret. Though his heart seemed to labour in his throat, he would allow no delight or agitation to turn him from his task. Looking still in her face, he passed on to the mightiest charm he knew. Suddenly the lady turned and walked out of the door of her reflected chamber. A moment after, she entered his room with veritable presence; and, forgetting all his precautions, he sprang from the charmed circle, and knelt before her. There she stood, the living lady of his passionate visions, alone beside him, in a thundery twilight, and the glow of a magic fire.

"Why," said the lady, with a trembling voice, "didst thou bring a poor maiden through the rainy streets alone?"

"Because I am dying for love of thee; but I only brought thee from the mirror there."

"Ah, the mirror!" and she looked up at it, and shuddered. "Alas! I am but a slave, while that mirror exists. But do not think it was the power of thy spells that drew me; it was thy longing desire to see me, that beat at the door of my heart, till I was forced to yield."

"Canst thou love me then?" said Cosmo, in a voice calm as death, but almost inarticulate with emotion.

"I do not know," she replied sadly; "that I cannot tell, so long as I am bewildered with enchantments. It were indeed a joy too great, to lay my head on thy bosom and weep to death; for I think thou lovest me, though I do not know;—but——"

Cosmo rose from his knees.

"I love thee as—nay, I know not what—for since I have loved thee, there is nothing else."

He seized her hand : she withdrew it.

"No, better not; I am in thy power, and therefore I may not."

She burst into tears, and, kneeling before him in her turn, said—

"Cosmo, if thou lovest me, set me free, even from thyself : break the mirror."

"And shall I see thyself instead?"

"That I cannot tell, I will not deceive thee; we may never meet again."

A fierce struggle arose in Cosmo's bosom. Now she was in his power. She did not dislike him at least; and he could see her when he would. To break the mirror would be to destroy his very life, to banish out of his universe the only glory it possessed. The whole world would be but a prison, if he annihilated the one window that looked into the paradise of love. Not yet pure in love, he hesitated.

With a wail of sorrow, the lady rose to her feet. "Ah! he loves me not; he loves me not even as I love him; and alas! I care more for his love than even for the freedom I ask."

"I will not wait to be willing," cried Cosmo; and sprang to the corner where the great sword stood.

Meantime it had grown very dark; only the embers cast a red glow through the room. He seized the sword by the steel scabbard, and stood before the mirror; but as he heaved a great blow at it with the heavy pommel, the blade slipped half-way out of the scabbard, and the pommel struck the wall above the mirror. At that moment, a terrible clap of thunder seemed to burst in the very room beside them; and ere Cosmo could repeat the blow, he fell senseless on the hearth. When he came to himself, he found that the lady and the mirror had both disappeared. He was seized with a brain fever, which kept him to his couch for weeks.

When he recovered his reason, he began to think what could have become of the mirror. For the lady, he hoped she had found her way back as she came; but as the mirror involved her fate with its own, he was more immediately anxious about that. He could not think she had carried it away. It was much too heavy, even if it had not been too firmly fixed in the wall, for her to remove it. Then again, he remembered the thunder; which made him believe that it was not the lightning, but some other blow that had struck him down. He concluded that, either by supernatural agency, he having exposed himself to the vengeance of the demons in leaving the circle of safety, or in some other mode, the mirror had probably found its way back to its former owner; and, horrible to think of, might have been by this time once more disposed of, delivering up the lady into the power of another man; who, if he used his power no worse than he himself had done, might yet give Cosmo abundant cause to curse the selfish indecision which prevented him from shattering the miror at once. Indeed, to think that she whom he loved, and who had prayed to him for freedom, should be still at the mercy, in some degree, of the possessor of the mirror, and was at least exposed to his constant observation, was in itself enough to madden a chary lover.

Anxiety to be well retarded his recovery; but at length he was able to creep abroad. He first made his way to the old broker's, pretending to be in search of something else. A laughing sneer on the creature's face convinced him that he knew all about it; but he could not see it amongst his furniture, or get any information out of him as to what had become of it. He expressed the

utmost surprise at hearing it had been stolen; a surprise which
Cosmo saw at once to be counterfeited; while, at the same time,
he fancied that the old wretch was not at all anxious to have it
mistaken for genuine. Full of distress, which he concealed as well
as he could, he made many searches, but with no avail. Of course
he could ask no questions; but he kept his ears awake for any
remotest hint that might set him in a direction of search. He
never went out without a short heavy hammer of steel about him,
that he might shatter the mirror the moment he was made happy
by the sight of his lost treasure, if ever that blessed moment
should arrive. Whether he should see the lady again, was now a
thought altogether secondary, and postponed to the achievement
of her freedom. He wandered here and there, like an anxious
ghost, pale and haggard; gnawed ever at the heart, by the
thought of what she might be suffering—all from his fault.

One night, he mingled with a crowd that filled the rooms of
one of the most distinguished mansions in the city; for he
accepted every invitation, that he might lose no chance, however
poor, of obtaining some information that might expedite his discovery. Here he wandered about, listening to every stray word
that he could catch, in the hope of a revelation. As he
approached some ladies who were talking quietly in a corner,
one said to another : "Have you heard of the strange illness of
the Princess von Hohenweiss?"

"Yes; she has been ill for more than a year now. It is very sad
for so fine a creature to have such a terrible malady. She was
better for some weeks lately, but within the last few days the
same attacks have returned, apparently accompanied with more
suffering than ever. It is altogether an inexplicable story."

"Is there a story connected with her illness?"

"I have only heard imperfect reports of it; but it is said that
she gave offence some eighteen months ago to an old woman
who had held an office of trust in the family, and who, after
some incoherent threats, disappeared. This peculiar affection
followed soon after. But the strangest part of the story is its
association with the loss of an antique mirror, which stood in
her dressing-room, and of which she constantly made use."

Here the speaker's voice sank to a whisper; and Cosmo,
although his very soul sat listening in his ears, could hear no
more. He trembled too much to dare to address the ladies, even

if it had been advisable to expose himself to their curiosity. The
name of the Princess was well known to him, but he had never
seen her; except indeed it was she, which now he hardly doubted,
who had knelt before him on that dreadful night. Fearful of
attracting attention, for, from the weak state of his health, he
could not recover an appearance of calmness, he made his way
to the open air, and reached his lodgings; glad in this, that he
at least knew where she lived, although he never dreamed of
approaching her openly, even if he should be happy enough to
free her from her hateful bondage. He hoped, too, that as he
had unexpectedly learned so much, the other and far more
important part might be revealed to him ere long.

.   .   .   .   .   .

"Have you seen Steinwald lately?"

"No, I have not seen him for some time. He is almost a match
for me at the rapier, and I suppose he thinks he needs no more
lessons."

"I wonder what has become of him. I want to see him very
much. Let me see; the last time I saw him he was coming out
of that old broker's den, to which, if you remember, you accompanied me once, to look at some armour. That is fully three
weeks ago."

This hint was enough for Cosmo. Von Steinwald was a man
of influence in the court, well known for his reckless habits and
fierce passions. The very possibility that the mirror should be in
his possession was hell itself to Cosmo. But violent or hasty
measures of any sort were most unlikely to succeed. All that he
wanted was an opportunity of breaking the fatal glass; and to
obtain this he must bide his time. He revolved many plans in his
mind, but without being able to fix upon any.

At length, one evening, as he was passing the house of Von
Steinwald, he saw the windows more than usually brilliant. He
watched for a while, and seeing that company began to arrive,
hastened home, and dressed as richly as he could, in the hope of
mingling with the guests unquestioned : in effecting which, there
could be no difficulty for a man of his carriage.

.   .   .   .   .   .

In a lofty, silent chamber, in another part of the city, lay a
form more like marble than a living woman. The loveliness of
death seemed frozen upon her face, for her lips were rigid, and

her eyelids closed. Her long white hands were crossed over her breast, and no breathing disturbed their repose. Beside the dead, men speak in whispers, as if the deepest rest of all could be broken by the sound of a living voice. Just so, though the soul was evidently beyond the reach of all intimations from the senses, the two ladies, who sat beside her, spoke in the gentlest tones of subdued sorrow.

"She has lain so for an hour."

"This cannot last long, I fear."

"How much thinner she has grown within the last few weeks! If she would only speak, and explain what she suffers, it would be better for her. I think she has visions in her trances, but nothing can induce her to refer to them when she is awake."

"Does she ever speak in these trances?"

"I have never heard her; but they say she walks sometimes, and once put the whole household in a terrible fright by disappearing for a whole hour, and returned drenched with rain, and almost dead with exhaustion and fright. But even then she would give no account of what had happened."

A scarce audible murmur from the yet motionless lips of the lady here startled her attendants. After several ineffectual attempts at articulation, the word *"Cosmo!"* burst from her. Then she lay still as before; but only for a moment. With a wild cry, she sprang from the couch erect on the floor, flung her arms above her head, with clasped and straining hands, and, her wide eyes flashing with light, called aloud, with a voice exultant as that of a spirit bursting from a sepulchre, "I am free! I am free! I thank thee!" Then she flung herself on the couch, and sobbed; then rose, and paced wildly up and down the room, with gestures of mingled delight and anxiety. Then turning to her motionless attendants—"Quick, Lisa, my cloak and hood!" Then lower—"I must go to him. Make haste, Lisa! You may come with me, if you will."

In another moment they were in the street, hurrying along towards one of the bridges over the Moldau. The moon was near the zenith, and the streets were almost empty. The Princess soon outstripped her attendant, and was half-way over the bridge, before the other reached it.

"Are you free, lady? The mirror is broken : are you free?"

The words were spoken close beside her, as she hurried on.

She turned; and there, leaning on the parapet in a recess of the bridge, stood Cosmo, in a splendid dress, but with a white and quivering face.

"Cosmo!—I am free—and thy servant for ever. I was coming to you now."

"And I to you, for Death made me bold; but I could get no further. Have I atoned at all? Do I love you a little—truly?"

"Ah, I know now that you love me, my Cosmo; but what do you say about death?"

He did not reply. His hand was pressed against his side. She looked more closely : the blood was welling from between the fingers. She flung her arms around him with a faint bitter wail.

When Lisa came up, she found her mistress kneeling above a wan dead face, which smiled on in the spectral moonbeams.

And now I will say no more about these wondrous volumes; though I could tell many a tale out of them, and could, perhaps, vaguely represent some entrancing thoughts of a deeper kind which I found within them. From many a sultry noon till twilight, did I sit in that grand hall, buried and risen again in these old books. And I trust I have carried away in my soul some of the exhalations of their undying leaves. In after hours of deserved or needful sorrow, portions of what I read there have often come to me again, with an unexpected comforting; which was not fruitless, even though the comfort might seem in itself groundless and vain.

CHAPTER XIV

"Your gallery
Have we pass'd through, not without much content
In many singularities; but we saw not
That which my daughter came to look upon,
The statue of her mother."—*Winter's Tale.*

I T SEEMED TO me strange, that all this time I had heard no music in the fairy palace. I was convinced there must be music in it, but that my sense was as yet too gross to receive the influence of those mysterious motions that beget sound. Sometimes I felt sure, from the way the few figures of which I got such transitory glimpses passed me, or glided into vacancy before me, that they were moving to the law of music; and, in fact, several times I fancied for a moment that I heard a few wondrous tones coming I knew not whence. But they did not last long enough to convince me that I had heard them with the bodily sense. Such as they were, however, they took strange liberties with me, causing me to burst suddenly into tears, of which there was no presence to make me ashamed, or casting me into a kind of trance of speechless delight, which, passing as suddenly, left me faint and longing for more.

Now, on an evening, before I had been a week in the palace, I was wandering through one lighted arcade and corridor after another. At length I arrived, through a door that closed behind me, in another vast hall of the palace. It was filled with a subdued crimson light; by which I saw that slender pillars of black, built close to walls of white marble, rose to a great height, and then, dividing into innumerable divergent arches, supported a roof, like the walls, of white marble, upon which the arches intersected intricately, forming a fretting of black upon the white, like the network of a skeleton-leaf. The floor was black. Between several pairs of the pillars upon every side, the place of the wall behind was occupied by a crimson curtain of thick silk, hanging in heavy and rich folds. Behind each of these curtains burned a powerful light, and these were the sources of the glow that filled the hall. A peculiar delicious odour pervaded the place. As soon as I entered, the old inspiration seemed to return to me, for I felt a strong impulse to sing; or rather, it seemed as if some one else was singing a song in my soul, which wanted to come forth at my lips, imbodied in my breath. But I kept silence; and feeling somewhat overcome by the red light and the perfume, as well as by the emotion within me, and seeing at one end of the hall a great crimson chair, more like a throne than a chair, beside a table of white marble, I went to it, and, throwing myself in it, gave myself up to a succession of images of bewildering beauty, which passed before my inward eye, in a long and occasionally crowded train. Here I sat for hours, I suppose; till, returning somewhat to myself, I saw that the red light had paled away, and felt a cool gentle breath gliding over my forehead. I rose and left the hall with unsteady steps, finding my way with some difficulty to my own chamber, and faintly remembering, as I went, that only in the marble cave, before I found the sleeping statue, had I ever had a similar experience.

After this, I repaired every morning to the same hall; where I sometimes sat in the chair and dreamed deliciously, and sometimes walked up and down over the black floor. Sometimes I acted within myself a whole drama, during one of these perambulations; sometimes walked deliberately through the whole epic of a tale; sometimes ventured to sing a song, though with a shrinking fear of I knew not what. I was astonished at the beauty of my own voice as it rang through the place, or rather crept undulating, like a serpent of sound, along the walls and roof of this superb music-hall. Entrancing verses arose within me as of their own accord, chanting themselves to their own melodies, and requiring no addition of music to satisfy the inward sense. But, ever in the pauses of these, when the singing mood was upon me, I seemed to hear something like the distant sound of multitudes of dancers, and felt as if it was the unheard music, moving their rhythmic motion, that within me blossomed in verse and song. I felt, too, that could I but see the dance, I should, from the harmony of complicated movements, not of the dancers in relation to each other merely, but of each dancer individually in the manifested plastic power that moved the consenting harmonious form, understand the whole of the music on the billows of which they floated and swung.

At length, one night, suddenly, when this feeling of dancing came upon me, I bethought me of lifting one of the crimson curtains, and looking if, perchance, behind it there might not be hid some other mystery, which might at least remove a step further the bewilderment of the present one. Nor was I altogether disappointed. I walked to one of the magnificent draperies, lifted a corner, and peeped in. There, burned a great, crimson, globe-shaped light, high in the cubical centre of another hall, which might be larger or less than that in which I stood, for its dimensions were not easily perceived, seeing that floor and roof and walls were entirely of black marble. The roof was supported by the same arrangement of pillars radiating in arches, as that of the first hall; only, here, the pillars and arches were of dark red. But what absorbed my delighted gaze, was an innumerable assembly of white marble statues, of every form, and in multitudinous posture, filling the hall throughout. These stood, in the ruddy glow of the great lamp, upon pedestals of jet black. Around the lamp shone in golden letters, plainly legible from where I stood, the two words—

TOUCH NOT !

There was in all this, however, no solution to the sound of dancing; and now I was aware that the influence on my mind had ceased. I did not go in that evening, for I was weary and faint, but I hoarded up the expectation of entering, as of a great coming joy.

Next night I walked, as on the preceding, through the hall. My mind was filled with pictures and songs, and therewith so much absorbed, that I did not for some time think of looking within the curtain I had last night lifted. When the thought of doing so occurred to me first, I happened to be within a few yards of it. I became conscious, at the same moment, that the sound of dancing had been for some time in my ears. I approached the curtain quickly, and, lifting it, entered the black hall. Everything was still as death. I should have concluded that the sound must have proceeded from some other more distant quarter, which conclusion its faintness would, in ordinary circumstances, have necessitated from the first; but there was a something about the statues that caused me still to remain in doubt. As I said, each stood perfectly still upon its black pedestal : but there was about every one a certain air, not of motion, but as if it had just ceased from movement; as if the rest were not altogether of the marbly stillness of thousands of years. It was as if the peculiar atmosphere of each had yet a kind of invisible tremulousness; as if its agitated wavelets had not yet subsided into a perfect calm. I had the suspicion that they had anticipated my appearance, and had sprung, each, from the living joy of the dance, to the death-silence and blackness of its isolated pedestal, just before I entered. I walked across the central hall to the curtain opposite the one I had lifted, and, entering there, found all the appearances similar; only that the statues were different, and differently grouped. Neither did they produce on my mind that impression—of motion just expired, which I had experienced from the others. I found that behind every one of the crimson curtains was a similar hall, similarly lighted, and similarly occupied.

The next night, I did not allow my thoughts to be absorbed

as before with inward images, but crept stealthily along to the furthest curtain in the hall, from behind which, likewise, I had formerly seemed to hear the sound of dancing. I drew aside its edge as suddenly as I could, and, looking in, saw that the utmost stillness pervaded the vast place. I walked in, and passed through it to the other end. There I found that it communicated with a circular corridor, divided from it only by two rows of red columns. This corridor, which was black, with red niches holding statues, ran entirely about the statue-halls, forming a communication between the further ends of them all; further, that is, as regards the central hall of white whence they all diverged like radii, finding their circumference in the corridor. Round this corridor I now went, entering all the halls, of which there were twelve, and finding them all similarly constructed, but filled with quite various statues, of what seemed both ancient and modern sculpture. After I had simply walked through them, I found myself sufficiently tired to long for rest, and went to my own room.

In the night I dreamed that, walking close by one of the curtains, I was suddenly seized with the desire to enter, and darted in. This time I was too quick for them. All the statues were in motion, statues no longer, but men and women—all shapes of beauty that ever sprang from the brain of the sculptor, mingled in the convolutions of a complicated dance. Passing through them to the further end, I almost started from my sleep on beholding, not taking part in the dance with the others, nor seemingly endued with life like them, but standing in marble coldness and rigidity upon a black pedestal in the extreme left corner—my lady of the cave; the marble beauty who sprang from her tomb or her cradle at the call of my songs. While I gazed in speechless astonishment and admiration, a dark shadow, descending from above like the curtain of a stage, gradually hid her entirely from my view. I felt with a shudder that this shadow was perchance my missing demon, whom I had not seen for days. I awoke with a stifled cry.

Of course, the next evening I began my journey through the halls (for I knew not to which my dream had carried me), in the hope of proving the dream to be a true one, by discovering my marble beauty upon her black pedestal. At length, on reaching the tenth hall, I thought I recognised some of the forms I had seen dancing in my dream; and to my bewilderment, when

I arrived at the extreme corner on the left, there stood, the only
one I had yet seen, a vacant pedestal. It was exactly in the
position occupied, in my dream, by the pedestal on which the
white lady stood. Hope beat violently in my heart.

"Now," said I to myself, "if yet another part of the dream
would but come true, and I should succeed in surprising these
forms in their nightly dance; it might be the rest would follow,
and I should see on the pedestal my marble queen. Then surely
if my songs sufficed to give her life before, when she lay in the
bonds of alabaster, much more would they be sufficient then to
give her volition and motion, when she alone of assembled
crowds of marble forms, would be standing rigid and cold."

But the difficulty was, to surprise the dancers. I had found
that a premeditated attempt at surprise, though executed with
the utmost care and rapidity, was of no avail. And, in my
dream, it was effected by a sudden thought suddenly executed.
I saw, therefore, that there was no plan of operation offering
any probability of success, but this : to allow my mind to be
occupied with other thoughts, as I wandered around the great
centre-hall; and so wait till the impulse to enter one of the
others should happen to arise in me just at the moment when I
was close to one of the crimson curtains. For I hoped that if I
entered any one of the twelve halls at the right moment, that
would as it were give me the right of entrance to all the others,
seeing they all had communication behind. I would not diminish
the hope of the right chance, by supposing it necessary that a
desire to enter should awake within me, precisely when I was
close to the curtains of the tenth hall.

At first, the impulses to see recurred so continually, in spite of
the crowded imagery that kept passing through my mind, that
they formed too nearly a continuous chain, for the hope that
any one of them would succeed as a surprise. But as I persisted
in banishing them, they recurred less and less often; and after
two or three, at considerable intervals, had come when the spot
where I happened to be was unsuitable, the hope strengthened,
that soon one might arise just at the right moment; namely,
when, in walking round the hall, I should be close to one of the
curtains.

At length the right moment and the impulse coincided. I
darted into the ninth hall. It was full of the most exquisite

moving forms. The whole space wavered and swam with the involutions of an intricate dance. It seemed to break suddenly as I entered, and all made one or two bounds towards their pedestals; but, apparently on finding that they were thoroughly overtaken, they returned to their employment (for it seemed with them earnest enough to be called such) without further heeding me. Somewhat impeded by the floating crowd, I made what haste I could towards the bottom of the hall; whence, entering the corridor, I turned towards the tenth. I soon arrived at the corner I wanted to reach, for the corridor was comparatively empty; but, although the dancers here, after a little confusion, altogether disregarded my presence, I was dismayed at beholding, even yet, a vacant pedestal. But I had a conviction that she was near me. And as I looked at the pedestal, I thought I saw upon it, vaguely revealed as if through overlapping folds of drapery, the indistinct outlines of white feet. Yet there was no sign of drapery or concealing shadow whatever. But I remembered the descending shadow in my dream. And I hoped still in the power of my songs; thinking that what could dispel alabaster, might likewise be capable of dispelling what concealed my beauty now, even if it were the demon whose darkness had overshadowed all my life.

CHAPTER XV

"*Alexander.* When will you finish Campaspe?
"*Apelles.* Never finish: for always in absolute beauty there is somewhat above art."—LYLY's *Campaspe.*

AND NOW, WHAT song should I sing to unveil my Isis, if indeed she was present unseen? I hurried away to the white hall of Phantasy, heedless of the innumerable forms of beauty that crowded my way: these might cross my eyes, but the unseen filled my brain. I wandered long, up and down the silent space: no songs came. My soul was not still enough for songs. Only in the silence and darkness of the soul's night, do those stars of the inward firmament sink to its lower surface from the singing realms beyond, and shine upon the conscious spirit. Here all effort was unavailing. If they came not, they could not be found.

Next night, it was just the same. I walked through the red glimmer of the silent hall; but lonely as there I walked, as lonely trod my soul up and down the halls of the brain. At last I entered one of the statue-halls. The dance had just commenced, and I was delighted to find that I was free of their assembly. I walked on till I came to the sacred corner. There I found the pedestal just as I had left it, with the faint glimmer as of white feet still resting on the dead black. As soon as I saw it, I seemed to feel a presence which longed to become visible; and, as it were, called to me to gift it with self-manifestation, that it might shine on me. The power of song came to me. But the moment my voice, though I sang low and soft, stirred the air of the hall, the dancers started; the quick interweaving crowd shook, lost its form, divided; each figure sprang to its pedestal, and stood, a self-evolving life no more, but a rigid, life-like, marble shape, with the whole form composed into the expression of a single state or act. Silence rolled like a spiritual thunder through the grand space. My song had ceased, scared at its own influences. But I saw in the hand of one of the statues close by me, a harp whose chords yet quivered. I remembered that as she bounded past me, her harp had brushed against my arm; so the spell of the marble had not infolded it. I sprang to her, and with a gesture of entreaty, laid my hand on the harp. The marble hand, probably from its contact with the uncharmed harp, had strength enough to relax its hold, and yield the harp to me. No other motion indicated life.

Instinctively I struck the chords and sang. And not to break upon the record of my song, I mention here, that as I sang the first four lines, the loveliest feet became clear upon the black pedestal; and ever as I sang, it was as if a veil were being lifted up from before the form, but an invisible veil, so that the statue appeared to grow before me, not so much by evolution, as by infinitesimal degrees of added height. And, while I sang, I did not feel that I stood by a statue, as indeed it appeared to be, but that a real woman-soul was revealing itself by successive stages of imbodiment, and consequent manifestation and expression.

> Feet of beauty, firmly planting
> Arches white on rosy heel!
> Whence the life-spring, throbbing, panting,
> Pulses upward to reveal!

Fairest things know least despising;
　Foot and earth meet tenderly:
'Tis the woman, resting, rising
　Upward to sublimity.

Rise the limbs, sedately sloping,
　Strong and gentle, full and free;
Soft and slow, like certain hoping,
　Drawing nigh the broad firm knee.
Up to speech! As up to roses
　Pants the life from leaf to flower,
So each blending change discloses,
　Nearer still, expression's power.

Lo! fair sweeps, white surges, twining
　Up and outward fearlessly!
Temple columns, close combining,
　Lift a holy mystery.
Heart of mine! what strange surprises
　Mount aloft on such a stair!
Some great vision upward rises,
　Curving, bending, floating fair.

Bands and sweeps, and hill and hollow
　Lead my fascinated eye;
Some apocalypse will follow,
　Some new word of deity.
Zoned unseen, and outward swelling,
　With new thoughts and wonders rife,
Queenly majesty foretelling,
　See the expanding house of life!

Sudden heaving, unforbidden
　Sighs eternal, still the same—
Mounts of snow have summits hidden
　In the mists of uttered flame.
But the spirit, dawning nearly,
　Finds no speech for earnest pain;
Finds a soundless sighing merely—
　Builds its stairs, and mounts again.

Heart, the queen, with secret hoping,
　Sendeth out her waiting pair;
Hands, blind hands, half blindly groping,
　Half inclasping visions rare;

And the great arms, heartways bending;
  Might of Beauty, drawing home;
There returning, and re-blending,
  Where from roots of love they roam.

Build thy slopes of radiance beamy,
  Spirit, fair with womanhood!
Tower thy precipice, white-gleamy,
  Climb unto the hour of good.
Dumb space will be rent asunder,
  Now the shining column stands
Ready to be crowned with wonder
  By the builder's joyous hands.

All the lines abroad are spreading,
  Like a fountain's falling race.
Lo, the chin, first feature, treading,
  Airy foot to rest the face!
Speech is nigh; oh, see the blushing,
  Sweet approach of lip and breath!
Round the mouth dim silence, hushing,
  Waits to die ecstatic death.

Span across in treble curving,
  Bow of promise, upper lip!
Set them free, with gracious swerving;
  Let the wing-words float and dip.
Dumb art thou? O Love immortal,
  More than words thy speech must be;
Childless yet the tender portal
  Of the home of melody.

Now the nostrils open fearless,
  Proud in calm unconsciousness,
Sure it must be something peerless
  That the great Pan would express!
Deepens, crowds some meaning tender,
  In the pure, dear lady-face.
Lo, a blinding burst of splendour!—
  'Tis the free soul's issuing grace.

Two calm lakes of molten glory
  Circling round unfathomed deeps!
Lightning-flashes, transitory,
  Cross the gulfs where darkness sleeps.

This the gate, at last, of gladness,
  To the outward striving *me*:
In a rain of light and sadness,
  Out its loves and longings flee!

With a presence I am smitten
  Dumb, with a foreknown surprise;
Presence greater yet than written
  Even in the glorious eyes.
Through the gulfs, with inward gazes,
  I may look till I am lost;
Wandering deep in spirit-mazes,
  In a sea without a coast.

Windows open to the glorious!
  Time and space, oh, far beyond!
Woman, ah! thou art victorious,
  And I perish, overfond.
Springs aloft the yet Unspoken
  In the forehead's endless grace,
Full of silences unbroken;
  Infinite, unfeatured face.

Domes above, the mount of wonder;
  Height and hollow wrapt in night;
Hiding in its caverns under
  Woman-nations in their might.
Passing forms, the highest Human
  Faints away to the Divine:
Features none, of man or woman,
  Can unveil the holiest shine.

Sideways, grooved porches only
  Visible to passing eye,
Stand the silent, doorless, lonely
  Entrance-gates of melody.
But all sounds fly in as boldly,
  Groan and song, and kiss and cry,
At their galleries, lifted coldly,
  Darkly, 'twixt the earth and sky.

Beauty, thou art spent, thou knowest:
  So, in faint, half-glad despair,
From the summit thou o'erflowest
  In a fall of torrent hair;

Hiding what thou hast created
In a half-transparent shroud:
Thus, with glory soft-abated,
Shines the moon through vapoury cloud.

CHAPTER XVI

"Selbst der Styx, der neunfach sie umwindet,
    Wehrt die Rückkehr Ceres Tochter nicht:
Nach dem Apfel greift sie, und es bindet
    Ewig sie des Orkus Pflicht."
        SCHILLER.—*Das Ideal und das Leben.*

"Ev'n the Styx, which ninefold her infoldeth,
    Hems not Ceres' daughter in its flow;
But she grasps the apple—ever holdeth
    Her, sad Orcus, down below."

Ever as I sang, the veil was uplifted; ever as I sang, the
signs of life grew; till, when the eyes dawned upon me, it was
with that sunrise of splendour which my feeble song attempted to
re-imbody. The wonder is, that I was not altogether overcome,
but was able to complete my song as the unseen veil continued
to rise. This ability came solely from the state of mental elevation
in which I found myself. Only because uplifted in song, was I
able to endure the blaze of the dawn. But I cannot tell whether
she looked more of statue or more of woman; she seemed
removed into that region of phantasy where all is intensely vivid,
but nothing clearly defined. At last, as I sang of her descending
hair, the glow of soul faded away, like a dying sunset. A lamp
within had been extinguished, and the house of life shone blank
in a winter morn. She was a statue once more—but visible, and
that was much gained. Yet the revulsion from hope and fruition
was such, that, unable to restrain myself, I sprang to her, and,
in defiance of the law of the place, flung my arms around her,
as if I would tear her from the grasp of a visible Death, and
lifted her from the pedestal down to my heart. But no sooner had
her feet ceased to be in contact with the black pedestal, than
she shuddered and trembled all over; then, writhing from my
arms, before I could tighten their hold, she sprang into the
corridor, with the reproachful cry, "You should not have touched

me!" darted behind one of the exterior pillars of the circle, and
disappeared. I followed almost as fast; but ere I could reach
the pillar, the sound of a closing door, the saddest of all sounds
sometimes, fell on my ear; and, arriving at the spot where she
had vanished, I saw, lighted by a pale yellow lamp which hung
above it, a heavy, rough door, altogether unlike any others I had
seen in the palace; for they were all of ebony, or ivory, or
covered with silver-plates, or of some odorous wood, and very
ornate; whereas this seemed of old oak, with heavy nails and iron
studs. Notwithstanding the precipitation of my pursuit, I could
not help reading, in silver letters beneath the lamp: *"No one
enters here without the leave of the Queen."* But what was the
Queen to me, when I followed my white lady? I dashed the
door to the wall, and sprang through. Lo! I stood on a waste
windy hill. Great stones like tombstones stood all about me. No
door, no palace was to be seen. A white figure gleamed past me,
wringing her hands, and crying, "Ah! you should have sung to
me; you should have sung to me!" and disappeared behind one
of the stones. I followed. A cold gust of wind met me from
behind the stone; and when I looked, I saw nothing but a great
hole in the earth, into which I could find no way of entering.
Had she fallen in? I could not tell. I must wait for the daylight.
I sat down and wept, for there was no help.

CHAPTER XVII

"Anfangs wollt' ich fast verzagen,
   Und ich glaubt' ich trüg' es nie,
Und ich hab' es doch getragen,—
   Aber fragt mich nur nicht: wie?"
                              HEINE.

"First, I thought, almost despairing,
   This must crush my spirit now;
Yet I bore it, and am bearing—
   Only do not ask me how."

WHEN THE DAYLIGHT came, it brought the possibility of
action, but with it little of consolation. With the first visible
increase of light, I gazed into the chasm, but could not, for

more than an hour, see sufficiently well to discover its nature.
At last I saw it was almost a perpendicular opening, like a
roughly excavated well, only very large. I could perceive no
bottom; and it was not till the sun actually rose, that I discovered a sort of natural staircase, in many parts little more than
suggested, which led round and round the gulf, descending
spirally into its abyss. I saw at once that this was my path; and
without a moment's hesitation, glad to quit the sunlight, which
stared at me most heartlessly, I commenced my tortuous descent.
It was very difficult. In some parts I had to cling to the rocks
like a bat. In one place, I dropped from the track down upon
the next returning spire of the stair; which being broad in this
particular portion, and standing out from the wall at right
angles, received me upon my feet safe, though somewhat
stupefied by the shock. After descending a great way, I found
the stair ended at a narrow opening which entered the rock
horizontally. Into this I crept, and, having entered, had just
room to turn round. I put my head out into the shaft by which
I had come down, and surveyed the course of my descent. Looking up, I saw the stars; although the sun must by this time have
been high in the heavens. Looking below, I saw that the sides of
the shaft went sheer down, smooth as glass; and far beneath me,
I saw the reflection of the same stars I had seen in the heavens
when I looked up. I turned again, and crept inwards some
distance, when the passage widened, and I was at length able
to stand and walk upright. Wider and loftier grew the way; new
paths branched off on every side; great open halls appeared; till
at last I found myself wandering on through an underground
country, in which the sky was of rock, and instead of trees and
flowers, there were only fantastic rocks and stones. And ever as
I went, darker grew my thoughts, till at last I had no hope
whatever of finding the white lady : I no longer called her to
myself *my* white lady. Whenever a choice was necessary, I
always chose the path which seemed to lead downwards.

At length I began to find that these regions were inhabited.
From behind a rock a peal of harsh grating laughter, full of evil
humour, rang through my ears, and, looking round, I saw a
queer, goblin creature, with a great head and ridiculous features,
just such as those described, in German histories and travels, as
Kobolds. "What do you want with me?" I said. He pointed at

me with a long forefinger, very thick at the root, and sharpened
to a point, and answered, "He! he! he! what do *you* want
here?" Then, changing his tone, he continued, with mock
humility—"Honoured sir, vouchsafe to withdraw from thy slaves
the lustre of thy august presence, for thy slaves cannot support
its brightness." A second appeared, and struck in : "You are so
big, you keep the sun from us. We can't see for you, and we're
so cold." Thereupon arose, on all sides, the most terrific uproar
of laughter, from voices like those of children in volume, but
scrannel and harsh as those of decrepit age, though, unfortunately, without its weakness. The whole pandemonium of fairy
devils, of all varieties of fantastic ugliness, both in form and
feature, and of all sizes from one to four feet, seemed to have
suddenly assembled about me. At length, after a great babble of
talk among themselves, in a language unknown to me, and after
seemingly endless gesticulation, consultation, elbow-nudging, and
unmitigated peals of laughter, they formed into a circle about
one of their number, who scrambled upon a stone, and, much to
my surprise, and somewhat to my dismay, began to sing, in a
voice corresponding in its nature to his talking one, from
beginning to end, the song with which I had brought the light
into the eyes of the white lady. He sang the same air too; and,
all the time, maintained a face of mock entreaty and worship;
accompanying the song with the travestied gestures of one playing on the lute. The whole assembly kept silence, except at the
close of every verse, when they roared, and danced, and shouted
with laughter, and flung themselves on the ground, in real or
pretended convulsions of delight. When he had finished, the
singer threw himself from the top of the stone, turning heels over
head several times in his descent; and when he did alight, it was
on the top of his head, on which he hopped about, making the
most grotesque gesticulations with his legs in the air. Inexpressible laughter followed, which broke up in a shower of tiny stones
from innumerable hands. They could not materially injure me,
although they cut me on the head and face. I attempted to run
away, but they all rushed upon me, and, laying hold of every
part that afforded a grasp, held me tight. Crowding about me
like bees, they shouted an insect-swarm of exasperating speeches
up into my face, among which the most frequently recurring
were—"You shan't have her; you shan't have her; he! he! he!

She's for a better man; she's for a better man; how he'll kiss her! how he'll kiss her!"

The galvanic torrent of this battery of malevolence stung to life within me a spark of nobleness, and I said aloud, "Well, if he is a better man, let him have her."

They instantly let go their hold of me, and fell back a step or two, with a whole broadside of grunts and humphs, as of unexpected and disappointed approbation. I made a step or two forward, and a lane was instantly opened for me through the midst of the grinning little antics, who bowed most politely to me on every side as I passed. After I had gone a few yards, I looked back, and saw them all standing quite still, looking after me, like a great school of boys; till suddenly one turned round, and with a loud whoop, rushed into the midst of the others. In an instant, the whole was one writhing and tumbling heap of contortion, reminding me of the live pyramids of intertwined snakes of which travellers make report. As soon as one was worked out of the mass, he bounded off a few paces, and then, with a somersault and a run, threw himself gyrating into the air, and descended with all his weight on the summit of the heaving and struggling chaos of fantastic figures. I left them still busy at this fierce and apparently aimless amusement. And as I went, I sang—

> If a nobler waits for thee,
>   I will weep aside;
> It is well that thou shouldst be,
>   Of the nobler, bride.
>
> For if love builds up the home,
>   Where the heart is free,
> Homeless yet the heart must roam,
>   That has not found thee.
>
> One must suffer: I, for her,
>   Yield in her my part.
> Take her, thou art worthier—
>   Still! be still, my heart!
>
> Gift ungotten! largess high
>   Of a frustrate will!
> But to yield it lovingly
>   Is a something still.

Then a little song arose of itself in my soul; and I felt for the moment, while it sang sadly within me, as if I was once more walking up and down the white hall of Phantasy in the Fairy Palace. But this lasted no longer than the song, as will be seen.

> Do not vex thy violet
>   Perfume to afford:
> Else no odour thou wilt get
>   From its little hoard.
>
> In thy lady's gracious eyes
>   Look not thou too long;
> Else from them the glory flies,
>   And thou dost her wrong.
>
> Come not thou too near the maid,
>   Clasp her not too wild;
> Else the splendour is allayed,
>   And thy heart beguiled.

A crash of laughter, more discordant and deriding than any I had yet heard, invaded my ears. Looking on in the direction of the sound, I saw a little elderly woman, much taller, however, than the goblins I had just left, seated upon a stone by the side of the path. She rose, as I drew near, and came forward to meet me. She was very plain and commonplace in appearance, without being hideously ugly. Looking up in my face with a stupid sneer, she said: "Isn't it a pity you haven't a pretty girl to walk all alone with you through this sweet country? How different everything would look? wouldn't it? Strange that one can never have what one would like best! How the roses would bloom and all that, even in this infernal hole! wouldn't they, Anodos? Her eyes would light up the old cave, wouldn't they?"

"That depends on who the pretty girl should be," replied I.

"Not so very much matter that," she answered; "look here."

I had turned to go away as I gave my reply, but now I stopped and looked at her. As a rough unsightly bud might suddenly blossom into the most lovely flower; or rather, as a sunbeam bursts through a shapeless cloud, and transfigures the earth; so burst a face of resplendent beauty, as it were *through* the unsightly visage of the woman, destroying it with light as it dawned through it. A summer sky rose above me, gray with heat; across a shining slumberous landscape, looked from afar the

peaks of snow-capped mountains; and down from a great rock
beside me, fell a sheet of water mad with its own delight.

"Stay with me," she said, lifting up her exquisite face, and
looking full in mine.

I drew back. Again the infernal laugh grated upon my ears;
again the rocks closed in around me, and the ugly woman
looked at me with wicked, mocking hazel eyes.

"You shall have your reward," said she. "You shall see your
white lady again."

"That lies not with you," I replied, and turned and left her.

She followed me with shriek upon shriek of laughter, as I
went on my way.

I may mention here, that although there was always light
enough to see my path and a few yards on every side of me, I
never could find out the source of this sad sepulchral
illumination.

CHAPTER XVIII

"Im Sausen des Windes, im Brausen des Meers,
  Und im Seufzen der eigenen Brust."—HEINE.

"In the wind's uproar, the sea's raging grim,
  And the sighs that are born in him."

"Ja, es wird zwar ein anderes Zeitalter kommen, wo es Licht wird,
und wo der Mensch aus erhabnen Traümen erwacht, und die Traüme
—wieder findet, weil er nichts verlor als den Schlaf."—JEAN PAUL,
Hesperus.

"From dreams of bliss shall men awake
  One day, but not to weep:
The dreams remain; they only break
  The mirror of the sleep."

HOW I GOT THROUGH this dreary part of my travels, I do not
know. I do not think I was upheld by the hope that any moment
the light might break in upon me; for I scarcely thought about
that. I went on with a dull endurance, varied by moments of
uncontrollable sadness; for more and more the conviction grew
upon me that I should never see the white lady again. It may
seem strange that one with whom I had held so little communion should have so engrossed my thoughts; but benefits

conferred awaken love in some minds, as surely as benefits received in others. Besides being delighted and proud that *my* songs had called the beautiful creature to life, the same fact caused me to feel a tenderness unspeakable for her, accompanied with a kind of feeling of property in her; for so the goblin Selfishness would reward the angel Love. When to all this is added, an overpowering sense of her beauty, and an unquestioning conviction that this was a true index to inward loveliness, it may be understood how it come to pass that my imagination filled my whole soul with the play of its own multitudinous colours and harmonies around the form which yet stood, a gracious marble radiance, in the midst of *its* white hall of phantasy. The time passed by unheeded; for my thoughts were busy. Perhaps this was also in part the cause of my needing no food, and never thinking how I should find any, during this subterraneous part of my travels. How long they endured I could not tell, for I had no means of measuring time; and when I looked back, there was such a discrepancy between the decisions of my imagination and my judgment, as to the length of time that had passed, that I was bewildered, and gave up all attempts to arrive at any conclusion on the point.

A gray mist continually gathered behind me. When I looked back towards the past, this mist was the medium through which my eyes had to strain for a vision of what had gone by; and the form of the white lady had receded into an unknown region. At length the country of rock began to close again around me, gradually and slowly narrowing, till I found myself walking in a gallery of rock once more, both sides of which I could touch with my outstretched hands. It narrowed yet, until I was forced to move carefully, in order to avoid striking against the projecting pieces of rock. The roof sank lower and lower, until I was compelled, first to stoop, and then to creep on my hands and knees. It recalled terrible dreams of childhood; but I was not much afraid, because I felt sure that this was my path, and my only hope of leaving Fairy Land, of which I was now almost weary.

At length, on getting past an abrupt turn in the passage, through which I had to force myself, I saw, a few yards ahead of me, the long-forgotten daylight shining through a small opening, to which the path, if path it could now be called, led me. With

great difficulty I accomplished these last few yards, and came
forth to the day. I stood on the shore of a wintry sea, with a
wintry sun just a few feet above its horizon-edge. It was bare,
and waste, and gray. Hundreds of hopeless waves rushed constantly shorewards, falling exhausted upon a beach of great loose
stones, that seemed to stretch miles and miles in both directions.
There was nothing for the eye but mingling shades of gray;
nothing for the ear but the rush of the coming, the roar of the
breaking, and the moan of the retreating wave. No rock lifted
up a sheltering severity above the dreariness around; even that
from which I had myself emerged rose scarcely a foot above the
opening by which I had reached the dismal day, more dismal
even than the tomb I had left. A cold, death-like wind swept
across the shore, seeming to issue from a pale mouth of cloud
upon the horizon. Sign of life was nowhere visible. I wandered
over the stones, up and down the beach, a human imbodiment of
the nature around me. The wind increased; its keen waves flowed
through my soul; the foam rushed higher up the stones; a few
dead stars began to gleam in the east; the sound of the waves
grew louder and yet more despairing. A dark curtain of cloud
was lifted up, and a pale blue rent shone between its foot and
the edge of the sea, out from which rushed an icy storm of
frozen wind, that tore the waters into spray as it passed, and
flung the billows in raving heaps upon the desolate shore. I
could bear it no longer.

"I will not be tortured to death," I cried; "I will meet it
half-way. The life within me is yet enough to bear me up to the
face of Death, and then I die unconquered."

Before it had grown so dark, I had observed, though without
any particular interest, that on one part of the shore a low
platform of rock seemed to run out far into the midst of the
breaking waters. Towards this I now went, scrambling over
smooth stones, to which scarce even a particle of sea-weed
clung; and having found it, I got on it, and followed its direction, as near as I could guess, out into the tumbling chaos. I
could hardly keep my feet against the wind and sea. The waves
repeatedly all but swept me off my path; but I kept on my way,
till I reached the end of the low promontory, which, in the fall
of the waves, rose a good many feet above the surface, and, in
their rise, was covered with their waters. I stood one moment

and gazed into the heaving abyss beneath me; then plunged headlong into the mounting wave below. A blessing, like the kiss of a mother, seemed to alight on my soul; a calm, deeper than that which accompanies a hope deferred, bathed my spirit. I sank far in the waters, and sought not to return. I felt as if once more the great arms of the beech-tree were around me, soothing me after the miseries I had passed through, and telling me, like a little sick child, that I should be better to-morrow. The waters of themselves lifted me, as with loving arms, to the surface. I breathed again, but did not unclose my eyes. I would not look on the wintry sea, and the pitiless gray sky. Thus I floated, till something gently touched me. It was a little boat floating beside me. How it came there I could not tell; but it rose and sank on the waters, and kept touching me in its fall, as if with a human will to let me know that help was by me. It was a little gay-coloured boat, seemingly covered with glistering scales like those of a fish, all of brilliant rainbow hues. I scrambled into it, and lay down in the bottom, with a sense of exquisite repose. Then I drew over me a rich, heavy, purple cloth that was beside me; and, lying still, knew, by the sound of the waters, that my little bark was fleeting rapidly onwards. Finding, however, none of that stormy motion which the sea had manifested when I beheld it from the shore, I opened my eyes; and, looking first up, saw above me the deep violet sky of a warm southern night; and then, lifting my head, saw that I was sailing fast upon a summer sea, in the last border of a southern twilight. The aureole of the sun yet shot the extreme faint tips of its longest rays above the horizon-waves, and withdrew them not. It was a perpetual twilight. The stars, great and earnest, like children's eyes, bent down lovingly towards the waters; and the reflected stars within seemed to float up, as if longing to meet their embraces. But when I looked down, a new wonder met my view. For, vaguely revealed beneath the wave, I floated above my whole Past. The fields of my childhood flitted by; the halls of my youthful labours; the streets of great cities where I had dwelt; and the assemblies of men and women wherein I had wearied myself seeking for rest. But so indistinct were the visions, that sometimes I thought that I was sailing on a shallow sea, and that strange rocks and forests of sea-plants beguiled my eye, sufficiently to be transformed, by the magic of the phantasy, into well-known

objects and regions. Yet, at times, a beloved form seemed to lie
close beneath me in sleep; and the eyelids would tremble as if
about to forsake the conscious eye; and the arms would heave
upwards, as if in dreams they sought for a satisfying presence.
But these motions might come only from the heaving of the
waters between those forms and me. Soon I fell asleep, overcome
with fatigue and delight. In dreams of unspeakable joy—of
restored friendships; of revived embraces; of love which said it
had never died; of faces that had vanished long ago, yet said
with smiling lips that they knew nothing of the grave; of pardons
implored, and granted with such bursting floods of love, that I
was almost glad I had sinned—thus I passed through this wondrous twilight. I awoke with the feeling that I had been kissed
and loved to my heart's content; and found that my boat was
floating motionless by the grassy shore of a little island.

CHAPTER XIX

"In stiller Ruhe, in wechselloser Einfalt führ ich ununterbrochen das
Bewusstseyn der ganzen Menschheit in mir."
                                    SCHLEIERMACHER—*Monologen.*

"In still rest, in changeless simplicity, I bear, uninterrupted, the
consciousness of the whole of Humanity within me."

> "—such a sweetness, such a grace
>   In all thy speech appear,
> That what to th' eye a beauteous face,
>   That thy tongue is to the ear."—COWLEY.

THE WATER WAS deep to the very edge; and I sprang from
the little boat upon a soft grassy turf. The island seemed rich
with a profusion of all grasses and low flowers. All delicate lowly
things were most plentiful; but no trees rose skywards; not even
a bush overtopped the tall grasses, except in one place near the
cottage I am about to describe, where a few plants of the gum-
cistus, which drops every night all the blossoms that the day
brings forth, formed a kind of natural arbour. The whole island
lay open to the sky and sea. It rose nowhere more than a few
feet above the level of the waters, which flowed deep all around
its border. Here there seemed to be neither tide nor storm. A

sense of persistent calm and fulness arose in the mind at the sight of the slow, pulse-like rise and fall of the deep, clear, unrippled waters against the bank of the island, for shore it could hardly be called, being so much more like the edge of a full, solemn river. As I walked over the grass towards the cottage, which stood at a little distance from the bank, all the flowers of childhood looked at me with perfect child-eyes out of the grass. My heart, softened by the dreams through which it had passed, overflowed in a sad, tender love towards them. They looked to me like children impregnably fortified in a helpless confidence. The sun stood half-way down the western sky, shining very soft and golden; and there grew a second world of shadows amidst the world of grasses and wild flowers.

The cottage was square, with low walls, and a high pyramidal roof thatched with long reeds, of which the withered blossoms hung over all the eaves. It is noticeable that most of the buildings I saw in Fairy Land were cottages. There was no path to a door, nor, indeed, was there any track worn by footsteps in the island. The cottage rose right out of the smooth turf. It had no windows that I could see; but there was a door in the centre of the side facing me, up to which I went. I knocked, and the sweetest voice I had ever heard said, "Come in." I entered. A bright fire was burning on a hearth in the centre of the earthen floor, and the smoke found its way out at an opening in the centre of the pyramidal roof. Over the fire hung a little pot, and over the pot bent a woman-face, the most wonderful, I thought, that I had ever beheld. For it was older than any countenance I had ever looked upon. There was not a spot in which a wrinkle could lie, where a wrinkle lay not. And the skin was ancient and brown, like old parchment. The woman's form was tall and spare : and when she stood up to welcome me, I saw that she was straight as an arrow. Could that voice of sweetness have issued from those lips of age? Mild as they were, could they be the portals whence flowed such melody? But the moment I saw her eyes, I no longer wondered at her voice : they were absolutely young—those of a woman of five-and-twenty, large, and of a clear gray. Wrinkles had beset them all about; the eyelids themselves were old, and heavy, and worn; but the eyes were very incarnations of soft light. She held out her hand to me, and the voice of sweetness again greeted me, with the single word,

"Welcome." She set an old wooden chair for me, near the fire, and went on with her cooking. A wondrous sense of refuge and repose came upon me. I felt like a boy who has got home from school, miles across the hills, through a heavy storm of wind and snow. Almost, as I gazed on her, I sprang from my seat to kiss those old lips. And when, having finished her cooking, she brought some of the dish she had prepared, and set it on a little table by me, covered with a snow-white cloth, I could not help laying my head on her bosom, and bursting into happy tears. She put her arms round me, saying, "Poor child; poor child!"

As I continued to weep, she gently disengaged herself; and, taking a spoon, put some of the food (I did not know what it was) to my lips, entreating me most endearingly to swallow it. To please her, I made an effort, and succeeded. She went on feeding me like a baby, with one arm round me, till I looked up in her face and smiled : then she gave me the spoon, and told me to eat, for it would do me good. I obeyed her, and found myself wonderfully refreshed. Then she drew near the fire an old-fashioned couch that was in the cottage, and making me lie down upon it, sat at my feet, and began to sing. Amazing store of old ballads rippled from her lips, over the pebbles of ancient tunes; and the voice that sang was sweet as the voice of a tuneful maiden that singeth ever from very fulness of song. The songs were almost all sad, but with a sound of comfort. One I can faintly recall. It was something like this :

> Sir Aglovaile through the churchyard rode;
> *Sing, All alone I lie:*
> Little recked he where'er he yode,
> *All alone, up in the sky.*
>
> Swerved his courser, and plunged with fear;
> *All alone I lie:*
> His cry might have wakened the dead men near,
> *All alone, up in the sky.*
>
> The very dead that lay at his feet,
> Lapt in the mouldy winding-sheet.
>
> But he curbed him and spurred him, until he stood
> Still in his place, like a horse of wood,
>
> With nostrils uplift, and eyes wide and wan;
> But the sweat in streams from his fetlocks ran.

A ghost grew out of the shadowy air,
And sat in the midst of her moony hair.

In her gleamy hair she sat and wept;
In the dreamful moon they lay and slept;

The shadows above, and the bodies below,
Lay and slept in the moonbeams slow.

And she sang, like the moan of an autumn wind
Over the stubble left behind:

> *Alas, how easily things go wrong!*
> *A sigh too much, or a kiss too long,*
> *And there follows a mist and a weeping rain,*
> *And life is never the same again.*
>
> *Alas, how hardly things go right!*
> *'Tis hard to watch in a summer night,*
> *For the sigh will come, and the kiss will stay,*
> *And the summer night is a winter day.*

"Oh, lovely ghost, my heart is woe,
To see thee weeping and wailing so.

Oh, lovely ghost," said the fearless knight,
"Can the sword of a warrior set it right?

Or prayer of bedesman, praying mild,
As a cup of water a feverish child,

Sooth thee at last, in dreamless mood
To sleep the sleep a dead lady should?

Thine eyes they fill me with longing sore,
As if I had known thee for evermore.

Oh, lovely ghost, I could leave the day
To sit with thee in the moon away

If thou wouldst trust me, and lay thy head
To rest on a bosom that is not dead."

The lady sprang up with a strange ghost-cry,
And she flung her white ghost-arms on high:

And she laughed a laugh that was not gay,
And it lengthened out till it died away.

And the dead beneath turned and moaned,
And the yew-trees above they shuddered and groaned.

"Will he love me twice with a love that is vain?
Will he kill the poor ghost yet again?

I thought thou wert good; but I said, and wept:
'Can I have dreamed who have not slept?'

And I knew, alas! or ever I would,
Whether I dreamed, or thou wert good.

When my baby died, my brain grew wild.
I awoke, and found I was with my child."

"If thou art the ghost of my Adelaide,
How is it? Thou wert but a village maid,

And thou seemest an angel lady white,
Though thin, and wan, and past delight."

The lady smiled a flickering smile,
And she pressed her temples hard the while.

"Thou seest that Death for a woman can
Do more than knighthood for a man."

"But show me the child thou callest mine,
Is she out to-night in the ghost's sunshine?"

"In St. Peter's Church she is playing on,
At hide-and-seek, with Apostle John.

When the moonbeams right through the window go,
Where the twelve are standing in glorious show,

She says the rest of them do not stir,
But one comes down to play with her.

Then I can go where I list, and weep,
For good St. John my child will keep."

"Thy beauty filleth the very air,
Never saw I a woman so fair."

"Come, if thou darest, and sit by my side;
But do not touch me, or woe will betide.

Alas, I am weak: I well might know
This gladness betokens some further woe.

Yet come. It will come. I will bear it. I can.
For thou lovest me yet—though but as a man."

The knight dismounted in earnest speed;
Away through the tombstones thundered the steed,

And fell by the outer wall, and died.
But the knight he kneeled by the lady's side;

Kneeled beside her in wondrous bliss,
Rapt in an everlasting kiss:

Though never his lips come the lady nigh,
And his eyes alone on her beauty lie.

All the night long, till the cock crew loud,
He kneeled by the lady, lapt in her shroud.

And what they said, I may not say:
Dead night was sweeter than living day.

How she made him so blissful glad
Who made her and found her so ghostly sad,

I may not tell; but it needs no touch
To make them blessed who love so much.

"Come every night, my ghost, to me;
And one night I will come to thee.

'Tis good to have a ghostly wife:
She will not tremble at clang of strife;

She will only hearken, amid the din,
Behind the door, if he cometh in."

And this is how Sir Aglovaile
Often walked in the moonlight pale.

And oft when the crescent but thinned the gloom,
Full orbéd moonlight filled his room;

And through beneath his chamber door,
Fell a ghostly gleam on the outer floor;

And they that passed, in fear averred
That murmured words they often heard.

'Twas then that the eastern crescent shone
Through the chancel window, and good St. John

Played with the ghost-child all the night,
And the mother was free till the morning light,

And sped through the dawning night, to stay
With Aglovaile till the break of day.

And their love was a rapture, lone and high,
And dumb as the moon in the topmost sky.

One night Sir Aglovaile, weary, slept,
And dreamed a dream wherein he wept.

A warrior he was, not often wept he,
But this night he wept full bitterly.

He woke—beside him the ghost-girl shone
Out of the dark: 'twas the eve of St. John.

He had dreamed a dream of a still, dark wood,
Where the maiden of old beside him stood;

But a mist came down, and caught her away,
And he sought her in vain through the pathless day,

Till he wept with the grief that can do no more,
And thought he had dreamt the dream before.

From bursting heart the weeping flowed on;
And lo! beside him the ghost-girl shone;

Shone like the light on a harbour's breast,
Over the sea of his dream's unrest;

Shone like the wondrous, nameless boon,
That the heart seeks ever, night or noon:

Warnings forgotten, when needed most,
He clasped to his bosom the radiant ghost.

She wailed aloud, and faded, and sank.
With upturn'd white face, cold and blank,

In his arms lay the corpse of the maiden pale,
And she came no more to Sir Aglovaile.

Only a voice, when winds were wild,
Sobbed and wailed like a chidden child.

> *Alas, how easily things go wrong!*
> *A sigh too much, or a kiss too long,*
> *And there follows a mist and a weeping rain,*
> *And life is never the same again.*

This was one of the simplest of her songs, which, perhaps, is the cause of my being able to remember it better than most of the others.

While she sung, I was in Elysium, with the sense of a rich soul upholding, embracing, and overhanging mine, full of all plenty and bounty. I felt as if she could give me everything I wanted; as if I should never wish to leave her, but would be content to be sung to and fed by her, day after day, as years rolled by. At last I fell asleep while she sang.

When I awoke, I knew not whether it was night or day. The fire had sunk to a few red embers, which just gave light enough to show me the woman standing a few feet from me, with her back towards me, facing the door by which I had entered. She was weeping, but very gently and plentifully. The tears seemed to come freely from her heart. Thus she stood for a few minutes; then, slowly turning at right angles to her former position, she faced another of the four sides of the cottage. I now observed, for the first time, that here was a door likewise; and that, indeed, there was one in the centre of every side of the cottage. When she looked towards the second door, her tears ceased to flow, but sighs took their place. She often closed her eyes as she stood; and every time she closed her eyes, a gentle sigh seemed to be born in her heart, and to escape at her lips. But when her eyes were open, her sighs were deep and very sad, and shook her whole frame. Then she turned towards the third door, and a cry as of fear or suppressed pain broke from her; but she seemed to hearten herself against the dismay, and to front it steadily; for, although I often heard a slight cry, and sometimes a moan, yet she never moved or bent her head, and I felt sure that her eyes never closed. Then she turned to the fourth door, and I saw her shudder, and then stand still as a statue; till at last she turned towards me and approached the fire. I saw that her face was white as death. But she gave one look upwards, and smiled the sweetest, most child-innocent smile; then heaped fresh wood on the fire, and, sitting down by the blaze, drew her wheel near her, and began to spin. While she spun, she murmured a low strange song, to which the hum of the wheel made a kind of infinite symphony. At length, she paused in her spinning and singing, and glanced towards me, like a mother who looks whether or not her child gives signs of waking. She smiled when she saw that my eyes were open. I asked her whether it was day yet. She answered, "It is always day here, so long as I keep my fire burning."

I felt wonderfully refreshed; and a great desire to see more of the island awoke within me. I rose, and saying that I wished to look about me, went towards the door by which I had entered.

"Stay a moment," said my hostess, with some trepidation in

her voice. "Listen to me. You will not see what you expect when you go out of that door. Only remember this : whenever you wish to come back to me, enter wherever you see this mark."

She held up her left hand between me and the fire. Upon the palm, which appeared amost transparent, I saw, in dark red, a mark like this ⤸ , which I took care to fix in my mind.

She then kissed me, and bade me good-bye with a solemnity that awed me; and bewildered me too, seeing I was only going out for a little ramble in an island, which I did not believe larger than could easily be compassed in a few hours' walk at most. As I went she resumed her spinning.

I opened the door, and stepped out. The moment my foot touched the smooth sward, I seemed to issue from the door of an old barn on my father's estate, where, in the hot afternoons, I used to go and lie amongst the straw, and read. It seemed to me now that I had been asleep there. At a little distance in the field, I saw two of my brothers at play. The moment they caught sight of me, they called out to me to come and join them, which I did; and we played together as we had done years ago, till the red sun went down in the west, and the gray fog began to rise from the river. Then we went home together with a strange happiness. As we went, we heard the continually renewed larum of a landrail in the long grass. One of my brothers and I separated to a little distance, and each commenced running towards the part whence the sound appeared to come, in the hope of approaching the spot where the bird was, and so getting at least a sight of it, if we should not be able to capture the little creature. My father's voice recalled us from trampling down the rich long grass, soon to be cut down and laid aside for winter. I had quite forgotten all about Fairy Land, and the wonderful old woman, and the curious red mark.

My favourite brother and I shared the same bed. Some childish dispute arose between us; and our last words, ere we fell asleep, were not of kindness, notwithstanding the pleasures of the day. When I woke in the morning, I missed him. He had risen early, and had gone to bathe in the river. In another hour, he was brought home drowned. Alas! alas! if we had only gone to sleep as usual, the one with his arm about the other! Amidst the horror of the moment, a strange conviction flashed across my mind, that I had gone through the very same once before.

I rushed out of the house, I knew not why, sobbing and crying bitterly. I ran through the fields in aimless distress, till, passing the old barn, I caught sight of a red mark on the door. The merest trifles sometimes rivet the attention in the deepest misery; the intellect has so little to do with grief. I went up to look at this mark, which I did not remember ever to have seen before. As I looked at it, I thought I would go in and lie down amongst the straw, for I was very weary with running about and weeping. I opened the door; and there in the cottage sat the old woman as I had left her, at her spinning-wheel.

"I did not expect you quite so soon," she said, as I shut the door behind me. I went up to the couch, and threw myself on it with that fatigue wherewith one awakes from a feverish dream of hopeless grief.

The old woman sang :

> The great sun, benighted,
> May faint from the sky;
> But love, once uplighted,
> Will never more die.

> Form, with its brightness,
> From eyes will depart:
> It walketh, in whiteness,
> The halls of the heart.

Ere she had ceased singing, my courage had returned. I started from the couch, and, without taking leave of the old woman, opened the door of Sighs, and sprang into what should appear.

I stood in a lordly hall, where, by a blazing fire on the hearth, sat a lady, waiting, I knew, for some one long desired. A mirror was near me, but I saw that my form had no place within its depths, so I feared not that I should be seen. The lady wonderfully resembled my marble lady, but was altogether of the daughters of men, and I could not tell whether or not it was she. It was not for me she waited. The tramp of a great horse rang through the court without. It ceased, and the clang of armour told that his rider alighted, and the sound of his ringing heels approached the hall. The door opened; but the lady waited, for she would meet her lord alone. He strode in : she flew like a home-bound dove into his arms, and nestled on the hard steel. It was the knight of the soiled armour. But now the armour shone like polished glass; and strange to tell, though the mirror reflected not my form, I saw a dim shadow of myself in the shining steel.

"O my beloved, thou art come, and I am blessed."

Her soft fingers speedily overcame the hard clasp of his helmet; one by one she undid the buckles of his armour; and she toiled under the weight of the mail, as she *would* carry it aside. Then she unclasped his greaves, and unbuckled his spurs; and once more she sprang into his arms, and laid her head where she could now feel the beating of his heart. Then she disengaged herself from his embrace, and, moving back a step or two, gazed at him. He stood there a mighty form, crowned with a noble head, where all sadness had disappeared, or had been absorbed in solemn purpose. Yet I suppose that he looked more thoughtful than the lady had expected to see him, for she did not renew her caresses, although his face glowed with love, and the few words he spoke were as mighty deeds for strength; but she led him towards the hearth, and seated him in an ancient chair, and set wine before him, and sat at his feet.

"I am sad," he said, "when I think of the youth whom I met twice in the forests of Fairy Land; and who, you say, twice, with his songs, roused you from the death-sleep of an evil enchantment. There was something noble in him, but it was a nobleness of thought, and not of deed. He may yet perish of vile fear."

"Ah!" returned the lady, "you saved him once; and for that I thank you; for may I not say that I somewhat loved him? But tell me how you fared, when you struck your battle-axe into the ash-tree, and he came and found you; for so much of the story you had told me, when the beggar-child came and took you away."

"As soon as I saw him," rejoined the knight, "I knew that earthly arms availed not against such as he; and that my soul must meet him in its naked strength. So I unclasped my helm, and flung it on the ground; and, holding my good axe yet in my hand, gazed at him with steady eyes. On he came, a horror indeed, but I did not flinch. Endurance must conquer, where force could not reach. He came nearer and nearer, till the ghastly face was close to mine. A shudder as of death ran through me; but I think I did not move, for he seemed to quail, and retreated. As soon as he gave back, I struck one more sturdy blow on the stem of his tree, that the forest rang; and then looked at him again. He writhed and grinned with rage and apparent pain, and again approached me, but retreated sooner than before. I heeded him no more, but hewed with a will at the tree, till the trunk creaked, and the head bowed, and with a crash it fell to the earth. Then I looked up from my labour, and lo! the spectre had vanished, and I saw him no more; nor ever in my wanderings have I heard of him again."

"Well struck! well withstood! my hero," said the lady.

"But," said the knight, somewhat troubled, "dost thou love the youth still?"

"Ah!" she replied, "how can I help it? He woke me from worse than death; he loved me. I had never been for thee, if he had not sought me first. But I love him not as I love thee. He was but the moon of my night; thou art the sun of my day, O beloved."

"Thou art right," returned the noble man. "It were hard, indeed, not to have some love in return for such a gift as he hath given thee. I, too, owe him more than words can speak."

Humbled before them, with an aching and desolate heart, I yet could not restrain my words:

"Let me, then, be the moon of thy night still, O woman! And when thy day is beclouded, as the fairest days will be, let some song of mine comfort thee, as an old, withered, half-forgotten thing, that belongs to an ancient mournful hour of uncompleted birth, which yet was beautiful in its time."

They sat silent, and I almost thought they were listening. The colour of the lady's eyes grew deeper and deeper; the slow tears grew, and filled them, and overflowed. They rose, and passed, hand in hand, close to where I stood; and each looked towards me in passing. Then they disappeared through a door which closed behind them; but, ere it closed, I saw that the room into which it opened was a rich chamber, hung with gorgeous arras. I stood with an ocean of sighs frozen in my bosom. I could remain no longer. She was near me, and I could not see her; near me in the arms of one loved better than I, and I would not see her, and I would not be by her. But how to escape from the nearness of the best beloved? I had not this time forgotten the mark; for the fact that I could not enter the sphere of these living beings kept me aware that, for me, I moved in a vision, while they moved in life. I looked all about for the mark, but could see it nowhere; for I avoided looking just where it was. There the dull red cipher glowed, on the very door of their secret chamber. Struck with agony, I dashed it open, and fell at the feet of the ancient woman, who still spun on, the whole dissolved ocean of my sighs bursting from me in a storm of tearless sobs. Whether I fainted or slept, I do not know; but, as I returned to consciousness, before I seemed to have power to move, I heard the woman singing, and could distinguish the words :

> O light of dead and of dying days!
>   O Love; in thy glory go,
> In a rosy mist and a moony maze,
>   O'er the pathless peaks of snow.
>
> But what is left for the cold gray soul,
>   That moans like a wounded dove?
> One wine is left in the broken bowl—
>   'Tis—*To love, and love, and love.*

Now I could weep. When she saw me weeping, she sang :

> Better to sit at the waters' birth,
>   Than a sea of waves to win;
> To live in the love that floweth forth,
>   Than the love that cometh in.
>
> Be thy heart a well of love, my child,
>   Flowing, and free, and sure;
> For a cistern of love, though undefiled,
>   Keeps not the spirit pure.

I rose from the earth, loving the white lady as I had never loved her before.

Then I walked up to the door of Dismay, and opened it, and went out. And lo! I came forth upon a crowded street, where men and women went to and fro in multitudes. I knew it well; and, turning to one hand, walked sadly along the pavement. Suddenly I saw approaching me, a little way off, a form well known to me (*well-known!*—alas, how weak the word!) in the years when I thought my boyhood was left behind, and shortly before I entered the realm of Fairy Land. Wrong and Sorrow

had gone together, hand-in-hand as it is well they do. Unchange-
ably dear was that face. It lay in my heart as a child lies in its
own white bed; but I could not meet her.

"Anything but that," I said; and, turning aside, sprang up
the steps to a door, on which I fancied I saw the mystic sign. I
entered—not the mysterious cottage, but her home. I rushed
wildly on, and stood by the door of her room.

"She is out," I said, "I will see the old room once more."

I opened the door gently, and stood in a great solemn church.
A deep-toned bell, whose sounds throbbed and echoed and
swam through the empty building, struck the hour of midnight.
The moon shone through the windows of the clerestory, and
enough of the ghostly radiance was diffused through the church
to let me see, walking with a stately, yet somewhat trailing and
stumbling step, down the opposite aisle, for I stood in one of the
transepts, a figure dressed in a white robe, whether for the night,
or for that longer night which lies too deep for the day, I could
not tell. Was it she? and was this her chamber? I crossed the
church, and followed. The figure stopped, seemed to ascend as
it were a high bed, and lay down. I reached the place where
it lay, glimmering white. The bed was a tomb. The light was
too ghostly to see clearly, but I passed my hand over the face
and the hands and the feet, which were all bare. They were
cold—they were marble, but I knew them. It grew dark. I
turned to retrace my steps, but found, ere long, that I had
wandered into what seemed a little chapel. I groped about,
seeking the door. Everything I touched belonged to the dead.
My hands fell on the cold effigy of a knight who lay with his
legs crossed and his sword broken beside him. He lay in his
noble rest, and I lived on in ignoble strife. I felt for the left
hand and a certain finger; I found there the ring I knew : he
was one of my own ancestors. I was in the chapel over the
burial-vault of my race. I called aloud : "If any of the dead are
moving here, let them take pity upon me, for I, alas! am still
alive; and let some dead woman comfort me, for I am a stranger
in the land of the dead, and see no light." A warm kiss alighted on
my lips through the dark. And I said, "The dead kiss well; I will
not be afraid." And a great hand was reached out of the dark,
and grasped mine for a moment, mightily and tenderly. I said
to myself : "The veil between, though very dark, is very thin."

Groping my way further, I stumbled over the heavy stone that covered the entrance of the vault: and, in stumbling, descried upon the stone the mark, glowing in red fire. I caught the great ring. All my effort could not have moved the huge slab; but it opened the door of the cottage, and I threw myself once more, pale and speechless, on the couch beside the ancient dame. She sang once more:

> Thou dreamest: on a rock thou art,
>   High o'er the broken wave;
> Thou fallest with a fearful start,
>   But not into thy grave;
> For, waking in the morning's light,
> Thou smilest at the vanished night.
>
> So wilt thou sink, all pale and dumb,
>   Into the fainting gloom;
> But ere the coming terrors come,
>   Thou wak'st—where is the tomb?
> Thou wak'st—the dead ones smile above,
> With hovering arms of sleepless love.

She paused; then sang again:

> We weep for gladness, weep for grief;
>   The tears they are the same;
> We sigh for longing, and relief;
>   The sighs have but one name.
>
> And mingled in the dying strife,
>   Are moans that are not sad;
> The pangs of death are throbs of life,
>   Its sighs are sometimes glad.
>
> The face is very strange and white:
>   It is Earth's only spot
> That feebly flickers back the light
>   The living seëth not.

I fell asleep, and slept a dreamless sleep, for I know not how long. When I awoke, I found that my hostess had moved from where she had been sitting, and now sat between me and the fourth door. I guessed that her design was to prevent my entering there. I sprang from the couch, and darted past her to the door. I opened it at once and went out. All I remember is a cry of distress from the woman: "Don't go there, my child! Don't go there!" But I was gone.

I knew nothing more; or, if I did, I had forgot it all when I awoke to consciousness, lying on the floor of the cottage, with my head in the lap of the woman, who was weeping over me, and stroking my hair with both hands, talking to me as a mother might talk to a sick and sleeping, or a dead child. As soon as I looked up and saw her, she smiled through her tears; smiled with withered face and young eyes, till her countenance was irradiated with the light of the smile. Then she bathed my head and face and hands in an icy cold, colourless liquid, which smelt a little of damp earth. Immediately I was able to sit up. She rose and put some food before me. When I had eaten, she said:

"Listen to me, my child. You must leave me directly!"

"Leave you!" I said. "I am so happy with you. I never was so happy in my life."

"But you must go," she rejoined sadly. "Listen! What do you hear?"

"I hear the sound as of a great throbbing of water."

"Ah! you do hear it? Well, I had to go through that door—the door of the Timeless" (and she shuddered as she pointed to the fourth door)—"to find you; for if I had not gone, you would never have entered again; and because I went, the waters around my cottage will rise and rise, and flow and come, till they build a great firmament of waters over my dwelling. But as long as I keep my fire burning, they cannot enter. I have fuel enough for years; and after one year they will sink away again, and be just as they were before you came. I have not been buried for a hundred years now." And she smiled and wept.

"Alas! alas!" I cried. "I have brought this evil on the best and kindest of friends, who has filled my heart with great gifts."

"Do not think of that," she rejoined. "I can bear it very well. You will come back to me some day, I know. But I beg you, for my sake, my dear child, to do one thing. In whatever sorrow you may be, however inconsolable and irremediable it may appear, believe me that the old woman in the cottage, with the young eyes," (and she smiled,) "knows something, though she must not always tell it, that would quite satisfy you about it, even in the worst moments of your distress. Now you must go."

"But how can I go, if the waters are all about, and if the doors all lead into other regions and other worlds?"

"This is not an island," she replied; "but is joined to the land by a narrow neck; and for the door, I will lead you myself through the right one."

She took my hand, and led me through the third door; whereupon I found myself standing in the deep grassy turf on which I had landed from the little boat, but upon the opposite side of the cottage. She pointed out the direction I must take, to find the isthmus and escape the rising waters.

Then putting her arms around me, she held me to her bosom; and as I kissed her, I felt as if I were leaving my mother for the first time, and could not help weeping bitterly. At length she gently pushed me away, and with the words, "Go, my son, and do something worth doing," turned back, and, entering the cottage, closed the door behind her.

I felt very desolate as I went.

CHAPTER XX

"Thou hadst no fame; that which thou didst like good
Was but thy appetite that swayed thy blood
For that time to the best; for as a blast
That through a house comes, usually doth cast
Things out of order, yet by chance may come
And blow some one thing to his proper room,
So did thy appetite, and not thy zeal,
Sway thee by chance to do some one thing well."
                    FLETCHER's *Faithful Shepherdess.*

"The noble hart that harbours vertuous thought
And is with childe of glorious great intent,
Can never rest, until it forth have brought
Th' eternall brood of glorie excellent."
                    SPENSER—*The Faerie Queene.*

I HAD NOT GONE very far before I felt that the turf beneath my feet was soaked with the rising waters. But I reached the isthmus in safety. It was rocky, and so much higher than the level of the peninsula, that I had plenty of time to cross. I saw on each side of me the water rising rapidly, altogether without wind, or violent motion, or broken waves, but as if a slow strong fire were glowing beneath it. Ascending a steep acclivity, I found myself at last in an open, rocky country. After travelling for some hours, as nearly in a straight line as I could, I arrived at a lonely tower, built on the top of a little hill, which overlooked the whole neighbouring country. As I approached, I heard the clang of an anvil; and so rapid were the blows, that I despaired of making myself heard till a pause in the work should ensue. It was some minutes before a cessation took place; but when it did, I knocked loudly, and had not long to wait; for, a moment after, the door was partly opened by a noble-looking youth, half-undressed, glowing with heat, and begrimed with the blackness of the forge. In one hand he held a sword, so lately from the furnace that it yet shone with a dull fire. As soon as he saw me, he threw the door wide open, and standing aside, invited me very cordially to enter. I did so; when he shut and bolted the door most carefully, and then led the way inwards. He brought me into a rude hall, which seemed to occupy almost the whole of the ground floor of the little tower, and which I saw was now being used as a workshop. A huge fire roared on the hearth, beside which was an anvil. By the anvil stood, in similar undress, and in a waiting attitude, hammer in hand, a second youth, tall as the former, but far more slightly built. Reversing the usual course of perception in such meetings, I thought them, at first sight, very unlike; and at the second glance, knew that they were brothers. The former, and apparently the elder, was muscular and dark, with curling hair, and large hazel eyes, which sometimes grew wondrously soft. The second was slender and fair, yet with a countenance like an eagle, and an eye which, though pale blue, shone with an almost fierce expression. He stood erect, as if looking from a lofty mountain crag, over a vast plain outstretched below. As soon as we entered the hall, the elder turned to me, and I saw that a glow of satisfaction shone on both their faces. To my surprise and great pleasure, he addressed me thus :

"Brother, will you sit by the fire and rest, till we finish this part of our work?"

I signified my assent; and, resolved to await any disclosure they might be inclined to make, seated myself in silence near the hearth.

The elder brother then laid the sword in the fire, covered it well over, and when it had attained a sufficient degree of heat, drew it out and laid it on the anvil, moving it carefully about, while the younger, with a succession of quick smart blows, appeared either to be welding it, or hammering one part of it to a consenting shape with the rest. Having finished, they laid it carefully in the fire; and, when it was very hot indeed, plunged it into a vessel full of some liquid, whence a blue flame sprang upwards, as the glowing steel entered. There they left it; and drawing two stools to the fire, sat down, one on each side of me.

"We are very glad to see you, brother. We have been expecting you for some days," said the dark-haired youth.

"I am proud to be called your brother," I rejoined; "and you will not think I refuse the name, if I desire to know why you honour me with it?"

"Ah! then he does not know about it," said the younger. "We thought you had known of the bond betwixt us, and the work we have to do together. You must tell him, brother, from the first."

So the elder began:

"Our father is king of this country. Before we were born, three giant brothers had appeared in the land. No one knew exactly when, and no one had the least idea whence they came. They took possession of a ruined castle that had stood unchanged and unoccupied within the memory of any of the country people. The vaults of this castle had remained uninjured by time, and these, I presume, they made use of at first. They were rarely seen, and never offered the least injury to any one; so that they were regarded in the neighbourhood as at least perfectly harmless, if not rather benevolent beings. But it began to be observed, that the old castle had assumed somehow or other, no one knew when or how, a somewhat different look from what it used to have. Not only were several breaches in the lower part of the walls built up, but actually some of the battlements which yet stood, had been repaired, apparently to prevent them from falling into worse decay, while the more important parts were being restored. Of course, every one supposed the giants must have a hand in the work, but no one ever saw them engaged in it. The peasants became yet more uneasy, after one, who had concealed himself, and watched all night, in the neighbourhood of the castle, reported that he had seen, in full moonlight, the three huge giants working with might and main, all night long, restoring to their former position some massive stones, formerly

steps of a grand turnpike stair, a great portion of which had
long since fallen, along with part of the wall of the round tower
in which it had been built. This wall they were completing, foot
by foot, along with the stair. But the people said they had no
just pretext for interfering : although the real reason for letting
the giants alone was, that everybody was far too much afraid of
them to interrupt them.

"At length, with the help of a neighbouring quarry, the whole
of the external wall of the castle was finished. And now the
country folks were in greater fear than before. But for several
years the giants remained very peaceful. The reason of this was
afterwards supposed to be the fact, that they were distantly
related to several good people in the country; for, as long as
these lived, they remained quiet; but as soon as they were all
dead the real nature of the giants broke out. Having completed
the outside of their castle, they proceeded, by spoiling the
country houses around them, to make a quite luxurious provision
for their comfort within. Affairs reached such a pass, that the
news of their robberies came to my father's ears; but he, alas!
was so crippled in his resources, by a war he was carrying on
with a neighbouring prince, that he could only spare a very few
men, to attempt the capture of their stronghold. Upon these
the giants issued in the night, and slew every man of them. And
now, grown bolder by success and impunity, they no longer confined their depredations to property, but began to seize the
persons of their distinguished neighbours, knights and ladies,
and hold them in durance, the misery of which was heightened
by all manner of indignity, until they were redeemed by their
friends, at an exorbitant ransom. Many knights have adventured
their overthrow, but to their own instead; for they have all been
slain, or captured, or forced to make a hasty retreat. To crown
their enormities, if any man now attempts their destruction, they,
immediately upon his defeat, put one or more of their captives
to a shameful death, on a turret in sight of all passers-by; so
that they have been much less molested of late; and we, although
we have burned, for years, to attack these demons and destroy
them, dared not, for the sake of their captives, risk the adventure,
before we should have reached at least our earliest manhood.
Now, however, we are preparing for the attempt; and the
grounds of this preparation are these. Having only the resolution,

and not the experience necessary for the undertaking, we went and consulted a lonely woman of wisdom, who lives not very far from here, in the direction of the quarter from which you have come. She received us most kindly, and gave us what seems to us the best of advice. She first inquired what experience we had had in arms. We told her we had been well exercised from our boyhood, and for some years had kept ourselves in constant practice, with a view to this necessity.

" 'But you have not actually fought for life and death?' said she.

"We were forced to confess we had not.

" 'So much the better in some respects,' she replied. 'Now listen to me. Go first and work with an armourer, for as long time as you find needful to obtain a knowledge of his craft; which will not be long, seeing your hearts will be all in the work. Then go to some lonely tower, you two alone. Receive no visits from man or woman. There forge for yourselves every piece of armour that you wish to wear, or to use, in your coming encounter. And keep up your exercises. As, however, two of you can be no match for the three giants, I will find you, if I can, a third brother, who will take on himself the third share of the fight, and the preparation. Indeed, I have already seen one who will, I think, be the very man for your fellowship, but it will be some time before he comes to me. He is wandering now without an aim. I will show him to you in a glass, and, when he comes, you will know him at once. If he will share your endeavours, you must teach him all you know, and he will repay you well, in present song, and in future deeds.'

"She opened the door of a curious old cabinet that stood in the room. On the inside of this door was an oval convex mirror. Looking in it for some time, we at length saw reflected the place where we stood, and the old dame seated in her chair. Our forms were not reflected. But at the feet of the dame lay a young man, yourself, weeping.

" 'Surely this youth will not serve our ends,' said I, 'for he weeps.'

"The old woman smiled. 'Past tears are present strength,' said she.

" 'Oh!' said my brother, 'I saw you weep once over an eagle you shot.'

" 'That was because it was so like you, brother,' I replied; 'but indeed, this youth may have better cause for tears than that—I was wrong.'

" 'Wait a while,' said the woman; 'if I mistake not, he will make you weep till your tears are dry for ever. Tears are the only cure for weeping. And you may have need of the cure, before you go forth to fight the giants. You must wait for him, in your tower, till he comes.'

"Now if you will join us, we will soon teach you to make your armour; and we will fight together, and work together, and love each other as never three loved before. And you will sing to us, will you not?"

"That I will, when I can," I answered; "but it is only at times that the power of song comes upon me. For that I must wait; but I have a feeling that if I work well, song will not be far off to enliven the labour."

This was all the compact made : the brothers required nothing more, and I did not think of giving anything more. I rose, and threw off my upper garments.

"I know the uses of the sword," I said. "I am ashamed of my white hands beside yours so nobly soiled and hard; but that shame will soon be wiped away."

"No, no; we will not work to-day. Rest is as needful as toil. Bring the wine, brother; it is your turn to serve to-day."

The younger brother soon covered a table with rough viands, but good wine; and we ate and drank heartily, beside our work. Before the meal was over, I had learned all their story. Each had something in his heart which made the conviction, that he would victoriously perish in the coming conflict, a real sorrow to him. Otherwise they thought they would have lived enough. The causes of their trouble were respectively these :—

While they wrought with an armourer, in a city famed for workmanship in steel and silver, the elder had fallen in love with a lady as far beneath him in real rank, as she was above the station he had as apprentice to an armourer. Nor did he seek to further his suit by discovering himself; but there was simply so much manhood about him, that no one ever thought of rank when in his company. This is what his brother said about it. The lady could not help loving him in return. He told her when he left her, that he had a perilous adventure before him, and that

when it was achieved, she would either see him return to claim
her, or hear that he had died with honour. The younger brother's
grief arose from the fact, that, if they were both slain, his old
father, the king, would be childless. His love for his father was
so exceeding, that to one unable to sympathise with it, it would
have appeared extravagant. Both loved him equally at heart;
but the love of the younger had been more developed, because
his thoughts and anxieties had not been otherwise occupied.
When at home, he had been his constant companion; and, of
late, had ministered to the infirmities of his growing age. The
youth was never weary of listening to the tales of his sire's
youthful adventures; and had not yet in the smallest degree lost
the conviction, that his father was the greatest man in the world.
The grandest triumph possible to his conception was, to return
to his father, laden with the spoils of one of the hated giants.
But they both were in some dread, lest the thought of the
loneliness of these two might occur to them, in the moment
when decision was most necessary, and disturb, in some degree,
the self-possession requisite for the success of their attempt. For,
as I have said, they were yet untried in actual conflict. "Now,"
thought I, "I see to what the powers of my gift must minister."
For my own part, I did not dread death, for I had nothing to
care to live for; but I dreaded the encounter because of the
responsibility connected with it. I resolved however to work
hard, and thus grow cool, and quick, and forceful.

The time passed away in work and song, in talk and ramble,
in friendly fight and brotherly aid. I would not forge for myself
armour of heavy mail like theirs, for I was not so powerful as
they, and depended more for any success I might secure, upon
nimbleness of motion, certainty of eye, and ready response of
hand. Therefore I began to make for myself a shirt of steel
plates and rings; which work, while more troublesome, was
better suited to me than the heavier labour. Much assistance did
the brothers give me, even after, by their instructions, I was able
to make some progress alone. Their work was in a moment
abandoned, to render any required aid to mine. As the old
woman had promised, I tried to repay them with song; and
many were the tears they both shed over my ballads and dirges.
The songs they liked best to hear were two which I made for
them. They were not half so good as many others I knew,

especially some I had learned from the wise woman in the cottage; but what comes nearest to our needs we like the best.

I.

The king sat on his throne,
  Glowing in gold and red;
The crown in his right hand shone,
  And the gray hairs crowned his head.

His only son walks in,
  And in walls of steel he stands:
"Make me, O father, strong to win,
  With the blessing of holy hands."

He knelt before his sire,
  Who blessed him with feeble smile;
His eyes shone out with a kingly fire,
  But his old lips quivered the while.

"Go to the fight, my son,
  Bring back the giant's head;
And the crown with which my brows have done,
  Shall glitter on thine instead."

"My father, I seek no crown,
  But unspoken praise from thee;
For thy people's good, and thy renown,
  I will die to set them free."

The king sat down and waited there,
  And rose not, night nor day;
Till a sound of shouting filled the air,
  And cries of a sore dismay.

Then like a king he sat once more,
  With the crown upon his head;
And up to the throne the people bore
  A mighty giant dead.

And up to the throne the people bore
  A pale and lifeless boy.
The king rose up like a prophet of yore,
  In a lofty, deathlike joy.

He put the crown on the chilly brow:
  "Thou should'st have reigned with me;
But Death is the king of both, and now
  I go to obey with thee.

"Surely some good in me there lay,
　　To beget the noble one."
The old man smiled like a winter day,
　　And fell beside his son.

II.

"O lady, thy lover is dead," they cried;
　　"He is dead, but hath slain the foe;
He hath left his name to be magnified
　　In a song of wonder and woe."

"Alas! I am well repaid," said she,
　　"With a pain that stings like joy;
For I feared, from his tenderness to me,
　　That he was but a feeble boy.

"Now I shall hold my head on high,
　　The queen among my kind;
If ye hear a sound, 'tis only a sigh
　　For a glory left behind."

The first three times I sang these songs they both wept passionately. But after the third time, they wept no more. Their eyes shone, and their faces grew pale, but they never wept at any of my songs again.

CHAPTER XXI

"I put my life in my hands."—The Book of Judges.

AT LENGTH, WITH much toil and equal delight, our armour was finished. We armed each other, and tested the strength of the defence, with many blows of loving force. I was inferior in strength to both my brothers, but a little more agile than either; and upon this agility, joined to precision in hitting with the point of my weapon, I grounded my hopes of success in the ensuing combat. I likewise laboured to develop yet more the keenness of sight with which I was naturally gifted; and, from the remarks of my companions, I soon learned that my endeavours were not in vain.

The morning arrived on which we had determined to make

the attempt, and succeed or perish—perhaps both. We had resolved to fight on foot; knowing that the mishap of many of the knights who had made the attempt, had resulted from the fright of their horses at the appearance of the giants; and believing with Sir Gawain, that, though mare's sons might be false to us, the earth would never prove a traitor. But most of our preparations were, in their immediate aim at least, frustrated.

We rose, that fatal morning, by day-break. We had rested from all labour the day before, and now were fresh as the lark. We bathed in cold spring water, and dressed ourselves in clean garments, with a sense of preparation, as for a solemn festivity. When we had broken our fast, I took an old lyre, which I had found in the tower and had myself repaired, and sung for the last time the two ballads of which I have said so much already. I followed them with this, for a closing song :—

> Oh, well for him who breaks his dream
>   With the blow that ends the strife;
> And, waking, knows the peace that flows
>   Around the pain of life!
>
> We are dead, my brothers! Our bodies clasp,
>   As an armour, our souls about;
> This hand is the battle-axe I grasp,
>   And this my hammer stout.
>
> Fear not, my brothers, for we are dead;
>   No noise can break our rest;
> The calm of the grave is about the head,
>   And the heart heaves not the breast.
>
> And our life we throw to our people back,
>   To live with, a further store;
> We leave it them, that there be no lack
>   In the land where we live no more.
>
> Oh, well for him who breaks his dream
>   With the blow that ends the strife;
> And, waking, knows the peace that flows
>   Around the noise of life!

As the last few tones of the instrument were following, like a dirge, the death of the song, we all sprang to our feet. For, through one of the little windows of the tower, towards which I had looked as I sang, I saw, suddenly rising over the edge of

the slope on which our tower stood, three enormous heads. The
brothers knew at once, by my looks, what caused my sudden
movement. We were utterly unarmed, and there was no time to
arm. But we seemed to adopt the same resolution simultaneously;
for each caught up his favourite weapon, and, leaving his
defence behind, sprang to the door. I snatched up a long rapier,
abruptly, but very finely pointed, in my sword-hand, and in the
other a sabre; the elder brother seized his heavy battle-axe; and
the younger, a great, two-handed sword, which he wielded in
one hand like a feather. We had just time to get clear of the
tower, embrace and say good-bye, and part to some little distance, that we might not encumber each other's motions, ere
the triple giant-brotherhood drew near to attack us. They were
about twice our height, and armed to the teeth. Through the
visors of their helmets their monstrous eyes shone with a horrible
ferocity. I was in the middle position, and the middle giant
approached me. My eyes were busy with his armour, and I was
not a moment in settling my mode of attack. I saw that his body-
armour was somewhat clumsily made, and that the overlappings
in the lower part had more play than necessary; and I hoped
that, in a fortunate moment, some joint would open a little, in
a visible and accessible part. I stood till he came near enough to
aim a blow at me with the mace, which has been, in all ages, the
favourite weapon of giants, when, of course, I leaped aside, and
let the blow fall upon the spot where I had been standing. I
expected this would strain the joints of his armour yet more. Full
of fury, he made at me again; but I kept him busy, constantly
eluding his blows, and hoping thus to fatigue him. He did not
seem to fear any assault from me, and I attempted none as yet;
but while I watched his motions in order to avoid his blows, I,
at the same time, kept equal watch upon those joints of his
armour, through some one of which I hoped to reach his life.
At length, as if somewhat fatigued, he paused a moment, and
drew himself slightly up; I bounded forward, foot and hand,
ran my rapier right through to the armour of his back, let go
the hilt, and passing under his right arm, turned as he fell, and
flew at him with my sabre. At one happy blow I divided the
band of his helmet, which fell off, and allowed me, with a second
cut across the eyes, to blind him quite; after which I clove his
head, and turned, uninjured, to see how my brothers had fared.

Both the giants were down, but so were my brothers. I flew first to the one and then to the other couple. Both pairs of combatants were dead, and yet locked together, as in the death-struggle. The elder had buried his battle-axe in the body of his foe, and had fallen beneath him as he fell. The giant had strangled him in his own death-agonies. The younger had nearly hewn off the left leg of his enemy; and, grappled with in the act, had, while they rolled together on the earth, found for his dagger a passage betwixt the gorget and cuirass of the giant, and stabbed him mortally in the throat. The blood from the giant's throat was yet pouring over the hand of his foe, which still grasped the hilt of the dagger sheathed in the wound. They lay silent. I, the least worthy, remained the sole survivor in the lists.

As I stood exhausted amidst the dead, after the first worthy deed of my life, I suddenly looked behind me, and there lay the Shadow, black in the sunshine. I went into the lonely tower, and there lay the useless armour of the noble youths—supine as they. Ah, how sad it looked! It was a glorious death, but it was death. My songs could not comfort me now. I was almost ashamed that I was alive, when they, the true-hearted, were no more. And yet I breathed freer to think that I had gone through the trial, and had not failed. And perhaps I may be forgiven, if some feelings of pride arose in my bosom, when I looked down on the mighty form that lay dead by my hand.

"After all, however," I said to myself, and my heart sank, "it was only skill. Your giant was but a blunderer."

I left the bodies of friends and foes, peaceful enough when the death-fight was over, and, hastening to the country below, roused the peasants. They came with shouting and gladness, bringing waggons to carry the bodies. I resolved to take the princes home to their father, each as he lay, in the arms of his country's foe. But first I searched the giants, and found the keys of their castle, to which I repaired, followed by a great company of the people. It was a place of wonderful strength. I released the prisoners, knights and ladies, all in a sad condition, from the cruelties and neglects of the giants. It humbled me to see them crowding round me with thanks, when in truth the glorious brothers, lying dead by their lonely tower, were those to whom the thanks belonged. I had but aided in carrying out the thought born in their brain, and uttered in visible form before ever I laid hold thereupon. Yet I did count myself happy to have been chosen for their brother in this great deed.

After a few hours spent in refreshing and clothing the prisoners, we all commenced our journey towards the capital. This was slow at first; but, as the strength and spirits of the prisoners returned, it became more rapid; and in three days we reached the palace of the king. As we entered the city gates, with the huge bulks lying each on a waggon drawn by horses, and two of them inextricably intertwined with the dead bodies of their princes, the people raised a shout and then a cry, and followed in multitudes the solemn procession.

I will not attempt to describe the behaviour of the grand old king. Joy and pride in his sons overcame his sorrow at their loss. On me he heaped every kindness that heart could devise or hand execute. He used to sit and question me, night after night, about everything that was in any way connected with them and their preparations. Our mode of life, and relation to each other, during the time we spent together, was a constant theme. He entered into the minutest details of the construction of the armour, even to a peculiar mode of riveting some of the plates, with unwearying interest. This armour I had intended to beg of the king, as my sole memorials of the contest; but, when I saw the delight he took in contemplating it, and the consolation it appeared to afford him in his sorrow, I could not ask for it; but, at his request, left my own, weapons and all, to be joined with theirs in a trophy, erected in the grand square of the palace. The king, with gorgeous ceremony, dubbed me knight with his own old hand, in which trembled the sword of his youth.

During the short time I remained, my company was, naturally, much courted by the young nobles. I was in a constant round of gaiety and diversion, notwithstanding that the court was in mourning. For the country was so rejoiced at the death of the giants, and so many of their lost friends had been restored to the nobility and men of wealth, that the gladness surpassed the grief. "Ye have indeed left your lives to your people, my great brothers!" I said.

But I was ever and ever haunted by the old shadow, which I had not seen all the time that I was at work in the tower. Even in the society of the ladies of the court, who seemed to think it only their duty to make my stay there as pleasant to me as possible, I could not help being conscious of its presence, although it might not be annoying me at the time. At length, somewhat weary of uninterrupted pleasure, and nowise strengthened thereby, either in body or mind, I put on a splendid suit of armour of steel inlaid with silver, which the old king had given me, and, mounting the horse on which it had been brought to me, took my leave of the palace, to visit the distant city in which the lady dwelt, whom the elder prince had loved. I anticipated a sore task, in conveying to her the news of his glorious fate : but this trial was spared me, in a manner as strange as anything that had happened to me in Fairy Land.

CHAPTER XXII

"Niemand hat meine Gestalt als der *Ich*."
Schoppe, in JEAN PAUL's *Titan*.

"No one has my form but the *I*."

"Joy's a subtil elf.
I think man's happiest when he forgets himself."
CYRIL TOURNEUR—*The Revenger's Tragedy*.

ON THE THIRD day of my journey, I was riding gently along a road, apparently little frequented, to judge from the grass that grew upon it. I was approaching a forest. Everywhere in Fairy Land forests are the places where one may most certainly expect adventures. As I drew near, a youth, unarmed, gentle, and beautiful, who had just cut a branch from a yew growing on the skirts of the wood, evidently to make himself a bow, met me, and thus accosted me :

"Sir knight, be careful as thou ridest through this forest; for it is said to be strangely enchanted, in a sort which even those who have been witnesses of its enchantment can hardly describe."

I thanked him for his advice, which I promised to follow, and rode on. But the moment I entered the wood it seemed to me that, if enchantment there was, it must be of a good kind; for the Shadow, which had been more than usually dark and distressing since I had set out on this journey, suddenly disappeared. I felt a wonderful elevation of spirits, and began to reflect on my past life, and especially on my combat with the giants, with such satisfaction, that I had actually to remind myself, that I had only killed one of them; and that, but for the brothers, I should never have had the idea of attacking them, not to mention the smallest power of standing to it. Still I rejoiced, and counted myself amongst the glorious knights of old; having even the unspeakable presumption—my shame and self-condemnation at the memory of it are such, that I write it as the only and sorest penance I can perform—to think of myself (will the world believe it?) as side by side with Sir Galahad! Scarcely had the thought been born in my mind, when, approaching me from the left, through the trees, I espied a resplendent knight, of mighty size, whose armour seemed to shine of itself, without the sun. When he drew near, I was astonished to see that this armour was like my own; nay, I could trace, line for line, the correspondence of the inlaid silver to the device on my own. His horse, too, was like mine in colour, form, and motion; save that, like his rider, he was greater and fiercer than his counterpart. The knight rode with beaver up. As he halted right opposite to me in the narrow path, barring my way, I saw the reflection of my countenance in the centre plate of shining steel on his breastplate. Above it rose the same face—his face—only, as I have said, larger and fiercer. I was bewildered. I could not help feeling some admiration of him, but it was mingled with a dim conviction that he was evil, and that I ought to fight with him.

"Let me pass," I said.

"When I will," he replied.

Something within me said : "Spear in rest, and ride at him! else thou art for ever a slave."

I tried, but my arm trembled so much that I could not couch my lance. To tell the truth, I, who had overcome the giant, shook like a coward before this knight. He gave a scornful laugh, that echoed through the wood, turned his horse, and said, without looking round, "Follow me."

I obeyed, abashed and stupefied. How long he led, and how long I followed, I cannot tell. "I never knew misery before," I said to myself. "Would that I had at least struck him, and had had my death-blow in return! Why, then, do I not call to him to wheel and defend himself? Alas! I know not why, but I cannot.

One look from him would cow me like a beaten hound." I followed, and was silent.

At length we came to a dreary square tower, in the middle of a dense forest. It looked as if scarce a tree had been cut down to make room for it. Across the very door, diagonally, grew the stem of a tree, so large that there was just room to squeeze past it in order to enter. One miserable square hole in the roof was the only visible suggestion of a window. Turret or battlement, or projecting masonry of any kind, it had none. Clear and smooth and massy, it rose from its base, and ended with a line straight and unbroken. The roof, carried to a centre from each of the four walls, rose slightly to the point where the rafters met. Round the base lay several little heaps of either bits of broken branches, withered and peeled, or half-whitened bones; I could not distinguish which. As I approached, the ground sounded hollow beneath my horse's hoofs. The knight took a great key from his pocket, and reaching past the stem of the tree, with some difficulty opened the door. "Dismount!" he commanded. I obeyed. He turned my horse's head away from the tower, gave him a terrible blow with the flat side of his sword, and sent him madly tearing through the forest.

"Now," said he, "enter, and take your companion with you."

I looked round : knight and horse had vanished, and behind me lay the horrible shadow. I entered, for I could not help myself; and the shadow followed me. I had a terrible conviction that the knight and he were one. The door closed behind me.

Now I was indeed in pitiful plight. There was literally nothing in the tower but my shadow and me. The walls rose right up to the roof; in which, as I had seen from without, there was one little square opening. This I now knew to be the only window the tower possessed. I sat down on the floor, in listless wretchedness. I think I must have fallen asleep, and have slept for hours; for I suddenly became aware of existence, in observing that the moon was shining through the hole in the roof. As she rose higher and higher, her light crept down the wall over me, till at last it shone right upon my head. Instantaneously the walls of the tower seemed to vanish away like a mist. I sat beneath a beech, on the edge of a forest, and the open country lay, in the moonlight, for miles and miles around me, spotted with glimmering houses and spires and towers. I thought with myself, "Oh, joy! it was only a dream; the horrible narrow waste is gone, and I wake beneath a beech-tree, perhaps one that loves me, and I can go where I will." I rose, as I thought, and walked about, and did what I would, but ever kept near the tree; for always, and, of course, since my meeting with the woman of the beech-tree far more than ever, I loved that tree. So the night wore on. I waited for the sun to rise, before I could venture to renew my journey. But as soon as the first faint light of the dawn appeared, instead of shining upon me from the eye of the morning, it stole like a fainting ghost through the little square hole above my head; and the walls came out as the light grew, and the glorious night was swallowed up of the hateful day. The long dreary day passed. My shadow lay black on the floor. I felt no hunger, no need of food. The night came. The moon shone. I watched her light slowly descending the wall, as I might have watched, adown the sky, the long, swift approach of a helping angel. Her rays touched me, and I was free. Thus night after night passed away. I should have died but for this. Every night the conviction returned, that I was free. Every morning I sat wretchedly disconsolate. At length, when the course of the moon no longer permitted her beams to touch me, the night was dreary as the day. When I slept, I was somewhat consoled by my dreams; but all the time I dreamed, I knew that I was only dreaming. But one night, at length, the moon, a mere shred of pallor, scattered a few thin ghostly rays upon me; and I think I fell asleep and dreamed. I sat in an autumn night, before the vintage, on a hill overlooking my own castle. My heart sprang with joy. Oh, to be a child again, innocent, fearless, without shame or desire! I walked down to the castle. All were in consternation at my absence. My sisters were weeping for my loss. They sprang up and clung to me, with incoherent cries, as I entered. My old friends came flocking round me. A gray light shone on the roof of the hall. It was the light of the dawn shining through the square window of my tower. More earnestly than ever, I longed for freedom after this dream; more drearily than ever, crept on the next wretched day. I measured by the sunbeams, caught through the little window in the trap of my tower, how it went by, waiting only for the dreams of the night.

About noon, I started as if something foreign to all my senses and all my experience, had suddenly invaded me; yet it was

only the voice of a woman singing. My whole frame quivered
with joy, surprise, and the sensation of the unforeseen. Like a
living soul, like an incarnation of Nature, the song entered my
prison-house. Each tone folded its wings, and laid itself, like a
caressing bird, upon my heart. It bathed me like a sea; inwrapt
me like an odorous vapour; entered my soul like a long draught
of clear spring-water; shone upon me like essential sunlight;
soothed me like a mother's voice and hand. Yet, as the clearest
forest-well tastes sometimes of the bitterness of decayed leaves,
so to my weary, prisoned heart, its cheerfulness had a sting of
cold, and its tenderness unmanned me with the faintness of long-
departed joys. I wept half-bitterly, half-luxuriously; but not long.
I dashed away the tears, ashamed of a weakness which I thought
I had abandoned. Ere I knew, I had walked to the door, and
seated myself with my ear against it, in order to catch every
syllable of the revelation from the unseen outer world. And now
I heard each word distinctly. The singer seemed to be standing
or sitting near the tower, for the sounds indicated no change of
place. The song was something like this :—

> The sun, like a golden knot on high,
> Gathers the glories of the sky,
> And binds them into a shining tent,
> Roofing the world with the firmament.
> And through the pavilion the rich winds blow,
> And through the pavilion the waters go.
> And the birds for joy, and the trees for prayer,
> Bowing their heads in the sunny air,
> And for thoughts, the gently talking springs,
> That come from the centre with secret things—
> All make a music, gentle and strong,
> Bound by the heart into one sweet song.
> And amidst them all, the mother Earth
> Sits with the children of her birth;
> She tendeth them all, as a mother hen
> Her little ones round her, twelve or ten:
> Oft she sitteth, with hands on knee,
> Idle with love for her family.
> Go forth to her from the dark and the dust,
> And weep beside her, if weep thou must;
> If she may not hold thee to her breast,
> Like a weary infant, that cries for rest;

At least she will press thee to her knee,
And tell a low, sweet tale to thee,
Till the hue to thy cheek, and the light to thine eye,
Strength to thy limbs, and courage high
To thy fainting heart, return amain,
And away to work thou goest again.
From the narrow desert, O man of pride,
Come into the house, so high and wide.

Hardly knowing what I did, I opened the door. Why had I not done so before? I do not know.

At first I could see no one; but when I had forced myself past the tree which grew across the entrance, I saw, seated on the ground, and leaning against the tree, with her back to my prison, a beautiful woman. Her countenance seemed known to me, and yet unknown. She looked up at me and smiled, when I made my appearance.

"Ah! were you the prisoner there? I am very glad I have wiled you out."

"Do you know me then?"

"Do you not know me? But you hurt me, and that, I suppose, makes it easy for a man to forget. You broke my globe. Yet I thank you. Perhaps I owe you many thanks for breaking it. I took the pieces, all black, and wet with crying over them, to the Fairy Queen. There was no music and no light in them now. But she took them from me, and laid them aside; and made me go to sleep in a great hall of white, with black pillars, and many red curtains. When I woke in the morning, I went to her, hoping to have my globe again, whole and sound; but she sent me away without it, and I have not seen it since. Nor do I care for it now. I have something so much better. I do not need the globe to play to me; for I can sing. I could not sing at all before. Now I go about everywhere through Fairy Land, singing till my heart is like to break, just like my globe, for very joy at my own songs. And wherever I go, my songs do good, and deliver people. And now I have delivered you, and I am so happy."

She ceased, and the tears came into her eyes.

All this time, I had been gazing at her; and now fully recognised the face of the child, glorified in the countenance of the woman. I was ashamed and humbled before her; but a great weight was lifted from my thoughts. I knelt before her, and thanked her, and begged her to forgive me.

"Rise, rise," she said; "I have nothing to forgive; I thank you. But now I must be gone, for I do not know how many may be waiting for me, here and there, through the dark forests; and they cannot come out till I come."

She rose, and with a smile and a farewell, turned and left me. I dared not ask her to stay; in fact, I could hardly speak to her. Between her and me, there was a great gulf. She was uplifted, by sorrow and well-doing, into a region I could hardly hope ever to enter. I watched her departure, as one watches a sunset. She went like a radiance through the dark wood, which was henceforth bright to me, from simply knowing that such a creature was in it. She was bearing the sun to the unsunned spots. The light and the music of her broken globe were now in her heart and her brain. As she went, she sang; and I caught these few words of her song; and the tones seemed to linger and wind about the trees after she had disappeared :—

> Thou goest thine, and I go mine—
>   Many ways we wend;
> Many days, and many ways,
>   Ending in one end.
>
> Many a wrong, and its curing song;
>   Many a road, and many an inn;
> Room to roam, but only one home
>   For all the world to win.

And so she vanished. With a sad heart, soothed by humility, and the knowledge of her peace and gladness, I bethought me what now I should do. First, I must leave the tower far behind me, lest, in some evil moment, I might be once more caged within its horrible walls. But it was ill walking in my heavy armour; and besides I had now no right to the golden spurs and the resplendent mail, fitly dulled with long neglect. I might do for a squire; but I honoured knighthood too highly, to call myself any longer one of the noble brotherhood. I stripped off all my armour, piled it under the tree, just where the lady had been seated, and took my unknown way, eastward through the woods. Of all my weapons, I carried only a short axe in my hand. Then first I knew the delight of being lowly; of saying to myself, "I am what I am, nothing more." "I have failed," I said; "I have lost myself—would it had been my shadow." I looked round : the shadow was nowhere to be seen. Ere long, I learned that it was not myself, but only my shadow, that I had lost. I learned that it is better, a thousand-fold, for a proud man to fall and be humbled, than to hold up his head in his pride and fancied innocence. I learned that he that will be a hero, will barely be a man; that he that will be nothing but a doer of his work, is sure of his manhood. In nothing was my ideal lowered, or dimmed, or grown less precious; I only saw it too plainly, to set myself for a moment beside it. Indeed, my ideal soon became my life; whereas, formerly, my life had consisted in a vain attempt to behold, if not my ideal in myself, at least myself in my ideal. Now, however, I took, at first, what perhaps was a mistaken pleasure, in despising and degrading myself. Another self seemed to arise, like a white spirit from a dead man, from the dumb and trampled self of the past. Doubtless, this self must again die and be buried, and again, from its tomb, spring a winged child; but of this my history as yet bears not the record. Self will come to life even in the slaying of self; but there is ever something deeper and stronger than it, which will emerge at last from the unknown abysses of the soul : will it be as a solemn gloom, burning with eyes? or a clear morning after the rain? or a smiling child, that finds itself nowhere, and everywhere?

CHAPTER XXIII

"High erected thought, seated in a heart of courtesy."
                                    SIR PHILIP SIDNEY.

"A sweet attractive kinde of grace,
    A full assurance given by lookes,
Continuall comfort in a face,
    The lineaments of Gospell bookes."
        MATTHEW ROYDON, on *Sir Philip Sidney*.

I HAD NOT GONE far, for I had but just lost sight of the hated tower, when a voice of another sort, sounding near or far, as the trees permitted or intercepted its passage, reached me. It was a full, deep, manly voice, but withal clear and melodious. Now it burst on the ear with a sudden swell, and anon, dying away as suddenly, seemed to come to me across a great space. Nevertheless, it drew nearer; till, at last, I could distinguish the words of the song, and get transient glimpses of the singer, between the columns of the trees. He came nearer, dawning upon me like a growing thought. He was a knight, armed from head to heel, mounted upon a strange-looking beast, whose form I could not understand. The words which I heard him sing were like these : —

> Heart be stout,
>   And eye be true;
> Good blade out!
>   And ill shall rue.
>
> Courage, horse!
>   Thou lackst no skill;
> Well thy force
>   Hath matched my will.
>
> For the foe
>   With fiery breath,
> At a blow,
>   Is still in death.
>
> Gently, horse!
>   Tread fearlessly;
> 'Tis his corse
>   That burdens thee.
>
> The sun's eye
>   Is fierce at noon;
> Thou and I
>   Will rest full soon.
>
> And new strength
>   New work will meet;
> Till, at length,
>   Long rest is sweet.

And now horse and rider had arrived near enough for me to see, fastened by the long neck to the hinder part of the saddle, and trailing its hideous length on the ground behind, the body of a great dragon. It was no wonder that, with such a drag at his heels, the horse could make but slow progress, notwithstanding his evident dismay. The horrid, serpent-like head, with its black tongue, forked with red, hanging out of its jaws, dangled against

the horse's side. Its neck was covered with long blue hair; its
sides with scales of green and gold. Its back was of corrugated
skin, of a purple hue. Its belly was similar in nature, but its
colour was leaden, dashed with blotches of livid blue. Its skinny,
bat-like wings and its tail were of a dull gray. It was strange to
see how so many gorgeous colours, so many curving lines, and
such beautiful things as wings and hair and scales, combined
to form the horrible creature, intense in ugliness.

The knight was passing me with a salutation; but, as I walked
towards him, he reined up, and I stood by his stirrup. When I
came near him, I saw to my surprise and pleasure likewise,
although a sudden pain, like a birth of fire, sprang up in my
heart, that it was the knight of the soiled armour, whom I knew
before, and whom I had seen in the vision, with the lady of the
marble. But I could have thrown my arms around him, because
she loved him. This discovery only strengthened the resolution
I had formed, before I recognised him, of offering myself to the
knight, to wait upon him as a squire, for he seemed to be
unattended. I made my request in as few words as possible. He
hesitated for a moment, and looked at me thoughtfully. I saw
that he suspected who I was, but that he continued uncertain
of his suspicion. No doubt he was soon convinced of its truth; but
all the time I was with him, not a word crossed his lips with
reference to what he evidently concluded I wished to leave
unnoticed, if not to keep concealed.

"Squire and knight should be friends," said he : "can you
take me by the hand?" And he held out the great gauntleted
right hand. I grasped it willingly and strongly. Not a word
more was said. The knight gave the sign to his horse, which
again began his slow march, and I walked beside and a little
behind.

We had not gone very far before we arrived at a little cottage;
from which, as we drew near, a woman rushed out with the cry :

"My child! my child! have you found my child?"

"I have found her," replied the knight, "but she is sorely hurt.
I was forced to leave her with the hermit, as I returned. You
will find her there, and I think she will get better. You see I
have brought you a present. This wretch will not hurt you
again." And he undid the creature's neck, and flung the frightful
burden down by the cottage-door.

The woman was now almost out of sight in the wood; but the husband stood at the door, with speechless thanks in his face.

"You must bury the monster," said the knight. "If I had arrived a moment later, I should have been too late. But now you need not fear, for such a creature as this very rarely appears, in the same part, twice during a life-time."

"Will you not dismount and rest you, Sir Knight?" said the peasant, who had, by this time, recovered himself a little.

"That I will, thankfully," said he; and, dismounting, he gave the reins to me, and told me to unbridle the horse, and lead him into the shade. "You need not tie him up," he added; "he will not run away."

When I returned, after obeying his orders, and entered the cottage, I saw the knight seated, without his helmet, and talking most familiarly with the simple host. I stood at the open door for a moment, and, gazing at him, inwardly justified the white lady in preferring him to me. A nobler countenance I never saw. Loving-kindness beamed from every line of his face. It seemed as if he would repay himself for the late arduous combat, by indulging in all the gentleness of a womanly heart. But when the talk ceased for a moment, he seemed to fall into a reverie. Then the exquisite curves of the upper lip vanished. The lip was lengthened and compressed at the same moment. You could have told that, within the lips, the teeth were firmly closed. The whole face grew stern and determined, all but fierce; only the eyes burned on like a holy sacrifice, uplift on a granite rock.

The woman entered, with her mangled child in her arms. She was pale as her little burden. She gazed, with a wild love and despairing tenderness, on the still, all but dead face, white and clear from loss of blood and terror.

The knight rose. The light that had been confined to his eyes, now shone from his whole countenance. He took the little thing in his arms, and, with the mother's help, undressed her, and looked to her wounds. The tears flowed down his face as he did so. With tender hands he bound them up, kissed the pale cheek, and gave her back to her mother. When he went home, all his tale would be of the grief and joy of the parents; while to me, who had looked on, the gracious countenance of the armed man, beaming from the panoply of steel, over the seemingly dead child, while the powerful hands turned it and shifted it, and bound it, if possible even more gently than the mother's, formed the centre of the story.

After we had partaken of the best they could give us, the knight took his leave, with a few parting instructions to the mother, as to how she should treat the child.

I brought the knight his steed, held the stirrup while he mounted, and then followed him through the wood. The horse, delighted to be free of his hideous load, bounded beneath the weight of man and armour, and could hardly be restrained from galloping on. But the knight made him time his powers to mine, and so we went on for an hour or two. Then the knight dismounted, and compelled me to get into the saddle, saying : "Knight and squire must share the labour."

Holding by the stirrup, he walked along by my side, heavily clad as he was, with apparent ease. As we went, he led a conversation, in which I took what humble part my sense of my condition would permit me.

"Somehow or other," said he, "notwithstanding the beauty of this country of Faerie, in which we are, there is much that is wrong in it. If there are great splendours, there are corresponding horrors; heights and depths; beautiful woman and awful fiends; noble men and weaklings. All a man has to do, is to better what he can. And if he will settle it with himself, that even renown and success are in themselves of no great value, and be content to be defeated, if so be that the fault is not his; and so go to his work with a cool brain and a strong will, he will get it done; and fare none the worse in the end, that he was not burdened with provision and precaution."

"But he will not always come off well," I ventured to say.

"Perhaps not," rejoined the knight, "in the individual act; but the result of his lifetime will content him."

"So it will fare with you, doubtless," thought I; "but for me——"

Venturing to resume the conversation after a pause, I said, hesitatingly :

"May I ask for what the little beggar girl wanted your aid, when she came to your castle to find you"

He looked at me for a moment in silence, and then said—

"I cannot help wondering how you know of that; but there is something about you quite strange enough to entitle you to the privilege of the country; namely, to go unquestioned. I, however, being only a man, such as you see me, am ready to tell you anything you like to ask me, as far as I can. The little beggar-girl came into the hall where I was sitting, and told me a very curious story, which I can only recollect very vaguely, it was so peculiar. What I can recall is, that she was sent to gather wings. As soon as she had gathered a pair of wings for herself, she was to fly away, she said, to the country she came from; but where that was, she could give no information. She said she had to beg her wings from the butterflies and moths; and whenever she begged, no one refused her. But she needed a great many of the wings of butterflies and moths to make a pair for her; and so she had to wander about day after day, looking for butterflies, and night after night, looking for moths; and then she begged for their wings. But the day before, she had come into a part of the forest, she said, where there were multitudes of splendid butterflies flitting about, with wings which were just fit to make the eyes in the shoulders of hers; and she knew she could have as many of them as she liked for the asking; but as soon as she began to beg, there came a great creature right up to her, and threw her down, and walked over her. When she got up, she saw the wood was full of these beings stalking about, and seeming to have nothing to do with each other. As soon as ever she began to beg, one of them walked over her; till at last in dismay, and in growing horror of the senseless creatures, she had run away to look for somebody to help her. I asked her what they were like. She said, like great men, made of wood, without knee or elbow-joints, and without any noses or mouths or eyes in their faces. I laughed at the little maiden, thinking she was making child's game of me; but, although she burst out laughing too, she persisted in asserting the truth of her story.

" 'Only come, knight, come and see; I will lead you.'

"So I armed myself, to be ready for anything that might happen, and followed the child; for, although I could make nothing of her story, I could see she was a little human being in need of some help or other. As she walked before me, I looked attentively at her. Whether or not it was from being so often knocked down and walked over, I could not tell, but her clothes were very much torn, and in several places her white skin was peeping through. I thought she was hump-backed; but on looking more closely, I saw, through the tatters of her frock—do not laugh at me—a bunch on each shoulder, of the most gorgeous colours. Looking yet more closely, I saw that they were of the shape of folded wings, and were made of all kinds of butterfly-wings and moth-wings, crowded together like the feathers on the individual butterfly pinion; but, like them, most beautifully arranged, and producing a perfect harmony of colour and shade. I could now more easily believe the rest of her story; especially as I saw, every now and then, a certain heaving motion in the wings, as if they longed to be uplifted and out-spread. But beneath her scanty garments complete wings could not be concealed, and indeed, from her own story, they were yet unfinished.

"After walking for two or three hours (how the little girl found her way, I could not imagine), we came to a part of the forest, the very air of which was quivering with the motions of multitudes of resplendent butterflies; as gorgeous in colour, as if the eyes of peacocks' feathers had taken to flight, but of infinite variety of hue and form, only that the appearance of some kind of eye on each wing predominated. 'There they are, there they are!' cried the child, in a tone of victory mingled with terror. Except for this tone, I should have thought she referred to the butterflies, for I could see nothing else. But at that moment an enormous butterfly, whose wings had great eyes of blue sur-rounded by confused cloudy heaps of more dingy colouring, just like a break in the clouds on a stormy day towards evening, settled near us. The child instantly began murmuring: 'Butter-fly, butterfly, give me your wings'; when, the moment after, she fell to the ground, and began crying as if hurt. I drew my sword and heaved a great blow in the direction in which the child had fallen. It struck something, and instantly the most grotesque imitation of a man became visible. You see this Fairy Land is full of oddities and all sorts of incredibly ridiculous things, which a man is compelled to meet and treat as real existences, although all the time he feels foolish for doing so. This being, if being it could be called, was like a block of wood roughly hewn into the mere outlines of a man; and hardly so, for it had but head, body, legs, and arms—the head without a face, and the limbs utterly formless. I had hewn off one of its legs, but the two portions moved on as best they could, quite independent of each other; so that I had done no good. I ran after it, and clove it in twain from the head downwards; but it could not be convinced that its vocation was not to walk over people; for, as soon as the little girl began her begging again, all three parts came bustling up; and if I had not interposed my weight between her and them, she would have been trampled again under them. I saw that something else must be done. If the wood was full of the creatures, it would be an endless work to chop them so small that they could do no injury; and then, besides, the parts would be so numerous, that the butterflies would be in danger from the drift of flying chips. I served this one so, however; and then told the girl to beg again, and point out the direction in which one was coming. I was glad to find, however, that I could now see him myself, and wondered how they could have been invisible before. I would not allow him to walk over the child; but while I kept him off, and she began begging again, another appeared; and it was all I could do, from the weight of my armour, to protect her from the stupid, persevering efforts of the two. But suddenly the right plan occurred to me. I tripped one of them up, and, taking him by the legs, set him up on his head, with his heels against a tree. I was delighted to find he could not move. Meantime the poor child was walked over by the other, but it was for the last time. Whenever one appeared, I followed the same plan—tripped him up and set him on his head; and so the little beggar was able to gather her wings without any trouble, which occupation she continued for several hours in my company."

"What became of her?" I asked.

"I took her home with me to my castle, and she told me all her story; but it seemed to me, all the time, as if I were hearing a child talk in its sleep. I could not arrange her story in my mind at all, although it seemed to leave hers in some certain order of its own. My wife——"

Here the knight checked himself, and said no more. Neither did I urge the conversation further.

Thus we journeyed for several days, resting at night in such shelter as we could get; and when no better was to be had, lying in the forest under some tree, on a couch of old leaves.

I loved the knight more and more. I believe never squire served his master with more care and joyfulness than I. I tended his horse; I cleaned his armour; my skill in the craft enabled me to repair it when necessary; I watched his needs; and was well repaid for all, by the love itself which I bore him.

"This," I said to myself, "is a true man. I will serve him, and give him all worship, seeing in him the imbodiment of what I would fain become. If I cannot be noble myself, I will yet be servant to his nobleness." He, in return, soon showed me such signs of friendship and respect, as made my heart glad; and I felt that, after all, mine would be no lost life, if I might wait on him to the world's end, although no smile but his should greet me, and no one but him should say, "Well done! he was a good servant!" at last. But I burned to do something more for him than the ordinary routine of a squire's duty permitted.

One afternoon, we began to observe an appearance of roads in the wood. Branches had been cut down, and openings made, where footsteps had worn no path below. These indications increased as we passed on; till, at length, we came into a long, narrow avenue, formed by felling the trees in its line, as the remaining roots evidenced. At some little distance, on both hands, we observed signs of similar avenues, which appeared to converge with ours, towards one spot. Along these we indistinctly saw several forms moving, which seemed, with ourselves, to approach the common centre. Our path brought us, at last, up to a wall of yew trees, growing close together, and intertwining their branches so, that nothing could be seen beyond it. An opening was cut in it like a door, and all the wall was trimmed smooth and perpendicular. The knight dismounted, and waited till I had provided for his horse's comfort; upon which we entered the place together.

It was a great space, bare of trees, and enclosed by four walls of yew, similar to that through which we had entered. These trees grew to a very great height, and did not divide from each other till close to the top, where their summits formed a row of conical battlements all around the walls. The space contained was a parallelogram of great length. Along each of the two longer sides of the interior, were ranged three ranks of men, in white robes, standing silent and solemn, each with a sword by his side, although the rest of his costume and bearing was more priestly than soldierly. For some distance inwards, the space between these opposite rows was filled with a company of men

and women and children, in holiday attire. The looks of all were
directed inwards, towards the further end. Far beyond the crowd,
in a long avenue, seeming to narrow in the distance, went the
long rows of the white-robed men. On what the attention of the
multitude was fixed, we could not tell, for the sun had set before
we arrived, and it was growing dark within. It grew darker and
darker. The multitude waited in silence. The stars began to
shine down into the enclosure, and they grew brighter and
larger every moment. A wind arose, and swayed the pinnacles of
the tree-tops; and made a strange sound, half like music, half
like moaning, through the close branches and leaves of the tree-
walls. A young girl who stood beside me, clothed in the same
dress as the priests, bowed her head, and grew pale with awe.

The knight whispered to me, "How solemn it is! Surely they
wait to hear the voice of a prophet. There is something good
near!"

But I, though somewhat shaken by the feeling expressed by
my master, yet had an unaccountable conviction that here was
something bad. So I resolved to be keenly on the watch for what
should follow.

Suddenly a great star, like a sun, appeared high in the air
over the temple, illuminating it throughout; and a great song
arose from the men in white, which went rolling round and
round the building, now receding to the end, and now approaching, down the other side, the place where we stood. For some of
the singers were regularly ceasing, and the next to them as
regularly taking up the song; so that it crept onwards with
gradations produced by changes which could not themselves be
detected, for only a few of those who were singing ceased at the
same moment. The song paused; and I saw a company of six of
the white-robed men walk up the centre of the human avenue,
surrounding a youth gorgeously attired beneath his robe of white,
and wearing a chaplet of flowers on his head. I followed them
closely, with my keenest observation; and, by accompanying
their slow progress with my eyes, I was able to perceive more
clearly what took place when they arrived at the other end. I
knew that my sight was so much more keen than that of most
people, that I had good reason to suppose I should see more than
the rest could, at such a distance. At the further end a throne
stood upon a platform, high above the heads of the surrounding

priests. To this platform I saw the company begin to ascend, apparently by an inclined plane of gentle slope. The throne itself was elevated again, on a kind of square pedestal, to the top of which led a flight of steps. On the throne sat a majestic-looking figure, whose posture seemed to indicate a mixture of pride and benignity, as he looked down on the multitude below. The company ascended to the foot of the throne, where they all kneeled for some minutes; then they rose and passed round to the side of the pedestal upon which the throne stood. Here they crowded close behind the youth, putting him in the foremost place; and one of them opened a door in the pedestal, for the youth to enter. I was sure I saw him shrink back, and those crowding behind pushed him in. Then, again, arose a burst of song from the multitude in white, which lasted some time. When it ceased, a new company of seven commenced its march up the centre. As they advanced, I looked up at my master : his noble countenance was full of reverence and awe. Incapable of evil himself, he could scarcely suspect it in another, much less in a multitude such as this, and surrounded with such appearances of solemnity. I was certain it was the really grand accompaniments that overcame him; that the stars overhead, the dark towering tops of the yew-trees, and the wind that, like an unseen spirit, sighed through their branches, bowed his spirit to the belief, that in all these ceremonies lay some great mystical meaning, which, his humility told him, his ignorance prevented him from understanding.

More convinced than before, that there was evil here, I could not endure that my master should be deceived; that one like him, so pure and noble, should respect what, if my suspicions were true, was worse than the ordinary deceptions of priestcraft. I could not tell how far he might be led to countenance, and otherwise support their doings, before he should find cause to repent bitterly of his error. I watched the new procession yet more keenly, if possible, than the former. This time, the central figure was a girl; and, at the close, I observed, yet more indubitably, the shrinking back, and the crowding push. What happened to the victims, I never learned; but I had learned enough, and I could bear it no longer. I stooped, and whispered to the young girl who stood by me, to lend me her white garment. I wanted it, that I might not be entirely out of keeping

with the solemnity, but might have at least this help to passing
unquestioned. She looked up, half-amused and half-bewildered,
as if doubting whether I was in earnest or not. But in her
perplexity, she permitted me to unfasten it, and slip it down
from her shoulders. I easily got possession of it; and, sinking
down on my knees in the crowd, I rose apparently in the habit
of one of the worshippers.

Giving my battle-axe to the girl, to hold in pledge for the
return of her stole, for I wished to test the matter unarmed, and,
if it was a man that sat upon the throne, to attack him with
hands bare, as I supposed his must be, I made my way through
the crowd to the front, while the singing yet continued, desirous
of reaching the platform while it was unoccupied by any of the
priests. I was permitted to walk up the long avenue of white
robes unmolested, though I saw questioning looks in many of
the faces as I passed. I presume my coolness aided my passage;
for I felt quite indifferent as to my own fate; not feeling, after
the late events of my history, that I was at all worth taking care
of; and enjoying, perhaps, something of an evil satisfaction, in
the revenge I was thus taking upon the self which had fooled
me so long. When I arrived on the platform, the song had just
ceased, and I felt as if all were looking towards me. But instead
of kneeling at its foot, I walked right up the stairs to the throne,
laid hold of a great wooden image that seemed to sit upon it,
and tried to hurl it from its seat. In this I failed at first, for I
found it firmly fixed. But in dread lest, the first shock of amazement passing away, the guards would rush upon me before I had
effected my purpose, I strained with all my might; and, with a
noise as of cracking, and breaking, and tearing of rotten wood,
something gave way, and I hurled the image down the steps. Its
displacement revealed a great hole in the throne, like the hollow
of a decayed tree, going down apparently a great way. But I had
no time to examine it, for, as I looked into it, up out of it rushed
a great brute, like a wolf, but twice the size, and tumbled me
headlong with itself, down the steps of the throne. As we fell,
however, I caught it by the throat, and the moment we reached
the platform, a struggle commenced, in which I soon got uppermost, with my hand upon its throat, and knee upon its heart. But
now arose a wild cry of wrath and revenge and rescue. A
universal hiss of steel, as every sword was swept from its scab-

bard, seemed to tear the very air in shreds. I heard the rush of hundreds towards the platform on which I knelt. I only tightened my grasp on the brute's throat. His eyes were already starting from his head, and his tongue was hanging out. My anxious hope was, that, even after they had killed me, they would be unable to undo my grip of his throat, before the monster was past breathing. I therefore threw all my will, and force, and purpose, into the grasping hand. I remember no blow. A faintness came over me, and my consciousness departed.

CHAPTER XXIV

"We are ne'er like angels till our passions die."
DEKKER.

"This wretched *Inn,* where we scarce stay to bait,
We call our *Dwelling-Place*:
We call one *Step* a *Race*:
But angels in their full enlightened state,
Angels, who *Live,* and know what 'tis to *Be,*
Who all the nonsense of our language see,
Who speak *things,* and our *words,* their ill-drawn *pictures,*
scorn,
When we, by a foolish figure say,
Behold an old man dead! then they
Speak properly, and cry, *Behold a man-child born!*"
COWLEY.

I WAS DEAD, AND right content. I lay in my coffin, with my hands folded in peace. The knight, and the lady I loved, wept over me. Her tears fell on my face.

"Ah!" said the knight, "I rushed amongst them like a madman. I hewed them down like brushwood. Their swords battered on me like hail, but hurt me not. I cut a lane through to my friend. He was dead. But he had throttled the monster, and I had to cut the handful out of its throat, before I could disengage and carry off his body. They dared not molest me as I brought him back."

"He has died well," said the lady.

My spirit rejoiced. They left me to my repose. I felt as if a cool hand had been laid upon my heart, and had stilled it. My soul was like a summer evening, after a heavy fall of rain, when the drops are yet glistening on the trees in the last rays of the down-going sun, and the wind of the twilight has begun to blow. The hot fever of life had gone by, and I breathed the clear mountain-air of the land of Death. I had never dreamed of such blessedness. It was not that I had in any way ceased to be what I had been. The very fact that anything can die, implies the existence of something that cannot die; which must either take to itself another form, as when the seed that is sown dies, and arises again; or, in conscious existence, may, perhaps, continue to lead a purely spiritual life. If my passions were dead, the souls of the passions, those essential mysteries of the spirit which had imbodied themselves in the passions, and had given to them all their glory and wonderment, yet lived, yet glowed, with a pure, undying fire. They rose above their vanishing earthly garments, and disclosed themselves angels of light. But oh, how beautiful beyond the old form! I lay thus for a time, and lived as it were an unradiating existence; my soul a motionless lake, that received all things and gave nothing back; satisfied in still contemplation, and spiritual consciousness.

Ere long, they bore me to my grave. Never tired child lay down in his white bed, and heard the sound of his playthings being laid aside for the night, with a more luxurious satisfaction of repose than I knew, when I felt the coffin settle on the firm earth, and heard the sound of the falling mould upon its lid. It has not the same hollow rattle within the coffin, that it sends up to the edge of the grave. They buried me in no graveyard. They loved me too much for that, I thank them; but they laid me in the grounds of their own castle, amid many trees; where, as it was spring-time, were growing primroses, and blue-bells, and all the families of the woods.

Now that I lay in her bosom, the whole earth, and each of her many births, was as a body to me, at my will. I seemed to feel the great heart of the mother beating into mine, and feeding me with her own life, her own essential being and nature. I heard the footsteps of my friends above, and they sent a thrill through my heart. I knew that the helpers had gone, and that the knight and the lady remained, and spoke low, gentle, tearful words of him who lay beneath the yet wounded sod. I rose into a single large primrose that grew by the edge of the grave, and from the window of its humble, trusting face, looked full in the countenance of the lady. I felt that I could manifest myself in the primrose; that it said a part of what I wanted to say; just as in the old time, I had used to betake myself to a song for the same end. The flower caught her eye. She stooped and plucked it, saying, "Oh, you beautiful creature!" and, lightly kissing it, put it in her bosom. It was the first kiss she had ever given me. But the flower soon began to wither, and I forsook it.

It was evening. The sun was below the horizon; but his rosy beams yet illuminated a feathery cloud, that floated high above the world. I arose, I reached the cloud; and, throwing myself upon it, floated with it in sight of the sinking sun. He sank, and the cloud grew gray; but the grayness touched not my heart. It carried its rose-hue within; for now I could love without needing to be loved again. The moon came gliding up with all the past in her wan face. She changed my couch into a ghostly pallor, and threw all the earth below as to the bottom of a pale sea of dreams. But she could not make me sad. I knew now, that it is by loving, and not by being loved, that one can come nearest the soul of another; yea, that, where two love, it is the loving of each other, and not the being beloved by each other, that originates and perfects and assures their blessedness. I knew that love gives to him that loveth, power over any soul beloved, even if that soul know him not, bringing him inwardly close to that spirit; a power that cannot be but for good; for in proportion as selfishness intrudes, the love ceases, and the power which springs therefrom dies. Yet all love will, one day, meet with its return. All true love will, one day, behold its own image in the eyes of the beloved, and be humbly glad. This is possible in the realms of lofty Death. "Ah! my friends," thought I, "how I will tend you, and wait upon you, and haunt you with my love."

My floating chariot bore me over a great city. Its faint dull sound steamed up into the air—a sound—how composed? "How many hopeless cries," thought I, "and how many mad shouts go to make up the tumult, here so faint where I float in eternal peace, knowing that they will one day be stilled in the surrounding calm, and that despair dies into infinite hope, and that the seeming impossible there, is the law here! But, O pale-faced women, and gloomy-browed men, and forgotten children, how I will wait on you, and minister to you, and, putting my arms about you in the dark, think hope unto your hearts, when you fancy no one is near! Soon as my senses have all come back, and have grown accustomed to this new blessed life, I will be among you with the love that healeth."

With this, a pang and a terrible shudder went through me; a writhing as of death convulsed me; and I became once again conscious of a more limited, even a bodily and earthly life.

CHAPTER XXV

"Unser Leben ist kein Traum, aber es soll und wird vielleicht einer werden."—NOVALIS.

"Our life is no dream; but it ought to become one, and perhaps will."

"And on the ground, which is my modres gate,
I knocke with my staf, erlich and late,
And say to hire, Leve mother, let me in."
CHAUCER, *The Pardoneres Tale.*

SINKING FROM SUCH a state of ideal bliss, into the world of shadows which again closed around and infolded me, my first dread was, not unnaturally, that my own shadow had found me again, and that my torture had commenced anew. It was a sad revulsion of feeling. This, indeed, seemed to correspond to what we think death is, before we die. Yet I felt within me a power of calm endurance to which I had hitherto been a stranger. For, in truth, that I should be able if only to think such things as I had been thinking, was an unspeakable delight. An hour of such peace made the turmoil of a life-time worth striving through.

I found myself lying in the open air, in the early morning, before sunrise. Over me rose the summer heaven, expectant of the sun. The clouds already saw him, coming from afar; and soon every dewdrop would rejoice in his individual presence within it. I lay motionless for a few minutes; and then slowly rose and looked about me. I was on the summit of a little hill; a valley lay beneath, and a range of mountains closed up the view upon that side. But, to my horror, across the valley, and up the height of the opposing mountains, stretched, from my very feet, a hugely expanding shade. There it lay, long and large, dark and mighty. I turned away with a sick despair; when lo! I beheld the sun just lifting his head above the eastern hill, and the shadow that fell from me, lay only where his beams fell not. I danced for joy. It was only the natural shadow, that goes with every man who walks in the sun. As he arose, higher and higher, the shadow-head sank down the side of the opposite hill, and crept in across the valley towards my feet.

Now that I was so joyously delivered from this fear, I saw and recognised the country around me. In the valley below, lay my own castle, and the haunts of my childhood were all about me. I hastened home. My sisters received me with unspeakable joy; but I suppose they observed some change in me, for a kind of respect, with a slight touch of awe in it, mingled with their joy, and made me ashamed. They had been in great distress about me. On the morning of my disappearance, they had found the floor of my room flooded; and, all that day, a wondrous and nearly impervious mist had hung about the castle and grounds. I had been gone, they told me, twenty-one days. To me it seemed twenty-one years. Nor could I yet feel quite secure in my new experiences. When, at night, I lay down once more in my own bed, I did not feel at all sure that when I awoke, I should not find myself in some mysterious region of Fairy Land. My dreams were incessant and perturbed; but when I did awake, I saw clearly that I was in my own home.

My mind soon grew calm; and I began the duties of my new position, somewhat instructed, I hoped, by the adventures that had befallen me in Fairy Land. Could I translate the experience of my travels there, into common life? This was the question. Or must I live it all over again, and learn it all over again, in the other forms that belong to the world of men, whose experience yet runs parallel to that of Fairy Land? These questions I cannot yet answer. But I fear.

Even yet, I find myself looking round sometimes with anxiety, to see whether my shadow falls right away from the sun or no. I have never yet discovered any inclination to either side. And if I am not unfrequently sad, I yet cast no more of a shade on the earth, than most men who have lived in it as long as I. I have a strange feeling sometimes, that I am a ghost, sent into the world to minister to my fellow-men, or, rather, to repair the wrongs I have already done. May the world be brighter for me, at least in those portions of it, where my darkness falls not.

Thus I, who set out to find my Ideal, came back rejoicing that I had lost my Shadow.

When the thought of the blessedness I experienced, after my death in Fairy Land, is too high for me to lay hold upon it and hope in it, I often think of the wise woman in the cottage, and of her solemn assurance that she knew something too good to be told. When I am oppressed by any sorrow or real perplexity, I often feel as if I had only left her cottage for a time, and would soon return out of the vision, into it again. Sometimes, on such occasions, I find myself, unconsciously almost, looking about for the mystic mark of red, with the vague hope of entering her door, and being comforted by her wise tenderness. I then console myself by saying : "I have come through the door of Dismay; and the way back from the world into which that has led me, is through my tomb. Upon that the red sign lies, and I shall find it one day, and be glad."

I will end my story with the relation of an incident which befell me a few days ago. I had been with my reapers, and, when they ceased their work at noon, I had lain down under the shadow of a great, ancient beech-tree, that stood on the edge of the field. As I lay, with my eyes closed, I began to listen to the sound of the leaves overhead. At first, they made sweet inarticulate music alone; but, by and by, the sound seemed to begin to take shape, and to be gradually moulding itself into words; till, at last, I seemed able to distinguish these, half-dissolved in a little ocean of circumfluent tones : "A great good is coming—is coming—is coming to thee, Anodos"; and so over and over again. I fancied that the sound reminded me of the voice of the ancient woman, in the cottage that was four-square. I opened my eyes, and, for a moment, almost believed that I saw her face, with its many wrinkles and its young eyes, looking at me from between two hoary branches of the beech overhead. But when I looked more keenly, I saw only twigs and leaves, and the infinite sky, in tiny spots, gazing through between. Yet I know that good is coming to me—that good is always coming; though few have at all times the simplicity and the courage to believe it. What we call evil, is the only and best shape, which, for the person and his condition at the time, could be assumed by the best good. And so, *Farewell*.

LILITH

A Romance

"Off, Lilith!"—*The Kabala*

I TOOK A WALK on Spaulding's Farm the other afternoon. I saw the setting sun lighting up the opposite side of a stately pine wood. Its golden rays straggled into the aisles of the wood as into some noble hall. I was impressed as if some ancient and altogether admirable and shining family had settled there in that part of the land called Concord, unknown to me,—to whom the sun was servant,—who had not gone into society in the village,— who had not been called on. I saw their park, their pleasure-ground, beyond through the wood, in Spaulding's cranberry-meadow. The pines furnished them with gables as they grew. Their house was not obvious to vision; their trees grew through it. I do not know whether I heard the sounds of a suppressed hilarity or not. They seemed to recline on the sunbeams. They have sons and daughters. They are quite well. The farmer's cart-path, which leads directly through their hall, does not in the least put them out,—as the muddy bottom of a pool is sometimes seen through the reflected skies. They never heard of Spaulding, and do not know that he is their neighbor,—notwithstanding I heard him whistle as he drove his team through the house. Nothing can equal the serenity of their lives. Their coat of arms is simply a lichen. I saw it painted on the pines and oaks. Their attics were in the tops of the trees. They are of no politics. There was no noise of labor. I did not perceive that they were weaving or spinning. Yet I did detect, when the wind lulled and hearing was done away, the finest imaginable sweet musical hum,—as of a distant hive in May, which perchance was the sound of their thinking. They had no idle thoughts, and no one without could see their work, for their industry was not as in knots and excrescences embayed.

But I find it difficult to remember them. They fade irrevocably out of my mind even now while I speak and endeavor to recall them, and recollect myself. It is only after a long and serious effort to recollect my best thoughts that I become again aware of their cohabitancy. If it were not for such families as this, I think I should move out of Concord.

THOREAU : *"Walking."*

CHAPTER I

THE LIBRARY

I HAD JUST FINISHED my studies at Oxford, and was taking a brief holiday from work before assuming definitely the management of the estate. My father died when I was yet a child; my mother followed him within a year; and I was nearly as much alone in the world as a man might find himself.

I had made little acquaintance with the history of my ancestors. Almost the only thing I knew concerning them was, that a notable number of them had been given to study. I had myself so far inherited the tendency as to devote a good deal of my time, though, I confess, after a somewhat desultory fashion, to the physical sciences. It was chiefly the wonder they woke that drew me. I was constantly seeing, and on the outlook to see, strange analogies, not only between the facts of different sciences of the same order, or between physical and metaphysical facts, but between physical hypotheses and suggestions glimmering out of the metaphysical dreams into which I was in the habit of falling. I was at the same time much given to a premature indulgence of the impulse to turn hypothesis into theory. Of my mental peculiarities there is no occasion to say more.

The house as well as the family was of some antiquity, but no description of it is necessary to the understanding of my narrative. It contained a fine library, whose growth began before the invention of printing, and had continued to my own time, greatly influenced, of course, by changes of taste and pursuit. Nothing surely can more impress upon a man the transitory nature of possession than his succeeding to an ancient property! Like a moving panorama mine has passed from before many eyes, and is now slowly flitting from before my own.

The library, although duly considered in many alterations of the house and additions to it, had nevertheless, like an encroaching state, absorbed one room after another until it occupied the greater part of the ground floor. Its chief room was large, and the walls of it were covered with books almost to the ceiling; the rooms into which it overflowed were of various sizes and shapes, and communicated in modes as various—by doors, by open arches, by short passages, by steps up and steps down.

In the great room I mainly spent my time, reading books of science, old as well as new; for the history of the human mind in relation to supposed knowledge was what most of all interested me. Ptolemy, Dante, the two Bacons, and Boyle were even more to me than Darwin or Maxwell, as so much nearer the vanished van breaking into the dark of ignorance.

In the evening of a gloomy day of August I was sitting in my usual place, my back to one of the windows, reading. It had rained the greater part of the morning and afternoon, but just as the sun was setting, the clouds parted in front of him, and he shone into the room. I rose and looked out of the window. In the centre of the great lawn the feathering top of the fountain column was filled with his red glory. I turned to resume my seat, when my eye was caught by the same glory on the one picture in the room—a portrait, in a sort of niche or little shrine sunk for it in the expanse of book-filled shelves. I knew it as the likeness of one of my ancestors, but had never even wondered why it hung there alone, and not in the gallery, or one of the great rooms, among the other family portraits. The direct sunlight brought out the painting wonderfully; for the first time I seemed to see it, and for the first time it seemed to respond to my look. With my eyes full of the light reflected from it, something, I cannot tell what, made me turn and cast a glance to the farther end of the room, when I saw, or seemed to see, a tall figure reaching up a hand to a bookshelf. The next instant, my vision apparently rectified by the comparative dusk, I saw no one, and concluded that my optic nerves had been momentarily affected from within.

I resumed my reading, and would doubtless have forgotten the vague, evanescent impression, had it not been that, having occasion a moment after to consult a certain volume, I found but a gap in the row where it ought to have stood, and the same instant remembered that just there I had seen, or fancied I saw, the old man in search of a book. I looked all about the spot but

in vain. The next morning, however, there it was, just where I
had thought to find it! I knew of no one in the house likely to
be interested in such a book.

Three days after, another and yet odder thing took place.

In one of the walls was the low, narrow door of a closet, containing some of the oldest and rarest of the books. It was a very
thick door, with a projecting frame, and it had been the fancy
of some ancestor to cross it with shallow shelves, filled with book-
backs only. The harmless trick may be excused by the fact that
the titles on the sham backs were either humorously original, or
those of books lost beyond hope of recovery. I had a great liking
for the masked door.

To complete the illusion of it, some inventive workman
apparently had shoved in, on the top of one of the rows, a part
of a volume thin enough to lie between it and the bottom of the
next shelf : he had cut away diagonally a considerable portion,
and fixed the remnant with one of its open corners projecting beyond the book-backs. The binding of the mutilated volume was
limp vellum, and one could open the corner far enough to see
that it was manuscript upon parchment.

Happening, as I sat reading, to raise my eyes from the page,
my glance fell upon this door, and at once I saw that the book
described, if book it may be called, was gone. Angrier than any
worth I knew in it justified, I rang the bell, and the butler
appeared. When I asked him if he knew what had befallen it,
he turned pale, and assured me he did not. I could less easily
doubt his word than my own eyes, for he had been all his life
in the family, and a more faithful servant never lived. He left
on me the impression, nevertheless, that he could have said something more.

In the afternoon I was again reading in the library, and coming to a point which demanded reflection, I lowered the book
and let my eyes go wandering. The same moment I saw the back
of a slender old man, in a long, dark coat, shiny as from much
wear, in the act of disappearing through the masked door into
the closet beyond. I darted across the room, found the door shut,
pulled it open, looked into the closet, which had no other issue,
and, seeing nobody, concluded, not without uneasiness, that I
had had a recurrence of my former illusion, and sat down again
to my reading.

Naturally, however, I could not help feeling a little nervous, and presently glancing up to assure myself that I was indeed alone, started again to my feet, and ran to the masked door—for there was the mutilated volume in its place! I laid hold of it and pulled : it was firmly fixed as usual!

I was now utterly bewildered. I rang the bell; the butler came; I told him all I had seen, and he told me all he knew.

He had hoped, he said, that the old gentleman was going to be forgotten; it was well no one but myself had seen him. He had heard a good deal about him when first he served in the house, but by degrees he had ceased to be mentioned, and he had been very careful not to allude to him.

"The place was haunted by an old gentleman, was it?" I said.

He answered that at one time everybody believed it, but the fact that I had never heard of it seemed to imply that the thing had come to an end and was forgotten.

I questioned him as to what he had seen of the old gentleman.

He had never seen him, he said, although he had been in the house from the day my father was eight years old. My grandfather would never hear a word on the matter, declaring that whoever alluded to it should be dismissed without a moment's warning : it was nothing but a pretext of the maids, he said, for running into the arms of the men! but old Sir Ralph believed in nothing he could not see or lay hold of. Not one of the maids ever said she had seen the apparition, but a footman had left the place because of it.

An ancient woman in the village had told him a legend concerning a Mr. Raven, long time librarian to "that Sir Upward whose portrait hangs there among the books." Sir Upward was a great reader, she said—not of such books only as were wholesome for men to read, but of strange, forbidden, and evil books; and in so doing, Mr. Raven, who was probably the devil himself, encouraged him. Suddenly they both disappeared, and Sir Upward was never after seen or heard of, but Mr. Raven continued to show himself at uncertain intervals in the library. There were some who believed he was not dead; but both he and the old woman held it easier to believe that a dead man might revisit the world he had left, than that one who went on living for hundreds of years should be a man at all.

He had never heard that Mr. Raven meddled with anything

in the house, but he might perhaps consider himself privileged in regard to the books. How the old woman had learned so much about him he could not tell; but the description she gave of him corresponded exactly with the figure I had just seen.

"I hope it was but a friendly call on the part of the old gentleman!" he concluded, with a troubled smile.

I told him I had no objection to any number of visits from Mr. Raven, but it would be well he should keep to his resolution of saying nothing about him to the servants. Then I asked him if he had ever seen the mutilated volume out of its place; he answered that he never had, and had always thought it a fixture. With that he went to it, and gave it a pull : it seemed immovable.

CHAPTER II

THE MIRROR

Nothing more happened for some days. I think it was about a week after, when what I have now to tell took place.

I had often thought of the manuscript fragment, and repeatedly tried to discover some way of releasing it, but in vain : I could not find out what held it fast.

But I had for some time intended a thorough overhauling of the books in the closet, its atmosphere causing me uneasiness as to their condition. One day the intention suddenly became a resolve, and I was in the act of rising from my chair to make a beginning, when I saw the old librarian moving from the door of the closet toward the farther end of the room. I ought rather to say only that I caught sight of something shadowy from which I received the impression of a slight, stooping man, in a shabby dress-coat reaching almost to his heels, the tails of which, disparting a little as he walked, revealed thin legs in black stockings, and large feet in wide, slipper-like shoes.

At once I followed him : I might be following a shadow, but I never doubted I was following something. He went out of the library into the hall, and across to the foot of the great staircase, then up the stairs to the first floor, where lay the chief rooms. Past these rooms, I following close, he continued his way, through a wide corridor, to the foot of a narrower stair leading to the second floor. Up that he went also, and when I reached the top, strange as it may seem, I found myself in a region almost unknown to me. I never had brother or sister to incite to such romps as make children familiar with nook and cranny; I was a mere child when my guardian took me away; and I had never seen the house again until, about a month before, I returned to take possession.

Through passage after passage we came to a door at the bottom of a winding wooden stair, which we ascended. Every step creaked under my foot, but I heard no sound from that of my guide. Somewhere in the middle of the stair I lost sight of him, and from the top of it the shadowy shape was nowhere visible. I could not even imagine I saw him. The place was full of shadows, but he was not one of them.

I was in the main garret, with huge beams and rafters over my head, great spaces around me, a door here and there in sight, and long vistas whose gloom was thinned by a few lurking cob-webbed windows and small dusky skylights. I gazed with a strange mingling of awe and pleasure : the wide expanse of garret was my own, and unexplored!

In the middle of it stood an unpainted inclosure of rough planks, the door of which was ajar. Thinking Mr. Raven might be there, I pushed the door, and entered.

The small chamber was full of light, but such as dwells in places deserted : it had a dull, disconsolate look, as if it found itself of no use, and regretted having come. A few rather dim sunrays, marking their track through the cloud of motes that had just been stirred up, fell upon a tall mirror with a dusty face, old-fashioned and rather narrow—in appearance an ordinary glass. It had an ebony frame, on the top of which stood a black eagle with outstretched wings, in his beak a golden chain, from whose end hung a black ball.

I had been looking at rather than into the mirror, when suddenly I became aware that it reflected neither the chamber nor my own person. I have an impression of having seen the wall melt away, but what followed is enough to account for any un-certainty :—could I have mistaken for a mirror the glass that protected a wonderful picture?

I saw before me a wild country, broken and heathy. Desolate

hills of no great height, but somehow of strange appearance, occupied the middle distance; along the horizon stretched the tops of a far-off mountain range; nearest me lay a tract of moorland, flat and melancholy.

Being short-sighted, I stepped closer to examine the texture of a stone in the immediate foreground, and in the act espied, hopping toward me with solemnity, a large and ancient raven, whose purply black was here and there softened with gray. He seemed looking for worms as he came. Nowise astonished at the appearance of a live creature in a picture, I took another step forward to see him better, stumbled over something—doubtless the frame of the mirror—and stood nose to beak with the bird: I was in the open air, on a houseless heath!

CHAPTER III

THE RAVEN

I TURNED AND LOOKED behind me : all was vague and uncertain, as when one cannot distinguish between fog and field, between cloud and mountain-side. One fact only was plain— that I saw nothing I knew. Imagining myself involved in a visual illusion, and that touch would correct sight, I stretched my arms and felt about me, walking in this direction and that, if haply, where I could see nothing, I might yet come in contact with something; but my search was vain. Instinctively then, as to the only living thing near me, I turned to the raven, which stood a little way off, regarding me with an expression at once respectful and quizzical. Then the absurdity of seeking counsel from such a one struck me, and I turned again, overwhelmed with bewilderment, not unmingled with fear. Had I wandered into a region where both the material and psychical relations of our world had ceased to hold? Might a man at any moment step beyond the realm of order, and become the sport of the lawless? Yet I saw the raven, felt the ground under my feet, and heard a sound as of wind in the lowly plants around me!

"How *did* I get here?" I said—apparently aloud, for the question was immediately answered.

"You came through the door," replied an odd, rather harsh voice.

I looked behind, then all about me, but saw no human shape. The terror that madness might be at hand laid hold upon me : must I henceforth place no confidence either in my senses or my consciousness? The same instant I knew it was the raven that had spoken, for he stood looking up at me with an air of waiting. The sun was not shining, yet the bird seemed to cast a shadow, and the shadow seemed part of himself.

I beg my reader to aid me in the endeavour to make myself intelligible—if here understanding be indeed possible between us. I was in a world, or call it a state of things, an economy of conditions, an idea of existence, so little correspondent with the ways and modes of this world—which we are apt to think the only world, that the best choice I can make of word or phrase is but an adumbration of what I would convey. I begin indeed to fear that I have undertaken an impossibility, undertaken to tell what I cannot tell because no speech at my command will fit the forms in my mind. Already I have set down statements I would gladly change did I know how to substitute a truer utterance; but as often as I try to fit the reality with nearer words, I find myself in danger of losing the things themselves, and feel like one in process of awaking from a dream, with the thing that seemed familiar gradually yet swiftly changing through a succession of forms until its very nature is no longer recognisable.

I bethought me that a bird capable of addressing a man must have the right of a man to a civil answer; perhaps, as a bird, even a greater claim.

A tendency to croak caused a certain roughness in his speech, but his voice was not disagreeable, and what he said, although conveying little enlightenment, did not sound rude.

"I did not come through any door," I rejoined.

"I saw you come through it !—saw you with my own ancient eyes !" asserted the raven, positively but not disrespectfully.

"I never saw any door !" I persisted.

"Of course not !" he returned; "all the doors you had yet seen —and you haven't seen many—were doors in; here you came upon a door out ! The strange thing to you," he went on thoughtfully, "will be, that the more doors you go out of, the farther you get in !"

"Oblige me by telling me where I am."

"That is impossible. You know nothing about whereness. The only way to come to know where you are is to begin to make yourself at home."

"How am I to begin that where everything is so strange?"

"By doing something."

"What?"

"Anything; and the sooner you begin the better! for until you are at home, you will find it as difficult to get out as it is to get in."

"I have, unfortunately, found it too easy to get in; once out I shall not try again!"

"You have stumbled in, and may, possibly, stumble out again. Whether you have got in *unfortunately* remains to be seen."

"Do you never go out, sir?"

"When I please I do, but not often, or for long. Your world is such a half-baked sort of place, it is at once so childish and so self-satisfied—in fact, it is not sufficiently developed for an old raven—at your service!"

"Am I wrong, then, in presuming that a man is superior to a bird?"

"That is as it may be. We do not waste our intellects in generalising, but take man or bird as we find him.—I think it is now my turn to ask you a question!"

"You have the best of rights," I replied, "in the fact that you *can* do so!"

"Well answered!" he rejoined. "Tell me, then, who you are— if you happen to know."

"How should I help knowing? I am myself, and must know!"

"If you know you are yourself, you know that you are not somebody else; but do you know that you are yourself? Are you sure you are not your own father?—or, excuse me, your own fool?—Who are you, pray?"

I became at once aware that I could give him no notion of who I was. Indeed, who was I? It would be no answer to say I was who! Then I understood that I did not know myself, did not know what I was, had no grounds on which to determine that I was one and not another. As for the name I went by in my own world, I had forgotten it, and did not care to recall it, for it meant nothing, and what it might be was plainly of no consequence here. I had indeed almost forgotten that there it was a custom for everybody to have a name! So I held my peace, and it was my wisdom; for what should I say to a creature such as this raven, who saw through accident into entity?

"Look at me," he said, "and tell me who I am."

As he spoke, he turned his back, and instantly I knew him. He was no longer a raven, but a man above the middle height with a stoop, very thin, and wearing a long black tail-coat. Again he turned, and I saw him a raven.

"I have seen you before, sir," I said, feeling foolish rather than surprised.

"How can you say so from seeing me behind?" he rejoined. "Did you ever see yourself behind? You have never seen yourself at all!—Tell me now, then, who I am."

"I humbly beg your pardon," I answered: "I believe you were once the librarian of our house, but more *who* I do not know."

"Why do you beg my pardon?"

"Because I took you for a raven," I said—seeing him before me as plainly a raven as bird or man could look.

"You did me no wrong," he returned. "Calling me a raven, or thinking me one, you allowed me existence, which is the sum of what one can demand of his fellowbeings. Therefore, in return, I will give you a lesson:—No one can say he is himself, until first he knows that he *is,* and then what *himself* is. In fact, nobody is himself, and himself is nobody. There is more in it than you can see now, but not more than you need to see. You have, I fear, got into this region too soon, but none the less you must get to be at home in it; for home, as you may or may not know, is the only place where you can go out and in. There are places you can go into, and places you can go out of; but the one place, if you do but find it, where you may go out and in both, is home."

He turned to walk away, and again I saw the librarian. He did not appear to have changed, only to have taken up his shadow. I know this seems nonsense, but I cannot help it.

I gazed after him until I saw him no more; but whether distance hid him, or he disappeared among the heather, I cannot tell.

Could it be that I was dead, I thought, and did not know it?

Was I in what we used to call the world beyond the grave? and must I wander about seeking my place in it? How was I to find myself at home? The raven said I must do something : what could I do here?—And would that make me somebody? for now, alas, I was nobody!

I took the way Mr. Raven had gone, and went slowly after him. Presently I saw a wood of tall slender pine-trees, and turned towards it. The odour of it met me on my way, and I made haste to bury myself in it.

Plunged at length in its twilight glooms, I spied before me something with a shine, standing between two of the stems. It had no colour, but was like the translucent trembling of the hot air that rises, in a radiant summer noon, from the sun-baked ground, vibrant like the smitten chords of a musical instrument. What it was grew no plainer as I went nearer, and when I came close up, I ceased to see it, only the form and colour of the trees beyond seemed strangely uncertain. I would have passed between the stems, but received a slight shock, stumbled, and fell. When I rose, I saw before me the wooden wall of the garret chamber. I turned, and there was the mirror, on whose top the black eagle seemed but that moment to have perched.

Terror seized me, and I fled. Outside the chamber the wide garret spaces had an *uncanny* look. They seemed to have long been waiting for something; it had come, and they were waiting again! A shudder went through me on the winding stair : the house had grown strange to me! something was about to leap upon me from behind! I darted down the spiral, struck against the wall and fell, rose and ran. On the next floor I lost my way, and had gone through several passages a second time ere I found the head of the stair. At the top of the great stair I had come to myself a little, and in a few moments I sat recovering my breath in the library.

Nothing should ever again make me go up that last terrible stair! The garret at the top of it pervaded the whole house! It sat upon it, threatening to crush me out of it! The brooding brain of the building, it was full of mysterious dwellers, one or other of whom might any moment appear in the library where I sat! I was nowhere safe! I would let, I would sell the dreadful place, in which an aërial portal stood ever open to creatures whose life was other than human! I would purchase a crag in

Switzerland, and thereon build a wooden nest of one story with
never a garret above it, guarded by some grand old peak that
would send down nothing worse than a few tons of whelming
rock!

I knew all the time that my thinking was foolish, and was
even aware of a certain undertone of contemptuous humour in
it; but suddenly it was checked, and I seemed again to hear the
croak of the raven.

"If I know nothing of my own garret," I thought, "what is
there to secure me against my own brain? Can I tell what it is
even now generating?—what thought it may present me the next
moment, the next month, or a year away? What is at the heart
of my brain? What is behind my *think*? Am *I* there at all?—
Who, what am I?"

I could no more answer the question now than when the
raven put it to me in—at—"Where in?—where at?" I said, and
gave myself up as knowing anything of myself or the universe.

I started to my feet, hurried across the room to the masked
door, where the mutilated volume, sticking out from the flat of
soulless, bodiless, non-existent books, appeared to beckon me,
went down on my knees, and opened it as far as its position
would permit, but could see nothing. I got up again, lighted a
taper, and peeping as into a pair of reluctant jaws, perceived
that the manuscript was verse. Further I could not carry discovery. Beginnings of lines were visible on the left-hand page,
and ends of lines on the other; but I could not, of course, get at
the beginning and end of a single line, and was unable, in what
I could read, to make any guess at the sense. The mere words,
however, woke in me feelings which to describe was, from their
strangeness, impossible. Some dreams, some poems, some musical
phrases, some pictures, wake feelings such as one never had
before, new in colour and form—spiritual sensations, as it were,
hitherto unproved : here, some of the phrases, some of the senseless half-lines, some even of the individual words affected me in
similar fashion—as with the aroma of an idea, rousing in me a
great longing to know what the poem or poems might, even yet
in their multilation, hold or suggest.

I copied out a few of the larger shreds attainable, and tried
hard to complete some of the lines, but without the least success.
The only thing I gained in the effort was so much weariness

that, when I went to bed, I fell asleep at once and slept soundly.

In the morning all that horror of the empty garret spaces had left me.

CHAPTER IV

SOMEWHERE OR NOWHERE?

THE SUN WAS very bright, but I doubted if the day would long be fine, and looked into the milky sapphire I wore, to see whether the star in it was clear. It was even less defined than I had expected. I rose from the breakfast-table, and went to the window to glance at the stone again. There had been heavy rain in the night, and on the lawn was a thrush breaking his way into the shell of a snail.

As I was turning my ring about to catch the response of the star to the sun, I spied a keen black eye gazing at me out of the milky misty blue. The sight startled me so that I dropped the ring, and when I picked it up the eye was gone from it. The same moment the sun was obscured; a dark vapour covered him, and in a minute or two the whole sky was clouded. The air had grown sultry, and a gust of wind came suddenly. A moment more and there was a flash of lightning, with a single sharp thunder-clap. Then the rain fell in torrents.

I had opened the window, and stood there looking out at the precipitous rain, when I descried a raven walking toward me over the grass, with solemn gait, and utter disregard of the falling deluge. Suspecting who he was, I congratulated myself that I was safe on the ground-floor. At the same time I had a conviction that, if I were not careful, something would happen.

He came nearer and nearer, made a profound bow, and with a sudden winged leap stood on the window sill. Then he stepped over the ledge, jumped down into the room, and walked to the door. I thought he was on his way to the library, and followed him, determined, if he went up the stair, not to take one step after him. He turned, however, neither toward the library nor the stair, but to a little door that gave upon a grass-patch in a nook between two portions of the rambling old house. I made haste to open it for him. He stepped out into its creeper-covered porch, and stood looking at the rain, which fell like a huge thin cataract; I stood in the door behind him. The second flash came, and was followed by a lengthened roll of more distant thunder. He turned his head over his shoulder and looked at me, as much as to say, "You hear that?" then swivelled it round again, and anew contemplated the weather, apparently with approbation. So human were his pose and carriage and the way he kept turning his head, that I remarked almost involuntarily,

"Fine weather for the worms, Mr. Raven!"

"Yes," he answered, in the rather croaky voice I had learned to know, "the ground will be nice for them to get out and in!— It must be a grand time on the steppes of Uranus!" he added, with a glance upward; "I believe it is raining there too; it was, all the last week!"

"Why should that make it a grand time?" I asked.

"Because the animals there are all burrowers," he answered, "—like the field-mice and the moles here.—They will be, for ages to come."

"How do you know that, if I may be so bold?" I rejoined.

"As any one would who had been there to see," he replied. "It is a great sight, until you get used to it, when the earth gives a heave, and out comes a beast. You might think it a hairy elephant or a deinotherium—but none of the animals are the same as we have ever had here. I was almost frightened myself the first time I saw the dry-bog-serpent come wallowing out—such a head and mane! and *such* eyes!—but the shower is nearly over. It will stop directly after the next thunder-clap. There it is!"

A flash came with the words, and in about half a minute the thunder. Then the rain ceased.

"Now we should be going!" said the raven, and stepped to the front of the porch.

"Going where?" I asked.

"Going where we have to go," he answered. "You did not surely think you had got home? I told you there was no going out and in at pleasure until you were at home!"

"I do not want to go," I said.

"That does not make any difference—at least not much," he answered. "This is the way!"

"I am quite content where I am."

"You think so, but you are not. Come along."

He hopped from the porch on the grass, and turned, waiting.

"I will not leave the house to-day," I said with obstinacy.

"You will come into the garden!" rejoined the raven.

"I give in so far," I replied, and stepped from the porch.

The sun broke through the clouds, and the raindrops flashed and sparkled on the grass. The raven was walking over it.

"You will wet your feet!" I cried.

"And mire my beak," he answered, immediately plunging it deep in the sod, and drawing out a great wriggling red worm. He threw back his head, and tossed it in the air. It spread great wings, gorgeous in red and black, and soared aloft.

"Tut! tut!" I exclaimed; "you mistake, Mr. Raven: worms are not the larvæ of butterflies!"

"Never mind," he croaked; "it will do for once! I'm not a reading man at present, but sexton at the—at a certain grave-yard—cemetery, more properly—in—at—no matter where!"

"I see! you can't keep your spade still: and when you have nothing to bury, you must dig something up! Only you should mind what it is before you make it fly! No creature should be allowed to forget what and where it came from!"

"Why?" said the raven.

"Because it will grow proud, and cease to recognise its superiors."

No man knows it when he is making an idiot of himself.

"Where *do* the worms come from?" said the raven, as if suddenly grown curious to know.

"Why, from the earth, as you have just seen!" I answered.

"Yes, last!" he replied. "But they can't have come from it first—for that will never go back to it!" he added, looking up.

I looked up also, but could see nothing save a little dark cloud, the edges of which were red, as if with the light of the sunset.

"Surely the sun is not going down!" I exclaimed, struck with amazement.

"Oh, no!" returned the raven. "That red belongs to the worm."

"You see what comes of making creatures forget their origin!" I cried with some warmth.

"It is well, surely, if it be to rise higher and grow larger!" he returned. "But indeed I only teach them to find it!"

"Would you have the air full of worms?"

"That is the business of a sexton. If only the rest of the clergy understood it as well!"

In went his beak again through the soft turf, and out came the wriggling worm. He tossed it in the air, and away it flew.

I looked behind me, and gave a cry of dismay : I had but that moment declared I would not leave the house, and already I was a stranger in the strange land!

"What right have you to treat me so, Mr. Raven?" I said with deep offence. "Am I, or am I not, a free agent?"

"A man is as free as he chooses to make himself, never an atom freer," answered the raven.

"You have no right to make me do things against my will!"

"When you have a will, you will find that no one can."

"You wrong me in the very essence of my individuality!" I persisted.

"If you were an individual I could not, therefore now I do not. You are but beginning to become an individual."

All about me was a pine-forest, in which my eyes were already searching deep, in the hope of discovering an unaccountable glimmer, and so finding my way home. But, alas! how could I any longer call that house *home*, where every door, every window opened into—*Out*, and even the garden I could not keep inside!

I suppose I looked discomfited.

"Perhaps it may comfort you," said the raven, "to be told that you have not yet left your house, neither has your house left you. At the same time it cannot contain you, or you inhabit it!"

"I do not understand you," I replied. "Where am I?"

"In the region of the seven dimensions," he answered, with a curious noise in his throat, and a flutter of his tail. "You had better follow me carefully now for a moment, lest you should hurt some one!"

"There is nobody to hurt but yourself, Mr. Raven! I confess I should rather like to hurt you!"

"That you see nobody is where the danger lies. But you see that large tree to your left, about thirty yards away?"

"Of course I do : why should I not?" I answered testily.

"Ten minutes ago you did not see it, and now you do not know where it stands!"

"I do."

"Where do you think it stands?"

"Why *there*, where you know it is!"

"Where is *there*?"

"You bother me with your silly questions!" I cried. "I am growing tired of you!"

"That tree stands on the hearth of your kitchen, and grows nearly straight up its chimney," he said.

"Now I *know* you are making game of me!" I answered, with a laugh of scorn.

"Was I making game of you when you discovered me looking out of your star-sapphire yesterday?"

"That was this morning—not an hour ago!"

"I have been widening your horizon longer than that, Mr. Vane; but never mind!"

"You mean you have been making a fool of me!" I said, turning from him.

"Excuse me : no one can do that but yourself!"

"And I decline to do it."

"You mistake."

"How?"

"In declining to acknowledge yourself one already. You make yourself such by refusing what is true, and for that you will sorely punish yourself."

"How, again?"

"By believing what is not true."

"Then, if I walk to the other side of that tree, I shall walk through the kitchen fire?"

"Certainly. You would first, however, walk through the lady at the piano in the breakfast-room. That rosebush is close by her. You would give her a terrible start!"

"There is no lady in the house!"

"Indeed! Is not your housekeeper a lady? She is counted such in a certain country where all are servants, and the liveries one and multitudinous!"

"She cannot use the piano, anyhow!"

"Her niece can : she is there—a well-educated girl and a capital musician."

"Excuse me; I cannot help it : you seem to me to be talking sheer nonsense!"

"If you could but hear the music! Those great long heads of wild hyacinth are inside the piano, among the strings of it, and give that peculiar sweetness to her playing!—Pardon me: I forgot your deafness!"

"Two objects," I said, "cannot exist in the same place at the same time!"

"Can they not? I did not know!—I remember now they do teach that with you. It is a great mistake—one of the greatest ever wiseacre made! No man of the universe, only a man of the world could have said so!"

"You a librarian, and talk such rubbish!" I cried. "Plainly, you did not read many of the books in your charge!"

"Oh, yes! I went through all in your library—at the time, and came out at the other side not much the wiser. I was a bookworm then, but when I came to know it, I awoke among the butterflies. To be sure I have given up reading for a good many years—ever since I was made sexton.—There! I smell Grieg's Wedding March in the quiver of those rose-petals!"

I went to the rose-bush and listened hard, but could not hear the thinnest ghost of a sound; I only smelt something I had never before smelt in any rose. It was still rose-odour, but with a difference, caused, I suppose, by the Wedding March.

When I looked up, there was the bird by my side.

"Mr. Raven," I said, "forgive me for being so rude: I was irritated. Will you kindly show me my way home? I must go, for I have an appointment with my bailiff. One must not break faith with his servants!"

"You cannot break what was broken days ago!" he answered.

"Do show me the way," I pleaded.

"I cannot," he returned. "To go back, you must go through yourself, and that way no man can show another."

Entreaty was vain. I must accept my fate! But how was life to be lived in a world of which I had all the laws to learn? There would, however, be adventure! that held consolation; and whether I found my way home or not, I should at least have the rare advantage of knowing two worlds!

I had never yet done anything to justify my existence; my former world was nothing the better for my sojourn in it: here, however, I must earn, or in some way find, my bread! But I reasoned that, as I was not to blame in being here, I might expect to be taken care of here as well as there! I had had nothing to do with getting into the world I had just left, and in it I had found myself heir to a large property! If that world, as I now saw, had a claim upon me because I had eaten, and could eat again, upon this world I had a claim because I must eat—when it would in return have a claim on me!

"There is no hurry," said the raven, who stood regarding me; "we do not go much by the clock here. Still, the sooner one begins to do what has to be done, the better! I will take you to my wife."

"Thank you. Let us go!" I answered, and immediately he led the way.

CHAPTER V

THE OLD CHURCH

I FOLLOWED HIM DEEP into the pine-forest. Neither of us said much while yet the sacred gloom of it closed us round. We came to larger and yet larger trees—older, and more individual, some of them grotesque with age. Then the forest grew thinner.

"You see that hawthorn?" said my guide at length, pointing with his beak.

I looked where the wood melted away on the edge of an open heath.

"I see a gnarled old man, with a great white head," I answered.

"Look again," he rejoined : "it is a hawthorn."

"It seems indeed an ancient hawthorn; but this is not the season for the hawthorn to blossom!" I objected.

"The season for the hawthorn to blossom," he replied, "is when the hawthorn blossoms. That tree is in the ruins of the church on your home-farm. You were going to give some directions to the bailiff about its churchyard, were you not, the morning of the thunder?"

"I was going to tell him I wanted it turned into a wilderness of rose-trees, and that the plough must never come within three yards of it."

"Listen!" said the raven, seeming to hold his breath.

I listened, and heard—was it the sighing of a far-off musical wind—or the ghost of a music that had once been glad? Or did I indeed hear anything?

"They go there still," said the raven.

"Who goes there? and where do they go?" I asked.

"Some of the people who used to pray there, go to the ruins still," he replied. "But they will not go much longer, I think."

"What makes them go now?"

"They need help from each other to get their thinking done, and their feelings hatched, so they talk and sing together; and then, they say, the big thought floats out of their hearts like a great ship out of the river at high water."

"Do they pray as well as sing?"

"No; they have found that each can best pray in his own silent heart.—Some people are always at their prayers.—Look! look! There goes one!"

He pointed right up into the air. A snow-white pigeon was mounting, with quick and yet quicker wing-flap, the unseen spiral of an ethereal stair. The sunshine flashed quivering from its wings.

"I see a pigeon!" I said.

"Of course you see a pigeon," rejoined the raven, "for there is the pigeon! *I* see a prayer on its way.—I wonder now what heart is that dove's mother! Some one may have come awake in my cemetery!"

"How can a pigeon be a prayer?" I said. "I understand, of course, how it should be a fit symbol or likeness for one; but a live pigeon to come out of a heart!"

"It *must* puzzle you! It cannot fail to do so!"

"A prayer is a thought, a thing spiritual!" I pursued.

"Very true! But if you understood any world besides your own, you would understand your own much better.—When a heart is really alive, then it is able to think live things. There is one heart all whose thoughts are strong, happy creatures, and whose very dreams are lives. When some pray, they lift heavy thoughts from the ground, only to drop them on it again; others send up their prayers in living shapes, this or that, the nearest likeness to each. All live things were thoughts to begin with, and are fit therefore to be used by those that think. When one says to the great Thinker:—"Here is one of thy thoughts: I am thinking it now!" that is a prayer—a word to the big heart from one of its own little hearts.—Look, there is another!"

This time the raven pointed his beak downward—to something at the foot of a block of granite. I looked, and saw a little flower. I had never seen one like it before, and cannot utter the feeling it woke in me by its gracious, trusting form, its colour, and its odour as of a new world that was yet the old. I can only say that it suggested an anemone, was of a pale rose-hue, and had a golden heart.

"That is a prayer-flower," said the raven.

"I never saw such a flower before!" I rejoined.

"There is no other such. Not one prayer-flower is ever quite like another," he returned.

"How do you know it a prayer-flower?" I asked.

"By the expression of it," he answered. "More than that I cannot tell you. If you know it, you know it; if you do not, you do not."

"Could you not teach me to know a prayer-flower when I see it?" I said.

"I could not. But if I could, what better would you be? you would not know it of *your*self and *it*self! Why know the name of a thing when the thing itself you do not know? Whose work is it but your own to open your eyes? But indeed the business of the universe is to make such a fool of you that you will know yourself for one, and so begin to be wise!"

But I did see that the flower was different from any flower I had ever seen before; therefore I knew that I must be seeing a shadow of the prayer in it; and a great awe came over me to think of the heart listening to the flower.

CHAPTER VI

THE SEXTON'S COTTAGE

WE HAD BEEN for some time walking over a rocky moorland covered with dry plants and mosses, when I descried a little cottage in the farthest distance. The sun was not yet down, but he was wrapt in a gray cloud. The heath looked as if it had never been warm, and the wind blew strangely cold, as if from some region where it was always night.

"Here we are at last!" said the raven. "What a long way it is! In half the time I could have gone to Paradise and seen my cousin—him, you remember, who never came back to Noah! Dear! dear! it is almost winter!"

"Winter!" I cried; "it seems but half a day since we left home!"

"That is because we have travelled so fast," answered the raven. "In your world you cannot pull up the plumb-line you call gravitation, and let the world spin round under your feet! But here is my wife's house! She is very good to let me live with her, and call it the sexton's cottage!"

"But where is your churchyard—your cemetery—where you make your graves, I mean?" said I, seeing nothing but the flat heath.

The raven stretched his neck, held out his beak horizontally, turned it slowly round to all points of the compass, and said nothing.

I followed the beak with my eyes, and lo, without church or graves, all was a churchyard! Wherever the dreary wind swept, there was the raven's cemetery! He was sexton of all he surveyed! lord of all that was laid aside! I stood in the burial-ground of the universe; its compass the unenclosed heath, its wall the gray horizon, low and starless! I had left spring and summer, autumn and sunshine behind me, and come to the winter that waited for me! I had set out in the prime of my youth, and here I was already!—But I mistook. The day might well be long in that region, for it contained the seasons. Winter slept there, the night through, in his winding-sheet of ice; with childlike smile, Spring came awake in the dawn; at noon, Summer blazed abroad in her gorgeous beauty; with the slow-changing afternoon, old Autumn crept in, and died at the first breath of the vaporous, ghosty night.

As we drew near the cottage, the clouded sun was rushing down the steepest slope of the west, and he sank while we were yet a few yards from the door. The same instant I was assailed by a cold that seemed almost a material presence, and I struggled across the threshold as if from the clutches of an icy death. A wind swelled up on the moor, and rushed at the door as with difficulty I closed it behind me. Then all was still, and I looked about me.

A candle burned on a deal table in the middle of the room, and the first thing I saw was the lid of a coffin, as I thought, set up against the wall; but it opened, for it was a door, and a woman entered. She was all in white—as white as new-fallen snow; and her face was as white as her dress, but not like snow, for at once it suggested warmth. I thought her features were perfect, but her eyes made me forget them. The life of her face and her whole person was gathered and concentrated in her eyes, where it became light. It might have been coming death that made her face luminous, but the eyes had life in them for a nation—large, and dark with a darkness ever deepening as I gazed. A whole night-heaven lay condensed in each pupil; all the stars were in its blackness, and flashed; while round it for a horizon lay coiled an iris of the eternal twilight. What any eye *is*, God only knows : her eyes must have been coming direct out of his own ! the still face might be a primeval perfection; the live eyes were a continuous creation.

"Here is Mr. Vane, wife !" said the raven.

"He is welcome," she answered, in a low, rich, gentle voice. Treasures of immortal sound seemed to lie buried in it.

I gazed, and could not speak.

"I knew you would be glad to see him !" added the raven.

She stood in front of the door by which she had entered, and did not come nearer.

"Will he sleep?" she asked.

"I fear not," he replied; "he is neither weary nor heavy laden."

"Why then have you brought him?"

"I have my fears it may prove precipitate."

"I do not quite understand you," I said, with an uneasy foreboding as to what she meant, but a vague hope of some escape. "Surely a man must do a day's work first !"

I gazed in the white face of the woman, and my heart fluttered. She returned my gaze in silence.

"Let me first go home," I resumed, "and come again after I have found or made, invented, or at least discovered something !"

"He has not yet learned that the day begins with sleep !" said the woman, turning to her husband. "Tell him he must rest before he can do anything !"

"Men," he answered, "think so much of having done, that

they fall asleep upon it. They cannot empty an egg but they turn into the shell, and lie down!"

The words drew my eyes from the woman to the raven.

I saw no raven, but the librarian—the same slender elderly man, in a rusty black coat, large in the body and long in the tails. I had seen only his back before; now for the first time I saw his face. It was so thin that it showed the shape of the bones under it, suggesting the skulls his last-claimed profession must have made him familiar with. But in truth I had never before seen a face so alive, or a look so keen or so friendly as that in his pale blue eyes, which yet had a haze about them as if they had done much weeping.

"You knew I was not a raven!" he said with a smile.

"I knew you were Mr. Raven," I replied; "but somehow I thought you a bird too!"

"What made you think me a bird?"

"You looked a raven, and I saw you dig worms out of the earth with your beak."

"And then?"

"Toss them in the air."

"And then?"

"They grew butterflies, and flew away."

"Did you ever see a raven do that? I told you I was a sexton!"

"Does a sexton toss worms in the air, and turn them into butterflies?"

"Yes."

"I never saw one do it!"

"You saw me do it!—But I am still librarian in your house, for I never was dismissed, and never gave up the office. Now I am librarian here as well."

"But you have just told me you were sexton here!"

"So I am. It is much the same profession. Except you are a true sexton, books are but dead bodies to you, and a library nothing but a catacomb!"

"You bewilder me!"

"That's all right!"

A few moments he stood silent. The woman, moveless as a statue, stood silent also by the coffin-door.

"Upon occasion," said the sexton at length, "it is more convenient to put one's bird-self in front. Every one, as you ought to know, has a beast-self—and a bird-self, and a stupid fish-self, ay, and a creeping serpent-self too—which it takes a deal of crushing to kill! In truth he has also a tree-self and a crystal-self, and I don't know how many selves more—all to get into harmony. You can tell what sort a man is by his creature that comes oftenest to the front."

He turned to his wife, and I considered him more closely. He was above the ordinary height, and stood more erect than when last I saw him. His face was, like his wife's, very pale; its nose handsomely encased the beak that had retired within it; its lips were very thin, and even they had no colour, but their curves were beautiful, and about them quivered a shadowy smile that had humour in it as well as love and pity.

"We are in want of something to eat and drink, wife," he said; "we have come a long way!"

"You know, husband," she answered, "we can give only to him that asks."

She turned her unchanging face and radiant eyes upon mine.

"Please give me something to eat, Mrs. Raven," I said, "and something—what you will—to quench my thirst."

"Your thirst must be greater before you can have what will quench it," she replied; "but what I can give you, I will gladly."

She went to a cupboard in the wall, brought from it bread and wine, and set them on the table.

We sat down to the perfect meal; and as I ate, the bread and wine seemed to go deeper than the hunger and thirst. Anxiety and discomfort vanished; expectation took their place.

I grew very sleepy, and now first felt weary.

"I have earned neither food nor sleep, Mrs. Raven," I said, "but you have given me the one freely, and now I hope you will give me the other, for I sorely need it."

"Sleep is too fine a thing ever to be earned," said the sexton; "it must be given and accepted, for it is a necessity. But it would be perilous to use this house as a half-way hostelry—for the repose of a night, that is, merely."

A wild-looking little black cat jumped on his knee as he spoke. He patted it as one pats a child to make it go to sleep : he seemed to me patting down the sod upon a grave—patting it lovingly, with an inward lullaby.

"Here is one of Mara's kittens!" he said to his wife : "will you give it something and put it out? she may want it!"

The woman took it from him gently, gave it a little piece of bread, and went out with it, closing the door behind her.

"How then am I to make use of your hospitality?" I asked.

"By accepting it to the full," he answered.

"I do not understand."

"In this house no one wakes of himself."

"Why?"

"Because no one anywhere ever wakes of himself. You can wake yourself no more than you can make yourself."

"Then perhaps you or Mrs. Raven would kindly call me!" I said, still nowise understanding, but feeling afresh that vague foreboding.

"We cannot."

"How dare I then go to sleep?" I cried.

"If you would have the rest of this house, you must not trouble yourself about waking. You must go to sleep heartily, altogether and outright."

My soul sank within me.

The sexton sat looking me in the face. His eyes seemed to say, "Will you not trust me?" I returned his gaze, and answered,

"I will."

"Then come," he said; "I will show you your couch."

As we rose, the woman came in. She took up the candle, turned to the inner door, and led the way. I went close behind her, and the sexton followed.

CHAPTER VII

THE CEMETERY

THE AIR AS of an ice-house met me crossing the threshold. The door fell-to behind us. The sexton said something to his wife that made her turn towards us.—What a change had passed upon her! It was as if the splendour of her eyes had grown too much for them to hold, and, sinking into her countenance, made it flash with a loveliness like that of

Beatrice in the white rose of the redeemed. Life itself, life eternal, immortal, streamed from it, an unbroken lightning. Even her hands shone with a white radiance, every "pearl-shell helmet" gleaming like a moonstone. Her beauty was over-powering; I was glad when she turned it from me.

But the light of the candle reached such a little way, that at first I could see nothing of the place. Presently, however, it fell on something that glimmered, a little raised from the floor. Was it a bed? Could live thing sleep in such a mortal cold? Then surely it was no wonder it should not wake of itself! Beyond that appeared a fainter shine; and then I thought I descried uncertain gleams on every side.

A few paces brought us to the first; it was a human form under a sheet, straight and still—whether of man or woman I could not tell, for the light seemed to avoid the face as we passed.

I soon perceived that we were walking along an aisle of couches, on almost every one of which, with its head to the passage, lay something asleep or dead, covered with a sheet white as snow. My soul grew silent with dread. Through aisle after aisle we went, among couches innumerable. I could see only a few of them at once, but they were on all sides, vanishing, as it seemed, in the infinite.—Was it here lay my choice of a bed? Must I go to sleep among the unwaking, with no one to rouse me? Was this the sexton's library? were these his books? Truly it was no half-way house, this chamber of the dead!

"One of the cellars I am placed to watch!" remarked Mr. Raven—in a low voice, as if fearing to disturb his silent guests. "Much wine is set here to ripen!—But it is dark for a stranger!" he added.

"The moon is rising; she will soon be here," said his wife, and her clear voice, low and sweet, sounded of ancient sorrow long bidden adieu.

Even as she spoke the moon looked in at an opening in the wall, and a thousand gleams of white responded to her shine. But not yet could I descry beginning or end of the couches. They stretched away and away, as if for all the disparted world to sleep upon. For along the far receding narrow ways, every couch stood by itself, and on each slept a lonely sleeper. I thought at first their sleep was death, but I soon saw it was something deeper still—a something I did not know.

The moon rose higher, and shone through other openings, but I could never see enough of the place at once to know its shape or character; now it would resemble a long cathedral nave, now a huge barn made into a dwelling of tombs. She looked colder than any moon in the frostiest night of the world, and where she shone direct upon them, cast a bluish, icy gleam on the white sheets and the pallid countenances—but it might be the faces that made the moon so cold!

Of such as I could see, all were alike in the brotherhood of death, all unlike in the character and history recorded upon them. Here lay a man who had died—for although this was not death, I have no other name to give it—in the prime of manly strength; his dark beard seemed to flow like a liberated stream from the glacier of his frozen countenance; his forehead was smooth as polished marble; a shadow of pain lingered about his lips, but only a shadow. On the next couch lay the form of a girl, passing lovely to behold. The sadness left on her face by parting was not yet absorbed in perfect peace, but absolute submission possessed the placid features, which bore no sign of wasting disease, of "killing care or grief of heart" : if pain had been there, it was long charmed asleep, never again to awake. Many were the beautiful that there lay very still—some of them mere children; but I did not see one infant. The most beautiful of all was a lady whose white hair, and that alone, suggested her old when first she fell asleep. On her stately countenance rested —not submission, but a right noble acquiescence, an assurance, firm as the foundations of the universe, that all was as it should be. On some faces lingered the almost obliterated scars of strife, the marrings of hopeless loss, the fading shadows of sorrows that had seemed inconsolable : the aurora of the great morning had not yet quite melted them away; but those faces were few, and every one that bore such brand of pain seemed to plead, "Pardon me : I died only yesterday!" or, "Pardon me : I died but a century ago!" That some had been dead for ages I knew, not merely by their unutterable repose, but by something for which I have neither word nor symbol.

We came at last to three empty couches, immediately beyond which lay the form of a beautiful woman, a little past the prime

of life. One of her arms was outside the sheet, and her hand lay
with the palm upward, in its centre a dark spot. Next to her was
the stalwart figure of a man of middle age. His arm too was
outside the sheet, the strong hand almost closed, as if clenched
on the grip of a sword. I thought he must be a king who had
died fighting for the truth.

"Will you hold the candle nearer, wife?" whispered the
sexton, bending down to examine the woman's hand.

"It heals well," he murmured to himself: "the nail found in
her nothing to hurt!"

At last I ventured to speak.

"Are they not dead?" I asked softly.

"I cannot answer you," he replied in a subdued voice. "I
almost forget what they mean by *dead* in the old world. If I said
a person was dead, my wife would understand one thing, and
you would imagine another.—This is but one of my treasure
vaults," he went on, "and all my guests are not laid in vaults:
out there on the moor they lie thick as the leaves of a forest after
the first blast of your winter—thick, let me say rather, as if the
great white rose of heaven had shed its petals over it. All night
the moon reads their faces, and smiles."

"But why leave them in the corrupting moonlight?" I asked.

"Our moon," he answered, "is not like yours—the old cinder
of a burnt-out world; her beams embalm the dead, not corrupt
them. You observe that here the sexton lays his dead on the
earth; he buries very few under it! In your world he lays huge
stones on them, as if to keep them down; I watch for the hour to
ring the resurrection-bell, and wake those that are still asleep.
Your sexton looks at the clock to know when to ring the dead-
alive to church; I hearken for the cock on the spire to crow:
'Awake, thou that sleepest, and arise from the dead!'"

I began to conclude that the self-styled sexton was in truth
an insane parson: the whole thing was too mad! But how was
I to get away from it? I was helpless! In this world of the dead,
the raven and his wife were the only living I had yet seen:
whither should I turn for help? I was lost in a space larger than
imagination; for if here two things, or any parts of them, could
occupy the same space, why not twenty or ten thousand?—But
I dared not think further in that direction.

"You seem in your dead to see differences beyond my perception!" I ventured to remark.

"None of those you see," he answered, "are in truth quite dead yet, and some have but just begun to come alive and die. Others had begun to die, that is to come alive, long before they came to us; and when such are indeed dead, that instant they will wake and leave us. Almost every night some rise and go. But I will not say more, for I find my words only mislead you!— This is the couch that has been waiting for you," he ended, pointing to one of the three.

"Why just this?" I said, beginning to tremble, and anxious by parley to delay.

"For reasons which one day you will be glad to know," he answered.

"Why not know them now?"

"That also you will know when you wake."

"But these are all dead, and I am alive!" I objected, shuddering.

"Not much," rejoined the sexton with a smile, "—not nearly enough! Blessed be the true life that the pauses between its throbs are not death!"

"The place is too cold to let one sleep!" I said.

"Do these find it so?" he returned. "They sleep well—or will soon. Of cold they feel not a breath : it heals their wounds.—Do not be a coward, Mr. Vane. Turn your back on fear, and your face to whatever may come. Give yourself up to the night, and you will rest indeed. Harm will not come to you, but a good you cannot foreknow."

The sexton and I stood by the side of the couch, his wife, with the candle in her hand, at the foot of it. Her eyes were full of light, but her face was again of a still whiteness; it was no longer radiant.

"Would they have me make of a charnel-house my bed-chamber?" I cried aloud. "I will not. I will lie abroad on the heath; it cannot be colder there!"

"I have just told you that the dead are there also,

> 'Thick as autumnal leaves that strow the brooks
> In Vallombrosa,' "

said the librarian.

"I will *not*," I cried again; and in the compassing dark, the two gleamed out like spectres that waited on the dead; neither answered me; each stood still and sad, and looked at the other.

"Be of good comfort; we watch the flock of the great shepherd," said the sexton to his wife.

Then he turned to me.

"Didst thou not find the air of the place pure and sweet when thou enteredst it?" he asked.

"Yes; but oh, so cold!" I answered.

"Then know," he returned, and his voice was stern, "that thou who callest thyself alive, hast brought into this chamber the odours of death, and its air will not be wholesome for the sleepers until thou art gone from it!"

They went farther into the great chamber, and I was left alone in the moonlight with the dead.

I turned to escape.

What a long way I found it back through the dead! At first I was too angry to be afraid, but as I grew calm, the still shapes grew terrible. At last, with loud offence to the gracious silence, I ran, I fled wildly, and, bursting out, flung-to the door behind me. It closed with an awful silence.

I stood in pitch-darkness. Feeling about me, I found a door, opened it, and was aware of the dim light of a lamp. I stood in my library, with the handle of the masked door in my hand.

Had I come to myself out of a vision?—or lost myself by going back to one? Which was the real—what I now saw, or what I had just ceased to see? Could both be real, inter-penetrating yet unmingling?

I threw myself on a couch, and fell asleep.

In the library was one small window to the east, through which, at this time of the year, the first rays of the sun shone upon a mirror whence they were reflected on the masked door: when I woke, there they shone, and thither they drew my eyes. With the feeling that behind it must lie the boundless chamber I had left by that door, I sprang to my feet, and opened it. The light, like an eager hound, shot before me into the closet, and pounced upon the gilded edges of a large book.

"What idiot," I cried, "has put that book in the shelf the wrong way?"

But the gilded edges, reflecting the light a second time, flung it on a nest of drawers in a dark corner, and I saw that one of them was half open.

"More meddling!" I cried, and went to close the drawer.

It contained old papers, and seemed more than full, for it would not close. Taking the topmost one out, I perceived that it was in my father's writing and of some length. The words on which first my eyes fell, at once made me eager to learn what it contained. I carried it to the library, sat down in one of the western windows, and read what follows.

CHAPTER VIII

MY FATHER'S MANUSCRIPT

I AM FILLED WITH awe of what I have to write. The sun is shining golden above me; the sea lies blue beneath his gaze; the same world sends its growing things up to the sun, and its flying things into the air which I have breathed from my infancy; but I know the outspread splendour a passing show, and that at any moment it may, like the drop-scene of a stage, be lifted to reveal more wonderful things.

Shortly after my father's death, I was seated one morning in the library. I had been, somewhat listlessly, regarding the portrait that hangs among the books, which I knew only as that of a distant ancestor, and wishing I could learn something of its original. Then I had taken a book from the shelves and begun to read.

Glancing up from it, I saw coming toward me—not between me and the door, but between me and the portrait—a thin pale man in rusty black. He looked sharp and eager, and had a notable nose, at once reminding me of a certain jug my sisters used to call Mr. Crow.

"Finding myself in your vicinity, Mr. Vane, I have given myself the pleasure of calling," he said, in a peculiar but not disagreeable voice. "Your honoured grandfather treated me—I may say it without presumption—as a friend, having known me from childhood as his father's librarian."

It did not strike me at the time how old the man must be.

"*May I ask where you live now, Mr. Crow?*" I said.

He smiled an amused smile.

"*You nearly hit my name,*" he rejoined, "*which shows the family insight. You have seen me before, but only once, and could not then have heard it!*"

"*Where was that?*"

"*In this very room. You were quite a child, however!*"

I could not be sure that I remembered him, but for a moment I fancied I did, and I begged him to set me right as to his name.

"*There is such a thing as remembering without recognising the memory in it,*" he remarked. "*For my name—which you have near enough—it used to be Raven.*"

I had heard the name, for marvellous tales had brought it me.

"*It is very kind of you to come and see me,*" I said. "*Will you not sit down?*"

He seated himself at once.

"*You knew my father, then, I presume?*"

"*I knew him,*" he answered with a curious smile, "*but he did not care about my acquaintance, and we never met.—That gentleman, however,*" he added, pointing to the portrait,—"*old Sir Up'ard, his people called him,—was in his day a friend of mine yet more intimate than ever your grandfather became.*"

Then at length I began to think the interview a strange one. But in truth it was hardly stranger that my visitor should remember Sir Upward, than that he should have been my great-grandfather's librarian!

"*I owe him much,*" he continued; "*for, although I had read many more books than he, yet, through the special direction of his studies, he was able to inform me of a certain relation of modes which I should never have discovered of myself, and could hardly have learned from any one else.*"

"*Would you mind telling me all about that?*" I said.

"*By no means—as much at least as I am able: there are not such things as wilful secrets,*" he answered—and went on.

"*That closet held his library—a hundred manuscripts or so, for printing was not then invented. One morning I sat there, working at a catalogue of them, when he looked in at the door, and said, "Come." I laid down my pen and followed him—across the great hall, down a steep rough descent, and along an underground passage to a tower he had lately built, consisting of*

a stair and a room at the top of it. *The door of this room had a
tremendous lock, which he undid with the smallest key I ever
saw. I had scarcely crossed the threshold after him, when, to
my eyes, he began to dwindle, and grew less and less. All at
once my vision seemed to come right, and I saw that he was
moving swiftly away from me. In a minute more he was the
merest speck in the distance, with the tops of blue mountains
beyond him, clear against a sky of paler blue. I recognised the
country, for I had gone there and come again many a time,
although I had never known this way to it.*

"Many years after, when the tower had long disappeared, I
taught one of his descendants what Sir Upward had taught me;
and now and then to this day I use your house when I want to
go the nearest way home. I must indeed—without your leave, for
which I ask your pardon—have by this time well established a
right of way through it—not from front to back, but from bottom
to top!"

"You would have me then understand, Mr. Raven," I said,
"that you go through my house into another world, heedless of
disparting space?"

"That I go through it is an incontrovertible acknowledgment
of space," returned the old librarian.

"Please do not quibble, Mr. Raven," I rejoined. "Please to
take my question as you know I mean it."

"There is in your house a door, one step through which carries
me into a world very much another than this."

"A better?"

"Not throughout; but so much another that most of its
physical, and many of its mental laws are different from those
of this world. As for moral laws, they must everywhere be
fundamentally the same."

"You try my power of belief!" I said.

"You take me for a madman, probably?"

"You do not look like one."

"A liar then?"

"You give me no ground to think you such."

"Only you do not believe me?"

"I will go out of that door with you if you like: I believe in
you enough to risk the attempt."

"*The blunder all my children make!*" *he murmured.* "*The only door out is the door in!*"

I began to think he must be crazy. He sat silent for a moment, his head resting on his hand, his elbow on the table, and his eyes on the books before him.

"*A book,*" *he said louder,* "*is a door in, and therefore a door out.—I see old Sir Up'ard,*" *he went on, closing his eyes,* "*and my heart swells with love to him:—what world is he in?*"

"*The world of your heart!*" *I replied;* "*—that is, the idea of him is there.*"

"*There is one world then at least on which your hall-door does not open?*"

"*I grant you so much; but the things in that world are not things to have and to hold.*"

"*Think a little farther,*" *he rejoined:* "*did anything ever become yours, except by getting into that world?—The thought is beyond you, however, at present!—I tell you there are more worlds, and more doors to them, than you will think of in many years!*"

He rose, left the library, crossed the hall, and went straight up to the garret, familiar evidently with every turn. I followed, studying his back. His hair hung down long and dark, straight and glossy. His coat was wide and reached to his heels. His shoes seemed too large for him.

In the garret a light came through at the edges of the great roofing slabs, and showed us parts where was no flooring, and we must step from joist to joist: in the middle of one of these spaces rose a partition, with a door: through it I followed Mr. Raven into a small, obscure chamber, whose top contracted as it rose, and went slanting through the roof.

"*That is the door I spoke of,*" *he said, pointing to an oblong mirror that stood on the floor and leaned against the wall. I went in front of it, and saw our figures dimly reflected in its dusty face. There was something about it that made me uneasy. It looked old-fashioned and neglected, but, notwithstanding its ordinary seeming, the eagle, perched with outstretched wings on the top, appeared threatful.*

"*As a mirror,*" *said the librarian,* "*it has grown dingy with age; but that is no matter: its doorness depends on the light.*"

"*Light!*" *I rejoined;* "*there is no light here!*"

He did not answer me, but began to pull at a little chain on the opposite wall. I heard a creaking: the top of the chamber was turning slowly round. He ceased pulling, looked at his watch, and began to pull again.

"We arrive almost to the moment!" he said; "it is on the very stroke of noon!"

The top went creaking and revolving for a minute or so. Then he pulled two other chains, now this, now that, and returned to the first. A moment more and the chamber grew much clearer: a patch of sunlight had fallen upon a mirror on the wall opposite that against which the other leaned, and on the dust I saw the path of the reflected rays to the mirror on the ground. But from the latter none were returned; they seemed to go clean through; there was nowhere in the chamber a second patch of light!

"Where are the sunrays gone?" I cried.

"That I cannot tell," returned Mr. Raven; "—back, perhaps, to where they came from first. They now belong, I fancy, to a sense not yet developed in us."

He then talked of the relations of mind to matter, and of sense to qualities, in a way I could only a little understand, whence he went on to yet stranger things which I could not at all comprehend. He spoke much about dimensions, telling me that there were many more than three, some of them concerned with powers which were indeed in us, but of which as yet we knew absolutely nothing. His words, however, I confess, took little more hold of me than the light did of the mirror, for I thought he hardly knew what he was saying.

Suddenly I was aware that our forms had gone from the mirror, which seemed full of a white mist. As I gazed I saw, growing gradually visible beyond the mist, the tops of a range of mountains, which became clearer and clearer. Soon the mist vanished entirely, uncovering the face of a wide heath, on which, at some distance, was the figure of a man moving swiftly away. I turned to address my companion; he was no longer by my side. I looked again at the form in the mirror, and recognised the wide coat flying, the black hair lifting in a wind that did not touch me. I rushed in terror from the place.

CHAPTER IX

I REPENT

I LAID THE MANUSCRIPT down, consoled to find that my father had had a peep into that mysterious world, and that he knew Mr. Raven.

Then I remembered that I had never heard the cause or any circumstance of my father's death, and began to believe that he must at last have followed Mr. Raven, and not come back; whereupon I speedily grew ashamed of my flight. What wondrous facts might I not by this time have gathered concerning life and death, and wide regions beyond ordinary perception! Assuredly the Ravens were good people, and a night in their house would nowise have hurt me! They were doubtless strange, but it was faculty in which the one was peculiar, and beauty in which the other was marvellous! And I had not believed in them! had treated them as unworthy of my confidence, as harbouring a design against me! The more I thought of my behaviour to them, the more disgusted I became with myself. Why should I have feared such dead? To share their holy rest was an honour of which I had proved myself unworthy! What harm could that sleeping king, that lady with the wound in her palm, have done me? I felt a longing after the sweet and stately stillness of their two countenances, and wept. Weeping I threw myself on a couch, and suddenly fell asleep.

As suddenly I woke, feeling as if some one had called me. The house was still as an empty church. A blackbird was singing on the lawn. I said to myself, "I will go and tell them I am ashamed, and will do whatever they would have me do!" I rose and went straight up the stairs to the garret.

The wooden chamber was just as when first I saw it, the mirror dimly reflecting everything before it. It was nearly noon, and the sun would be a little higher than when first I came : I must raise the hood a little, and adjust the mirrors accordingly! If I had but been in time to see Mr. Raven do it!

I pulled the chains, and let the light fall on the first mirror.

I turned then to the other : there were the shapes of the former vision—distinguishable indeed, but tremulous like a landscape in a pool ruffled by "a small pipling wind!" I touched the glass; it was impermeable.

Suspecting polarisation as the thing required, I shifted and shifted the mirrors, changing their relation, until at last, in a great degree, so far as I was concerned, by chance, things came right between them, and I saw the mountains blue and steady and clear. I stepped forward, and my feet were among the heather.

All I knew of the way to the cottage was that we had gone through a pine-forest. I passed through many thickets and several small fir-woods, continually fancying afresh that I recognised something of the country; but I had come upon no forest, and now the sun was near the horizon, and the air had begun to grow chill with the coming winter, when, to my delight, I saw a little black object coming toward me : it was indeed the raven!

I hastened to meet him.

"I beg your pardon, sir, for my rudeness last night," I said. "Will you take me with you now? I heartily confess I do not deserve it."

"Ah!" he returned, and looked up. Then, after a brief pause, "My wife does not expect you to-night," he said. "She regrets that we at all encouraged your staying last week."

"Take me to her that I may tell her how sorry I am," I begged humbly.

"It is of no use," he answered. "Your night was not come then, or you would not have left us. It is not come now, and I cannot show you the way. The dead were rejoicing under their daisies—they all lie among the roots of the flowers of heaven—at the thought of your delight when the winter should be past, and the morning with its birds come : ere you left them, they shivered in their beds. When the spring of the universe arrives,—but that cannot be for ages yet! how many, I do not know—and do not care to know."

"Tell me one thing, I beg of you, Mr. Raven : is my father with you? Have you seen him since he left the world?"

"Yes; he is with us, fast asleep. That was he you saw with his arm on the coverlet, his hand half closed."

"Why did you not tell me? That I should have been so near him, and not know!"

"And turn your back on him!" corrected the raven.

"I would have lain down at once had I known!"

"I doubt it. Had you been ready to lie down, you would have known him!—Old Sir Up'ard," he went on, "and your twice great-grandfather, both are up and away long ago. Your great-grandfather has been with us for many a year; I think he will soon begin to stir. You saw him last night, though of course you did not know him."

"Why *of course*?"

"Because he is so much nearer waking than you. No one who will not sleep can ever wake."

"I do not at all understand you!"

"You turned away, and would not understand!"

I held my peace.—But if I did not say something, he would go!

"And my grandfather—is he also with you?" I asked.

"No; he is still in the Evil Wood, fighting the dead."

"Where is the Evil Wood, that I may find him?"

"You will not find him; but you will hardly miss the wood. It is the place where those who will not sleep, wake up at night, to kill their dead and bury them."

"I cannot understand you!"

"Naturally not. Neither do I understand you; I can read neither your heart nor your face. When my wife and I do not understand our children, it is because there is not enough of them to be understood. God alone can understand foolishness."

"Then," I said, feeling naked and very worthless, "will you be so good as show me the nearest way home? There are more ways than one, I know, for I have gone by two already."

"There are indeed many ways."

"Tell me, please, how to recognise the nearest."

"I cannot," answered the raven; "you and I use the same words with different meanings. We are often unable to tell people what they *need* to know, because they *want* to know something else, and would therefore only misunderstand what we said. Home is ever so far away in the palm of your hand, and how to get there it is of no use to tell you. But you will get there; you must get there; you have to get there. Everybody who is not at home, has to go home. You thought you were at home where I found you: if that had been your home, you could not have left it. Nobody can leave home. And nobody ever was or ever will be at home without having gone there."

"Enigma treading on enigma!" I exclaimed. "I did not come here to be asked riddles."

"No; but you came, and found the riddles waiting for you! Indeed you are yourself the only riddle. What you call riddles are truths, and seem riddles because you are not true."

"Worse and worse!" I cried.

"And you *must* answer the riddles!" he continued. "They will go on asking themselves until you understand yourself. The universe is a riddle trying to get out, and you are holding your door hard against it."

"Will you not in pity tell me what I am to do—where I must go?"

"How should I tell *your* to-do, or the way to it?"

"If I am not to go home, at least direct me to some of my kind."

"I do not know of any. The beings most like you are in that direction."

He pointed with his beak. I could see nothing but the setting sun, which blinded me.

"Well," I said bitterly, "I cannot help feeling hardly treated —taken from my home, abandoned in a strange world, and refused instruction as to where I am to go or what I am to do!"

"You forget," said the raven, "that, when I brought you and you declined my hospitality, you reached what you call home in safety : now you are come of yourself! Good night."

He turned and walked slowly away, with his beak toward the ground. I stood dazed. It was true I had come of myself, but had I not come with intent of atonement? My heart was sore, and in my brain was neither quest nor purpose, hope nor desire. I gazed after the raven, and would have followed him, but felt it useless.

All at once he pounced on a spot, throwing the whole weight of his body on his bill, and for some moments dug vigorously. Then with a flutter of his wings he threw back his head, and something shot from his bill, cast high in the air. That moment the sun set, and the air at once grew very dusk, but the something opened into a soft radiance, and came pulsing toward me like a fire-fly, but with a much larger and a yellower light. It flew over my head. I turned and followed it.

Here I interrupt my narrative to remark that it involves a constant struggle to say what cannot be said with even an approach to precision, the things recorded being, in their nature and in that of the creatures concerned in them, so inexpressibly different from any possible events of this economy, that I can present them only by giving, in the forms and language of life in this world, the modes in which they affected me—not the things themselves, but the feelings they woke in me. Even this much, however, I do with a continuous and abiding sense of failure, finding it impossible to present more than one phase of a multitudinously complicated significance, or one concentric sphere of a graduated embodiment. A single thing would sometimes seem to be and mean many things, with an uncertain identity at the heart of them, which kept constantly altering their look. I am indeed often driven to set down what I know to be but a clumsy and doubtful representation of the mere feeling aimed at, none of the communicating media of this world being fit to convey it, in its peculiar strangeness, with even an approach to clearness or certainty. Even to one who knew the region better than myself, I should have no assurance of transmitting the reality of my experience in it. While without a doubt, for instance, that I was actually regarding a scene of activity, I might be, at the same moment, in my consciousness aware that I was perusing a metaphysical argument.

CHAPTER X

THE BAD BURROW

As the air grew black and the winter closed swiftly around me, the fluttering fire blazed out more luminous, and arresting its flight, hovered waiting. So soon as I came under its radiance, it flew slowly on, lingering now and then above spots where the ground was rocky. Every time I looked up, it seemed to have grown larger, and at length gave me an attendant shadow. Plainly a bird-butterfly, it flew with a certain swallowy double. Its wings were very large, nearly square, and flashed all the colours of the rainbow. Wondering at their splendour, I became so absorbed in their beauty that I stumbled over a low rock, and lay stunned. When I came to myself, the creature was hovering over my head, radiating the whole chord of light, with multitudinous gradations and some kinds of colour I had never before seen. I rose and went on, but, unable to take my eyes off the shining thing to look to my steps, I struck my foot against a stone. Fearing then another fall, I sat down to watch the little glory, and a great longing awoke in me to have it in my hand. To my unspeakable delight, it began to sink toward me. Slowly at first, then swiftly it sank, growing larger as it came nearer. I felt as if the treasure of the universe were giving itself to me— put out my hand, and had it. But the instant I took it, its light went out; all was dark as pitch; a dead book with boards outspread lay cold and heavy in my hand. I threw it in the air— only to hear it fall among the heather. Burying my face in my hands, I sat in motionless misery.

But the cold grew so bitter that, fearing to be frozen, I got up. The moment I was on my feet, a faint sense of light awoke in me. "Is it coming to life?" I cried, and a great pang of hope shot through me. Alas, no! it was the edge of a moon peering up keen and sharp over a level horizon! She brought me light— but no guidance! *She* would not hover over me, would not wait on my faltering steps! She could but offer me an ignorant choice!

With a full face she rose, and I began to see a little about me. Westward of her, and not far from me, a range of low hills broke the horizon-line: I set out for it.

But what a night I had to pass ere I reached it! The moon seemed to know something, for she stared at me oddly. Her look was indeed icy-cold, but full of interest, or at least curiosity. She was not the same moon I had known on the earth; her face was strange to me, and her light yet stranger. Perhaps it came from an unknown sun! Every time I looked up, I found her staring at me with all her might! At first I was annoyed, as at the rudeness of a fellow creature; but soon I saw or fancied a certain wondering pity in her gaze: why was I out in her night? Then first I knew what an awful thing it was to be awake in the universe: I *was*, and could not help it!

As I walked, my feet lost the heather, and trod a bare spongy soil, something like dry, powdery peat. To my dismay it gave a momentary heave under me; then presently I saw what seemed the ripple of an earthquake running on before me, shadowy in the low moon. It passed into the distance; but, while yet I stared after it, a single wave rose up, and came slowly toward me. A yard or two away it burst, and from it, with a scramble and a bound, issued an animal like a tiger. About his mouth and ears hung clots of mould, and his eyes winked and flamed as he rushed at me, showing his white teeth in a soundless snarl. I stood fascinated, unconscious of either courage or fear. He turned his head to the ground, and plunged into it.

"That moon is affecting my brain," I said as I resumed my journey. "What life can be here but the phantasmic—the stuff of which dreams are made? I am indeed walking in a vain show!"

Thus I strove to keep my heart above the waters of fear, nor knew that she whom I distrusted was indeed my defence from the realities I took for phantoms : her light controlled the monsters, else had I scarce taken a second step on the hideous ground. "I will not be appalled by that which only seems!" I said to myself, yet felt it a terrible thing to walk on a sea where such fishes disported themselves below. With that, a step or two from me, the head of a worm began to come slowly out of the earth, as big as that of a polar bear and much resembling it, with a white mane to its red neck. The drawing wriggles with which its huge length extricated itself were horrible, yet I dared not turn my eyes from them. The moment its tail was free, it lay as if exhausted, wallowing in feeble effort to burrow again.

"Does it live on the dead," I wondered, "and is it unable to hurt the living? If they scent their prey and come out, why do they leave me unharmed?"

I know now it was that the moon paralysed them.

All the night through as I walked, hideous creatures, no two alike, threatened me. In some of them, beauty of colour enhanced loathliness of shape : one large serpent was covered from head to distant tail with feathers of glorious hues.

I became at length so accustomed to their hurtless menaces that I fell to beguiling the way with the invention of monstrosities, never suspecting that I owed each moment of life to the staring moon. Though hers was no primal radiance, it so hampered the evil things, that I walked in safety. For light is yet light, if but the last of a countless series of reflections! How swiftly would not my feet have carried me over the restless soil, had I known that, if still within their range when her lamp ceased to shine on the cursed spot, I should that moment be at the mercy of such as had no mercy, the centre of a writhing heap of hideousness, every individual of it as terrible as before it had but seemed! Fool of ignorance, I watched the descent of the weary, solemn anxious moon down the widening vault above me, with no worse uneasiness than the dread of losing my way—where as yet I had indeed no way to lose.

I was drawing near the hills I had made my goal, and she was now not far from their sky-line, when the soundless wallowing ceased, and the burrow lay motionless and bare. Then I saw, slowly walking over the light soil, the form of a woman. A white mist floated about her, now assuming, now losing to reassume the shape of a garment, as it gathered to her or was blown from her by a wind that dogged her steps.

She was beautiful, but with such a pride at once and misery on her countenance that I could hardly believe what yet I saw. Up and down she walked, vainly endeavouring to lay hold of the mist and wrap it around her. The eyes in the beautiful face were dead, and on her left side was a dark spot, against which she would now and then press her hand, as if to stifle pain or sickness. Her hair hung nearly to her feet, and sometimes the wind would so mix it with the mist that I could not distinguish the one from the other; but when it fell gathering together again, it shone a pale gold in the moonlight.

Suddenly pressing both hands on her heart, she fell to the ground, and the mist rose from her and melted in the air. I ran to her. But she began to writhe in such torture that I stood aghast. A moment more and her legs, hurrying from her body, sped away serpents. From her shoulders fled her arms as in terror, serpents also. Then something flew up from her like a bat, and when I looked again, she was gone. The ground rose like the sea in a storm; terror laid hold upon me; I turned to the hills and ran.

I was already on the slope of their base, when the moon sank behind one of their summits, leaving me in its shadow. Behind me rose a waste and sickening cry, as of frustrate desire—the only sound I had heard since the fall of the dead butterfly; it made my heart shake like a flag in the wind. I turned, saw many dark objects bounding after me, and made for the crest of a ridge on which the moon still shone. She seemed to linger there that I might see to defend myself. Soon I came in sight of her, and climbed the faster.

Crossing the shadow of a rock, I heard the creatures panting at my heels. But just as the foremost threw himself upon me with a snarl of greedy hate, we rushed into the moon together. She flashed out an angry light, and he fell from me a bodiless blotch. Strength came to me, and I turned on the rest. But one by one as they darted into the light, they dropped with a howl; and I saw or fancied a strange smile on the round face above me.

I climbed to the top of the ridge : far away shone the moon, sinking to a low horizon. The air was pure and strong. I descended a little way, found it warmer, and sat down to wait the dawn.

The moon went below, and the world again was dark.

CHAPTER XI

THE EVIL WOOD

I FELL FAST ASLEEP, and when I woke the sun was rising. I went to the top again, and looked back : the hollow I had crossed in the moonlight lay without sign of life. Could it be that the calm expanse before me swarmed with creatures of devouring greed?

I turned and looked over the land through which my way must lie. It seemed a wide desert, with a patch of a different colour in the distance that might be a forest. Sign of presence, human or animal, was none—smoke or dust or shadow of cultivation. Not a cloud floated in the clear heaven; no thinnest haze curtained any segment of its circling rim.

I descended, and set out for the imaginable forest : something alive might be there; on this side of it could not well be anything !

When I reached the plain, I found it, as far as my sight could go, of rock, here flat and channeled, there humped and pinnacled—evidently the wide bed of a vanished river, scored by innumerable water-runs, without a trace of moisture in them. Some of the channels bore a dry moss, and some of the rocks a few lichens almost as hard as themselves. The air, once "filled with pleasant noise of waters," was silent as death. It took me the whole day to reach the patch,—which I found indeed a forest—but not a rudiment of brook or runnel had I crossed! Yet through the glowing noon I seemed haunted by an aural mirage, hearing so plainly the voice of many waters that I could hardly believe the opposing testimony of my eyes.

The sun was approaching the horizon when I left the river-bed, and entered the forest. Sunk below the tree-tops, and sending his rays between their pillar-like boles, he revealed a world of blessed shadows waiting to receive me. I had expected a pine-wood, but here were trees of many sorts, some with strong resemblances to trees I knew, others with marvellous differences from any I had ever seen. I threw myself beneath the boughs of what seemed a eucalyptus in blossom : its flowers had a hard calyx much resembling a skull, the top of which rose like a lid to let the froth-like bloom-brain overfoam its cup. From beneath the shadow of its falchion-leaves my eyes went wandering into deep after deep of the forest.

Soon, however, its doors and windows began to close, shutting up aisle and corridor and roomier glade. The night was about me, and instant and sharp the cold. Again what a night I found it! How shall I make my reader share with me its wild ghostiness?

The tree under which I lay rose high before it branched, but the boughs of it bent so low that they seemed ready to shut me in as I leaned against the smooth stem, and let my eyes wander through the brief twilight of the vanishing forest. Presently, to my listless roving gaze, the varied outlines of the clumpy foliage began to assume or imitate—say rather *suggest* other shapes than their own. A light wind began to blow; it set the boughs of a neighbour tree rocking, and all their branches aswing, every twig and every leaf blending its individual motion with the sway of its branch and the rock of its bough. Among its leafy shapes was a pack of wolves that struggled to break from a wizard's leash : greyhounds would not have strained so savagely! I watched them with an interest that grew as the wind gathered force, and their motions life.

Another mass of foliage, larger and more compact, presented my fancy with a group of horses' heads and forequarters projecting caparisoned from their stalls. Their necks kept moving up and down, with an impatience that augmented as the growing wind broke their vertical rhythm with a wilder swaying from side to side. What heads they were! how gaunt, how strange!— several of them bare skulls—one with the skin tight on its bones! One had lost the under jaw and hung low, looking unutterably weary—but now and then hove high as if to ease the bit. Above them, at the end of a branch, floated erect the form of a woman, waving her arms in imperious gesture. The definiteness of these and other leaf masses first surprised and then discomposed me : what if they should overpower my brain with seeming reality? But the twilight became darkness; the wind ceased; every shape was shut up in the night; I fell asleep.

It was still dark when I began to be aware of a far-off, confused, rushing noise, mingled with faint cries. It grew and grew until a tumult as of gathering multitudes filled the wood. On all sides at once the sounds drew nearer; the spot where I lay seemed the centre of a commotion that extended throughout the forest. I scarce moved hand or foot lest I should betray my presence to hostile things.

The moon at length approached the forest, and came slowly into it : with her first gleam the noises increased to a deafening uproar, and I began to see dim shapes about me. As she ascended and grew brighter, the noises became yet louder, and the shapes clearer. A furious battle was raging around me. Wild cries and roars of rage, shock of onset, struggle prolonged, all mingled with words articulate, surged in my ears. Curses and credos, snarls and sneers, laughter and mockery, sacred names and howls of hate, came huddling in chaotic interpenetration. Skeletons and phantoms fought in maddest confusion. Swords swept through the phantoms : they only shivered. Maces crashed on the skeletons, shattering them hideously : not one fell or ceased to fight, so long as a single joint held two bones together. Bones of men and horses lay scattered and heaped; grinding and crunching them under foot fought the skeletons. Everywhere charged the bone-gaunt white steeds; everywhere on foot or on wind-blown misty battle-horses, raged and ravened and raved the indestructible spectres; weapons and hoofs clashed and crushed; while skeleton jaws and phantom-throats swelled the deafening tumult with the war-cry of every opinion, bad or good, that had bred strife, injustice, cruelty in any world. The holiest words went with the most hating blow. Lie-distorted truths flew hurtling in the wind of javelins and bones. Every moment some one would turn against his comrades, and fight more wildly than before, *The Truth! The Truth!* still his cry. One I noted who wheeled ever in a circle, and smote on all sides. Wearied out, a pair would sit for a minute side by side, then rise and renew the fierce combat. None stooped to comfort the fallen, or stepped wide to spare him.

The moon shone till the sun rose, and all the night long I had glimpses of a woman moving at her will above the strife-tormented multitude, now on this front now on that, one outstretched arm urging the fight, the other pressed against her side. "Ye are men : slay one another!" she shouted. I saw her dead eyes and her dark spot, and recalled what I had seen the night before.

Such was the battle of the dead, which I saw and heard as I lay under the tree.

Just before sunrise, a breeze went through the forest, and a voice cried, "Let the dead bury their dead!" At the word the contending thousands dropped noiseless, and when the sun looked in, he saw never a bone, but here and there a withered branch.

I rose and resumed my journey, through as quiet a wood as ever grew out of the quiet earth. For the wind of the morning had ceased when the sun appeared, and the trees were silent. Not a bird sang, not a squirrel, mouse, or weasel showed itself, not a belated moth flew athwart my path. But as I went I kept watch over myself, nor dared let my eyes rest on any forest-shape. All the time I seemed to hear faint sounds of mattock and spade and hurtling bones : any moment my eyes might open on things I would not see! Daylight prudence muttered that perhaps, to appear, ten thousand phantoms awaited only my consenting fancy.

In the middle of the afternoon I came out of the wood—to find before me a second net of dry water-courses. I thought at first that I had wandered from my attempted line, and reversed my direction; but I soon saw it was not so, and concluded presently that I had come to another branch of the same river-bed. I began at once to cross it, and was in the bottom of a wide channel when the sun set.

I sat down to await the moon, and growing sleepy, stretched myself on the moss. The moment my head was down, I heard the sounds of rushing streams—all sorts of sweet watery noises. The veiled melody of the molten music sang me into a dreamless sleep, and when I woke the sun was already up, and the wrinkled country widely visible. Covered with shadows it lay striped and mottled like the skin of some wild animal. As the sun rose the shadows diminished, and it seemed as if the rocks were re-absorbing the darkness that had oozed out of them during the night.

Hitherto I had loved my Arab mare and my books more, I fear, than live man or woman; now at length my soul was athirst for a human presence, and I longed even after those inhabitants of this alien world whom the raven had so vaguely described as nearest my sort. With heavy yet hoping heart, and mind haunted by a doubt whether I was going in any direction at all, I kept wearily travelling "north-west and by south."

CHAPTER XII

FRIENDS AND FOES

COMING, IN ONE of the channels, upon what seemed a little shrub, the outlying picket, I trusted, of an army behind it, I knelt to look at it closer. It bore a small fruit, which, as I did not recognise it, I feared to gather and eat. Little I thought that I was watched from behind the rocks by hundreds of eyes eager with the question whether I would or would not take it.

I came to another plant somewhat bigger, then to another larger still, and at length to clumps of a like sort; by which time I saw that they were not shrubs but dwarf-trees. Before I reached the bank of this second branch of the river-bed, I found the channels so full of them that it was with difficulty I crossed such as I could not jump. In one I heard a great rush, as of a multitude of birds from an ivied wall, but saw nothing.

I came next to some large fruit-bearing trees, but what they bore looked coarse. They stood on the edge of a hollow, which evidently had once been the basin of a lake. From the left a forest seemed to flow into and fill it; but while the trees above were of many sorts, those in the hollow were almost entirely fruit-bearing.

I went a few yards down the slope of grass mingled with moss, and stretched myself upon it weary. A little farther down stood a tiny tree full of rosiest apples no bigger than small cherries, its top close to my hand; I pulled and ate one of them. Finding it delicious, I was in the act of taking another, when a sudden shouting of children, mingled with laughter clear and sweet as the music of a brook, startled me with delight.

"He likes our apples! He likes our apples! He's a good giant! He's a good giant!" cried many little voices.

"He's a giant!" objected one.

"He *is* rather big," assented another, "but littleness isn't everything! It won't keep you from growing big and stupid except you take care!"

I rose on my elbow and stared. Above and about and below me stood a multitude of children, apparently of all ages, some just able to run alone, and some about twelve or thirteen. Three or four seemed older. They stood in a small knot, a little apart, and were less excited than the rest. The many were chattering in groups, declaiming and contradicting, like a crowd of grown people in a city, only with greater merriment, better manners, and more sense.

I gathered that, by the approach of my hand to a second apple, they knew that I liked the first; but how from that they argued me good, I did not see, nor wondered that one of them at least should suggest caution. I did not open my mouth, for I was afraid of frightening them, and sure I should learn more by listening than by asking questions. For I understood nearly all they said—at which I was not surprised : to understand is not more wonderful than to love.

There came a movement and slight dispersion among them, and presently a sweet, innocent-looking, lovingly roguish little fellow handed me a huge green apple. Silence fell on the noisy throng; all waited expectant.

"Eat, good giant," he said.

I sat up, took the apple, smiled thanks, and would have eaten; but the moment I bit into it, I flung it far away.

Again rose a shout of delight; they flung themselves upon me, so as nearly to smother me; they kissed my face and hands; they laid hold of my legs; they clambered about my arms and shoulders, embracing my head and neck. I came to the ground at last, overwhelmed with the lovely little goblins.

"Good, good giant!" they cried. "We knew you would come! Oh you dear, good, strong giant!"

The babble of their talk sprang up afresh, and ever the jubilant shout would rise anew from hundreds of clear little throats.

Again came a sudden silence. Those around me drew back; those atop of me got off and began trying to set me on my feet. Upon their sweet faces, concern had taken the place of merriment.

"Get up, good giant!" said a little girl. "Make haste! much haste! He saw you throw his apple away!"

Before she ended, I was on my feet. She stood pointing up the slope. On the brow of it was a clownish, bad-looking fellow, a few inches taller than myself. He looked hostile, but I saw no reason to fear him, for he had no weapon, and my little friends had vanished every one.

He began to descend, and I, in the hope of better footing and position, to go up. He growled like a beast as he turned toward me.

Reaching a more level spot, I stood and waited for him. As he came near, he held out his hand. I would have taken it in friendly fashion, but he drew it back, threatened a blow, and held it out again. Then I understood him to claim the apple I had flung away, whereupon I made a grimace of dislike and a gesture of rejection.

He answered with a howl of rage that seemed to say, 'Do you dare tell me my apple was not fit to eat?"

"One bad apple may grow on the best tree," I said.

Whether he perceived my meaning I cannot tell, but he made a stride nearer, and I stood on my guard. He delayed his assault, however, until a second giant, much like him, who had been stealing up behind me, was close enough, when he rushed upon me. I met him with a good blow in the face, but the other struck me on the back of the head, and between them I was soon overpowered.

They dragged me into the wood above the valley, where their tribe lived—in wretched huts, built of fallen branches and a few stones. Into one of these they pushed me, there threw me on the ground, and kicked me. A woman was present, who looked on with indifference.

I may here mention that during my captivity I hardly learned to distinguish the women from the men, they differed so little. Often I wondered whether I had not come upon a sort of fungoid people, with just enough mind to give them motion and the expressions of anger and greed. Their food, which consisted of tubers, bulbs, and fruits, was to me inexpressibly disagreeable, but nothing offended them so much as to show dislike to it. I was cuffed by the women and kicked by the men because I would not swallow it.

I lay on the floor that night hardly able to move, but I slept a good deal, and woke a little refreshed. In the morning they dragged me to the valley, and tying my feet, with a long rope, to a tree, put a flat stone with a saw-like edge in my left hand. I shifted it to the right; they kicked me, and put it again in the left; gave me to understand that I was to scrape the bark off every branch that had no fruit on it; kicked me once more, and left me.

I set about the dreary work in the hope that by satisfying them I should be left very much to myself—to make my observations and choose my time for escape. Happily one of the dwarf-trees grew close by me, and every other minute I plucked and ate a small fruit, which wonderfully refreshed and strengthened me.

CHAPTER XIII

THE LITTLE ONES

I HAD BEEN AT work but a few moments, when I heard small voices near me, and presently the Little Ones, as I soon found they called themselves, came creeping out from among the tiny trees that like brushwood filled the spaces between the big ones. In a minute there were scores and scores about me. I made signs that the giants had but just left me, and were not far off; but they laughed, and told me the wind was quite clean.

"They are too blind to see us," they said, and laughed like a multitude of sheep-bells.

"Do you like that rope about your ankles?" asked one.

"I want them to think I cannot take it off," I replied.

"They can scarcely see their own feet!" he rejoined. "Walk with short steps and they will think the rope is all right."

As he spoke, he danced with merriment.

One of the bigger girls got down on her knees to untie the clumsy knot. I smiled, thinking those pretty fingers could do nothing with it, but in a moment it was loose.

They then made me sit down, and fed me with delicious little fruits; after which the smaller of them began to play with me in the wildest fashion, so that it was impossible for me to resume my work. When the first grew tired, others took their places, and this went on until the sun was setting, and heavy steps were heard approaching. The little people started from me, and I made haste to put the rope round my ankles.

"We must have a care," said the girl who had freed me; "a crush of one of their horrid stumpy feet might kill a very little one!"

"Can they not perceive you at all then?"

"They might see something move; and if the children were in a heap on the top of you, as they were a moment ago, it would be terrible; for they hate every live thing but themselves. —Not that they are much alive either!"

She whistled like a bird. The next instant not one of them was to be seen or heard, and the girl herself had disappeared.

It was my master, as doubtless he counted himself, come to take me home. He freed my ankles, and dragged me to the door of his hut; there he threw me on the ground, again tied my feet, gave me a kick, and left me.

Now I might at once have made my escape; but at length I had friends, and could not think of leaving them. They were so charming, so full of winsome ways, that I must see more of them! I must know them better! "To-morrow," I said to myself with delight, "I shall see them again!" But from the moment there was silence in the huts until I fell asleep, I heard them whispering all about me, and knew that I was lovingly watched by a multitude. After that, I think they hardly ever left me quite alone.

I did not come to know the giants at all, and I believe there was scarcely anything in them to know. They never became in the least friendly, but they were much too stupid to invent cruelties. Often I avoided a bad kick by catching the foot and giving its owner a fall, upon which he never, on that occasion, renewed his attempt.

But the little people were constantly doing and saying things that pleased, often things that surprised me. Every day I grew more loath to leave them. While I was at work, they would keep coming and going, amusing and delighting me, and taking all the misery, and much of the weariness out of my monotonous toil. Very soon I loved them more than I can tell. They did not know much, but they were very wise, and seemed capable of learning anything. I had no bed save the bare ground, but almost as often as I woke, it was in a nest of children—one or other of them in my arms, though which I seldom could tell until the light came, for they ordered the succession among themselves. When one crept into my bosom, unconsciously I clasped him there, and the rest lay close around me, the smaller nearer. It is hardly necessary to say that I did not suffer much from the nightly cold! The first thing they did in the morning, and the last before sunset, was to bring the good giant plenty to eat.

One morning I was surprised on waking to find myself alone. As I came to my senses, however, I heard subdued sounds of approach, and presently the girl already mentioned, the tallest and gravest of the community, and regarded by all as their mother, appeared from the wood, followed by the multitude in jubilation manifest—but silent lest they should rouse the sleeping giant at whose door I lay. She carried a boy-baby in her arms: hitherto a girl-baby, apparently about a year old, had been the youngest. Three of the bigger girls were her nurses, but they shared their treasure with all the rest. Among the Little Ones, dolls were unknown; the bigger had the smaller, and the smaller the still less, to tend and play with.

Lona came to me and laid the infant in my arms. The baby opened his eyes and looked at me, closed them again, and fell asleep.

"He loves you already!" said the girl.

"Where did you find him?" I asked.

"In the wood, of course," she answered, her eyes beaming

with delight, "—where we always find them. Isn't he a beauty? We've been out all night looking for him. Sometimes it is not easy to find!"

"How do you know when there is one to find?" I asked.

"I cannot tell," she replied. "Every one makes haste to tell the other, but we never find out who told first. Sometimes I think one must have said it asleep, and another heard it half-awake. When there is a baby in the wood, no one can stop to ask questions; and when we have found it, then it is too late."

"Do more boy or girl babies come to the wood?"

"They don't come to the wood; we go to the wood and find them."

"Are there more boys or girls of you now?"

I had found that to ask precisely the same question twice, made them knit their brows.

"I do not know," she answered.

"You can count them, surely!"

"We never do that. We shouldn't like to be counted."

"Why?"

"It wouldn't be smooth. We would rather not know."

"Where do the babies come from first?"

"From the wood—always. There is no other place they can come from."

She knew where they came from last, and thought nothing else was to be known about their advent.

"How often do you find one?"

"Such a happy thing takes all the glad we've got, and we forget the last time. You too are glad to have him—are you not, good giant?"

"Yes, indeed, I am!" I answered. "But how do you feed him?"

"I will show you," she rejoined, and went away—to return directly with two or three ripe little plums. She put one to the baby's lips.

"He would open his mouth if he were awake," she said, and took him in her arms.

She squeezed a drop to the surface, and again held the fruit to the baby's lips. Without waking he began at once to suck it, and she went on slowly squeezing until nothing but skin and stone were left.

"There!" she cried, in a tone of gentle triumph. "A big-apple world it would be with nothing for the babies! We wouldn't stop in it—would we, darling? We would leave it to the bad giants!"

"But what if you let the stone into the baby's mouth when you were feeding him?" I said.

"No mother would do that," she replied. "I shouldn't be fit to have a baby!"

I thought what a lovely woman she would grow. But what became of them when they grew up? Where did they go? That brought me again to the question—where did they come from first?

"Will you tell me where you lived before?" I said.

"Here," she replied.

"Have you *never* lived anywhere else?" I ventured.

"Never. We all came from the wood. Some think we dropped out of the trees."

"How is it there are so many of you quite little?"

"I don't understand. Some are less and some are bigger. I am very big."

"Baby will grow bigger, won't he?"

"Of course he will!"

"And will you grow bigger?"

"I don't think so. I hope not. I am the biggest. It frightens me sometimes."

"Why should it frighten you?"

She gave me no answer.

"How old are you?" I resumed.

"I do not know what you mean. We are all just that."

"How big will the baby grow?"

"I cannot tell.—Some," she added, with a trouble in her voice, "begin to grow after we think they have stopped.—That is a frightful thing. We don't talk about it!"

"What makes it frightful?"

She was silent for a moment, then answered,

"We fear they may be beginning to grow giants."

"Why should you fear that?"

"Because it is so terrible—I don't want to talk about it!"

She pressed the baby to her bosom with such an anxious look that I dared not further question her.

Before long I began to perceive in two or three of the smaller children some traces of greed and selfishness, and noted that the bigger girls cast on these a not infrequent glance of anxiety.

None of them put a hand to my work : they would do nothing for the giants! But they never relaxed their loving ministrations to me. They would sing to me, one after another, for hours; climb the tree to reach my mouth and pop fruit into it with their dainty little fingers; and they kept constant watch against the approach of a giant.

Sometimes they would sit and tell me stories—mostly very childish, and often seeming to mean hardly anything. Now and then they would call a general assembly to amuse me. On one such occasion a moody little fellow sang me a strange crooning song, with a refrain so pathetic that, although unintelligible to me, it caused the tears to run down my face. This phenomenon made those who saw it regard me with much perplexity. Then first I bethought myself that I had not once, in that world, looked on water, falling or lying or running. Plenty there had been in some long vanished age—that was plain enough—but the Little Ones had never seen any before they saw my tears! They had, nevertheless, it seemed, some dim, instinctive perception of their origin; for a very small child went up to the singer, shook his clenched pud in his face, and said something like this: " 'Ou skeeze ze juice out of ze good giant's seeberries! Bad giant!"

"How is it," I said one day to Lona, as she sat with the baby in her arms at the foot of my tree, "that I never see any children among the giants?"

She stared a little, as if looking in vain for some sense in the question, then replied,

"They are giants; there are no little ones."

"Have they never any children?" I asked.

"No; there are never any in the wood for them. They do not love them. If they saw ours, they would stamp them."

"Is there always the same number of the giants then? I thought, before I had time to know better, that they were your fathers and mothers."

She burst into the merriest laughter, and said,

"No, good giant; *we* are *their* firsters."

But as she said it, the merriment died out of her, and she looked scared.

I stopped working, and gazed at her, bewildered.

"How *can* that be?" I exclaimed.

"I do not say; I do not understand," she answered. "But we were here and they not. They go from us. I am sorry, but we cannot help it. *They* could have helped it."

"How long have you been here?" I asked, more and more puzzled—in the hope of some side-light on the matter.

"Always, I think," she replied. "I think somebody made us always."

I turned to my scraping.

She saw I did not understand.

"The giants were not made always," she resumed. "If a Little One doesn't care, he grows greedy, and then lazy, and then big, and then stupid, and then bad. The dull creatures don't know that they come from us. Very few of them believe we are any-where. They say *Nonsense!*—Look at little Blunty: he is eating one of their apples! He will be the next! Oh! oh! he will soon be big and bad and ugly, and not know it!"

The child stood by himself a little way off, eating an apple nearly as big as his head. I had often thought he did not look so good as the rest; now he looked disgusting.

"I will take the horrid thing from him!" I cried.

"It is no use," she answered sadly. "We have done all we can, and it is too late! We were afraid he was growing, for he would not believe anything told him; but when he refused to share his berries, and said he had gathered them for himself, then we knew it! He is a glutton, and there is no hope of him.—It makes me sick to see him eat!"

"Could not some of the boys watch him, and not let him touch the poisonous things?"

"He may have them if he will: it is all one—to eat the apples, and to be a boy that would eat them if he could. No; he must go to the giants! He belongs to them. You can see how much bigger he is than when first you came! He is bigger since yesterday."

"He is as like that hideous green lump in his hand as boy could look!"

"It suits what he is making himself."

"His head and it might change places!"

"Perhaps they do!"

"Does he want to be a giant?"

"He hates the giants, but he is making himself one all the same: he likes their apples! Oh baby, baby, he was just such a darling as you when we found him!"

"He will be very miserable when he find himself a giant!"

"Oh, no; he will like it well enough! That is the worst of it."

"Will he hate the Little Ones?"

"He will be like the rest; he will not remember us—most likely will not believe there are Little Ones. He will not care; he will eat his apples."

"Do tell me how it will come about. I understand your world so little! I come from a world where everything is different."

"I do not know about *world*. What is it? What more but a word in your beautiful big mouth?—That makes it something!"

"Never mind about the word; tell me what next will happen to Blunty."

"He will wake one morning and find himself a giant—not like you, good giant, but like any other bad giant. You will hardly know him, but I will tell you which. He will think he has been a giant always, and will not know you, or any of us. The giants have lost themselves, Peony says, and that is why they never smile. I wonder whether they are not glad because they are bad, or bad because they are not glad. But they can't be glad when they have no babies! I wonder what *bad* means, good giant!"

"I wish I knew no more about it than you!" I returned. "But I try to be good, and mean to keep on trying."

"So do I—and that is how I know you are good."

A long pause followed.

"Then you do not know where the babies come from into the wood?" I said, making one attempt more.

"There is nothing to know there," she answered. "They are in the wood; they grow there."

"Then how is it you never find one before it is quite grown?" I asked.

She knitted her brows and was silent a moment:

"They're not there till they're finished," she said.

"It is a pity the little sillies can't speak till they've forgotten everything they had to tell!" I remarked.

"Little Tolma, the last before this baby, looked as if she had something to tell, when I found her under a beech-tree, sucking her thumb, but she hadn't. She only looked up at me—oh, so sweetly! *She* will never go bad and grow big! When they begin to grow big they care for nothing but bigness; and when they cannot grow any bigger, they try to grow fatter. The bad giants are very proud of being fat."

"So they are in my world," I said; "only they do not say *fat* there, they say *rich*."

"In one of their houses," continued Lona, "sits the biggest and fattest of them—so proud that nobody can see him; and the giants go to his house at certain times, and call out to him, and tell him how fat he is, and beg him to make them strong to eat more and grow fat like him."

The rumour at length reached my ears that Blunty had vanished. I saw a few grave faces among the bigger ones, but he did not seem to be much missed.

The next morning Lona came to me and whispered,

"Look! look there—by that quince-tree : that is the giant that was Blunty!—Would you have known him?"

"Never," I answered. "—But now you tell me, I could fancy it might be Blunty staring through a fog! He *does* look stupid!"

"He is for ever eating those apples now!" she said. "That is what comes of Little Ones that *won't* be little!"

"They call it growing-up in my world!" I said to myself. "If only she would teach me to grow the other way, and become a Little One!—Shall I ever be able to laugh like them?"

I had had the chance, and had flung it from me! Blunty and I were alike! He did not know his loss, and I had to be taught mine!

CHAPTER XIV

A CRISIS

For a time I had no desire save to spend my life with the Little Ones. But soon other thoughts and feelings began to influence me. First awoke the vague sense that I ought to be doing something; that I was not meant for the fattening of boors! Then it came to me that I was in a marvellous world, of which it was assuredly my business to discover the ways and laws; and that, if I would do anything in return for the children's goodness, I must learn more about them than they could tell me, and to that end must be free. Surely, I thought, no suppression of their growth can be essential to their loveliness and truth and purity! Not in any world could the possibility exist of such a discord between constitution and its natural outcome! Life and law cannot be so at variance that perfection must be gained by thwarting development! But the growth of the Little Ones *was* arrested! something interfered with it: what was it? Lona seemed the eldest of them, yet not more than fifteen, and had been long in charge of a multitude, in semblance and mostly in behaviour merest children, who regarded her as their mother! Were they growing at all? I doubted it. Of time they had scarcely the idea; of their own age they knew nothing! Lona herself thought she had lived always! Full of wisdom and empty of knowledge, she was at once their Love and their Law! But what seemed to me her ignorance might in truth be my own lack of insight! Her one anxiety plainly was, that her Little Ones should not grow, and change into bad giants! Their "good giant" was bound to do his best for them : without more knowledge of their nature, and some knowledge of their history, he could do nothing, and must therefore leave them! They would only be as they were before; they had in no way become dependent on me; they were still my protectors, I was not theirs; my presence but brought them more in danger of their idiotic neighbours! I longed to teach them many things : I must first understand more of those I would teach! Knowledge no doubt made bad people worse, but it must make good people better! I was convinced they would learn mathematics; and might they not be taught to write down the dainty melodies they murmured and forgot?

The conclusion was, that I must rise and continue my travels, in the hope of coming upon some elucidation of the fortunes and destiny of the bewitching little creatures.

My design, however, would not so soon have passed into action, but for what now occurred.

To prepare them for my temporary absence, I was one day telling them while at work that I would long ago have left the bad giants, but that I loved the Little Ones so much—when, as by one accord, they came rushing and crowding upon me; they scrambled over each other and up the tree and dropped on my head, until I was nearly smothered. With three very little ones in my arms, one on each shoulder clinging to my neck, one standing straight up on my head, four or five holding me fast by the legs, others grappling my body and arms, and a multitude climbing and descending upon these, I was helpless as one overwhelmed by lava. Absorbed in the merry struggle, not one of them saw my tyrant coming until he was almost upon me. With just one cry of "Take care, good giant!" they ran from me like mice, they dropped from me like hedgehogs, they flew from me up the tree like squirrels, and the same moment, sharp round the stem came the bad giant, and dealt me such a blow on the head with a stick that I fell to the ground. The children told me afterwards that they sent him "such a many bumps of big apples and stones" that he was frightened, and ran blundering home.

When I came to myself it was night. Above me were a few pale stars that expected the moon. I thought I was alone. My head ached badly, and I was terribly athirst.

I turned wearily on my side. The moment my ear touched the ground, I heard the gushing and gurgling of water, and the soft noises made me groan with longing. At once I was amid a multitude of silent children, and delicious little fruits began to visit my lips. They came and came until my thirst was gone.

Then I was aware of sounds I had never heard there before; the air was full of little sobs.

I tried to sit up. A pile of small bodies instantly heaped itself at my back. Then I struggled to my feet, with much pushing and pulling from the Little Ones, who were wonderfully strong for their size.

"You must go away, good giant," they said. "When the bad giants see you hurt, they will all trample on you."

"I think I must," I answered.

"Go and grow strong, and come again," they said.

"I will," I replied—and sat down.

"Indeed you must go at once!" whispered Lona, who had been supporting me, and now knelt beside me.

"I listened at his door," said one of the bigger boys, "and heard the bad giant say to his wife that he had found you idle, talking to a lot of moles and squirrels, and when he beat you,

they tried to kill him. He said you were a wizard, and they must
knock you, or they would have no peace."

"I will go at once," I said, "and come back as soon as I have
found out what is wanted to make you bigger and stronger."

"We don't want to be bigger," they answered, looking very
serious. "We *won't* grow bad giants!—We are strong now; you
don't know how much strong!"

It was no use holding them out a prospect that had not any
attraction for them! I said nothing more, but rose and moved
slowly up the slope of the valley. At once they formed themselves
into a long procession; some led the way, some walked with me
helping me, and the rest followed. They kept feeding me as we
went.

"You are broken," they said, "and much red juice has run
out of you : put some in."

When we reached the edge of the valley, there was the moon
just lifting her forehead over the rim of the horizon.

"She has come to take care of you, and show you the way,"
said Lona.

I questioned those about me as we walked, and learned there
was a great place with a giant-girl for queen. When I asked if
it was a city, they said they did not know. Neither could they
tell how far off, or in what direction it was, or what was the
giant-girl's name; all they knew was, that she hated the Little
Ones, and would like to kill them, only she could not find them.
I asked how they knew that; Lona answered that she had always
known it. If the giant-girl came to look for them, they must hide
hard, she said. When I told them I should go and ask her why
she hated them, they cried out,

"No, no! she will kill you, good giant; she will kill you! She
is an awful bad-giant witch!"

I asked them where I was to go then. They told me that,
beyond the baby-forest, away where the moon came from, lay a
smooth green country, pleasant to the feet, without rocks or trees.
But when I asked how I was to set out for it,

"The moon will tell you, we think," they said.

They were taking me up the second branch of the river bed :
when they saw that the moon had reached her height, they
stopped to return.

"We have never gone so far from our trees before," they said.

"Now mind you watch how you go, that you may see inside your eyes how to come back to us."

"And beware of the giant-woman that lives in the desert," said one of the bigger girls as they were turning. "I suppose you have heard of her!"

"No," I answered.

"Then take care not to go near her. She is called the Cat-woman. She is awfully ugly—*and scratches.*"

As soon as the bigger ones stopped, the smaller had begun to run back. The others now looked at me gravely for a moment, and then walked slowly away. Last to leave me, Lona held up the baby to be kissed, gazed in my eyes, whispered, "The Cat-woman will not hurt *you*," and went without another word. I stood a while, gazing after them through the moonlight, then turned and, with a heavy heart, began my solitary journey. Soon the laughter of the Little Ones overtook me, like sheep-bells innumerable, rippling the air, and echoing in the rocks about me. I turned again, and again gazed after them : they went gamboling along, with never a care in their sweet souls. But Lona walked apart with her baby.

Pondering as I went, I recalled many traits of my little friends.

Once when I suggested that they should leave the country of the bad giants, and go with me to find another, they answered, "But that would be to *not* ourselves!"—so strong in them was the love of place that their country seemed essential to their very being! Without ambition or fear, discomfort or greed, they had no motive to desire any change; they knew of nothing amiss; and, except their babies, they had never had a chance of helping any one but myself :—How were they to grow? But again, Why should they grow? In seeking to improve their conditions, might I not do them harm, and only harm? To enlarge their minds after the notions of my world—might it not be to distort and weaken them? Their fear of growth as a possible start for giant-hood might be instinctive!

The part of philanthropist is indeed a dangerous one; and the man who would do his neighbour good must first study how not to do him evil, and must begin by pulling the beam out of his own eye.

CHAPTER XV

A STRANGE HOSTESS

I TRAVELLED ON ATTENDED by the moon. As usual she was full—I had never seen her other—and to-night as she sank I thought I perceived something like a smile on her countenance.

When her under edge was a little below the horizon, there appeared in the middle of her disc, as if it had been painted upon it, a cottage, through the open door and window of which she shone; and with the sight came the conviction that I was expected there. Almost immediately the moon was gone, and the cottage had vanished; the night was rapidly growing dark, and my way being across a close succession of small ravines, I resolved to remain where I was and expect the morning. I stretched myself, therefore, in a sandy hollow, made my supper off the fruits the children had given me at parting, and was soon asleep.

I woke suddenly, saw above me constellations unknown to my former world, and had lain for a while gazing at them, when I became aware of a figure seated on the ground a little way from and above me. I was startled, as one is on discovering all at once that he is not alone. The figure was between me and the sky, so that I saw its outline well. From where I lay low in the hollow, it seemed larger than human.

It moved its head, and then first I saw that its back was toward me.

"Will you not come with me?" said a sweet, mellow voice, unmistakably a woman's.

Wishing to learn more of my hostess,

"I thank you," I replied, "but I am not uncomfortable here. Where would you have me go? I like sleeping in the open air."

"There is no hurt in the air," she returned; "but the creatures that roam the night in these parts are not such as a man would willingly have about him while he sleeps."

"I have not been disturbed," I said.

"No; I have been sitting by you ever since you lay down."

"That is very kind of you! How came you to know I was here? Why do you show me such favour?"

"I saw you," she answered, still with her back to me, "in the light of the moon, just as she went down. I see badly in the day, but at night perfectly. The shadow of my house would have hidden you, but both its doors were open. I was out on the waste, and saw you go into this hollow. You were asleep, however, before I could reach you, and I was not willing to disturb you. People are frightened if I come on them suddenly. They call me the Cat-woman. It is not my name."

I remembered what the children had told me—that she was very ugly, and scratched. But her voice was gentle, and its tone a little apologetic : she could not be a bad giantess!

"You shall not hear it from me," I answered. "Please tell me what I *may* call you!"

"When you know me, call me by the name that seems to you to fit me," she replied : "that will tell me what sort you are. People do not often give me the right one. It is well when they do."

"I suppose, madam, you live in the cottage I saw in the heart of the moon?"

"I do. I live there alone, except when I have visitors. It is a poor place, but I do what I can for my guests, and sometimes their sleep is sweet to them."

Her voice entered into me, and made me feel strangely still.

"I will go with you, madam," I said, rising.

She rose at once, and without a glance behind her led the way. I could see her just well enough to follow. She was taller than myself, but not so tall as I had thought her. That she never turned her face to me made me curious—nowise apprehensive, her voice rang so true. But how was I to fit her with a name who could not see her? I strove to get alongside of her, but failed : when I quickened my pace she quickened hers, and kept easily ahead of me. At length I did begin to grow a little afraid. Why was she so careful not to be seen? Extraordinary ugliness would account for it : she might fear terrifying me! Horror of an inconceivable monstrosity began to assail me : was I following through the dark an unheard of hideousness? Almost I repented of having accepted her hospitality.

Neither spoke, and the silence grew unbearable. I *must* break it!

"I want to find my way," I said, "to a place I have heard of, but whose name I have not yet learned. Perhaps you can tell it me!"

"Describe it, then, and I will direct you. The stupid Bags know nothing, and the careless little Lovers forget almost everything."

"Where do those live?"

"You are just come from them!"

"I never heard those names before!"

"You would not hear them. Neither people knows its own name!"

"Strange!"

"Perhaps so! but hardly any one anywhere knows his own name! It would make many a fine gentleman stare to hear himself addressed by what is really his name!"

I held my peace, beginning to wonder what my name might be.

"What now do you fancy yours?" she went on, as if aware of my thought. "But, pardon me, it is a matter of no consequence."

I had actually opened my mouth to answer her, when I discovered that my name was gone from me. I could not even recall the first letter of it! This was the second time I had been asked my name and could not tell it!

"Never mind," she said; "it is not wanted. Your real name, indeed, is written on your forehead, but at present it whirls about so irregularly that nobody can read it. I will do my part to steady it. Soon it will go slower, and, I hope, settle at last."

This startled me, and I was silent.

We had left the channels and walked a long time, but no sign of the cottage yet appeared.

"The Little Ones told me," I said at length, "of a smooth green country, pleasant to the feet!"

"Yes?" she returned.

"They told me too of a girl giantess that was queen somewhere: is that her country?"

"There is a city in that grassy land," she replied, "where a woman is princess. The city is called Bulika. But certainly the princess is not a girl! She is older than this world, and came to it from yours—with a terrible history, which is not over yet. She is an evil person, and prevails much with the Prince of the Power of the Air. The people of Bulika were formerly simple folk, tilling the ground and pasturing sheep. She came among them, and they received her hospitably. She taught them to dig for diamonds and opals and sell them to strangers, and made them give up tillage and pasturage and build a city. One day they found a huge snake and killed it; which so enraged her that she declared herself their princess, and became terrible to them. The name of the country at that time was *The Land of Waters*; for the dry channels, of which you have crossed so many, were then overflowing with live torrents; and the valley, where now the Bags and the Lovers have their fruit-trees, was a lake that received a great part of them. But the wicked princess gathered up in her lap what she could of the water over the whole country, closed it in an egg, and carried it away. Her lap, however, would not hold more than half of it; and the instant she was gone, what she had not yet taken fled away underground, leaving the country as dry and dusty as her own heart. Were it not for the waters under it, every living thing would long ago have perished from it. For where no water is, no rain falls; and where no rain falls, no springs rise. Ever since then, the princess has lived in Bulika, holding the inhabitants in constant terror, and doing what she can to keep them from multiplying. Yet they boast and believe themselves a prosperous, and certainly are a self-satisfied people—good at bargaining and buying, good at selling and cheating; holding well together for a common interest, and utterly treacherous where interests clash; proud of their princess and her power, and despising every one they get the better of; never doubting themselves the most honourable of all the nations, and each man counting himself better than any other. The depth of their worthlessness and height of their vainglory no one can understand who has not been there to see, who has not learned to know the miserable misgoverned and self-deceived creatures."

"I thank you, madam. And now, if you please, will you tell me something about the Little Ones—the Lovers? I long heartily to serve them. Who and what are they? and how do they come to be there? Those children are the greatest wonder I have found in this world of wonders."

"In Bulika you may, perhaps, get some light on those matters. There is an ancient poem in the library of the palace, I am told, which of course no one there can read, but in which it is plainly written that after the Lovers have gone through great troubles and learned their own name, they will fill the land, and make the giants their slaves."

"By that time they will have grown a little, will they not?" I said.

"Yes, they will have grown; yet I think too they will not have grown. It is possible to grow and not to grow, to grow less and to grow bigger, both at once—yes, even to grow by means of not growing!"

"Your words are strange, madam!" I rejoined. "But I have heard it said that some words, because they mean more, appear to mean less!"

"That is true, and such words *have* to be understood. It were well for the princess of Bulika if she heard what the very silence of the land is shouting in her ears all day long! But she is far too clever to understand anything."

"Then I suppose, when the little Lovers are grown, their land will have water again?"

"Not exactly so : when they are thirsty enough, they will have water, and when they have water, they will grow. To grow, they must have water. And, beneath, it is flowing still."

"I have heard that water twice," I said; "—once when I lay down to wait for the moon—and when I woke the sun was shining! and once when I fell, all but killed by the bad giant. Both times came the voices of the water, and healed me."

The woman never turned her head, and kept always a little before me, but I could hear every word that left her lips, and her voice much reminded me of the woman's in the house of death. Much of what she said, I did not understand, and therefore cannot remember. But I forgot that I had ever been afraid of her.

We went on and on, and crossed yet a wide tract of sand before reaching the cottage. Its foundation stood in deep sand, but I could see that it was a rock. In character the cottage resembled the sexton's, but had thicker walls. The door, which was heavy and strong, opened immediately into a large bare room, which had two little windows opposite each other, without glass. My hostess walked in at the open door out of which the moon had looked, and going straight to the farthest corner, took a long white cloth from the floor, and wound it about her head and face. Then she closed the other door, in at which the moon had looked, trimmed a small horn lantern that stood on the hearth, and turned to receive me.

"You are very welcome, Mr. Vane!" she said, calling me by the name I had forgotten. "Your entertainment will be scanty, but, as the night is not far spent, and the day not at hand, it is better you should be indoors. Here you will be safe, and a little lack is not a great misery."

"I thank you heartily, madam," I replied. "But, seeing you know the name I could not tell you, may I not know yours?"

"My name is Mara," she answered.

Then I remembered the sexton and the little black cat.

"Some people," she went on, "take me for Lot's wife, lamenting over Sodom; and some think I am Rachel, weeping for her children; but I am neither of those."

"I thank you again, Mara," I said. "—May I lie here on your floor till the morning?"

"At the top of that stair," she answered, "you will find a bed—on which some have slept better than they expected, and some have waked all the night and slept all the next day. It is not a very soft one, but it is better than the sand—and there are no hyenas sniffing about it!"

The stair, narrow and steep, led straight up from the room to an unceiled and unpartitioned garret, with one wide, low dormer window. Close under the sloping roof stood a narrow bed, the sight of which with its white coverlet made me shiver, so vividly it recalled the couches in the chamber of death. On the table was a dry loaf, and beside it a cup of cold water. To me, who had tasted nothing but fruit for months, they were a feast.

"I must leave you in the dark," my hostess called from the bottom of the stair. "This lantern is all the light I have, and there are things to do to-night."

"It is of no consequence, thank you, madam," I returned. "To eat and drink, to lie down and sleep, are things that can be done in the dark."

"Rest in peace," she said.

I ate up the loaf, drank the water every drop, and laid myself down. The bed was hard, the covering thin and scanty, and the night cold : I dreamed that I lay in the chamber of death, between the warrior and the lady with the healing wound.

I woke in the middle of the night, thinking I heard low noises of wild animals.

"Creatures of the desert scenting after me, I suppose!" I said to myself, and, knowing I was safe, would have gone to sleep again. But that instant a rough purring rose to a howl under my window, and I sprang from my bed to see what sort of beast uttered it.

Before the door of the cottage, in the full radiance of the moon, a tall woman stood, clothed in white, with her back toward me. She was stooping over a large white animal like a panther, patting and stroking it with one hand, while with the other she pointed to the moon half-way up the heaven, then drew a perpendicular line to the horizon. Instantly the creature darted off with amazing swiftness in the direction indicated. For a moment my eyes followed it, then sought the woman; but she was gone, and not yet had I seen her face! Again I looked after the animal, but whether I saw or only fancied a white speck in the distance, I could not tell.—What did it mean? What was the monster-cat sent off to do? I shuddered, and went back to my bed. Then I remembered that, when I lay down in the sandy hollow outside, the moon was setting; yet here she was, a few hours after, shining in all her glory! "Everything is uncertain here," I said to myself, "—even the motions of the heavenly bodies!"

I learned afterwards that there were several moons in the service of this world, but the laws that ruled their times and different orbits I failed to discover.

Again I fell asleep, and slept undisturbed.

When I went down in the morning, I found bread and water waiting me, the loaf so large that I ate only half of it. My hostess sat muffled beside me while I broke my fast, and except to greet me when I entered, never opened her mouth until I asked her to instruct me how to arrive at Bulika. She then told me to go up the bank of the river-bed until it disappeared; then verge to the right until I came to a forest—in which I might spend a night, but which I must leave with my face to the rising moon. Keeping in the same direction, she said, until I reached a running stream, I must cross that at right angles, and go straight on until I saw the city on the horizon.

I thanked her, and ventured the remark that, looking out of the window in the night, I was astonished to see her messenger understand her so well, and go so straight and so fast in the direction she had indicated.

"If I had but that animal of yours to guide me—" I went on, hoping to learn something of its mission, but she interrupted me, saying,

"It was to Bulika she went—the shortest way."

"How wonderfully intelligent she looked!"

"Astarte knows her work well enough to be sent to do it," she answered.

"Have you many messengers like her?"

"As many as I require."

"Are they hard to teach?"

"They need no teaching. They are all of a certain breed, but not one of the breed is like another. Their origin is so natural it would seem to you incredible."

"May I not know it?"

"A new one came to me last night—from your head while you slept."

I laughed.

"All in this world seem to love mystery!" I said to myself. "Some chance word of mine suggested an idea—and in this form she embodies the small fact!"

"Then the creature is mine!" I cried.

"Not at all!" she answered. "That only can be ours in whose existence our will is a factor."

"Ha! a metaphysician too!" I remarked inside, and was silent.

"May I take what is left of the loaf?" I asked presently.

"You will want no more to-day," she replied.

"To-morrow I may!" I rejoined.

She rose and went to the door, saying as she went,

"It has nothing to do with to-morrow—but you may take it if you will."

She opened the door, and stood holding it. I rose, taking up the bread—but lingered, much desiring to see her face.

"Must I go, then?" I asked.

"No one sleeps in my house two nights together!" she answered.

"I thank you, then, for your hospitality, and bid you fare-well!" I said, and turned to go.

"The time will come when you must house with me many days and many nights," she murmured sadly through her muffling.

"Willingly," I replied.

"Nay, *not* willingly!" she answered.

I said to myself that she was right—I would not willingly be her guest a second time! but immediately my heart rebuked me, and I had scarce crossed the threshold when I turned again.

She stood in the middle of the room; her white garments lay like foamy waves at her feet, and among them the swathings of her face : it was lovely as a night of stars. Her great gray eyes looked up to heaven; tears were flowing down her pale cheeks. She reminded me not a little of the sexton's wife, although the one looked as if she had not wept for thousands of years, and the other as if she wept constantly behind the .wrappings of her beautiful head. Yet something in the very eyes that wept seemed to say, "Weeping may endure for a night, but joy cometh in the morning."

I had bowed my head for a moment, about to kneel and beg her forgiveness, when, looking up in the act, I found myself outside a doorless house. I went round and round it, but could find no entrance.

I had stopped under one of the windows, on the point of calling aloud my repentant confession, when a sudden wailing, howling scream invaded my ears, and my heart stood still. Something sprang from the window above my head, and lighted beyond me. I turned, and saw a large gray cat, its hair on end, shooting toward the river-bed. I fell with my face in the sand, and seemed to hear within the house the gentle sobbing of one who suffered but did not repent.

CHAPTER XVI

A GRUESOME DANCE

I ROSE TO RESUME my journey, and walked many a desert mile. How I longed for a mountain, or even a tall rock, from whose summit I might see across the dismal plain or the dried-up channels to some bordering hope! Yet what could such foresight have availed me? That which is within a man, not that which lies beyond his vision, is the main factor in what is about to befall him : the operation upon him is the event. Foreseeing is not understanding, else surely the prophecy latent in man would come oftener to the surface!

The sun was half-way to the horizon when I saw before me a rugged rocky ascent; but ere I reached it my desire to climb was over, and I longed to lie down. By that time the sun was almost set, and the air had begun to grow dark. At my feet lay a carpet of softest, greenest moss, couch for a king : I threw myself upon it, and weariness at once began to ebb, for, the moment my head was down, the third time I heard below me many waters, playing broken airs and ethereal harmonies with the stones of their buried channels. Loveliest chaos of music-stuff the harp aquarian kept sending up to my ears! What might not a Händel have done with that ever-recurring gurgle and bell-like drip, to the mingling and mutually destructive melodies their common refrain!

As I lay listening, my eyes went wandering up and down the rocky slope abrupt above me, reading on its face the record that down there, ages ago, rushed a cataract, filling the channels that had led me to its foot. My heart swelled at the thought of the splendid tumult, where the waves danced revelling in helpless fall, to mass their music in one organ-roar below. But soon the hidden brooks lulled me to sleep, and their lullabies mingled with my dreams.

I woke before the sun, and eagerly climbed to see what lay beyond. Alas, nothing but a desert of finest sand! Not a trace was left of the river that had plunged adown the rocks! The powdery drift had filled its course to the level of the dreary expanse! As I looked back I saw that the river had divided into two branches as it fell, that whose bank I had now followed to the foot of the rocky scaur, and that which first I crossed to the Evil Wood. The wood I descried between the two on the far horizon. Before me and to the left, the desert stretched beyond my vision, but far to the right I could see a lift in the sky-line, giving hope of the forest to which my hostess had directed me.

I sat down, and sought in my pocket the half-loaf I had brought with me—then first to understand what my hostess had meant concerning it. Verily the bread was not for the morrow : it had shrunk and hardened to a stone! I threw it away, and set out again.

About noon I came to a few tamarisk and juniper trees, and

then to a few stunted firs. As I went on, closer thickets and larger firs met me, and at length I was in just such a forest of pines and other trees as that in which the Little Ones found their babies, and believed I had returned upon a farther portion of the same. But what mattered *where* while *everywhere* was the same as *nowhere*! I had not yet, by doing something in it, made *anywhere* into a place! I was not yet alive; I was only dreaming I lived! I was but a consciousness with an outlook! Truly I had been nothing else in the world I had left, but now I knew the fact! I said to myself that if in this forest I should catch the faint gleam of the mirror, I would turn far aside lest it should entrap me unawares, and give me back to my old existence : here I might learn to be something by doing something! I could not endure the thought of going back, with so many beginnings and not an end achieved. The Little Ones would meet what fate was appointed them; the awful witch I should never meet; the dead would ripen and arise without me; I should but wake to know that I had dreamed, and that all my going was nowhither! I would rather go on and on than come to such a close!

I went deeper into the wood : I was weary, and would rest in it.

The trees were now large, and stood in regular, almost geometric, fashion, with roomy spaces between. There was little undergrowth, and I could see a long way in every direction. The forest was like a great church, solemn and silent and empty, for I met nothing on two feet or four that day. Now and then, it is true, some swift thing, and again some slow thing, would cross the space on which my eye happened that moment to settle; but it was always at some distance, and only enhanced the sense of wideness and vacancy. I heard a few birds, and saw plenty of butterflies, some of marvellously gorgeous colouring and combinations of colour, some of a pure and dazzling whiteness.

Coming to a spot where the pines stood farther apart and gave room for flowering shrubs, and hoping it a sign of some dwelling near, I took the direction where yet more and more roses grew, for I was hungry after the voice and face of my kind—after any live soul, indeed, human or not, which I might in some measure understand. What a hell of horror, I thought, to wander alone, a bare existence never going out of itself, never widening its life in another life, but, bound with the cords of its

poor peculiarities, lying an eternal prisoner in the dungeon of
its own being! I began to learn that it was impossible to live for
oneself even, save in the presence of others—then, alas, fearfully
possible! evil was only through good! selfishness but a parasite
on the tree of life! In my own world I had the habit of solitary
song; here not a crooning murmur ever parted my lips! There I
sang without thinking; here I thought without singing! there I
had never had a bosom-friend; here the affection of an idiot
would be divinely welcome! "If only I had a dog to love!" I
sighed—and regarded with wonder my past self, which preferred
the company of book or pen to that of man or woman; which,
if the author of a tale I was enjoying appeared, would wish him
away that I might return to his story. I had chosen the dead
rather than the living, the thing thought rather than the thing
thinking! "Any man," I said now, "is more than the greatest of
books!" I had not cared for my live brothers and sisters, and
now I was left without even the dead to comfort me!

The wood thinned yet more, and the pines grew yet larger,
sending up huge stems, like columns eager to support the
heavens. More trees of other kinds appeared; the forest was
growing richer! The roses were now trees, and their flowers of
astonishing splendour.

Suddenly I spied what seemed a great house or castle; but its
forms were so strangely indistinct, that I could not be certain it
was more than a chance combination of tree-shapes. As I drew
nearer, its lines yet held together, but neither they nor the body
of it grew at all more definite; and when at length I stood in
front of it, I remained as doubtful of its nature as before. House
or castle habitable, it certainly was not; it might be a ruin overgrown with ivy and roses! Yet of building hid in the foliage, not
the poorest wall-remnant could I discern. Again and again I
seemed to descry what must be building, but it always vanished
before closer inspection. Could it be, I pondered, that the ivy
had embraced a huge edifice and consumed it, and its interlaced
branches retained the shapes of the walls it had assimilated?—
I could be sure of nothing concerning the appearance.

Before me was a rectangular vacancy—the ghost of a doorway
without a door: I stepped through it, and found myself in an
open space like a great hall, its floor covered with grass and
flowers, its walls and roof of ivy and vine, mingled with roses.

There could be no better place in which to pass the night! I gathered a quantity of withered leaves, laid them in a corner, and threw myself upon them. A red sunset filled the hall, the night was warm, and my couch restful; I lay gazing up at the live ceiling, with its tracery of branches and twigs, its clouds of foliage, and peeping patches of loftier roof. My eyes went wading about as if tangled in it, until the sun was down, and the sky beginning to grow dark. Then the red roses turned black, and soon the yellow and white alone were visible. When they vanished, the stars came instead, hanging in the leaves like live topazes, throbbing and sparkling and flashing many colours : I was canopied with a tree from Aladdin's cave!

Then I discovered that it was full of nests, whence tiny heads, nearly indistinguishable, kept popping out with a chirp or two, and disappearing again. For a while there were rustlings and stirrings and little prayers; but as the darkness grew, the small heads became still, and at last every feathered mother had her brood quiet under her wings, the talk in the little beds was over, and God's bird-nursery at rest beneath the waves of sleep. Once more a few flutterings made me look up : an owl went sailing across. I had only a glimpse of him, but several times felt the cool wafture of his silent wings. The mother birds did not move again; they saw that he was looking for mice, not children.

About midnight I came wide awake, roused by a revelry, whose noises were not yet loud. Neither were they distant; they were close to me, but attenuate. My eyes were so dazzled, however, that for a while I could see nothing; at last they came to themselves.

I was lying on my withered leaves in the corner of a splendid hall. Before me was a crowd of gorgeously dressed men and gracefully robed women, none of whom seemed to see me. In dance after dance they vaguely embodied the story of life, its meetings, its passions, its partings. A student of Shakspere, I had learned something of every dance alluded to in his plays, and hence partially understood several of those I now saw— the minuet, the pavin, the hey, the coranto, the lavolta. The dancers were attired in fashion as ancient as their dances.

A moon had risen while I slept, and was shining through the countless-windowed roof; but her light was crossed by so many shadows that at first I could distinguish almost nothing of the faces of the multitude; I could not fail, however, to perceive that there was something odd about them : I sat up to see them better.—Heavens! could I call them faces? They were skull fronts!—hard, gleaming bone, bare jaws, truncated noses, lipless teeth which could no more take part in any smile! Of these, some flashed set and white and murderous; others were clouded with decay, broken and gapped, coloured of the earth in which they seemed so long to have lain! Fearfuller yet, the eye-sockets were not empty; in each was a lidless living eye! In those wrecks of faces, glowed or flashed or sparkled eyes of every colour, shape, and expression. The beautiful, proud eye, dark and lustrous, condescending to whatever it rested upon, was the more terrible; the lovely, languishing eye, the more repulsive; while the dim, sad eyes, less at variance with their setting, were sad exceedingly, and drew the heart in spite of the horror out of which they gazed.

I rose and went among the apparitions, eager to understand something of their being and belongings. Were they souls, or were they and their rhythmic motions but phantasms of what had been? By look nor by gesture, not by slightest break in the measure, did they show themselves aware of me; I was not present to them : how much were they in relation to each other? Surely they saw their companions as I saw them! Or was each only dreaming itself and the rest? Did they know each how they appeared to the others—a death with living eyes? Had they used their faces, not for communication, not to utter thought and feeling, not to share existence with their neighbours, but to appear what they wished to appear, and conceal what they were? and, having made their faces masks, were they therefore deprived of those masks, and condemned to go without faces until they repented?

"How long must they flaunt their facelessness in faceless eyes?" I wondered. "How long will the frightful punition endure? Have they at length begun to love and be wise? Have they yet yielded to the shame that has found them?

I heard not a word, saw not a movement of one naked mouth. Were they because of lying bereft of speech? With their eyes they spoke as if longing to be understood : was it truth or was it falsehood that spoke in their eyes? They seemed to know one another : did they see one skull beautiful, and another plain?

Difference must be there, and they had had long study of skulls!

My body was to theirs no obstacle : was I a body, and were they but forms? or was I but a form, and were they bodies? The moment one of the dancers came close against me, that moment he or she was on the other side of me, and I could tell, without seeing, which, whether man or woman, had passed through my house.

On many of the skulls the hair held its place, and however dressed, or in itself however beautiful, to my eyes looked frightful on the bones of the forehead and temples. In such case, the outer ear often remained also, and at its tip, the jewel of the ear as Sidney calls it, would hang, glimmering, gleaming, or sparkling, pearl or opal or diamond—under the night of brown or of raven locks, the sunrise of golden ripples, or the moonshine of pale, interclouded, fluffy cirri—lichenous all on the ivory-white or damp-yellow naked bone. I looked down and saw the daintily domed instep; I looked up and saw the plump shoulders basing the spring of the round full neck—which withered at half-height to the fluted shaft of a gibbose cranium.

The music became wilder, the dance faster and faster; eyes flared and flashed, jewels twinkled and glittered, casting colour and fire on the pallid grins that glode through the hall, weaving a ghastly rhythmic woof in intricate maze of multitudinous motion, when sudden came a pause, and every eye turned to the same spot :—in the doorway stood a woman, perfect in form, in holding, and in hue, regarding the company as from the pedestal of a goddess, while the dancers stood "like one forbid," frozen to a new death by the vision of a life that killed. "Dead things, I live!" said her scornful glance. Then, at once, like leaves in which an instant wind awakes, they turned each to another, and broke afresh into melodious consorted motion, a new expression in their eyes, late solitary, now filled with the interchange of a common triumph. "Thou also," they seemed to say, "wilt soon become weak as we! thou wilt soon become like unto us!" I turned mine again to the woman—and saw upon her side a small dark shadow.

She had seen the change in the dead stare; she looked down; she understood the talking eyes; she pressed both her lovely hands on the shadow, gave a smothered cry, and fled. The birds moved rustling in their nests, and a flash of joy lit up the eyes of the dancers, when suddenly a warm wind, growing in strength as it swept through the place, blew out every light. But the low moon yet glimmered on the horizon with "sick assay" to shine, and a turbid radiance yet gleamed from so many eyes, that I saw well enough what followed. As if each shape had been but a snow-image, it began to fall to pieces, ruining in the warm wind. In papery flakes the flesh peeled from its bones, dropping like soiled snow from under its garments; these fell fluttering in rags and strips, and the whole white skeleton, emerging from garment and flesh together, stood bare and lank amid the decay that littered the floor. A faint rattling shiver went through the naked company; pair after pair the lamping eyes went out; and the darkness grew round me with the loneliness. For a moment the leaves were still swept fluttering all one way; then the wind ceased, and the owl floated silent through the silent night.

Not for a moment had I been afraid. It is true that whoever would cross the threshold of any world, must leave fear behind him; but, for myself, I could claim no part in its absence. No conscious courage was operant in me; simply, I was not afraid. I neither knew why I was not afraid, nor wherefore I might have been afraid. I feared not even fear—which of all dangers is the most dangerous.

I went out into the wood, at once to resume my journey. Another moon was rising, and I turned my face toward it.

CHAPTER XVII

A GROTESQUE TRAGEDY

I HAD NOT GONE ten paces when I caught sight of a strange-looking object, and went nearer to know what it might be. I found it a mouldering carriage of ancient form, ruinous but still upright on its heavy wheels. On each side of the pole, still in its place, lay the skeleton of a horse; from their two grim white heads ascended the shrivelled reins to the hand of the skeleton-coachman seated on his tattered hammer-cloth; both doors had fallen away; within sat two skeletons, each leaning back in its corner.

Even as I looked, they started awake, and with a cracking rattle of bones, each leaped from the door next it. One fell and lay; the other stood a moment, its structure shaking perilously; then with difficulty, for its joints were stiff, crept, holding by the back of the carriage, to the opposite side, the thin leg-bones seeming hardly strong enough to carry its weight, where, kneeling by the other, it sought to raise it, almost falling itself again in the endeavour.

The prostrate one rose at length, as by a sudden effort, to the sitting posture. For a few moments it turned its yellowish skull to this side and that; then, heedless of its neighbour, got upon its feet by grasping the spokes of the hind wheel. Half erected thus, it stood with its back to the other, both hands holding one of its knee-joints. With little less difficulty and not a few contortions, the kneeling one rose next, and addressed its companion.

"Have you hurt yourself, my lord?" it said, in a voice that sounded far-off, and ill-articulated as if blown aside by some spectral wind.

"Yes, I have," answered the other, in like but rougher tone. "You would do nothing to help me, and this cursed knee is out!"

"I did my best, my lord."

"No doubt, my lady, for it was bad! I thought I should never find my feet again!—But, bless my soul, madam! are you out in your bones?"

She cast a look at herself.

"I have nothing else to be out in," she returned; '—and *you* at least cannot complain! But what on earth does it mean? Am I dreaming?"

"*You* may be dreaming, madam—I cannot tell; but this knee of mine forbids me the grateful illusion.—Ha! I too, I perceive, have nothing to walk in but bones!—Not so unbecoming to a man, however! I trust to goodness that they are not *my* bones! every one aches worse than another, and this loose knee worst of all! The bed must have been damp—and I too drunk to know it!"

"Probably, my lord of Cokayne!"

"What! what!—You make me think I too am dreaming— aches and all! How do *you* know the title my roistering bullies give me? I don't remember you!—Anyhow, you have no right to take liberties! My name is—I am lord——tut, tut! What do

you call me when I'm—I mean when you are sober? I cannot—
at the moment,—Why, what *is* my name?—I must have been
very drunk when I went to bed! I often am!"

"You come so seldom to mine, that I do not know, my lord;
but I may take your word for *that*!"

"I hope so!"

"—if for nothing else!"

"Hoity toity! I never told you a lie in my life!"

"You never told me anything but lies."

"Upon my honour!—Why, I never saw the woman before!"

"You knew me well enough to lie to, my lord!"

"I do seem to begin to dream I have met you before, but,
upon my oath, there is nothing to know you by! Out of your
clothes, who is to tell who you may not be?—One thing I *may*
swear—that I never saw you so much undressed before!—By
heaven, I have no recollection of you!"

"I am glad to hear it: my recollections of you are the less
distasteful!—Good morning, my lord!"

She turned away, hobbled, clacking, a few paces, and stood
again.

"You are just as heartless as—as—any other woman, madam!
—Where in this hell of a place shall I find my valet?—What
was the cursed name I used to call the fool?"

He turned his bare noddle this way and that on its creaking
pivot, still holding his knee with both hands.

"I will be your valet for once, my lord," said the lady, turning
once more to him. "—What can I do for you? It is not easy to
tell!"

"Tie my leg on, of course, you fool! Can't you see it is all
but off? Heigho, my dancing days!"

She looked about with her eyeless sockets and found a piece
of fibrous grass, with which she proceeded to bind together the
adjoining parts that had formed the knee. When she had done,
he gave one or two carefully tentative stamps.

"You used to stamp rather differently, my lord!" she said, as
she rose from her knees.

"Eh? what!—Now I look at you again, it seems to me I used
to hate you!—Eh?"

"Naturally, my lord! You hated a good many people!—your
wife, of course, among the rest!"

"Ah, I begin, I be-gin—— But—I must have been a long time somewhere!—I really forget!—There! your damned, miserable bit of grass is breaking!—We used to get on *pretty* well together—eh?"

"Not that I remember, my lord. The only happy moments I had in your company were scattered over the first week of our marriage."

"Was that the way of it? Ha! ha!—Well, it's over now, thank goodness!"

"I wish I could believe it! Why were we sitting there in that carriage together? It wakes apprehension!"

"I think we were divorced, my lady!"

"Hardly enough : we are still together!"

"A sad truth, but capable of remedy : the forest seems of some extent!"

"I doubt! I doubt!"

"I am sorry I cannot think of a compliment to pay you—without lying, that is. To judge by your figure and complexion you have lived hard since I saw you last! I cannot surely be *quite* so naked as your ladyship!—I beg your pardon, madam! I trust you will take it I am but jesting in a dream! It is of no consequence, however; dreaming or waking, all's one—all merest appearance! You can't be certain of anything, and that's as good as knowing there is nothing! Life may teach any fool that!"

"It has taught me the fool I was to love you!"

"You were not the only fool to do that! Women had a trick of falling in love with me :—I had forgotten that you were one of them!"

"I did love you, my lord—a little—at one time!"

"Ah, there was your mistake, my lady! You should have loved me much, loved me devotedly, loved me savagely—loved me eternally! Then I should have tired of you the sooner, and not hated you so much afterward!—But let bygones be bygones! —*Where* are we? Locality is the question! To be or not to be, is *not* the question!"

"We are in the other world, I presume!"

"Granted!—but in which or what sort of other world? This can't be hell!"

"It must : there's marriage in it! You and I are damned in each other."

"Then I'm not like Othello, damned in a fair wife!—Oh, I remember my Shakspere, madam!"

She picked up a broken branch that had fallen into a bush, and steadying herself with it, walked away, tossing her little skull.

"Give that stick to me," cried her late husband; "I want it more than you."

She returned him no answer.

"You mean to make me beg for it?"

"Not at all, my lord. I mean to keep it," she replied, continuing her slow departure.

"Give it to me at once; I mean to have it! I require it."

"Unfortunately, I think I require it myself!" returned the lady, walking a little quicker, with a sharper cracking of her joints and clinking of her bones.

He started to follow her, but nearly fell : his knee-grass had burst, and with an oath he stopped, grasping his leg again.

"Come and tie it up properly!" he would have thundered, but he only piped and whistled!

She turned and looked at him.

"Come and tie it up instantly!" he repeated.

She walked a step or two farther from him.

"I swear I will not touch you!" he cried.

"Swear on, my lord! there is no one here to believe you. But, pray, do not lose your temper, or you will shake yourself to pieces, and where to find string enough to tie up all your crazy joints, is more than I can tell."

She came back, and knelt once more at his side—first, however, laying the stick in dispute beyond his reach and within her own.

The instant she had finished retying the joint, he made a grab at her, thinking, apparently, to seize her by the hair; but his hard fingers slipped on the smooth poll.

"Disgusting!" he muttered, and laid hold of her upper arm-bone.

"You will break it!" she said, looking up from her knees.

"I will, then!" he answered, and began to strain at it.

"I shall not tie your leg again the next time it comes loose!" she threatened.

He gave her arm a vicious twist, but happily her bones were

in better condition than his. She stretched her other hand toward the broken branch.

"That's right : reach me the stick !" he grinned.

She brought it round with such a swing that one of the bones of the sounder leg snapped. He fell, choking with curses. The lady laughed.

"Now you will have to wear splints always !" she said; "such dry bones never mend !"

"You devil !" he cried.

"At your service, my lord ! Shall I fetch you a couple of wheel-spokes? Neat—but heavy, I fear !"

He turned his bone-face aside, and did not answer, but lay and groaned. I marvelled he had not gone to pieces when he fell. The lady rose and walked away—not all ungracefully, I thought.

"What can come of it?" I said to myself. "These are too wretched for any world, and this cannot be hell, for the Little Ones are in it, and the sleepers too ! What can it all mean? Can things ever come right for skeletons?"

"There are words too big for you and me : *all* is one of them, and *ever* is another," said a voice near me which I knew.

I looked about, but could not see the speaker.

"You are not in hell," it resumed. "Neither am I in hell. But those skeletons are in hell !"

Ere he ended I caught sight of the raven on the bough of a beech, right over my head. The same moment he left it, and alighting on the ground, stood there, the thin old man of the library, with long nose and long coat.

"The male was never a gentleman," he went on, "and in the bony stage of retrogression, with his skeleton through his skin, and his character outside his manners, does not look like one. The female is less vulgar, and has a little heart. But, the restraints of society removed, you see them now just as they are and always were !"

"Tell me, Mr. Raven, what will become of them," I said.

"We shall see," he replied. "In their day they were the handsomest couple at court; and now, even in their dry bones, they seem to regard their former repute as an inalienable possession; to see their faces, however, may yet do something for them ! They felt themselves rich too while they had pockets, but they have already begun to feel rather pinched ! My lord used to regard my lady as a worthless encumbrance, for he was tired of her beauty and had spent her money; now he needs her to cobble his joints for him! These changes have roots of hope in them. Besides, they cannot now get far away from each other, and they see none else of their own kind : they must at last grow weary of their mutual repugnance, and begin to love one another! for love, not hate, is deepest in what Love 'loved into being.' "

"I saw many more of their kind an hour ago, in the hall close by!" I said.

"Of their kind, but not of their sort," he answered. "For many years these will see none such as you saw last night. Those are centuries in advance of these. You saw that those could even dress themselves a little! It is true they cannot yet retain their clothes so long as they would—only, at present, for a part of the night; but they are pretty steadily growing more capable, and will by and by develop faces; for every grain of truthfulness adds a fibre to the show of their humanity. Nothing but truth can appear; and whatever is must seem."

"Are they upheld by this hope?" I asked.

"They are upheld by hope, but they do not in the least know their hope; to understand it, is yet immeasurably beyond them," answered Mr. Raven.

His unexpected appearance had caused me no astonishment. I was like a child, constantly wondering, and surprised at nothing.

"Did you come to find me, sir?" I asked.

"Not at all," he replied. "I have no anxiety about you. Such as you always come back to us."

"Tell me, please, who am I such as?" I said.

"I cannot make my friend the subject of conversation," he answered, with a smile.

"But when that friend is present!" I urged.

"I decline the more strongly," he rejoined.

"But when that friend asks you!" I persisted.

"Then most positively I refuse," he returned.

"Why?"

"Because he and I would be talking of two persons as if they were one and the same. Your consciousness of yourself and my knowledge of you are far apart!"

The lapels of his coat flew out, and the lappets lifted, and I thought the metamorphosis of *homo* to *corvus* was about to take place before my eyes. But the coat closed again in front of him, and he added, with seeming inconsequence,

"In this world never trust a person who has once deceived you. Above all, never do anything such a one may ask you to do."

"I will try to remember," I answered; "—but I may forget!"

"Then some evil that is good for you will follow."

"And if I remember?"

"Some evil that is not good for you, will not follow."

The old man seemed to sink to the ground, and immediately I saw the raven several yards from me, flying low and fast.

CHAPTER XVIII

DEAD OR ALIVE?

I WENT WALKING ON, still facing the moon, who, not yet high, was staring straight into the forest. I did not know what ailed her, but she was dark and dented, like a battered disc of old copper, and looked dispirited and weary. Not a cloud was nigh to keep her company, and the stars were too bright for her. "Is this going to last for ever?" she seemed to say. She was going one way and I was going the other, yet through the wood we went a long way together. We did not commune much, for my eyes were on the ground; but her disconsolate look was fixed on me : I felt without seeing it. A long time we were together, I and the moon, walking side by side, she the dull shine, and I the live shadow.

Something on the ground, under a spreading tree, caught my eye with its whiteness, and I turned toward it. Vague as it was in the shadow of the foliage, it suggested, as I drew nearer, a human body. "Another skeleton!" I said to myself, kneeling and laying my hand upon it. A body it was, however, and no skeleton, though as nearly one as body could well be. It lay on its side, and was very cold—not cold like a stone, but cold like that which was once alive, and is alive no more. The closer I looked at it, the oftener I touched it, the less it seemed possible it should be other than dead. For one bewildered moment, I fancied it one of the wild dancers, a ghostly Cinderella, perhaps, that had lost her way home, and perished in the strange night of an out-of-door world! It was quite naked, and so worn that, even in the shadow, I could, peering close, have counted, without touching them, every rib in its side. All its bones, indeed, were as visible as if tight-covered with only a thin elastic leather. Its beautiful yet terrible teeth, unseemly disclosed by the retracted lips, gleamed ghastly through the dark. Its hair was longer than itself, thick and very fine to the touch, and black as night.

It was the body of a tall, probably graceful woman.—How had she come there? Not of herself, and already in such wasted condition, surely! Her strength must have failed her; she had fallen, and lain there until she died of hunger! But how, even so, could she be thus emaciated? And how came she to be naked? Where were the savages to strip and leave her? or what wild beasts would have taken her garments? That her body should have been left was not wonderful!

I rose to my feet, stood, and considered. I must not, could not let her lie exposed and forsaken! Natural reverence forbade it. Even the garment of a woman claims respect; her body it were impossible to leave uncovered! Irreverent eyes might look on it! Brutal claws might toss it about! Years would pass ere the friendly rains washed it into the soil!—But the ground was hard, almost solid with interlacing roots, and I had but my bare hands!

At first it seemed plain that she had not long been dead : there was not a sign of decay about her! But then what had the slow wasting of life left of her to decay?

Could she be still alive? Might she not? What if she were! Things went very strangely in this strange world! Even then there would be little chance of bringing her back, but I must know she was dead before I buried her!

As I left the forest-hall, I had spied in the doorway a bunch of ripe grapes, and brought it with me, eating as I came : a few were yet left on the stalk, and their juice might possibly revive her! Anyhow it was all I had with which to attempt her rescue! The mouth was happily a little open; but the head was in such an awkward position that, to move the body, I passed my arm under the shoulder on which it lay, when I found the pine-needles beneath it warm : she could not have been any time dead, and *might* still be alive, though I could discern no motion of the heart, or any indication that she breathed ! One of her hands was clenched hard, apparently inclosing something small. I squeezed a grape into her mouth, but no swallowing followed.

To do for her all I could, I spread a thick layer of pine-needles and dry leaves, laid one of my garments over it, warm from my body, lifted her upon it, and covered her with my clothes and a great heap of leaves : I would save the little warmth left in her, hoping an increase to it when the sun came back. Then I tried another grape, but could perceive no slightest movement of mouth or throat.

"Doubt," I said to myself, "may be a poor encouragement to do anything, but it is a bad reason for doing nothing." So tight was the skin upon her bones that I dared not use friction.

I crept into the heap of leaves, got as close to her as I could, and took her in my arms. I had not much heat left in me, but what I had I would share with her ! Thus I spent what remained of the night, sleepless, and longing for the sun. Her cold seemed to radiate into me, but no heat to pass from me to her.

Had I fled from the beautiful sleepers, I thought, each on her "dim, straight" silver couch, to lie alone with such a bedfellow ! I had refused a lovely privilege : I was given over to an awful duty ! Beneath the sad, slow-setting moon, I lay with the dead, and watched for the dawn.

The darkness had given way, and the eastern horizon was growing dimly clearer, when I caught sight of a motion rather than of anything that moved—not far from me, and close to the ground. It was the low undulating of a large snake, which passed me in an unswerving line. Presently appeared, making as it seemed for the same point, what I took for a roebuck-doe and her calf. Again a while, and two creatures like bear-cubs came, with three or four smaller ones behind them. The light was now growing so rapidly that when, a few minutes after, a troop of horses went trotting past, I could see that, although the largest of them were no bigger than the smallest Shetland pony, they must yet be full-grown, so perfect were they in form, and so much had they all the ways and action of great horses. They were of many breeds. Some seemed models of cart-horses, others of chargers, hunters, racers. Dwarf cattle and small elephants followed.

"Why are the children not here!" I said to myself. "The moment I am free of this poor woman, I must go back and fetch them!"

Where were the creatures going? What drew them? Was this an exodus, or a morning habit? I must wait for the sun! Till he came I must not leave the woman!

I laid my hand on the body, and could not help thinking it felt a trifle warmer. It might have gained a little of the heat I had lost! it could hardly have generated any! What reason for hope there was had not grown less!

The forehead of the day began to glow, and soon the sun came peering up, as if to see for the first time what all this stir of a new world was about. At sight of his great innocent splendour, I rose full of life, strong against death. Removing the handkerchief I had put to protect the mouth and eyes from the pine-needles, I looked anxiously to see whether I had found a priceless jewel, or but its empty case.

The body lay motionless as when I found it. Then first, in the morning light, I saw how drawn and hollow was the face, how sharp were the bones under the skin, how every tooth shaped itself through the lips. The human garment was indeed worn to its threads, but the bird of heaven might yet be nestling within, might yet awake to motion and song!

But the sun was shining on her face! I re-arranged the handkerchief, laid a few leaves lightly over it, and set out to follow the creatures. Their main track was well beaten, and must have long been used—likewise many of the tracks that, joining it from both sides, merged in, and broadened it. The trees retreated as I went, and the grass grew thicker. Presently the forest was gone, and a wide expanse of loveliest green stretched away to the horizon. Through it, along the edge of the forest, flowed a small river, and to this the track led. At sight of the water a new though undefined hope sprang up in me. The stream looked everywhere deep, and was full to the brim, but nowhere more than a few yards wide. A bluish mist rose from it, vanishing as it rose. On the opposite side, in the plentiful grass, many small animals were feeding. Apparently they slept in the forest, and in the morning sought the plain, swimming the river to reach it.

I knelt and would have drunk, but the water was hot, and had a strange metallic taste.

I leapt to my feet : here was the warmth I sought—the first necessity of life ! I sped back to my helpless charge.

Without well considering my solitude, no one will understand what seemed to lie for me in the redemption of this woman from death. "Prove what she may," I thought with myself, "I shall at least be lonely no more !" I had found myself such poor company that now first I seemed to know what hope was. This blessed water would expel the cold death, and drown my desolation !

I bore her to the stream. Tall as she was, I found her marvellously light, her bones were so delicate, and so little covered them. I grew yet more hopeful when I found her so far from stiff that I could carry her on one arm, like a sleeping child, leaning against my shoulder. I went softly, dreading even the wind of my motion, and glad there was no other.

The water was too hot to lay her at once in it : the shock might scare from her the yet fluttering life ! I laid her on the bank, and dipping one of my garments, began to bathe the pitiful form. So wasted was it that, save for the plentifulness and blackness of the hair, it was impossible even to conjecture whether she was young or old. Her eyelids were just not shut, which made her look dead the more : there was a crack in the clouds of her night, at which no sun shone through !

The longer I went on bathing the poor bones, the less grew my hope that they would ever again be clothed with strength, that ever those eyelids would lift, and a soul look out; still I kept bathing continuously, allowing no part time to grow cold while I bathed another; and gradually the body became so much warmer, that at last I ventured to submerge it : I got into the stream and drew it in, holding the face above the water, and letting the swift, steady current flow all about the rest. I noted, but was able to conclude nothing from the fact, that, for all the heat, the shut hand never relaxed its hold.

After about ten minutes, I lifted it out and laid it again on the bank, dried it, and covered it as well as I could, then ran to the forest for leaves.

The grass and soil were dry and warm; and when I returned I thought it had scarcely lost any of the heat the water had given it. I spread the leaves upon it, and ran for more—then for a third and a fourth freight.

I could now leave it and go to explore, in the hope of discovering some shelter. I ran up the stream toward some rocky hills I saw in that direction, which were not far off.

When I reached them, I found the river issuing full grown from a rock at the bottom of one of them. To my fancy it seemed to have run down a stair inside, an eager cataract, at every landing wild to get out, but only at the foot finding a door of escape.

It did not fill the opening whence it rushed, and I crept through into a little cave, where I learned that, instead of hurrying tumultuously down a stair, it rose quietly from the ground at the back, like the base of a large column, and ran along one side, nearly filling a deep, rather narrow channel. I considered the place, and saw that, if I could find a few fallen boughs long enough to lie across the channel, and large enough to bear a little weight without bending much, I might, with smaller branches and plenty of leaves, make upon them a comfortable couch, which the stream under would keep constantly warm. Then I ran back to see how my charge fared.

She was lying as I had left her. The heat had not brought her to life, but neither had it developed anything to check further hope. I got a few boulders out of the channel, and arranged them at her feet and on both sides of her.

Running again to the wood, I had not to search long ere I found some small boughs fit for my purpose—mostly of beech, their dry yellow leaves yet clinging to them. With these I had soon laid the floor of a bridge-bed over the torrent. I crossed the boughs with smaller branches, interlaced these with twigs, and buried all deep in leaves and dry moss.

When thus at length, after not a few journeys to the forest, I had completed a warm, dry, soft couch, I took the body once more, and set out with it for the cave. It was so light that now and then as I went I almost feared lest, when I laid it down, I should find it a skeleton after all; and when at last I did lay it gently on the pathless bridge, it was a greater relief to part with that fancy than with the weight. Once more I covered the body with a thick layer of leaves; and trying again to feed her with a grape, found to my joy that I could open the mouth a little

LILITH 279

farther. The grape, indeed, lay in it unheeded, but I hoped some of the juice might find its way down.

After an hour or two on the couch, she was no longer cold. The warmth of the brook had interpenetrated her frame—truly it was but a frame!—and she was warm to the touch;—not, probably, with the warmth of life, but with a warmth which rendered it more possible, if she were alive, that she might live. I had read of one in a trance lying motionless for weeks!

In that cave, day after day, night after night, seven long days and nights, I sat or lay, now waking now sleeping, but always watching. Every morning I went out and bathed in the hot stream, and every morning felt thereupon as if I had eaten and drunk—which experience gave me courage to lay her in it also every day. Once as I did so, a shadow of discoloration on her left side gave me a terrible shock, but the next morning it had vanished, and I continued the treatment—every morning, after her bath, putting a fresh grape in her mouth.

I too ate of the grapes and other berries I found in the forest; but I believed that, with my daily bath in that river, I could have done very well without eating at all.

Every time I slept, I dreamed of finding a wounded angel, who, unable to fly, remained with me until at last she loved me and would not leave me; and every time I woke, it was to see, instead of an angel-visage with lustrous eyes, the white, motionless, wasted face upon the couch. But Adam himself, when first he saw her asleep, could not have looked more anxiously for Eve's awaking than I watched for this woman's. Adam knew nothing of himself, perhaps nothing of his need of another self; I, an alien from my fellows, had learned to love what I had lost! Were this one wasted shred of womanhood to disappear, I should have nothing in me but a consuming hunger after life! I forgot even the Little Ones : things were not amiss with them! here lay what might wake and be a woman! might actually open eyes, and look out of them upon me!

Now first I knew what solitude meant—now that I gazed on one who neither saw nor heard, neither moved nor spoke. I saw now that a man alone is but a being that may become a man —that he is but a need, and therefore a possibility. To be enough for himself, a being must be an eternal, self-existent worm! So superbly constituted, so simply complicate is man; he rises from and stands upon such a pedestal of lower physical organisms and spiritual structures, that no atmosphere will comfort or nourish his life, less divine than that offered by other souls; nowhere but in other lives can he ripen his specialty, develop the idea of himself, the individuality that distinguishes him from every other. Were all men alike, each would still have an individuality, secured by his personal consciousness, but there would be small reason why there should be more than two or three such; while, for the development of the differences which make a large and lofty unity possible, and which alone can make millions into a church, an endless and measureless influence and reaction are indispensable. A man to be perfect—complete, that is, in having reached the spiritual condition of persistent and universal growth, which is the mode wherein he inherits the infinitude of his Father—must have the education of a world of fellow-men. Save for the hope of the dawn of life in the form beside me, I should have fled for fellowship to the beasts that grazed and did not speak. Better to go about with them—infinitely better— than to live alone! But with the faintest prospect of a woman to my friend, I, poorest of creatures, was yet a possible man!

CHAPTER XIX

THE WHITE LEECH

I WOKE ONE MORNING from a profound sleep, with one of my hands very painful. The back of it was much swollen, and in the centre of the swelling was a triangular wound, like the bite of a leech. As the day went on, the swelling subsided, and by the evening the hurt was all but healed. I searched the cave, turning over every stone of any size, but discovered nothing I could imagine capable of injuring me.

Slowly the days passed, and still the body never moved, never opened its eyes. It could not be dead, for assuredly it manifested no sign of decay, and the air about it was quite pure. Moreover, I could imagine that the sharpest angles of the bones had begun to disappear, that the form was everywhere a little rounder, and the skin had less of a parchment-look : if such change was

indeed there, life must be there! the tide which had ebbed so
far toward the infinite, must have begun again to flow! Oh
joy to me, if the rising ripples of life's ocean were indeed burying
under lovely shape the bones it had all but forsaken! Twenty
times a day I looked for evidence of progress, and twenty times
a day I doubted—sometimes even despaired; but the moment
I recalled the mental picture of her as I found her, hope revived.

Several weeks had passed thus, when one night, after lying a
long time awake, I rose, thinking to go out and breathe the
cooler air; for, although from the running of the stream it was
always fresh in the cave, the heat was not seldom a little
oppressive. The moon outside was full, the air within shadowy
clear, and naturally I cast a lingering look on my treasure ere
I went. "Bliss eternal!" I cried aloud, "do I see her eyes?"
Great orbs, dark as if cut from the sphere of a starless night,
and luminous by excess of darkness, seemed to shine amid the
glimmering whiteness of her face. I stole nearer, my heart beating so that I feared the noise of it startling her. I bent over her.
Alas, her eyelids were close shut! Hope and Imagination had
wrought mutual illusion! my heart's desire would never be! I
turned away, threw myself on the floor of the cave, and wept.
Then I bethought me that her eyes had been a little open, and
that now the awful chink out of which nothingness had peered,
was gone : it might be that she had opened them for a moment,
and was again asleep!—it might be she was awake and holding
them close! In either case, life, less or more, must have shut
them! I was comforted, and fell fast asleep.

That night I was again bitten, and awoke with a burning
thirst.

In the morning I searched yet more thoroughly, but again in
vain. The wound was of the same character, and, as before,
was nearly well by the evening. I concluded that some large
creature of the leech kind came occasionally from the hot stream.
"But, if blood be its object," I said to myself, "so long as I am
there, I need hardly fear for my treasure!"

That same morning, when, having peeled a grape as usual and
taken away the seeds, I put it in her mouth, her lips made a
slight movement of reception, and I *knew* she lived!

My hope was now so much stronger that I began to think of
some attire for her : she must be able to rise the moment she

wished! I betook myself therefore to the forest, to investigate what material it might afford, and had hardly begun to look when fibrous skeletons, like those of the leaves of the prickly pear, suggested themselves as fit for the purpose. I gathered a stock of them, laid them to dry in the sun, pulled apart the reticulated layers, and of these had soon begun to fashion two loose garments, one to hang from her waist, the other from her shoulders. With the stiletto-point of an aloe-leaf and various filaments, I sewed together three thicknesses of the tissue.

During the week that followed, there was no further sign except that she more evidently took the grapes. But indeed all the signs became surer: plainly she was growing plumper, and her skin fairer. Still she did not open her eyes; and the horrid fear would at times invade me, that her growth was of some hideous fungoid nature, the few grapes being nowise sufficient to account for it.

Again I was bitten; and now the thing, whatever it was, began to pay me regular visits at intervals of three days. It now generally bit me in the neck or the arm, invariably with but one bite, always while I slept, and never, even when I slept, in the daytime. Hour after hour would I lie awake on the watch, but never heard it coming, or saw sign of its approach. Neither, I believe, did I ever feel it bite me. At length I became so hopeless of catching it, that I no longer troubled myself either to look for it by day, or lie in wait for it at night. I knew from my growing weakness that I was losing blood at a dangerous rate, but I cared little for that: in sight of my eyes death was yielding to life; a soul was gathering strength to save me from loneliness; we would go away together, and I should speedily recover!

The garments were at length finished, and, contemplating my handiwork with no small satisfaction, I proceded to mat layers of the fibre into sandals.

One night I woke suddenly, breathless and faint, and longing after air, and had risen to crawl from the cave, when a slight rustle in the leaves of the couch set me listening motionless.

"I caught the vile thing," said a feeble voice, in my mother-tongue; "I caught it in the very act!"

She was alive! she spoke! I dared not yield to my transport lest I should terrify her.

"What creature?" I breathed, rather than said.

"The creature," she answered, "that was biting you."

"What was it?"

"A great white leech."

"How big?" I pursued, forcing myself to be calm.

"Not far from six feet long, I should think," she answered.

"You have saved my life, perhaps!—But how could you touch the horrid thing! How brave of you!" I cried.

"I did!" was all her answer, and I thought she shuddered.

"Where is it? What could you do with such a monster?"

"I threw it in the river."

"Then it will come again, I fear!"

"I do not think I could have killed it, even had I known how!—I heard you moaning, and got up to see what disturbed you; saw the frightful thing at your neck, and pulled it away. But I could not hold it, and was hardly able to throw it from me. I only heard it splash in the water!"

"We'll kill it next time!" I said; but with that I turned faint, sought the open air, but fell.

When I came to myself the sun was up. The lady stood a little way off, looking, even in the clumsy attire I had fashioned for her, at once grand and graceful. I *had* seen those glorious eyes! Through the night they had shone! Dark as the darkness primeval, they now outshone the day! She stood erect as a column, regarding me. Her pale cheek indicated no emotion, only question. I rose.

"We must be going!" I said. "The white leech——"

I stopped: a strange smile had flickered over her beautiful face.

"Did you find me there?" she asked, pointing to the cave.

"No; I brought you there," I replied.

"You brought me?"

"Yes."

"From where?"

"From the forest."

"What have you done with my clothes—and my jewels?"

"You had none when I found you."

"Then why did you not leave me?"

"Because I hoped you were not dead."

"Why should you have cared?"

"Because I was very lonely, and wanted you to live."

"You would have kept me enchanted for my beauty!" she said, with proud scorn.

Her words and her look roused my indignation.

"There was no beauty left in you," I said.

"Why, then, again, did you not let me alone?"

"Because you were of my own kind."

"Of *your* kind?" she cried, in a tone of utter contempt.

"I thought so, but find I was mistaken!"

"Doubtless you pitied me!"

"Never had woman more claim on pity, or less on any other feeling!"

With an expression of pain, mortification, and anger unutterable, she turned from me and stood silent. Starless night lay profound in the gulfs of her eyes: hate of him who brought it back had slain their splendour. The light of life was gone from them.

"Had you failed to rouse me, what would you have done?" she asked suddenly without moving.

"I would have buried it."

"It! What?—You would have buried *this*?" she exclaimed, flashing round upon me in a white fury, her arms thrown out, and her eyes darting forks of cold lightning.

"Nay; that I saw not! That, weary weeks of watching and tending have brought back to you," I answered—for with such a woman I must be plain! "Had I seen the smallest sign of decay, I would at once have buried you."

"Dog of a fool!" she cried, "I was but in a trance!—Samoil! what a fate!—Go and fetch the she-savage from whom you borrowed this hideous disguise."

"I made it for you. It is hideous, but I did my best."

She drew herself up to her tall height.

"How long have I been insensible?" she demanded. "A woman could not have made that dress in a day!"

"Not in twenty days," I rejoined, "hardly in thirty!"

"Ha! How long do you pretend I have lain unconscious?—Answer me at once."

"I cannot tell how long you had lain when I found you, but there was nothing left of you save skin and bone: that is more than three months ago.—Your hair was beautiful, nothing else! I have done for it what I could."

"My poor hair!" she said, and brought a great armful of it round from behind her; "—it will be more than a three-months' care to bring *you* to life again!—I suppose I must thank you, although I cannot say I am grateful!"

"There is no need, madam: I would have done the same for any woman—yes, or for any man either!"

"How is it my hair is not tangled?" she said, fondling it.

"It always drifted in the current."

"How?—What do you mean?"

"I could not have brought you to life but by bathing you in the hot river every morning."

She gave a shudder of disgust, and stood for a while with her gaze fixed on the hurrying water. Then she turned to me:

"We must understand each other!" she said. "—You have done me the two worst of wrongs—compelled me to live, and put me to shame: neither of them can I pardon!"

She raised her left hand, and flung it out as if repelling me. Something ice-cold struck me on the forehead. When I came to myself, I was on the ground, wet and shivering.

CHAPTER XX

GONE!—BUT HOW?

I ROSE AND LOOKED around me, dazed at heart. For a moment I could not see her: she was gone, and loneliness had returned like the cloud after the rain! She whom I brought back from the brink of the grave, had fled from me, and left me with desolation! I dared not one moment remain thus hideously alone. Had I indeed done her a wrong? I must devote my life to sharing the burden I had compelled her to resume!

I descried her walking swiftly over the grass, away from the river, took one plunge for a farewell restorative, and set out to follow her. The last visit of the white leech, and the blow of the woman, had enfeebled me, but already my strength was reviving, and I kept her in sight without difficulty.

"Is this, then, the end?" I said as I went, and my heart brooded a sad song. Her angry, hating eyes haunted me. I could understand her resentment at my having forced life upon her, but how had I further injured her? Why should she loathe me? Could modesty itself be indignant with true service? How should the proudest woman, conscious of my every action, cherish against me the least sense of disgracing wrong? How reverently had I not touched her! As a father his motherless child, I had borne and tended her! Had all my labour, all my despairing hope gone to redeem only ingratitude? "No," I answered myself; "beauty must have a heart! However profoundly hidden, it must be there! The deeper buried, the stronger and truer will it wake at last in its beautiful grave! To rouse that heart were a better gift to her than the happiest life! It would be to give her a nobler, a higher life!

She was ascending a gentle slope before me, walking straight and steady as one that knew whither, when I became aware that she was increasing the distance between us. I summoned my strength, and it came in full tide. My veins filled with fresh life! My body seemed to become ethereal, and, following like an easy wind, I rapidly overtook her.

Not once had she looked behind. Swiftly she moved, like a Greek goddess to rescue, but without haste. I was within three yards of her, when she turned sharply, yet with grace unbroken, and stood. Fatigue or heat she showed none. Her paleness was not a pallor, but a pure whiteness; her breathing was slow and deep. Her eyes seemed to fill the heavens, and give light to the world. It was nearly noon, but the sense was upon me as of a great night in which an invisible dew makes the stars look large.

"Why do you follow me?" she asked, quietly but rather sternly, as if she had never before seen me.

"I have lived so long," I answered, "on the mere hope of your eyes, that I must want to see them again!"

"You *will* not be spared!" she said coldly. "I command you to stop where you stand."

"Not until I see you in a place of safety will I leave you," I replied.

"Then take the consequences," she said, and resumed her swift-gliding walk.

But as she turned she cast on me a glance, and I stood as if run through with a spear. Her scorn had failed: she would kill me with her beauty!

Despair restored my volition; the spell broke; I ran, and overtook her.

"Have pity upon me!" I cried.

She gave no heed. I followed her like a child whose mother pretends to abandon him. "I will be your slave!" I said, and laid my hand on her arm.

She turned as if a serpent had bit her. I cowered before the blaze of her eyes, but could not avert my own.

"Pity me," I cried again.

She resumed her walking.

The whole day I followed her. The sun climbed the sky, seemed to pause on its summit, went down the other side. Not a moment did she pause, not a moment did I cease to follow. She never turned her head, never relaxed her pace.

The sun went below, and the night came up. I kept close to her: if I lost sight of her for a moment, it would be for ever!

All day long we had been walking over thick soft grass; abruptly she stopped, and threw herself upon it. There was yet light enough to show that she was utterly weary. I stood behind her, and gazed down on her for a moment.

Did I love her? I knew she was not good! Did I hate her? I could not leave her! I knelt beside her.

"Begone! Do not dare touch me," she cried.

Her arms lay on the grass by her sides as if paralysed.

Suddenly they closed about my neck, rigid as those of the torture-maiden. She drew down my face to hers, and her lips clung to my cheek. A sting of pain shot somewhere through me, and pulsed. I could not stir a hair's breadth. Gradually the pain ceased. A slumberous weariness, a dreamy pleasure stole over me, and then I knew nothing.

All at once I came to myself. The moon was a little way above the horizon, but spread no radiance; she was but a bright thing set in blackness. My cheek smarted; I put my hand to it, and found a wet spot. My neck ached: there again was a wet spot! I sighed heavily, and felt very tired. I turned my eyes listlessly around me—and saw what had become of the light of the moon: it was gathered about the lady! she stood in a shimmering nimbus! I rose and staggered toward her.

"Down!" she cried imperiously, as to a rebellious dog. "Follow me a step if you dare!"

"I will!" I murmured, with an agonised effort.

"Set foot within the gates of my city, and my people will stone you : they do not love beggars!"

I was deaf to her words. Weak as water, and half awake, I did not know that I moved, but the distance grew less between us. She took one step back, raised her left arm, and with the clenched hand seemed to strike me on the forehead. I received as it were a blow from an iron hammer, and fell.

I sprang to my feet, cold and wet, but clear-headed and strong. Had the blow revived me? it had left neither wound nor pain!—But how came I wet?—I could not have lain long, for the moon was no higher!

The lady stood some yards away, her back toward me. She was doing something, I could not distinguish what. Then by her sudden gleam I knew she had thrown off her garments, and stood white in the dazed moon. One moment she stood—and fell forward.

A streak of white shot away in a swift-drawn line. The same instant the moon recovered herself, shining out with a full flash, and I saw that the streak was a long-bodied thing, rushing in great, low-curved bounds over the grass. Dark spots seemed to run like a stream adown its back, as if it had been fleeting along under the edge of a wood, and catching the shadows of the leaves.

"God of mercy!" I cried, "is the terrible creature speeding to the night-infolded city?" and I seemed to hear from afar the sudden burst and spread of outcrying terror, as the pale savage bounded from house to house, rending and slaying.

While I gazed after it fear-stricken, past me from behind, like a swift, all but noiseless arrow, shot a second large creature, pure white. Its path was straight for the spot where the lady had fallen, and, as I thought, lay. My tongue clave to the roof of my mouth. I sprang forward pursuing the beast. But in a moment the spot I made for was far behind it.

"It was well," I thought, "that I could not cry out : if she had risen, the monster would have been upon her!"

But when I reached the place, no lady was there; only the garments she had dropped lay dusk in the moonlight.

I stood staring after the second beast. It tore over the ground with yet greater swiftness than the former—in long, level, skimming leaps, the very embodiment of wasteless speed. It followed the line the other had taken, and I watched it grow smaller and smaller, until it disappeared in the uncertain distance.

But where was the lady? Had the first beast surprised her, creeping upon her noiselessly? I had heard no shriek! and there had not been time to devour her! Could it have caught her up as it ran, and borne her away to its den? So laden it could not have run so fast! and I should have seen that it carried something!

Horrible doubts began to wake in me. After a thorough but fruitless search, I set out in the track of the two animals.

CHAPTER XXI

THE FUGITIVE MOTHER

As I hastened along, a cloud came over the moon, and from the gray dark suddenly emerged a white figure, clasping a child to her bosom, and stooping as she ran. She was on a line parallel with my own, but did not perceive me as she hurried along, terror and anxiety in every movement of her driven speed.

"She is chased!" I said to myself. "Some prowler of this terrible night is after her!"

To follow would have added to her fright: I stepped into her track to stop her pursuer.

As I stood for a moment looking after her through the dusk, behind me came a swift, soft-footed rush, and ere I could turn, something sprang over my head, struck me sharply on the forehead, and knocked me down. I was up in an instant, but all I saw of my assailant was a vanishing whiteness. I ran after the beast, with the blood trickling from my forehead; but had run only a few steps, when a shriek of despair tore the quivering night. I ran the faster, though I could not but fear it must already be too late.

In a minute or two I spied a low white shape approaching me through the vapour-dusted moonlight. It must be another beast, I thought at first, for it came slowly, almost crawling, with strange, floundering leaps, as of a creature in agony! I drew aside from its path, and waited. As it neared me, I saw it was going on three legs, carrying its left fore-paw high from the ground. It had many dark, oval spots on a shining white skin, and was attended by a low rushing sound, as of water falling upon grass. As it went by me, I saw something streaming from the lifted paw.

"It is blood!" I said to myself, "some readier champion than I has wounded the beast!" But, strange to tell, such a pity seized me at sight of the suffering creature, that, though an axe had been in my hand I could not have struck at it. In a broken succession of hobbling leaps it went out of sight, its blood, as it seemed, still issuing in a small torrent, which kept flowing back softly through the grass beside me. "If it go on bleeding like that," I thought, "it will soon be hurtless!"

I went on, for I might yet be useful to the woman, and hoped also to see her deliverer.

I descried her a little way off, seated on the grass, with her child in her lap.

"Can I do anything for you?" I asked.

At the sound of my voice she started violently, and would have risen. I threw myself on the ground.

"You need not be frightened," I said. "I was following the beast when happily you found a nearer protector! It passed me now with its foot bleeding so much that by this time it must be all but dead!"

"There is little hope of that!" she answered, trembling. "Do you not know whose beast she is?"

Now I had certain strange suspicions, but I answered that I knew nothing of the brute, and asked what had become of her champion.

"What champion?" she rejoined. "I have seen no one."

"Then how came the monster to grief?"

"I pounded her foot with a stone—as hard as I could strike. Did you not hear her cry?"

"Well, you are a brave woman!" I answered. "I thought it was you gave the cry!"

"It was the leopardess."

"I never heard such a sound from the throat of an animal! it was like the scream of a woman in torture!"

"My voice was gone; I could not have shrieked to save my baby! When I saw the horrid mouth at my darling's little white neck, I caught up a stone and mashed her lame foot."

"Tell me about the creature," I said; "I am a stranger in these parts."

"You will soon know about her if you are going to Bulika!" she answered. "Now, I must never go back there!"

"Yes, I am going to Bulika," I said, "—to see the princess."

"Have a care; you had better not go!—But perhaps you are—! The princess is a very good, kind woman!"

I heard a little movement. Clouds had by this time gathered so thick over the moon that I could scarcely see my companion : I feared she was rising to run from me.

"You are in no danger of any sort from me," I said "What oath would you like me to take?"

"I know by your speech that you are not of the people of Bulika," she replied; "I will trust you!—I am not of them, either, else I should not be able : they never trust any one—If only I could see you! But I like your voice!—There, my darling is asleep! The foul beast has not hurt her!—Yes : it was my baby she was after!" she went on, caressing the child. "And then she would have torn her mother to pieces for carrying her off!—Some say the princess has two white leopardesses," she continued : "I know only one—with spots. Everybody knows *her*! If the princess hear of a baby, she sends her immediately to suck its blood, and then it either dies or grows up an idiot. I would have gone away with my baby, but the princess was from home, and I thought I might wait until I was a little stronger. But she must have taken the beast with her, and been on her way home when I left, and come across my track. I heard the *sniff-snuff* of the leopardess behind me, and ran;—oh, how I ran!— But my darling will not die! There is no mark on her!"

"Where are you taking her?"

"Where no one ever tells!"

"Why is the princess so cruel?"

"There is an old prophecy that a child will be the death of her. That is why she will listen to no offer of marriage, they say."

"But what will become of her country if she kills all the babies?"

"She does not care about her country. She sends witches

around to teach the women spells that keep babies away, and give them horrible things to eat. Some say she is in league with the Shadows to put an end to the race. At night we hear the questing beast, and lie awake and shiver. She can tell at once the house where a baby is coming, and lies down at the door, watching to get in. There are words that have power to shoo her away, only they do not always work—But here I sit talking, and the beast may by this time have got home, and her mistress be sending the other after us!"

As thus she ended, she rose in haste.

"I do not think she will ever get home.—Let me carry the baby for you!" I said, as I rose also.

She returned me no answer, and when I would have taken it, only clasped it the closer.

"I cannot think," I said, walking by her side, "how the brute could be bleeding so much!"

"Take my advice, and don't go near the palace," she answered. "There are sounds in it at night as if the dead were trying to shriek, but could not open their mouths!"

She bade me an abrupt farewell. Plainly she did not want more of my company; so I stood still, and heard her footsteps die away on the grass.

CHAPTER XXII

BULIKA

I HAD LOST ALL notion of my position, and was walking about in pure, helpless impatience, when suddenly I found myself in the path of the leopardess, wading in the blood from her paw. It ran against my ankles with the force of a small brook, and I got out of it the more quickly because of an unshaped suspicion in my mind as to whose blood it might be. But I kept close to the sound of it, walking up the side of the stream, for it would guide me in the direction of Bulika.

I soon began to reflect, however, that no leopardess, no elephant, no hugest animal that in our world preceded man, could keep such a torrent flowing, except every artery in its body were open, and its huge system went on filling its vessels

from fields and lakes and forests as fast as they emptied themselves : it could not be blood ! I dipped a finger in it, and at once
satisfied myself that it was not. In truth, however it might have
come there, it was a softly murmuring rivulet of water that
ran, without channel, over the grass ! But sweet as was its song,
I dared not drink of it; I kept walking on, hoping after the
light, and listening to the familiar sound so long unheard—for
that of the hot stream was very different. The mere wetting of
my feet in it, however, had so refreshed me, that I went on without fatigue till the darkness began to grow thinner, and I knew
the sun was drawing nigh. A few minutes more, and I could
discern, against the pale aurora, the wall-towers of a city—
seemingly old as time itself. Then I looked down to get a sight
of the brook.

It was gone. I had indeed for a long time noted its sound
growing fainter, but at last had ceased to attend to it. I looked
back : the grass in its course lay bent as it had flowed, and here
and there glimmered a small pool. Toward the city, there was
no trace of it. Near where I stood, the flow of its fountain must
at least have paused !

Around the city were gardens, growing many sorts of vegetables, hardly one of which I recognised. I saw no water, no
flowers, no sign of animals. The gardens came very near the
walls, but were separated from them by huge heaps of gravel
and refuse thrown from the battlements.

I went up to the nearest gate, and found it but half-closed,
nowise secured, and without guard or sentinel. To judge by its
hinges, it could not be farther opened or shut closer. Passing
through, I looked down a long ancient street. It was utterly
silent, and with scarce an indication in it of life present. Had I
come upon a dead city? I turned and went out again, toiled a
long way over the dust-heaps, and crossed several roads, each
leading up to a gate : I would not re-enter until some of the
inhabitants should be stirring.

What was I there for? what did I expect or hope to find?
what did I mean to do?

I must see, if but once more, the woman I had brought to
life ! I did not desire her society : she had waked in me frightful
suspicions; and friendship, not to say love, was wildly impossible
between us ! But her presence had had a strange influence upon

me, and in her presence I must resist, and at the same time analyse that influence! The seemingly inscrutable in her I would fain penetrate : to understand something of her mode of being would be to look into marvels such as imagination could never have suggested! In this I was too daring : a man must not, for knowledge, of his own will encounter temptation! On the other hand, I had reinstated an evil force about to perish, and was, to the extent of my opposing faculty, accountable for what mischief might ensue! I had learned that she was the enemy of children : the Little Ones might be in her danger! It was in the hope of finding out something of their history that I had left them; on that I had received a little light : I must have more; I must learn how to protect them!

Hearing at length a little stir in the place, I walked through the next gate, and thence along a narrow street of tall houses to a little square, where I sat down on the base of a pillar with a hideous bat-like creature atop. Ere long, several of the inhabitants came sauntering past. I spoke to one : he gave me a rude stare and ruder word, and went on.

I got up and went through one narrow street after another, gradually filling with idlers, and was not surprised to see no children. By and by, near one of the gates, I encountered a group of young men who reminded me not a little of the bad giants. They came about me staring, and presently began to push and hustle me, then to throw things at me. I bore it as well as I could, wishing not to provoke enmity where I wanted to remain for a while. Oftener than once or twice I appealed to passers-by whom I fancied more benevolent-looking, but none would halt a moment to listen to me. I looked poor, and that was enough : to the citizens of Bulika, as to house-dogs, poverty was an offence! Deformity and sickness were taxed; and no legislation of their princess was more heartily approved of than what tended to make poverty subserve wealth.

I took to my heels at last, and no one followed me beyond the gate. A lumbering fellow, however, who sat by it eating a hunch of bread, picked up a stone to throw after me, and happily, in his stupid eagerness, threw, not the stone but the bread. I took it, and he did not dare follow to reclaim it : beyond the walls they were cowards every one. I went off a few hundred yards, threw myself down, ate the bread, fell asleep, and slept soundly in the grass, where the hot sunlight renewed my strength.

It was night when I woke. The moon looked down on me in friendly fashion, seeming to claim with me old acquaintance. She was very bright, and the same moon, I thought, that saw me through the terrors of my first night in that strange world. A cold wind blew from the gate, bringing with it an evil odour; but it did not chill me, for the sun had plenished me with warmth. I crept again into the city. There I found the few that were still in the open air crouched in corners to escape the shivering blast.

I was walking slowly through the long narrow street, when, just before me, a huge white thing bounded across it, with a single flash in the moonlight, and disappeared. I turned down the next opening, eager to get sight of it again.

It was a narrow lane, almost too narrow to pass through, but it led me into a wider street. The moment I entered the latter, I saw on the opposite side, in the shadow, the creature I had followed, itself following like a dog what I took for a man. Over his shoulder, every other moment, he glanced at the animal behind him, but neither spoke to it, nor attempted to drive it away. At a place where he had to cross a patch of moonlight, I saw that he cast no shadow, and was himself but a flat superficial shadow, of two dimensions. He was, nevertheless, an opaque shadow, for he not merely darkened any object on the other side of him, but rendered it, in fact, invisible. In the shadow he was blacker than the shadow; in the moonlight he looked like one who had drawn his shadow up about him, for not a suspicion of it moved beside or under him; while the gleaming animal, which followed so close at his heels as to seem the white shadow of his blackness, and which I now saw to be a leopardess, drew her own gliding shadow black over the ground by her side. When they passed together from the shadow into the moonlight, the Shadow deepened in blackness, the animal flashed into radiance. I was at the moment walking abreast of them on the opposite side, my bare feet sounding on the flat stones : the leopardess never turned head or twitched ear; the shadow seemed once to look at me, for I lost his profile, and saw for a second only a sharp upright line. That instant the wind found me and blew through me : I shuddered from head to foot, and my heart went from wall to wall of my bosom, like a pebble in a child's rattle.

CHAPTER XXIII

A WOMAN OF BULIKA

I TURNED ASIDE INTO an alley, and sought shelter in a small archway. In the mouth of it I stopped, and looked out at the moonlight which filled the alley. The same instant a woman came gliding in after me, turned, trembling, and looked out also. A few seconds passed; then a huge leopard, its white skin dappled with many blots, darted across the archway. The woman pressed close to me, and my heart filled with pity. I put my arm round her.

"If the brute come here, I will lay hold of it," I said, "and you must run."

"Thank you!" she murmured.

"Have you ever seen it before?" I asked.

"Several times," she answered, still trembling. "She is a pet of the princess's. You are a stranger, or you would know her!"

"I am a stranger," I answered. "But is she, then, allowed to run loose?"

"She is kept in a cage, her mouth muzzled, and her feet in gloves of crocodile leather. Chained she is too; but she gets out often, and sucks the blood of any child she can lay hold of. Happily there are not many mothers in Bulika!"

Here she burst into tears.

"I wish I were at home!" she sobbed. "The princess returned only last night, and there is the leopardess out already! How am I to get into the house? It is me she is after, I know! She will be lying at my own door, watching for me!—But I am a fool to talk to a stranger!"

"All strangers are not bad!" I said. "The beast shall not touch you till she has done with me, and by that time you will be in. You are happy to have a house to go to! What a terrible wind it is!"

"Take me home safe, and I will give you shelter from it," she rejoined. "But we must wait a little!"

I asked her many questions. She told me the people never

did anything except dig for precious stones in their cellars. They were rich, and had everything made for them in other towns.

"Why?" I asked.

"Because it is a disgrace to work," she answered. "Everybody in Bulika knows that!"

I asked how they were rich if none of them earned money. She replied that their ancestors had saved for them, and they never spent. When they wanted money they sold a few of their gems.

"But there must be some poor!" I said.

"I suppose there must be, but we never think of such people. When one goes poor, we forget him. That is how we keep rich. We mean to be rich always."

"But when you have dug up all your precious stones and sold them, you will have to spend your money, and one day you will have none left!"

"We have so many, and there are so many still in the ground, that that day will never come," she replied.

"Suppose a strange people were to fall upon you, and take everything you have!"

"No strange people will dare; they are all horribly afraid of our princess. She it is who keeps us safe and free and rich!"

Every now and then as she spoke, she would stop and look behind her.

I asked why her people had such a hatred of strangers. She answered that the presence of a stranger defiled the city.

"How is that?" I said.

"Because we are more ancient and noble than any other nation.—Therefore," she added, "we always turn strangers out before night."

"How, then, can you take me into your house?" I asked.

"I will make an exception of you," she replied.

"Is there no place in the city for the taking in of strangers?"

"Such a place would be pulled down, and its owner burned. How is purity to be preserved except by keeping low people at a proper distance? Dignity is such a delicate thing!"

She told me that their princess had reigned for thousands of years; that she had power over the air and the water as well as the earth—and, she believed, over the fire too; that she could do what she pleased, and was answerable to nobody.

When at length she was willing to risk the attempt, we took

our way through lanes and narrow passages, and reached her door without having met a single live creature. It was in a wider street, between two tall houses, at the top of a narrow, steep stair, up which she climbed slowly, and I followed. Ere we reached the top, however, she seemed to take fright, and darted up the rest of the steps : I arrived just in time to have the door closed in my face, and stood confounded on the landing, where was about length enough, between the opposite doors of the two houses, for a man to lie down.

Weary, and not scrupling to defile Bulika with my presence, I took advantage of the shelter, poor as it was.

CHAPTER XXIV

THE WHITE LEOPARDESS

AT THE FOOT of the stair lay the moonlit street, and I could hear the unwholesome, inhospitable wind blowing about below. But not a breath of it entered my retreat, and I was composing myself to rest, when suddenly my eyes opened, and there was the head of the shining creature I had seen following the Shadow, just rising above the uppermost step! The moment she caught sight of my eyes, she stopped and began to retire, tail foremost. I sprang up; whereupon, having no room to turn, she threw herself backward, head over tail, scrambled to her feet, and in a moment was down the stair and gone. I followed her to the bottom, and looked all up and down the street. Not seeing her, I went back to my hard couch.

There were, then, two evil creatures prowling about the city, one with, and one without spots! I was not inclined to risk much for man or woman in Bulika, but the life of a child might well be worth such a poor one as mine, and I resolved to keep watch at that door the rest of the night.

Presently I heard the latch move, slow, slow : I looked up, and seeing the door half-open, rose and slid softly in. Behind it stood, not the woman I had befriended, but the muffled woman of the desert. Without a word she led me a few steps to an empty stone-paved chamber, and pointed to a rug on the floor. I wrapped myself in it, and once more lay down. She shut the door of the room, and I heard the outer door open and close again. There was no light save what came from the moonlit air.

As I lay sleepless, I began to hear a stifled moaning. It went on for a good while, and then came the cry of a child, followed by a terrible shriek. I sprang up and darted into the passage : from another door in it came the white leopardess with a new-born baby in her mouth, carrying it like a cub of her own. I threw myself upon her, and compelled her to drop the infant, which fell on the stone slabs with a piteous wail.

At the cry appeared the muffled woman. She stepped over us, the beast and myself, where we lay struggling in the narrow passage, took up the child, and carried it away. Returning, she lifted me off the animal, opened the door, and pushed me gently out. At my heels followed the leopardess.

"She too has failed me!" thought I; "—given me up to the beast to be settled with at her leisure! But we shall have a tussle for it!"

I ran down the stair, fearing she would spring on my back, but she followed me quietly. At the foot I turned to lay hold of her, but she sprang over my head; and when again I turned to face her, she was crouching at my feet! I stooped and stroked her lovely white skin; she responded by licking my bare feet with her hard dry tongue. Then I patted and fondled her, a well of tenderness overflowing in my heart : she might be treacherous too, but if I turned from every show of love lest it should be feigned, how was I ever to find the real love which must be somewhere in every world?

I stood up; she rose, and stood beside me.

A bulky object fell with a heavy squelch in the middle of the street, a few yards from us. I ran to it, and found a pulpy mass, with just form enough left to show it the body of a woman. It must have been thrown from some neighbouring window! I looked around me : the Shadow was walking along the other side of the way, with the white leopardess again at his heel!

I followed and gained upon them, urging in my heart for the leopardess that probably she was not a free agent. When I got near them, however, she turned and flew at me with such a hideous snarl, that instinctively I drew back : instantly she resumed her place behind the Shadow. Again I drew near; again she flew at me, her eyes flaming like live emeralds. Once more I made the experiment : she snapped at me like a dog, and bit me. My heart gave way, and I uttered a cry; whereupon the creature looked round with a glance that plainly meant—"Why *would* you make me do it?"

I turned away angry with myself : I had been losing my time ever since I entered the place ! night as it was, I would go straight to the palace ! From the square I had seen it—high above the heart of the city, compassed with many defences, more a fortress than a palace !

But I found its fortifications, like those of the city, much neglected, and partly ruinous. For centuries, clearly, they had been of no account ! It had great and strong gates, with something like a drawbridge to them over a rocky chasm; but they stood open, and it was hard to believe that water had ever occupied the hollow before them. All was so still that sleep seemed to interpenetrate the structure, causing the very moonlight to look discordantly awake. I must either enter like a thief, or break a silence that rendered frightful the mere thought of a sound !

Like an outcast dog I was walking about the walls, when I came to a little recess with a stone bench : I took refuge in it from the wind, lay down, and in spite of the cold fell fast asleep.

I was wakened by something leaping upon me, and licking my face with the rough tongue of a feline animal. "It is the white leopardess !" I thought. "She is come to suck my blood ! —and why should she not have it?—it would cost me more to defend than to yield it !" So I lay still, expecting a shoot of pain. But the pang did not arrive; a pleasant warmth instead began to diffuse itself through me. Stretched at my back, she lay as close to me as she could lie, the heat of her body slowly penetrating mine, and her breath, which had nothing of the wild beast in it, swathing my head and face in a genial atmosphere. A full conviction that her intention toward me was good, gained possession of me. I turned like a sleepy boy, threw my arm over her, and sank into profound unconsciousness.

When I began to come to myself, I fancied I lay warm and soft in my own bed. "Is it possible I am at home?" I thought. The well-known scents of the garden seemed to come crowding in. I rubbed my eyes, and looked out : I lay on a bare stone, in the heart of a hateful city !

I sprang from the bench. Had I indeed had a leopardess for my bedfellow, or had I but dreamed it? She had but just left me, for the warmth of her body was with me yet!

I left the recess with a new hope, as strong as it was shapeless. One thing only was clear to me : I must find the princess! Surely I had some power with her, if not over her! Had I not saved her life, and had she not prolonged it at the expense of my vitality? The reflection gave me courage to encounter her, be she what she might.

CHAPTER XXV

THE PRINCESS

MAKING A CIRCUIT of the castle, I came again to the open gates, crossed the ravine-like moat, and found myself in a paved court, planted at regular intervals with towering trees like poplars. In the centre was one taller than the rest, whose branches, near the top, spread a little and gave it some resemblance to a palm. Between their great stems I got glimpses of the palace, which was of a style strange to me, but suggested Indian origin. It was long and low, with lofty towers at the corners, and one huge dome in the middle, rising from the roof to half the height of the towers. The main entrance was in the centre of the front—a low arch that seemed half an ellipse. No one was visible, the doors stood wide open, and I went unchallenged into a large hall, in the form of a longish ellipse. Toward one side stood a cage, in which couched, its head on its paws, a huge leopardess, chained by a steel collar, with its mouth muzzled and its paws muffled. It was white with dark oval spots, and lay staring out of wide-open eyes, with canoe-shaped pupils, and great green irids. It appeared to watch me, but not an eyeball, not a foot, not a whisker moved, and its tail stretched out behind it rigid as an iron bar. I could not tell whether it was a live thing or not.

From this vestibule two low passages led; I took one of them, and found it branch into many, all narow and irregular. At a spot where was scarce room for two to pass, a page ran against me. He started back in terror, but having scanned me, gathered impudence, puffed himself out, and asked my business.

"To see the princess," I answered.

"A likely thing!" he returned. "I have not seen her highness this morning myself!"

I caught him by the back of the neck, shook him, and said,

"Take me to her at once, or I will drag you with me till I find her. She shall know how her servants receive her visitors."

He gave a look at me, and began to pull like a blind man's dog, leading me thus to a large kitchen, where were many servants, feebly busy, and hardly awake. I expected them to fall upon me and drive me out, but they stared instead, with wide eyes—not at me, but at something behind me, and grew more ghastly as they stared. I turned my head, and saw the white leopardess, regarding them in a way that might have feared stouter hearts.

Presently, however, one of them, seeing, I suppose, that attack was not imminent, began to recover himself; I turned to him, and let the boy go.

"Take me to the princess," I said.

"She has not yet left her room, your lordship," he replied.

"Let her know that I am here, waiting audience of her."

"Will your lordship please to give me your name?"

"Tell her that one who knows the white leech desires to see her."

"She will kill me if I take such a message : I must not. I dare not."

"You refuse?"

He cast a glance at my attendant, and went.

The others continued staring—too much afraid of her to take their eyes off her. I turned to the graceful creature, where she stood, her muzzle dropped to my heel, white as milk, a warm splendour in the gloomy place, and stooped and patted her. She looked up at me; the mere movement of her head was enough to scatter them in all directions. She rose on her hind legs, and put her paws on my shoulders; I threw my arms round her. She pricked her ears, broke from me, and was out of sight in a moment.

The man I had sent to the princess entered.

"Please to come this way, my lord," he said.

My heart gave a throb, as if bracing itself to the encounter.

I followed him through many passages, and was at last shown into a room so large and so dark that its walls were invisible. A single spot on the floor reflected a little light, but around that spot all was black. I looked up, and saw at a great height an oval aperture in the roof, on the periphery of which appeared the joints between blocks of black marble. The light on the floor showed close fitting slabs of the same material. I found afterwards that the elliptical wall as well was of black marble, absorbing the little light that reached it. The roof was the long half of an ellipsoid, and the opening in it was over one of the foci of the ellipse of the floor. I fancied I caught sight of reddish lines, but when I would have examined them, they were gone.

All at once, a radiant form stood in the centre of the darkness, flashing a splendour on every side. Over a robe of soft white, her hair streamed in a cataract, black as the marble on which it fell. Her eyes were a luminous blackness; her arms and feet like warm ivory. She greeted me with the innocent smile of a girl—and in face, figure, and motion seemed but now to have stepped over the threshold of womanhood. "Alas," thought I, "ill did I reckon my danger! Can this be the woman I rescued—she who struck me, scorned me, left me?" I stood gazing at her out of the darkness; she stood gazing into it, as if searching for me.

She disappeared. "She will not acknowledge me!" I thought. But the next instant her eyes flashed out of the dark straight into mine. She had descried me and come to me!

"You have found me at last!" she said, laying her hand on my shoulder. "I knew you would!"

My frame quivered with conflicting consciousnesses, to analyse which I had no power. I was simultaneously attracted and repelled : each sensation seemed either.

"You shiver!" she said. "This place is cold for you! Come."

I stood silent : she had struck me dumb with beauty; she held me dumb with sweetness.

Taking me by the hand, she drew me to the spot of light, and again flashed upon me. An instant she stood there.

"You have grown brown since last I saw you," she said.

"This is almost the first roof I have been under since you left me," I replied.

"Whose was the other?" she rejoined.

"I do not know the woman's name."

"I would gladly learn it! The instinct of hospitality is not strong in my people!"

She took me again by the hand, and led me through the darkness many steps to a curtain of black. Beyond it was a white stair, up which she conducted me to a beautiful chamber.

"How you must miss the hot flowing river!" she said. "But there is a bath in the corner with no white leeches in it! At the foot of your couch you will find a garment. When you come down, I shall be in the room to your left at the foot of the stair."

I stood as she left me, accusing my presumption : how was I to treat this lovely woman as a thing of evil, who behaved to me like a sister?—Whence the marvellous change in her? She left me with a blow; she received me almost with an embrace! She had reviled me; she said she knew I would follow and find her! Did she know my doubts concerning her—how much I should want explained? *Could* she explain all? Could I believe her if she did? As to her hospitality, I had surely earned and might accept that —at least until I came to a definite judgment concerning her!

Could such beauty as I saw, and such wickedness as I suspected, exist in the same person? If they could, *how* was it possible? Unable to answer the former question, I must let the latter wait!

Clear as crystal, the water in the great white bath sent a sparkling flash from the corner where it lay sunk in the marble floor, and seemed to invite me to its embrace. Except the hot stream, two draughts in the cottage of the veiled woman, and the pools in the track of the wounded leopardess, I had not seen water since leaving home; it looked a thing celestial. I plunged in.

Immediately my brain was filled with an odour strange and delicate, which yet I did not altogether like. It made me doubt the princess afresh : had she medicated it? had she enchanted it? was she in any way working on me unlawfully? And how was there water in the palace, and not a drop in the city? I remembered the crushed paw of the leopardess, and sprang from the bath.

What had I been bathing in? Again I saw the fleeing mother, again I heard the howl, again I saw the limping beast. But what matter whence it flowed? was not the water sweet? Was it not very water the pitcher-plant secreted from its heart, and stored for the weary traveller? Water came from heaven : what mattered the well where it gathered, or the spring whence it burst? But I did not re-enter the bath.

I put on the robe of white wool, embroidered on the neck and hem, that lay ready for me, and went down the stair to the room whither my hostess had directed me. It was round, all of alabaster, and without a single window : the light came through everywhere, a soft, pearly shimmer rather than shine. Vague shadowy forms went flitting about over the walls and low dome, like loose rain-clouds over a grey-blue sky.

The princess stood waiting me, in a robe embroidered with argentine rings and discs, rectangles and lozenges, close together —a silver mail. It fell unbroken from her neck and hid her feet, but its long open sleeves left her arms bare.

In the room was a table of ivory, bearing cakes and fruit, an ivory jug of milk, a crystal jug of wine of a pale rose-colour, and a white loaf.

"Here we do not kill to eat," she said; "but I think you will like what I can give you."

I told her I could desire nothing better than what I saw. She seated herself on a couch by the table, and made me a sign to sit by her.

She poured me out a bowlful of milk, and, handing me the loaf, begged me to break from it such a piece as I liked. Then she filled from the wine-jug two silver goblets of grotesquely graceful workmanship.

"You have never drunk wine like this !" she said.

I drank, and wondered : every flower of Hybla and Hymettus must have sent its ghost to swell the soul of that wine !

"And now that you will be able to listen," she went on, "I must do what I can to make myself intelligible to you. Our natures, however, are so different, that this may not be easy. Men and women live but to die; we, that is such as I—we are but a few—live to live on. Old age is to you a horror; to me it is a dear desire : the older we grow, the nearer we are to our perfection. Your perfection is a poor thing, comes soon, and lasts but a little while; ours is a ceaseless ripening. I am not yet ripe, and have lived thousands of your years—how many, I never cared to note. The everlasting will not be measured.

"Many lovers have sought me; I have loved none of them : they sought but to enslave me; they sought me but as the men of my city seek gems of price.—When you found me, I found a man ! I put you to the test; you stood it; your love was genuine !

—It was, however, far from ideal—far from such love as I
would have. You loved me truly, but not with true love. Pity
has, but is not love. What woman of any world would return
love for pity? Such love as yours was then, is hateful to me. I
knew that, if you saw me as I am, you would love me—like the
rest of them—to have and to hold : I would none of that either!
I would be otherwise loved! I would have a love that outlived
hopelessness, outmeasured indifference, hate, scorn! Therefore
did I put on cruelty, despite, ingratitude. When I left you, I had
shown myself such as you could at least no longer follow from
pity : I was no longer in need of you! But you must satisfy my
desire or set me free—prove yourself priceless or worthless! To
satisfy the hunger of my love, you must follow me, looking for
nothing, not gratitude, not even pity in return!—follow and find
me, and be content with merest presence, with scantest for-
bearance!—I, not you, have failed; I yield the contest."

She looked at me tenderly, and hid her face in her hands. But
I had caught a flash and a sparkle behind the tenderness, and
did not believe her. She laid herself out to secure and enslave
me; she only fascinated me!

"Beautiful princess," I said, "let me understand how you
came to be found in such evil plight."

"There are things I cannot explain," she replied, "until you
have become capable of understanding them—which can only
be when love is grown perfect. There are many things so hidden
from you that you cannot even wish to know them; but any
question you can put, I can in some measure answer.

"I had set out to visit a part of my dominions occupied by a
savage dwarf-people, strong and fierce, enemies to law and order,
opposed to every kind of progress—an evil race. I went alone,
fearing nothing, unaware of the least necessity for precaution. I
did not know that upon the hot stream beside which you found
me, a certain woman, by no means so powerful as myself, not
being immortal, had cast what you call a spell—which is merely
the setting in motion of a force as natural as any other, but
operating primarily in a region beyond the ken of the mortal
who makes use of the force.

"I set out on my journey, reached the stream, bounded across
it—"

A shadow of embarrassment darkened her cheek : I understood it, but showed no sign. Checked for the merest moment, she went on :

"—you know what a step it is in parts !—But in the very act, an indescribable cold invaded me. I recognised at once the nature of the assault, and knew it could affect me but temporarily. By sheer force of will I dragged myself to the wood—nor knew anything more until I saw you asleep, and the horrible worm at your neck. I crept out, dragged the monster from you, and laid my lips to the wound. You began to wake; I buried myself among the leaves."

She rose, her eyes flashing as never human eyes flashed, and threw her arms high over her head.

"What you have made me is yours !" she cried. "I will repay you as never yet did woman ! My power, my beauty, my love are your own : take them."

She dropt kneeling beside me, laid her arms across my knees, and looked up in my face.

Then first I noted on her left hand a large clumsy glove. In my mind's eye I saw hair and claws under it, but I knew it was a hand shut hard—perhaps badly bruised. I glanced at the other : it was lovely as hand could be, and I felt that, if I did less than loathe her, I should love her. Not to dally with usurping emotions, I turned my eyes aside.

She started to her feet. I sat motionless, looking down.

"To me she may be true !" said my vanity. For a moment I was tempted to love a lie.

An odour, rather than the gentlest of airy pulses, was fanning me. I glanced up. She stood erect before me waving her lovely arms in seemingly mystic fashion.

A frightful roar made my heart rebound against walls of its cage. The alabaster trembled as if it would shake into shivers. The princess shuddered visibly.

"My wine was too strong for you !" she said, in a quavering voice; "I ought not to have let you take a full draught ! Go and sleep now, and when you wake ask me what you please—I will go with you : come."

As she preceded me up the stair,—

"I do not wonder that roar startled you !" she said. "It startled me, I confess : for a moment I feared she had escaped. But that is impossible."

The roar seemed to me, however—I could not tell why—to come from the *white* leopardess, and to be meant for me, not the princess.

With a smile she left me at the door of my room, but as she turned I read anxiety on her beautiful face.

CHAPTER XXVI

A BATTLE ROYAL

I THREW MYSELF ON the bed, and began to turn over in my mind the tale she had told me. She had forgotten herself, and, by a single incautious word, removed one perplexity as to the condition in which I found her in the forest! The leopardess *bounded* over; the princess lay prostrate on the bank: the running stream had dissolved her self-enchantment! Her own account of the object of her journey revealed the danger of the Little Ones then imminent: I had saved the life of their one fearful enemy!

I had but reached this conclusion when I fell asleep. The lovely wine may not have been quite innocent.

When I opened my eyes, it was night. A lamp, suspended from the ceiling, cast a clear, although soft light through the chamber. A delicious languor infolded me. I seemed floating, far from land, upon the bosom of a twilight sea. Existence was in itself pleasure. I had no pain. Surely I was dying!

No pain!—ah, what a shoot of mortal pain was that! what a sickening sting! It went right through my heart! Again! That was sharpness itself!—and so sickening! I could not move my hand to lay it on my heart; something kept it down!

The pain was dying away, but my whole body seemed paralysed. Some evil thing was upon me!—something hateful! I would have struggled, but could not reach a struggle. My will agonised, but in vain, to assert itself. I desisted, and lay passive. Then I became aware of a soft hand on my face, pressing my head into the pillow, and of a heavy weight lying across me.

I began to breathe more freely; the weight was gone from my chest; I opened my eyes.

The princess was standing above me on the bed, looking out

into the room, with the air of one who dreamed. Her great eyes were clear and calm. Her mouth wore a look of satisfied passion; she wiped from it a streak of red.

She caught my gaze, bent down, and struck me on the eyes with the handkerchief in her hand : it was like drawing the edge of a knife across them, and for a moment of two I was blind.

I heard a dull heavy sound, as of a large soft-footed animal alighting from a little jump. I opened my eyes, and saw the great swing of a long tail as it disappeared through the half-open doorway. I sprang after it.

The creature had vanished quite. I shot down the stair, and into the hall of alabaster. The moon was high, and the place like the inside of a faint, sun-blanched moon. The princess was not there. I must find her : in her presence I might protect myself; out of it I could not ! I was a tame animal for her to feed upon; a human fountain for a thirst demoniac ! She showed me favour the more easily to use me ! My waking eyes did not fear her, but they would close, and she would come ! Not seeing her, I felt her everywhere, for she might be anywhere—might even now be waiting me in some secret cavern of sleep ! Only with my eyes upon her could I feel safe from her !

Outside the alabaster hall it was pitch-dark, and I had to grope my way along with hands and feet. At last I felt a curtain, put it aside, and entered the black hall. There I found a great silent assembly. How it was visible I neither saw nor could imagine, for the walls, the floor, the roof, were shrouded in what seemed an infinite blackness, blacker than the blackest of moonless, starless nights; yet my eyes could separate, although vaguely, not a few of the individuals in the mass interpenetrated and divided, as well as surrounded, by the darkness. It seemed as if my eyes would never come quite to themselves. I pressed their balls and looked and looked again, but what I saw would not grow distinct. Blackness mingled with form, silence and un-defined motion possessed the wide space. All was a dim, con-fused dance, filled with recurrent glimpses of shapes not un-known to me. Now appeared a woman, with glorious eyes looking out of a skull; now an armed figure on a skeleton horse; now one now another of the hideous burrowing phantasms. I could trace no order and little relation in the mingling and crossing currents and eddies. If I seemed to catch the shape and rhythm of a dance, it was but to see it break, and confusion prevail. With the shifting colours of the seemingly more solid shapes, mingled a multitude of shadows, independent apparently of originals, each moving after its own free shadow-will. I looked everywhere for the princess, but throughout the wildly changing kaleidoscopic scene, could not see her nor discover indication of her presence. Where was she? What might she not be doing? No one took the least notice of me as I wandered hither and thither seeking her. At length losing hope, I turned away to look elsewhere. Finding the wall, and keeping to it with my hand, for even then I could not see it, I came, groping along, to a curtained opening into the vestibule.

Dimly moonlighted, the cage of the leopardess was the arena of what seemed a desperate although silent struggle. Two vastly differing forms, human and bestial, with entangled confusion of mingling bodies and limbs, writhed and wrestled in closest embrace. It had lasted but an instant when I saw the leopardess out of the cage, walking quietly to the open door. As I hastened after her I threw a glance behind me : there was the leopardess in the cage, couching motionless as when I saw her first.

The moon, half-way up the sky, was shining round and clear; the bodiless shadow I had seen the night before, was walking through the trees toward the gate; and after him went the leopardess, swinging her tail. I followed, a little way off, as silently as they, and neither of them once looked round. Through the open gate we went down to the city, lying quiet as the moonshine upon it. The face of the moon was very still, and its stillness looked like that of expectation.

The Shadow took his way straight to the stair at the top of which I had lain the night before. Without a pause he went up, and the leopardess followed. I quickened my pace, but, a moment after, heard a cry of horror. Then came the fall of something soft and heavy between me and the stair, and at my feet lay a body, frightfully blackened and crushed, but still recognisable as that of the woman who had led me home and shut me out. As I stood petrified, the spotted leopardess came bounding down the stair with a baby in her mouth. I darted to seize her ere she could turn at the foot; but that instant, from behind me, the white leopardess, like a great bar of glowing silver, shot through the moonlight, and had her by the neck. She dropped the child;

I caught it up, and stood to watch the battle between them.

What a sight it was—now the one, now the other uppermost, both too intent for any noise beyond a low growl, a whimpered cry, or a snarl of hate—followed by a quicker scrambling of claws, as each, worrying and pushing and dragging, struggled for foothold on the pavement! The spotted leopardess was larger than the white, and I was anxious for my friend; but I soon saw that, though neither stronger nor more active, the white leopardess had the greater endurance. Not once did she lose her hold on the neck of the other. From the spotted throat at length issued a howl of agony, changing, by swift-crowded gradations, into the long-drawn *crescendo* of a woman's uttermost wail. The white one relaxed her jaws; the spotted one drew herself away, and rose on her hind legs. Erect in the moonlight stood the princess, a confused rush of shadows careering over her whiteness—the spots of the leopard crowding, hurrying, fleeing to the refuge of her eyes, where merging they vanished. The last few, outsped and belated, mingled with the cloud of her streamy hair, leaving her radiant as the moon when a legion of little vapours has flown, wind-hunted, off her silvery disc—save that, adown the white column of her throat, a thread of blood still trickled from every wound of her adversary's terrible teeth. She turned away, took a few steps with the gait of a Hecate, fell, covered afresh with her spots, and fled at a long, stretching gallop.

The white leopardess turned also, sprang upon me, pulled my arms asunder, caught the baby as it fell, and flew with it along the street toward the gate.

CHAPTER XXVII

THE SILENT FOUNTAIN

I TURNED AND FOLLOWED the spotted leopardess, catching but one glimpse of her as she tore up the brow of the hill to the gate of the palace. When I reached the entrance-hall, the princess was just throwing the robe around her which she had left on the floor. The blood had ceased to flow from her wounds, and had dried in the wind of her flight.

When she saw me, a flash of anger crossed her face, and she turned her head aside. Then, with an attempted smile, she looked at me, and said,

"I have met with a small accident! Happening to hear that the cat-woman was again in the city, I went down to send her away. But she had one of her horrid creatures with her : it sprang upon me, and had its claws in my neck before I could strike it!"

She gave a shiver, and I could not help pitying her, although I knew she lied, for her wounds were real, and her face reminded me of how she looked in the cave. My heart began to reproach me that I had let her fight unaided, and I suppose I looked the compassion I felt.

"Child of folly!" she said, with another attempted smile, "—not crying, surely!—Wait for me here; I am going into the black hall for a moment. I want you to get me something for my scratches."

But I followed her close. Out of my sight I feared her.

The instant the princess entered, I heard a buzzing sound as of many low voices, and, one portion after another, the assembly began to be shiftingly illuminated, as by a ray that went travelling from spot to spot. Group after group would shine out for a space, then sink back into the general vagueness, while another part of the vast company would grow momently bright.

Some of the actions going on when thus illuminated, were not unknown to me; I had been in them, or had looked on them, and so had the princess : present with every one of them I now saw her. The skull-headed dancers footed the grass in the forest-hall : there was the princess looking in at the door! The fight went on in the Evil Wood : there was the princess urging it! Yet I was close behind her all the time, she standing motionless, her head sunk on her bosom. The confused murmur continued, the confused commotion of colours and shapes; and still the ray went shifting and showing. It settled at last on the hollow in the heath, and there was the princess, walking up and down, and trying in vain to wrap the vapour around her! Then first I was startled at what I saw : the old librarian walked up to her, and stood for a moment regarding her; she fell; her limbs forsook her and fled; her body vanished.

A wild shriek rang through the echoing place, and with the fall of her eidolon, the princess herself, till then standing like a statue in front of me, fell heavily, and lay still. I turned at once and went out : not again would I seek to restore her ! As I stood trembling beside the cage, I knew that in the black ellipsoid I had been in the brain of the princess !—I saw the tail of the leopardess quiver once.

While still endeavouring to compose myself, I heard the voice of the princess beside me.

"Come now," she said; "I will show you what I want you to do for me."

She led the way into the court. I followed in dazed compliance.

The moon was near the zenith, and her present silver seemed brighter than the gold of the absent sun. She brought me through the trees to the tallest of them, the one in the centre. It was not quite like the rest, for its branches, drawing their ends together at the top, made a clump that looked from beneath like a fir-cone. The princess stood close under it, gazing up, and said, as if talking to herself,

"On the summit of that tree grows a tiny blossom which would at once heal my scratches ! I might be a dove for a moment and fetch it, but I see a little snake in the leaves whose bite would be worse to a dove than the bite of a tiger to me !—How I hate that cat-woman !"

She turned to me quickly, saying with one of her sweetest smiles,

"Can you climb?"

The smile vanished with the brief question, and her face changed to a look of sadness and suffering. I ought to have left her to suffer, but the way she put her hand to her wounded neck went to my heart.

I considered the tree. All the way up to the branches, were projections on the stem like the remnants on a palm of its fallen leaves.

"I can climb that tree," I answered.

"Not with bare feet !" she returned.

In my haste to follow the leopardess disappearing, I had left my sandals in my room.

"It is no matter," I said; "I have long gone barefoot !"

Again I looked at the tree, and my eyes went wandering up the stem until my sight lost itself in the branches. The moon shone like silvery foam here and there on the rugged bole, and a little rush of wind went through the top with a murmurous sound as of water falling softly into water. I approached the tree to begin my ascent of it. The princess stopped me.

"I cannot let you attempt it with your feet bare!" she insisted. "A fall from the top would kill you!"

"So would a bite from the snake!" I answered—not believing, I confess, that there was any snake.

"It would not hurt *you*!" she replied. "—Wait a moment."

She tore from her garment the two wide borders that met in front, and kneeling on one knee, made me put first my left foot, then my right on the other, and bound them about with the thick embroidered strips.

"You have left the ends hanging, princess!" I said.

"I have nothing to cut them off with; but they are not long enough to get entangled," she replied.

I turned to the tree, and began to climb.

Now in Bulika the cold after sundown was not so great as in certain other parts of the country—especially about the sexton's cottage; yet when I had climbed a little way, I began to feel very cold, grew still colder as I ascended, and became coldest of all when I got among the branches. Then I shivered, and seemed to have lost my hands and feet.

There was hardly any wind, and the branches did not sway in the least, yet, as I approached the summit, I became aware of a peculiar unsteadiness : every branch on which I placed foot or laid hold, seemed on the point of giving way. When my head rose above the branches near the top, and in the open moonlight I began to look about for the blossom, that instant I found myself drenched from head to foot. The next, as if plunged in a stormy water, I was flung about wildly, and felt myself sinking. Tossed up and down, tossed this way and tossed that way, rolled over and over, checked, rolled the other way and tossed up again, I was sinking lower and lower. Gasping and gurgling and choking, I fell at last upon a solid bottom.

"I told you so!" croaked a voice in my ear.

CHAPTER XXVIII

I AM SILENCED

I RUBBED THE WATER out of my eyes, and saw the raven on the edge of a huge stone basin. With the cold light of the dawn reflected from his glossy plumage, he stood calmly looking down upon me. I lay on my back in water, above which, leaning on my elbows, I just lifted my face. I was in the basin of the large fountain constructed by my father in the middle of the lawn. High over me glimmered the thick, steel-shiny stalk, shooting, with a torrent uprush, a hundred feet into the air, to spread in a blossom of foam.

Nettled at the coolness of the raven's remark,

"You told me nothing!" I said.

"I told you to do nothing any one you distrusted asked you!"

"Tut! how was mortal to remember that?"

"You will not forget the consequences of having forgotten it!" replied Mr. Raven, who stood leaning over the margin of the basin, and stretched his hand across to me.

I took it, and was immediately beside him on the lawn, dripping and streaming.

"You must change your clothes at once!" he said. "A wetting does not signify where you come from—though at present such an accident is unusual; here it has its inconveniences!"

He was again a raven, walking, with something stately in his step, toward the house, the door of which stood open.

"I have not much to change!" I laughed; for I had flung aside my robe to climb the tree.

"It is a long time since I moulted a feather!" said the raven.

In the house no one seemed awake. I went to my room, found a dressing-gown, and descended to the library.

As I entered, the librarian came from the closet. I threw myself on a couch. Mr. Raven drew a chair to my side and sat down. For a minute or two neither spoke. I was the first to break the silence.

"What does it all mean?" I said.

"A good question!" he rejoined: "nobody knows what any-

thing is; a man can learn only what a thing means! Whether he
do, depends on the use he is making of it."

"I have made no use of anything yet!"

"Not much; but you know the fact, and that is something!
Most people take more than a lifetime to learn that they have
learned nothing, and done less! At least you have not been
without the desire to be of use!"

"I did want to do something for the children—the precious
Little Ones, I mean."

"I know you did—and started the wrong way!"

"I did not know the right way."

"That is true also—but you are to blame that you did not."

"I am ready to believe whatever you tell me—as soon as I
understand what it means."

"Had you accepted our invitation, you would have known the
right way. When a man will not act where he is, he must go far
to find his work."

"Indeed I have gone far, and got nowhere, for I have not
found my work! I left the children to learn how to serve them,
and have only learned the danger they are in."

"When you were with them, you were where you could help
them : you left your work to look for it! It takes a wise man
to know when to go away; a fool may learn to go back at once!"

"Do you mean, sir, I could have done something for the Little
Ones by staying with them?"

"Could you teach them anything by leaving them?"

"No; but how could I teach them? I did not know how to
begin. Besides, they were far ahead of me!"

"That is true. But you were not a rod to measure them with!
Certainly, if they knew what you know, not to say what you
might have known, they would be ahead of you—out of sight
ahead! but you saw they were not growing—or growing so
slowly that they had not yet developed the idea of growing! they
were even afraid of growing!—You had never seen children
remain children!"

"But surely I had no power to make them grow!"

"You might have removed some of the hindrances to their
growing!"

"What are they? I do not know them. I did think perhaps it
was the want of water!"

"Of course it is! they have none to cry with!"

"I would gladly have kept them from requiring any for that purpose!"

"No doubt you would—the aim of all stupid philanthropists! Why, Mr. Vane, but for the weeping in it, your world would never have become worth saving! You confess you thought it might be water they wanted : why did not you dig them a well or two?"

"That never entered my mind!"

"Not when the sounds of the waters under the earth entered your ears?"

"I believe it did once. But I was afraid of the giants for them. That was what made me bear so much from the brutes myself!"

"Indeed you almost taught the noble little creatures to be afraid of the stupid Bags! While they fed and comforted and worshipped you, all the time you submitted to be the slave of bestial men! You gave the darlings a seeming coward for their hero! A worse wrong you could hardly have done them. They gave you their hearts; you owed them your soul!—You might by this time have made the Bags hewers of wood and drawers of water to the Little Ones!"

"I fear what you say is true, Mr. Raven! But indeed I was afraid that more knowledge might prove an injury to them— render them less innocent, less lovely."

"They had given you no reason to harbour such a fear!"

"Is not a little knowledge a dangerous thing?"

"That is one of the pet falsehoods of your world! Is man's greatest knowledge more than a little? or is it therefore danger-ous? The fancy that knowledge is in itself a great thing, would make any degree of knowledge more dangerous than any amount of ignorance. To know all things would not be greatness."

"At least it was for love of them, not from cowardice that I served the giants!"

"Granted. But you ought to have served the Little Ones, not the giants! You ought to have given the Little Ones water; then they would soon have taught the giants their true position. In the meantime you could yourself have made the giants cut down two-thirds of their coarse fruit-trees to give room to the little delicate ones! You lost your chance with the Lovers, Mr. Vane! You speculated about them instead of helping them!"

CHAPTER XXIX

THE PERSIAN CAT

I SAT IN SILENCE and shame. What he said was true : I had not been a wise neighbour to the Little Ones!

Mr. Raven resumed :

"You wronged at the same time the stupid creatures themselves. For them slavery would have been progress. To them a few such lessons as you could have given them with a stick from one of their own trees, would have been invaluable."

"I did not know they were cowards!"

"What difference does that make? The man who grounds his action on another's cowardice, is essentially a coward himself.—I fear worse will come of it! By this time the Little Ones might have been able to protect themselves from the princess, not to say the giants—they were always fit enough for that; as it was they laughed at them! but now, through your relations with her——"

"I hate her!" I cried.

"Did you let her know you hated her?"

Again I was silent.

"Not even to her have you been faithful!—But hush! we were followed from the fountain, I fear!"

"No living creature did I see!—except a disreputable-looking cat that bolted into the shrubbery."

"It was a magnificent Persian—so wet and draggled, though, as to look what she was—worse than disreputable!"

"What do you mean, Mr. Raven?" I cried, a fresh horror taking me by the throat. "—There was a beautiful blue Persian about the house, but she fled at the very sound of water!— Could she have been after the goldfish?"

"We shall see!" returned the librarian. "I know a little about cats of several sorts, and there is that in the room which will unmask this one, or I am mistaken in her."

He rose, went to the door of the closet, brought from it the mutilated volume, and sat down again beside me. I stared at the book in his hand : it was a whole book, entire and sound!

"Where was the other half of it?" I gasped.

"Sticking through into my library," he answered.

I held my peace. A single question more would have been a plunge into a bottomless sea, and there might be no time!

"Listen," he said: "I am going to read a stanza or two. There is one present who, I imagine, will hardly enjoy the reading!"

He opened the vellum cover, and turned a leaf or two. The parchment was discoloured with age, and one leaf showed a dark stain over two-thirds of it. He slowly turned this also, and seemed looking for a certain passage in what appeared a continuous poem. Somewhere about the middle of the book he began to read.

But what follows represents—not what he read, only the impression it made upon me. The poem seemed in a language I had never before heard, which yet I understood perfectly, although I could not write the words, or give their meaning save in poor approximation. These fragments, then, are the shapes which those he read have finally taken in passing again through my brain :—

> "But if I found a man that could believe
>   In what he saw not, felt not, and yet knew,
> From him I should take substance, and receive
>   Firmness and form relate to touch and view;
>   Then should I clothe me in the likeness true
> Of that idea where his soul did cleave!"

He turned a leaf and read again :—

> "In me was every woman. I had power
>   Over the soul of every living man,
> Such as no woman ever had in dower—
>   Could what no woman ever could, or can;
> All women, I, the woman, still outran,
>   Outsoared, outsank, outreigned, in hall or bower.

> "For I, though me he neither saw nor heard,
>   Nor with his hand could touch finger of mine,
> Although not once my breath had ever stirred
>   A hair of him, could trammel brain and spine
>   With rooted bonds which Death could not untwine—
> Or life, though hope was evermore deferred."

Again he paused, again turned a leaf, and again began :—

"For by his side I lay, a bodiless thing;
  I breathed not, saw not, felt not, only thought,
And made him love me—with a hungering
  After he knew not what—if it was aught
  Or but a nameless something that was wrought
By him out of himself; for I did sing

"A song that had no sound into his soul;
  I lay a heartless thing against his heart,
Giving him nothing where he gave his whole
  Being to clothe me human, every part:
  That I at last into his sense might dart,
Thus first into his living mind I stole.

"Ah, who was ever conquering Love but I!
  Who else did ever throne in heart of man!
To visible being, with a gladsome cry
  Waking, life's tremor through me throbbing ran!"

A strange, repulsive feline wail arose somewhere in the room.
I started up on my elbow and stared about me, but could see
nothing.

Mr. Raven turned several leaves, and went on :—

"Sudden I woke, nor knew the ghastly fear
  That held me—not like serpent coiled about,
But like a vapour moist, corrupt, and drear,
  Filling heart, soul, and breast and brain throughout;
  My being lay motionless in sickening doubt,
Nor dared to ask how came the horror here.

"My past entire I knew, but not my now;
  I understood nor what I was, nor where;
I knew what I had been: still on my brow
  I felt the touch of what no more was there!
  I was a fainting, dead, yet live Despair;
A life that flouted life with mop and mow!

"That I was a queen I knew right well,
  And sometimes wore a splendour on my head
Whose flashing even dead darkness could not quell—
  The like on neck and arms and girdle-stead:
  And men declared a light my closed eyes shed
That killed the diamond in its silver cell."

Again I heard the ugly cry of feline pain. Again I looked, but saw neither shape nor motion. Mr. Raven seemed to listen a moment, but again turned several pages, and resumed :—

"Hideously wet, my hair of golden hue
    Fouled my fair hands: to have it swiftly shorn
I had given my rubies, all for me dug new—
    No eyes had seen, and such no waist had worn!
    For a draught of water from a drinking horn,
For one blue breath, I had given my sapphires blue!

"Nay, I had given my opals for a smock,
    A peasant-maiden's garment, coarse and clean:
My shroud was rotting! Once I heard a cock
    Lustily crow upon the hillock green
    Over my coffin. Dulled by space between,
Came back an answer like a ghostly mock."

Once more arose the bestial wail.

"I thought some foul thing was in the room!" said the librarian, casting a glance around him; but instantly he turned a leaf or two, and again read :—

"For I had bathed in milk and honey-dew,
    In rain from roses shook, that ne're touched earth,
And ointed me with nard of amber hue;
    Never had spot me spotted from my birth,
    Or mole, or scar of hurt, or fret of dearth;
Never one hair superfluous on me grew.

"Fleeing cold whiteness, I would sit alone—
    Not in the sun—I feared his bronzing light,
But in his radiance back around me thrown
    By fulgent mirrors tempering his might;
    Thus bathing in a moon-bath not too bright,
My skin I tinted slow to ivory tone.

"But now, all round was dark, dark all within!
    My eyes not even gave out a phantom-flash;
My fingers sank in pulp through pulpy skin;
    My body lay death-weltered in a mash
    Of slimy horrors——"

With a fearsome yell, her clammy fur staring in clumps, her tail thick as a cable, her eyes flashing green as a chrysoprase, her distended claws entangling themselves so that she floundered across the carpet, a huge white cat rushed from somewhere, and made for the chimney. Quick as thought the librarian threw the manuscript between her and the hearth. She crouched instantly, her eyes fixed on the book. But his voice went on as if still he read, and his eyes seemed also fixed on the book :—

> "Ah, the two worlds! so strangely are they one,
>   And yet so measurelessly wide apart!
> Oh, had I lived the bodiless alone
>   And from defiling sense held safe my heart,
>   Then had I scaped the canker and the smart,
> Scaped life-in-death, scaped misery's endless moan!"

At these words such a howling, such a prolonged yell of agony burst from the cat, that we both stopped our ears. When it ceased, Mr. Raven walked to the fire-place, took up the book, and, standing between the creature and the chimney, pointed his finger at her for a moment. She lay perfectly still. He took a half-burnt stick from the hearth, drew with it some sign on the floor, put the manuscript back in its place, with a look that seemed to say, "Now we have her, I think!" and, returning to the cat, stood over her and said, in a still, solemn voice :—

"Lilith, when you came here on the way to your evil will, you little thought into whose hands you were delivering yourself !— Mr. Vane, when God created me—not out of Nothing, as say the unwise, but out of His own endless glory—He brought me an angelic splendour to be my wife : there she lies ! For her first thought was *power*; she counted it slavery to be one with me, and bear children for Him who gave her being. One child, indeed, she bore; then, puffed with the fancy that she had created her, would have me fall down and worship her ! Finding, however, that I would but love and honour, never obey and worship her, she poured out her blood to escape me, fled to the army of the aliens, and soon had so ensnared the heart of the great Shadow, that he became her slave, wrought her will, and made her queen of Hell. How it is with her now, she best knows, but I know also. The one child of her body she fears and hates, and would kill, asserting a right, which is a lie, over what God sent through her into His new world. Of creating, she knows no more than the crystal that takes its allotted shape, or the worm that makes two worms when it is cloven asunder. Vilest of God's creatures, she lives by the blood and lives and souls of men. She consumes and slays, but is powerless to destroy as to create."

The animal lay motionless, its beryl eyes fixed flaming on the man : his eyes on hers held them fixed that they could not move from his.

"Then God gave me another wife—not an angel but a woman—who is to this as light is to darkness."

The cat gave a horrible screech, and began to grow bigger. She went on growing and growing. At last the spotted leopardess uttered a roar that made the house tremble. I sprang to my feet. I do not think Mr. Raven started even with his eyelids.

"It is but her jealousy that speaks," he said, "jealousy self-kindled, foiled and fruitless; for here I am, her master now whom she would not have for her husband ! while my beautiful Eve yet lives, hoping immortally ! Her hated daughter lives also, but beyond her evil ken, one day to be what she counts her destruction—for even Lilith shall be saved by her childbearing. Meanwhile she exults that my human wife plunged herself and me in despair, and has borne me a countless race of miserables; but my Eve repented, and is now beautiful as never was woman or angel, while her groaning, travailing world is the nursery of our Father's children. I too have repented, and am blessed.— Thou, Lilith, hast not yet repented; but thou must.—Tell me, is the great Shadow beautiful? Knowest thou how long thou wilt thyself remain beautiful?—Answer me, if thou knowest."

Then at last I understood that Mr. Raven was indeed Adam, the old and the new man; and that his wife, ministering in the house of the dead, was Eve, the mother of us all, the lady of the New Jerusalem.

The leopardess reared; the flickering and fleeing of her spots began; the princess at length stood radiant in her perfect shape.

"I *am* beautiful—and immortal !" she said—and she looked the goddess she would be.

"As a bush that burns, and is consumed," answered he who had been her husband. "—What is that under thy right hand?"

For her arm lay across her bosom, and her hand was pressed to her side.

A swift pang contorted her beautiful face, and passed.

"It is but a leopard-spot that lingers! it will quickly follow those I have dismissed," she answered.

"Thou art beautiful because God created thee, but thou art the slave of sin: take thy hand from thy side."

Her hand sank away, and as it dropt she looked him in the eyes with a quailing fierceness that had in it no surrender.

He gazed a moment at the spot.

"It is not on the leopard; it is in the woman!" he said. "Nor will it leave thee until it hath eaten to thy heart, and thy beauty hath flowed from thee through the open wound!"

She gave a glance downward, and shivered.

"Lilith," said Adam, and his tone had changed to a tender beseeching, "hear me, and repent, and He who made thee will cleanse thee!"

Her hand returned quivering to her side. Her face grew dark. She gave the cry of one from whom hope is vanishing. The cry passed into a howl. She lay writhing on the floor, a leopardess covered with spots.

"The evil thou meditatest," Adam resumed, "thou shalt never compass, Lilith, for Good and not Evil is the Universe. The battle between them may last for countless ages, but it must end: how will it fare with thee when Time hath vanished in the dawn of the eternal morn? Repent, I beseech thee; repent, and be again an angel of God!"

She rose, she stood upright, a woman once more, and said,

"I will not repent. I will drink the blood of thy child."

My eyes were fastened on the princess; but when Adam spoke, I turned to him: he stood towering above her; the form of his visage was altered, and his voice was terrible.

"Down!" he cried; "or by the power given me I will melt thy very bones."

She flung herself on the floor, dwindled and dwindled, and was again a gray cat. Adam caught her up by the skin of her neck, bore her to the closet, and threw her in. He described a strange figure on the threshold, and closing the door, locked it.

Then he returned to my side the old librarian, looking sad and worn, and furtively wiping tears from his eyes.

CHAPTER XXX

ADAM EXPLAINS

'WE MUST BE on our guard," he said, "or she will again outwit us. She would befool the very elect!"

"How are we to be on our guard?" I asked.

"Every way," he answered. "She fears, therefore hates her child, and is in this house on her way to destroy her. The birth of children is in her eyes the death of their parents, and every new generation the enemy of the last. Her daughter appears to her an open channel through which her immortality—which yet she counts self-inherent—is flowing fast away : to fill it up, almost from her birth she has pursued her with an utter enmity. But the result of her machinations hitherto is, that in the region she claims as her own, has appeared a colony of children, to which that daughter is heart and head and sheltering wings. My Eve longed after the child, and would have been to her as a mother to her first-born, but we were then unfit to train her : she was carried into the wilderness, and for ages we knew nothing of her fate. But she was divinely fostered, and had young angels for her playmates; nor did she ever know care until she found a baby in the wood, and the mother-heart in her awoke. One by one she has found many children since, and that heart is not yet full. Her family is her absorbing charge, and never children were better mothered. Her authority over them is without appeal, but it is unknown to herself, and never comes to the surface except in watchfulness and service. She has forgotten the time when she lived without them, and thinks she came herself from the wood, the first of the family.

"You have saved the life of her and their enemy; therefore your life belongs to her and them. The princess was on her way to destroy them, but as she crossed that stream, vengeance overtook her, and she would have died had you not come to her aid. You did; and ere now she would have been raging among the Little Ones, had she dared again cross the stream. But there was yet a way to the blessed little colony through the world of the three dimensions; only, from that, by the slaying of her former body, she had excluded herself, and except in personal contact with one belonging to it, could not re-enter it. You provided the opportunity : never, in all her long years, had she had one before. Her hand, with lightest touch, was on one or other of your muffled feet, every step as you climbed. In that little chamber, she is now watching to leave it as soon as ever she may."

"She cannot know anything about the door!—she cannot at least know how to open it!" I said; but my heart was not so confident as my words.

"Hush, hush!" whispered the librarian, with uplifted hand; "she can hear through anything!—You must go at once, and make your way to my wife's cottage. I will remain to keep guard over her."

"Let me go to the Little Ones!" I cried.

"Beware of that, Mr. Vane. Go to my wife, and do as she tells you."

His advice did not recommend itself : why haste to encounter measureless delay? If not to protect the children, why go at all? Alas, even now I believed him only enough to ask him questions, not to obey him!

"Tell me first, Mr. Raven," I said, "why, of all places, you have shut her up there! The night I ran from your house, it was immediately into that closet!"

"The closet is no nearer our cottage, and no farther from it, than any or every other place."

"But," I returned, hard to persuade where I could not understand, "how is it then that, when you please, you take from that same door a whole book where I saw and felt only a part of one? The other part, you have just told me, stuck through into your library : when you put it again on the shelf, will it not again stick through into that? Must not then the two places, in which parts of the same volume can at the same moment exist, lie close together? Or can one part of the book be in space, or *somewhere*, and the other out of space, or *nowhere*?"

"I am sorry I cannot explain the thing to you," he answered; "but there is no provision in you for understanding it. Not merely, therefore, is the phenomenon inexplicable to you, but the very nature of it is inapprehensible by you. Indeed I but partially apprehend it myself. At the same time you are constantly experiencing things which you not only do not, but cannot understand. You think you understand them, but your understanding of them is only your being used to them, and therefore not surprised at them. You accept them, not because you understand them, but because you must accept them : they are there, and have unavoidable relations with you ! The fact is, no man understands anything; when he knows he does not understand, that is his first tottering step—not toward understanding, but toward the capability of one day understanding. To such things as these you are not used, therefore you do not fancy you understand them. Neither I nor any man can here help you to understand; but I may, perhaps, help you a little to believe !"

He went to the door of the closet, gave a low whistle, and stood listening. A moment after, I heard, or seemed to hear, a soft whir of wings, and, looking up, saw a white dove perch for an instant on the top of the shelves over the portrait, thence drop to Mr. Raven's shoulder, and lay her head against his cheek. Only by the motions of their two heads could I tell that they were talking together; I heard nothing. Neither had I moved my eyes from them, when suddenly she was not there, and Mr. Raven came back to his seat.

"Why did you whistle?" I asked. "Surely sound here is not sound there !"

"You are right," he answered. "I whistled that you might know I called her. Not the whistle, but what the whistle meant reached her.—There is not a minute to lose : you must go !"

"I will at once !" I replied, and moved for the door.

"You will sleep to-night at my hostelry !" he said—not as a question, but in a tone of mild authority.

"My heart is with the children," I replied. "But if you insist——"

"I do insist. You can otherwise effect nothing.—I will go with you as far as the mirror, and see you off."

He rose. There came a sudden shock in the closet. Apparently the leopardess had flung herself against the heavy door. I looked at my companion.

"Come; come !" he said.

Ere we reached the door of the library, a howling yell came after us, mingled with the noise of claws that scored at the hard oak. I hesitated, and half turned.

"To think of her lying there alone," I murmured, "—with that terrible wound!"

"Nothing will ever close that wound," he answered, with a sigh. "It must eat into her heart! Annihilation itself is no death to evil. Only good where evil was, is evil dead. An evil thing must live with its evil until it chooses to be good. That alone is the slaying of evil."

I held my peace until a sound I did not understand overtook us.

"If she should break loose!" I cried.

"Make haste!" he rejoined. "I shall hurry down the moment you are gone, and I have disarranged the mirrors."

We ran, and reached the wooden chamber breathless. Mr. Raven seized the chains and adjusted the hood. Then he set the mirrors in their proper relation, and came beside me in front of the standing one. Already I saw the mountain range emerging from the mist.

Between us, wedging us asunder, darted, with the yell of a demon, the huge bulk of the spotted leopardess. She leaped through the mirror as through an open window, and settled at once into a low, even, swift gallop.

I cast a look of dismay at my companion, and sprang through to follow her. He came after me leisurely.

"You need not run," he called; "you cannot overtake her. This is our way."

As he spoke he turned in the opposite direction.

"She has more magic at her finger-tips than I care to know!" he added quietly.

"We must do what we can!" I said, and ran on, but sickening as I saw her dwindle in the distance, stopped, and went back to him.

"Doubtless we must," he answered. "But my wife has warned Mara, and she will do her part; you must sleep first : you have given me your word!"

"Nor do I mean to break it. But surely sleep is not the first thing! Surely, surely, action takes precedence of repose!"

"A man can do nothing he is not fit to do.—See! did I not tell you Mara would do her part?"

I looked whither he pointed, and saw a white spot moving at an acute angle with the line taken by the leopardess.

"There she is!" he cried. "The spotted leopardess is strong, but the white is stronger!"

"I have seen them fight : the combat did not appear decisive
as to that."

"How should such eyes tell which have never slept? The
princess did not confess herself beaten—that she never does—
but she fled! When she confesses her last hope gone, that it is
indeed hard to kick against the goad, then will her day begin to
dawn! Come; come! He who cannot act must make haste to
sleep!"

CHAPTER XXXI

THE SEXTON'S OLD HORSE

I STOOD AND WATCHED the last gleam of the white leopardess
melt away, then turned to follow my guide—but reluctantly.
What had I to do with sleep? Surely reason was the same in
every world, and what reason could there be in going to sleep
with the dead, when the hour was calling the live man? Besides,
no one would wake me, and how could I be certain of waking
early—of waking at all?—the sleepers in that house let morning
glide into noon, and noon into night, nor ever stirred! I
murmured, but followed, for I knew not what else to do.

The librarian walked on in silence, and I walked silent as he.
Time and space glided past us. The sun set; it began to grow
dark, and I felt in the air the spreading cold of the chamber of
death. My heart sank lower and lower. I began to lose sight of
the lean, long-coated figure, and at length could no more hear
his swishing stride through the heather. But then I heard instead
the slow-flapping wings of the raven; and, at intervals, now a
firefly, now a gleaming butterfly rose into the rayless air.

By and by the moon appeared, slow crossing the far horizon.

"You are tired, are you not, Mr. Vane?" said the raven,
alighting on a stone. "You must make acquaintance with the
horse that will carry you in the morning!"

He gave a strange whistle through his long black beak. A spot
appeared on the face of the half-risen moon. To my ears came
presently the drumming of swift, soft-galloping hoofs, and in a
minute or two, out of the very disc of the moon, low-thundered
the terrible horse. His mane flowed away behind him like the

crest of a wind-fighting wave, torn seaward in hoary spray, and the whisk of his tail kept blinding the eye of the moon. Nineteen hands he seemed, huge of bone, tight of skin, hard of muscle—a steed the holy Death himself might choose on which to ride abroad and slay! The moon seemed to regard him with awe; in her scary light he looked a very skeleton, loosely roped together. Terrifically large, he moved with the lightness of a winged insect. As he drew near, his speed slackened, and his mane and tail drifted about him settling.

Now I was not merely a lover of horses, but I loved every horse I saw. I had never spent money except upon horses, and had never sold a horse. The sight of this mighty one, terrible to look at, woke in me longing to possess him. It was pure greed, nay, rank covetousness, an evil thing in all the worlds. I do not mean that I could have stolen him, but that, regardless of his proper place, I would have bought him if I could. I laid my hands on him, and stroked the protuberant bones that humped a hide smooth and thin, and shiny as satin—so shiny that the very shape of the moon was reflected in it; I fondled his sharp-pointed ears, whispered words in them, and breathed into his red nostrils the breath of a man's life. He in return breathed into mine the breath of a horse's life, and we loved one another. What eyes he had! Blue-filmy like the eyes of the dead, behind each was a glowing coal! The raven, with wings half extended, looked on pleased at my love-making to his magnificent horse.

"That is well! be friends with him," he said; "he will carry you all the better to-morrow!—Now we must hurry home!"

My desire to ride the horse had grown passionate.

"May I not mount him at once, Mr. Raven?" I cried.

"By all means!" he answered. "Mount, and ride him home."

The horse bent his head over my shoulder lovingly. I twisted my hands in his mane and scrambled on his back, not without aid from certain protuberant bones.

"He would outspeed any leopard in creation!" I cried.

"Not that way at night," answered the raven; "the road is difficult.—But come; loss now will be gain then! To wait is harder than to run, and its meed is the fuller. Go on, my son—straight to the cottage. I shall be there as soon as you. It will rejoice my wife's heart to see son of hers on that horse!"

I sat silent. The horse stood like a block of marble.

"Why do you linger?" asked the raven.

"I long so much to ride after the leopardess," I answered, "that I can scarce restrain myself!"

"You have promised!"

"My debt to the Little Ones appears, I confess, a greater thing than my bond to you."

"Yield to the temptation and you will bring mischief upon them—and on yourself also."

"What matters it for me? I love them; and love works no evil. I will go."

But the truth was, I forgot the children, infatuate with the horse.

Eyes flashed through the darkness, and I knew that Adam stood in his own shape beside me. I knew also by his voice that he repressed an indignation almost too strong for him.

"Mr. Vane," he said, "do you not know why you have not yet done anything worth doing?"

"Because I have been a fool," I answered.

"Wherein?"

"In everything."

"Which do you count your most indiscreet action?"

"Bringing the princess to life: I ought to have left her to her just fate."

"Nay, now you talk foolishly! You could not have done otherwise than you did, not knowing she was evil!—But you never brought any one to life! How could you, yourself dead?"

"I dead?" I cried.

"Yes," he answered; "and you will be dead, so long as you refuse to die."

"Back to the old riddling!" I returned scornfully.

"Be persuaded, and go home with me," he continued gently. "The most—nearly the only foolish thing you ever did, was to run from our dead."

I pressed the horse's ribs, and he was off like a sudden wind. I gave him a pat on the side of the neck, and he went about in a sharp-driven curve, "close to the ground, like a cat when scratchingly she wheels about after a mouse," leaning sideways till his mane swept the tops of the heather.

Through the dark I heard the wings of the raven. Five quick flaps I heard, and he perched on the horse's head. The horse checked himself instantly, ploughing up the ground with his feet.

"Mr. Vane," croaked the raven, "think what you are doing! Twice already has evil befallen you—once from fear, and once from heedlessness : breach of word is far worse; it is a crime."

"The Little Ones are in frightful peril, and I brought it upon them!" I cried. "—But indeed I will not break my word to you. I will return, and spend in your house what nights—what days—what years you please."

"I tell you once more you will do them other than good if you go to-night," he insisted.

But a false sense of power, a sense which had no root and was merely vibrated into me from the strength of the horse, had, alas, rendered me too stupid to listen to anything he said!

"Would you take from me my last chance of reparation?" I cried. "This time there shall be no shirking! It is my duty, and I will go—if I perish for it!"

"Go, then, foolish boy!" he returned, with anger in his croak. "Take the horse, and ride to failure! May it be to humility!"

He spread his wings and flew. Again I pressed the lean ribs under me.

"After the spotted leopardess!" I whispered in his ear.

He turned his head this way and that, snuffing the air; then started, and went a few paces in a slow, undecided walk. Suddenly he quickened his walk; broke into a trot; began to gallop, and in a few moments his speed was tremendous. He seemed to see in the dark; never stumbled, not once faltered, not once hesitated. I sat as on the ridge of a wave. I felt under me the play of each individual muscle : his joints were so elastic, and his every movement glided so into the next, that not once did he jar me. His growing swiftness bore him along until he flew rather than ran. The wind met and passed us like a tornado.

Across the evil hollow we sped like a bolt from an arblast. No monster lifted its neck; all knew the hoofs that thundered over their heads! We rushed up the hills, we shot down their farther slopes; from the rocky chasms of the river-bed he did not swerve; he held on over them his fierce, terrible gallop. The moon, half-way up the heaven, gazed with a solemn trouble in her pale countenance. Rejoicing in the power of my steed and in the pride of my life, I sat like a king and rode.

We were near the middle of the many channels, my horse

every other moment clearing one, sometimes two in his stride, and now and then gathering himself for a great bounding leap, when the moon reached the key-stone of her arch. Then came a wonder and a terror : she began to descend rolling like the nave of Fortune's wheel bowled by the gods, and went faster and faster. Like our own moon, this one had a human face, and now the broad forehead now the chin was uppermost as she rolled. I gazed aghast.

Across the ravines came the howling of wolves. An ugly fear began to invade the hollow places of my heart; my confidence was on the wane ! The horse maintained his headlong swiftness, with ears pricked forward, and thirsty nostrils exulting in the wind his career created. But there was the moon jolting like an old chariot-wheel down the hill of heaven, with awful boding ! She rolled at last over the horizon-edge and disappeared, carrying all her light with her.

The mighty steed was in the act of clearing a wide shallow channel when we were caught in the net of the darkness. His head dropped; its impetus carried his helpless bulk across, but he fell in a heap on the margin, and where he fell he lay. I got up, kneeled beside him, and felt him all over. Not a bone could I find broken, but he was a horse no more. I sat down on the body, and buried my face in my hands.

CHAPTER XXXII

THE LOVERS AND THE BAGS

Bitterly cold grew the night. The body froze under me. The cry of the wolves came nearer; I heard their feet soft-padding on the rocky ground; their quick panting filled the air. Through the darkness I saw the many glowing eyes; their half-circle contracted around me. My time was come ! I sprang to my feet.—Alas, I had not even a stick !

They came in a rush, their eyes flashing with fury of greed, their black throats agape to devour me. I stood hopelessly waiting them. One moment they halted over the horse—then came at me.

With a sound of swiftness all but silence, a cloud of green eyes

came down on their flank. The heads that bore them flew at
the wolves with a cry feebler yet fiercer than their howling snarl,
and by the cry I knew them : they were cats, led by a huge gray
one. I could see nothing of him but his eyes, yet I knew him—
and so knew his colour and bigness. A terrific battle followed,
whose tale alone came to me through the night. I would have
fled, for surely it was but a fight which should have me!—only
where was the use? my first step would be a fall! and my foes
of either kind could both see and scent me in the dark!

All at once I missed the howling, and the caterwauling grew
wilder. Then came the soft padding, and I knew it meant flight :
the cats had defeated the wolves! In a moment the sharpest of
sharp teeth were in my legs; a moment more and the cats were
all over me in a live cataract, biting wherever they could bite,
furiously scratching me anywhere and everywhere. A multitude
clung to my body; I could not flee. Madly I fell on the hateful
swarm, every finger instinct with destruction. I tore them off me,
I throttled at them in vain : when I would have flung them
from me, they clung to my hands like limpets. I trampled them
under my feet, thrust my fingers in their eyes, caught them in
jaws stronger than theirs, but could not rid myself of one. Without cease they kept discovering upon me space for fresh mouth-
fuls; they hauled at my skin with the widespread, horribly curved
pincers of clutching claws; they hissed and spat in my face—
but never touched it until, in my despair, I threw myself on the
ground, when they forsook my body, and darted at my face. I
rose, and immediately they left it, the more to occupy themselves
with my legs. In an agony I broke from them and ran, careless
whither, cleaving the solid dark. They accompanied me in a
surrounding torrent, now rubbing, now leaping up against me,
but tormenting me no more. When I fell, which was often, they
gave me time to rise; when from fear of falling I slackened my
pace, they flew afresh at my legs. All that miserable night they
kept me running—but they drove me by a comparatively smooth
path, for I tumbled into no gully, and passing the Evil Wood
without seeing it, left it behind in the dark. When at length the
morning appeared, I was beyond the channels, and on the verge
of the orchard valley. In my joy I would have made friends
with my persecutors, but not a cat was to be seen. I threw
myself on the moss, and fell fast asleep.

I was waked by a kick, to find myself bound hand and foot, once more the thrall of the giants!

"What fitter?" I said to myself; "to whom else should I belong?" and I laughed in the triumph of self-disgust. A second kick stopped my false merriment; and thus recurrently assisted by my captors, I succeeded at length in rising to my feet.

Six of them were about me. They undid the rope that tied my legs together, attached a rope to each of them, and dragged me away. I walked as well as I could, but, as they frequently pulled both ropes at once, I fell repeatedly, whereupon they always kicked me up again. Straight to my old labour they took me, tied my leg-ropes to a tree, undid my arms, and put the hateful flint in my left hand. Then they lay down and pelted me with fallen fruit and stones, but seldom hit me. If I could have freed my legs, and got hold of a stick I spied a couple of yards from me, I would have fallen upon all six of them! "But the Little Ones will come at night!" I said to myself, and was comforted.

All day I worked hard. When the darkness came, they tied my hands, and left me fast to the tree. I slept a good deal, but woke often, and every time from a dream of lying in the heart of a heap of children. With the morning my enemies reappeared, bringing their kicks and their bestial company.

It was about noon, and I was nearly failing from fatigue and hunger, when I heard a sudden commotion in the brushwood, followed by a burst of the bell-like laughter so dear to my heart. I gave a loud cry of delight and welcome. Immediately rose a trumpeting as of baby-elephants, a neighing as of foals, and a bellowing as of calves, and through the bushes came a crowd of Little Ones, on diminutive horses, on small elephants, on little bears; but the noises came from the riders, not the animals. Mingled with the mounted ones walked the bigger of the boys and girls, among the latter a woman with a baby crowing in her arms. The giants sprang to their lumbering feet, but were instantly saluted with a storm of sharp stones; the horses charged their legs; the bears rose and hugged them at the waist; the elephants threw their trunks round their necks, pulled them down, and gave them such a trampling as they had sometimes given, but never received before. In a moment my ropes were undone, and I was in the arms, seemingly innumerable, of the Little Ones. For some time I saw no more of the giants.

They made me sit down, and my Lona came, and without a word began to feed me with the loveliest red and yellow fruits. I sat and ate, the whole colony mounting guard until I had done. Then they brought up two of the largest of their elephants, and having placed them side by side, hooked their trunks and tied their tails together. The docile creatures could have untied their tails with a single shake, and unhooked their trunks by forgetting them; but tails and trunks remained as their little masters had arranged them, and it was clear the elephants understood that they must keep their bodies parallel. I got up, and laid myself in the hollow between their two backs; when the wise animals, counteracting the weight that pushed them apart, leaned against each other, and made for me a most comfortable litter. My feet, it is true, projected beyond their tails, but my head lay pillowed on an ear of each. Then some of the smaller children, mounting for a bodyguard, ranged themselves in a row along the back of each of my bearers; the whole assembly formed itself in train; and the procession began to move.

Whither they were carrying me, I did not try to conjecture; I yielded myself to their pleasure, almost as happy as they. Chattering and laughing and playing glad tricks innumerable at first, the moment they saw I was going to sleep, they became still as judges.

I woke: a sudden musical uproar greeted the opening of my eyes.

We were travelling through the forest in which they found the babies, and which, as I had suspected, stretched all the way from the valley to the hot stream.

A tiny girl sat with her little feet close to my face, and looked down at me coaxingly for a while, then spoke, the rest seeming to hang on her words.

"We make a petisson to king," she said.

"What is it, my darling?" I asked.

"Sut eyes one minute," she answered.

"Certainly I will! Here goes!" I replied, and shut my eyes close.

"No, no! not fore I tell oo!" she cried.

I opened them again, and we talked and laughed together for quite another hour.

"Close eyes!" she said suddenly.

I closed my eyes, and kept them close. The elephants stood still. I heard a soft scurry, a little rustle, and then a silence—for in that world *some* silences *are* heard.

"Open eyes!" twenty voices a little way off shouted at once; but when I obeyed, not a creature was visible except the elephants that bore me. I knew the children were marvellously quick in getting out of the way—the giants had taught them that; but when I raised myself, and looking about in the open shrubless forest, could descry neither hand nor heel, I stared in "blank astonishment."

The sun was set, and it was fast getting dark, yet presently a multitude of birds began to sing. I lay down to listen, pretty sure that, if I left them alone, the hiders would soon come out again.

The singing grew to a little storm of bird-voices. "Surely the children must have something to do with it!—And yet how could they set the birds singing?" I said to myself as I lay and listened. Soon, however, happening to look up into the tree under which my elephants stood, I thought I spied a little motion among the leaves, and looked more keenly. Sudden white spots appeared in the dark foliage, the music died down, a gale of childish laughter rippled the air, and white spots came out in every direction : the trees were full of children! In the wildest merriment they began to descend, some dropping from bough to bough so rapidly that I could scarce believe they had not fallen. I left my litter, and was instantly surrounded—a mark for all the artillery of their jubilant fun. With stately composure the elephants walked away to bed.

"But," said I, when their uproarious gladness had had scope for a while, "how is it that I never before heard you sing like the birds? Even when I thought it must be you, I could hardly believe it!"

"Ah," said one of the wildest, "but we were not birds then! We were run-creatures, not fly-creatures! We had our hide-places in the bushes then; but when we came to no-bushes, only trees, we had to build nests! When we built nests, we grew birds, and when we were birds, we had to do birds! We asked them to teach us their noises, and they taught us, and now we are real birds!—Come and see my nest. It's not big enough for king, but it's big enough for king to see me in it!"

I told him I could not get up a tree without the sun to show me the way; when he came, I would try.

"Kings seldom have wings!" I added.

"King! king!" cried one, "oo knows none of us hasn't no wings—foolis feddery tings! Arms and legs is better."

"That is true. I can get up without wings—and carry straws in my mouth too, to build my nest with!"

"Oo knows!" he answered, and went away sucking his thumb.

A moment after, I heard him calling out of his nest, a great way up a walnut tree of enormous size.

"Up adain, king! Dood night! I seepy!"

And I heard no more of him till he woke me in the morning.

CHAPTER XXXIII

LONA'S NARRATIVE

I LAY DOWN BY a tree, and one and one or in little groups, the children left me and climbed to their nests. They were always so tired at night and so rested in the morning, that they were equally glad to go to sleep and to get up again. I, although tired also, lay awake: Lona had not bid me good night, and I was sure she would come.

I had been struck, the moment I saw her again, with her resemblance to the princess, and could not doubt her the daughter of whom Adam had told me; but in Lona the dazzling beauty of Lilith was softened by childlikeness, and deepened by the sense of motherhood. "She is occupied probably," I said to myself, "with the child of the woman I met fleeing!" who, she had already told me, was not half mother enough.

She came at length, sat down beside me, and after a few moments of silent delight, expressed mainly by stroking my face and hands, began to tell me everything that had befallen since I went. The moon appeared as we talked, and now and then, through the leaves, lighted for a quivering moment her beautiful face—full of thought, and a care whose love redeemed and glorified it. How such a child should have been born of such a mother—such a woman of such a princess, was hard to understand; but then, happily, she had two parents—say rather, three! She drew my heart by what in me was likest herself, and I loved her as one who, grow to what perfection she might, could only become the more a child. I knew now that I loved her when I left her, and that the hope of seeing her again had been my main comfort. Every word she spoke seemed to go straight to my heart, and, like the truth itself, make it purer.

She told me that after I left the orchard valley, the giants began to believe a little more in the actual existence of their neighbours, and became in consequence more hostile to them. Sometimes the Little Ones would see them trampling furiously, perceiving or imagining some indication of their presence, while they indeed stood beside, and laughed at their foolish rage. By and by, however, their animosity assumed a more practical shape : they began to destroy the trees on whose fruit the Little Ones lived. This drove the mother of them all to meditate counteraction. Setting the sharpest of them to listen at night, she learned that the giants thought I was hidden somewhere near, intending, as soon as I recovered my strength, to come in the dark and kill them sleeping. Thereupon she concluded that the only way to stop the destruction was to give them ground for believing that they had abandoned the place. The Little Ones must remove into the forest—beyond the range of the giants, but within reach of their own trees, which they must visit by night! The main objection to the plan was, that the forest had little or no undergrowth to shelter—or conceal them if necessary.

But she reflected that where birds, there the Little Ones could find habitation. They had eager sympathies with all modes of life, and could learn of the wildest creatures : why should they not take refuge from the cold and their enemies in the tree-tops? why not, having lain in the low brushwood, seek now the lofty foliage? why not build nests where it would not serve to scoop hollows? All that the birds could do, the Little Ones could learn —except, indeed, to fly!

She spoke to them on the subject, and they heard with approval. They could already climb the trees, and they had often watched the birds building their nests! The trees of the forest, although large, did not look bad! They went up much nearer the sky than those of the giants, and spread out their arms—some even stretched them down—as if inviting them to come and live with them! Perhaps, in the top of the tallest, they might find that bird that laid the baby-eggs, and sat upon them till they were ripe, then tumbled them down to let the little ones out! Yes; they would build sleep-houses in the trees, where no giant would see them, for never by any chance did one throw back his dull head to look up! Then the bad giants would be sure they had left the country, and the Little Ones would gather their own apples and pears and figs and mesples and peaches when they were asleep!

Thus reasoned the Lovers, and eagerly adopted Lona's suggestion—with the result that they were soon as much at home in the tree-tops as the birds themselves, and that the giants came ere long to the conclusion that they had frightened them out of the country—whereupon they forgot their trees, and again almost ceased to believe in the existence of their small neighbours.

Lona asked me whether I had not observed that many of the children were grown. I answered I had not, but could readily believe it. She assured me it was so, but said the certain evidence that their minds too had grown since their migration upward, had gone far in mitigation of the alarm the discovery had occasioned her.

In the last of the short twilight, and later when the moon was shining, they went down to the valley, and gathered fruit enough to serve them the next day; for the giants never went out in the twilight : that to them was darkness; and they hated the moon : had they been able, they would have extinguished her. But soon the Little Ones found that fruit gathered in the night was not altogether good the next day; so the question arose whether it would not be better, instead of pretending to have left the country, to make the bad giants themselves leave it.

They had already, she said, in exploring the forest, made acquaintance with the animals in it, and with most of them personally. Knowing therefore how strong as well as wise and docile some of them were, and how swift as well as manageable many others, they now set themselves to secure their aid against the giants, and with loving, playful approaches, had soon made more than friends of most of them, from the first addressing horse or elephant as Brother or Sister Elephant, Brother or Sister Horse, until before long they had an individual name for each. It was some little time longer before they said Brother or Sister

Bear, but that came next, and the other day she had heard one little fellow cry, "Ah, Sister Serpent!" to a snake that bit him as he played with it too roughly. Most of them would have nothing to do with a caterpillar, except watch it through its changes; but when at length it came from its retirement with wings, all would immediately address it as Sister Butterfly, congratulating it on its metamorphosis—for which they used a word that meant something like *repentance*—and evidently regarding it as something sacred.

One moonlit evening, as they were going to gather their fruit, they came upon a woman seated on the ground with a baby in her lap—the woman I had met on my way to Bulika. They took her for a giantess that had stolen one of their babies, for they regarded all babies as their property. Filled with anger they fell upon her multitudinously, beating her after a childish, yet sufficiently bewildering fashion. She would have fled, but a boy threw himself down and held her by the feet. Recovering her wits, she recognised in her assailants the children whose hospitality she sought, and at once yielded the baby. Lona appeared, and carried it away in her bosom.

But while the woman noted that in striking her they were careful not to hurt the child, the Little Ones noted that, as she surrendered her, she hugged and kissed her just as they wanted to do, and came to the conclusion that she must be a giantess of the same kind as the good giant. The moment Lona had the baby, therefore, they brought the mother fruit, and began to show her every sort of childish attention.

Now the woman had been in perplexity whither to betake herself, not daring to go back to the city, because the princess was certain to find out who had lamed her leopardess : delighted with the friendliness of the little people, she resolved to remain with them for the present: she would have no trouble with her infant, and might find some way of returning to her husband, who was rich in money and gems, and very seldom unkind to her.

Here I must supplement, partly from conjecture, what Lona told me about the woman. With the rest of the inhabitants of Bulika, she was aware of the tradition that the princess lived in terror of the birth of an infant destined to her destruction. They were all unacquainted, however, with the frightful means by which she preserved her youth and beauty; and her deteriorating physical condition requiring a larger use of those means, they took the apparent increase of her hostility to children for a sign that she saw her doom approaching. This, although no one dreamed of any attempt against her, nourished in them hopes of change.

Now arose in the mind of the woman the idea of furthering the fulfilment of the shadowy prediction, or of using the myth at least for her own restoration to her husband. For what seemed more probable than that the fate foretold lay with these very children? They were marvellously brave, and the Bulikans cowards, in abject terror of animals! If she could rouse in the Little Ones the ambition of taking the city, then in the confusion of the attack, she would escape from the little army, reach her house unrecognised, and there lying hidden, await the result!

Should the children now succeed in expelling the giants, she would begin at once, while they were yet flushed with victory, to suggest the loftier aim! By disposition, indeed, they were unfit for warfare; they hardly ever quarrelled, and never fought; loved every live thing, and hated either to hurt or to suffer. Still, they were easily influenced, and could certainly be taught any exercise within their strength!—At once she set some of the smaller ones throwing stones at a mark; and soon they were all engrossed with the new game, and growing skilful in it.

The first practical result was their use of stones in my rescue. While gathering fruit, they found me asleep, went home, held a council, came the next day with their elephants and horses, overwhelmed the few giants watching me, and carried me off. Jubilant over their victory, the smaller boys were childishly boastful, the bigger boys less ostentatious, while the girls, although their eyes flashed more, were not so talkative as usual. The woman of Bulika no doubt felt encouraged.

We talked the greater part of the night, chiefly about the growth of the children, and what it might indicate. With Lona's power of recognising truth I had long been familiar; now I began to be astonished at her practical wisdom. Probably, had I been more of a child myself, I should have wondered less.

It was yet far from morning when I became aware of a slight fluttering and scrambling. I rose on my elbow, and looking about me, saw many Little Ones descend from their nests. They disappeared, and in a few moments all was again still.

"What are they doing?" I asked.

"They think," answered Lona, "that, stupid as they are, the giants will search the wood, and they are gone to gather stones with which to receive them. Stones are not plentiful in the forest, and they have to scatter far to find enow. They will carry them to their nests, and from the trees attack the giants as they come within reach. Knowing their habits, they do not expect them before the morning. If they do come, it will be the opening of a war of expulsion : one or the other people must go. The result, however, is hardly doubtful. We do not mean to kill them; indeed, their skulls are so thick that I do not think we could!—not that killing would do them much harm; they are so little alive! If one were killed, his giantess would not remember him beyond three days!"

"Do the children then throw so well that the thing *might* happen?" I asked.

"Wait till you see them!" she answered, with a touch of pride. "—But I have not yet told you," she went on, "of a strange thing that happened the night before last!—We had come home from gathering our fruit, and were asleep in our nests, when we were roused by the horrid noises of beasts fighting. The moon was bright, and in a moment our trees glittered with staring little eyes, watching two huge leopardesses, one perfectly white, the other covered with black spots, which worried and tore at each other with I do not know how many teeth and claws. To judge by her back, the spotted creature must have been climbing a tree when the other sprang upon her. When first I saw them, they were just under my own tree, rolling over and over each other. I got down on the lowest branch, and saw them perfectly. The children enjoyed the spectacle, siding some with this one, some with that, for we had never seen such beasts before, and thought they were only at play. But by degrees their roaring and growling almost ceased, and I saw that they were in deadly earnest, and heartily wished neither might be left able to climb a tree. But when the children saw the blood pouring from their flanks and throats, what do you think they did? They scurried down to comfort them, and gathering in a great crowd about the terrible creatures, began to pat and stroke them. Then I got down as well, for they were much too absorbed to heed my calling to them; but before I could reach them, the white one stopped fighting, and sprang among them with such a hideous yell that they flew up into the trees like birds. Before I got back into mine, the wicked beasts were at it again tooth and claw. Then Whitey had the best of it; Spotty ran away as fast as she could run, and Whitey came and lay down at the foot of my tree. But in a minute or two she was up again, and walking about as if she thought Spotty might be lurking somewhere. I waked often, and every time I looked out, I saw her. In the morning she went away."

"I know both the beasts," I said. "Spotty is a bad beast. She hates the children, and would kill every one of them. But Whitey loves them. She ran at them only to frighten them away, lest Spotty should get hold of any of them. No one needs be afraid of Whitey!"

By this time the Little Ones were coming back, and with much noise, for they had no care to keep quiet now that they were at open war with the giants, and laden with good stones. They mounted to their nests again, though with difficulty because of their burdens, and in a minute were fast asleep. Lona retired to her tree. I lay where I was, and slept the better that I thought most likely the white leopardess was still somewhere in the wood.

I woke soon after the sun, and lay pondering. Two hours passed, and then in truth the giants began to appear, in straggling companies of three and four, until I counted over a hundred of them. The children were still asleep, and to call them would draw the attention of the giants : I would keep quiet so long as they did not discover me. But by and by one came blundering upon me, stumbled, fell, and rose again. I thought he would pass heedless, but he began to search about. I sprang to my feet, and struck him in the middle of his huge body. The roar he gave roused the children, and a storm as of hail instantly came on, of which not a stone struck me, and not one missed the giant. He fell and lay. Others drew near, and the storm extended, each purblind creature becoming, as he entered the range of a garrisoned tree, a target for converging stones. In a short time almost every giant was prostrate, and a jubilant pæan of bird-song rose from the tops of fifty trees.

Many elephants came hurrying up, and the children descending the trees like monkeys, in a moment every elephant had three

or four of them on his back, and thus loaded, began to walk
over the giants, who lay and roared. Losing patience at length
with their noise, the elephants gave them a few blows of their
trunks, and left them.

Until night the bad giants remained where they had fallen,
silent and motionless. The next morning they had disappeared
every one, and the children saw no more of them. They removed
to the other end of the orchard valley, and never after ventured
into the forest.

CHAPTER XXXIV

PREPARATION

VICTORY THUS GAINED, the woman of Bulika began to speak
about the city, and talked much of its defenceless condition, of
the wickedness of its princess, of the cowardice of its inhabitants.
In a few days the children chattered of nothing but Bulika,
although indeed they had not the least notion of what a city
was. Then first I became aware of the design of the woman,
although not yet of its motive.

The idea of taking possession of the place, recommended itself
greatly to Lona—and to me also. The children were now so
rapidly developing faculty, that I could see no serious obstacle
to the success of the enterprise. For the terrible Lilith—woman
or leopardess, I knew her one vulnerable point, her doom
through her daughter, and the influence the ancient prophecy
had upon the citizens : surely whatever in the enterprise could
be called risk, was worth taking ! Successful,—and who could
doubt their success?—must not the Little Ones, from a crowd
of children, speedily become a youthful people, whose govern-
ment and influence would be all for righteousness? Ruling the
wicked with a rod of iron, would they not be the redemption of
the nation?

At the same time, I have to confess that I was not without
views of personal advantage, not without ambition in the undertaking. It was just, it seemed to me, that Lona should take her
seat on the throne that had been her mother's, and natural that
she should make of me her consort and minister. For me, I

would spend my life in her service; and between us, what might we not do, with such a core to it as the Little Ones, for the development of a noble state?

I confess also to an altogether foolish dream of opening a commerce in gems between the two worlds—happily impossible, for it could have done nothing but harm to both.

Calling to mind the appeal of Adam, I suggested to Lona that to find them water might perhaps expedite the growth of the Little Ones. She judged it prudent, however, to leave that alone for the present, as we did not know what its first consequences might be; while, in the course of time, it would almost certainly subject them to a new necessity.

"They are what they are without it!" she said: "when we have the city, we will search for water!"

We began, therefore, and pushed forward our preparations, constantly reviewing the merry troops and companies. Lona gave her attention chiefly to the commissariat, while I drilled the little soldiers, exercised them in stone-throwing, taught them the use of some other weapons, and did all I could to make warriors of them. The main difficulty was to get them to rally to their flag the instant the call was sounded. Most of them were armed with slings, some of the bigger boys with bows and arrows. The bigger girls carried aloe-spikes, strong as steel and sharp as needles, fitted to longish shafts—rather formidable weapons. Their sole duty was the charge of such as were too small to fight.

Lona had herself grown a good deal, but did not seem aware of it: she had always been, as she still was, the tallest! Her hair was much longer, and she was become almost a woman, but not one beauty of childhood had she outgrown. When first we met after our long separation, she laid down her infant, put her arms round my neck, and clung to me silent, her face glowing with gladness: the child whimpered; she sprang to him, and had him in her bosom instantly. To see her with any thoughtless, obstinate, or irritable little one, was to think of a tender grandmother. I seemed to have known her for ages—for always—from before time began! I hardly remembered my mother, but in my mind's eye she now looked like Lona; and if I imagined sister or child, invariably she had the face of Lona! My every imagination flew to her; she was my heart's wife! She hardly ever sought me, but was almost always within sound of my voice. What I did or thought, I referred constantly to her, and rejoiced to believe that, while doing her work in absolute independence, she was most at home by my side. Never for me did she neglect the smallest child, and my love only quickened my sense of duty. To love her and to do my duty, seemed, not indeed one, but inseparable. She might suggest something I should do; she might ask me what she ought to do; but she never seemed to suppose that I, any more than she, would like to do, or could care about anything except what must be done. Her love overflowed upon me—not in caresses, but in a closeness of recognition which I can compare to nothing but the devotion of a divine animal.

I never told her anything about her mother.

The wood was full of birds, the splendour of whose plumage, while it took nothing from their song, seemed almost to make up for the lack of flowers—which, apparently, could not grow without water. Their glorious feathers being everywhere about in the forest, it came into my heart to make from them a garment for Lona. While I gathered, and bound them in overlapping rows, she watched me with evident appreciation of my choice and arrangement, never asking what I was fashioning, but evidently waiting expectant the result of my work. In a week or two it was finished—a long loose mantle, to fasten at the throat and waist, with openings for the arms.

I rose and put it on her. She rose, took it off, and laid it at my feet—I imagine from a sense of propriety. I put it again on her shoulders, and showed her where to put her arms through. She smiled, looked at the feathers a little and stroked them—again took it off and laid it down, this time by her side. When she left me, she carried it with her, and I saw no more of it for some days. At length she came to me one morning wearing it, and carrying another garment which she had fashioned similarly, but of the dried leaves of a tough evergreen. It had the strength almost of leather, and the appearance of scale-armour. I put it on at once, and we always thereafter wore those garments when on horseback.

For, on the outskirts of the forest, had appeared one day a troop of full-grown horses, with which, as they were nowise alarmed at creatures of a shape so different from their own, I

had soon made friends, and two of the finest I had trained for
Lona and myself. Already accustomed to ride a small one, her
delight was great when first she looked down from the back of
an animal of the giant kind; and the horse showed himself proud
of the burden he bore. We exercised them every day until they
had such confidence in us as to obey instantly and fear nothing;
after which we always rode them at parade and on the march.

The undertaking did indeed at times appear to me a foolhardy
one, but the confidence of the woman of Bulika, real or simu-
lated, always overcame my hesitancy. The princess's magic, she
insisted, would prove powerless against the children; and as to
any force she might muster, our animal-allies alone would assure
our superiority : she was herself, she said, ready, with a good
stick, to encounter any two men of Bulika. She confessed to not
a little fear of the leopardess, but I was myself ready for her. I
shrank, however, from carrying *all* the children with us.

"Would it not be better," I said, "that you remained in the
forest with your baby and the smallest of the Little Ones?"

She answered that she greatly relied on the impression the
sight of them would make on the women, especially the mothers.

"When they see the darlings," she said, "their hearts will be
taken by storm; and I must be there encouraging them to make
a stand! If there be a remnant of hardihood in the place, it will
be found among the women!"

"*You* must not encumber yourself," I said to Lona, "with any
of the children; you will be wanted everywhere!"

For there were two babies besides the woman's, and even on
horseback she had almost always one in her arms.

"I do not remember ever being without a child to take care
of," she answered; "but when we reach the city, it shall be as
you wish!"

Her confidence in one who had failed so unworthily, shamed
me. But neither had I initiated the movement, nor had I any
ground for opposing it; I had no choice, but must give it the
best help I could! For myself, I was ready to live or die with
Lona. Her humility as well as her trust humbled me, and I gave
myself heartily to her purposes.

Our way lying across a grassy plain, there was no need to take
food for the horses, or the two cows which would accompany
us for the infants; but the elephants had to be provided for.

True, the grass was as good for them as for those other animals, but it was short, and with their one-fingered long noses, they could not pick enough for a single meal. We had, therefore, set the whole colony to gather grass and make hay, of which the elephants themselves could carry a quantity sufficient to last them several days, with the supplement of what we would gather fresh every time we halted. For the bears we stored nuts, and for ourselves dried plenty of fruits. We had caught and tamed several more of the big horses, and now having loaded them and the elephants with these provisions, we were prepared to set out.

Then Lona and I held a general review, and I made them a little speech. I began by telling them that I had learned a good deal about them, and knew now where they came from.

"We did not come from anywhere," they cried, interrupting me; "we are here!"

I told them that every one of them had a mother of his own, like the mother of the last baby; that I believed they had all been brought from Bulika when they were so small that they could not now remember it; that the wicked princess there was so afraid of babies, and so determined to destroy them, that their mothers had to carry them away and leave them where she could not find them; and that now we were going to Bulika, to find their mothers, and deliver them from the bad giantess.

"But I must tell you," I continued, "that there is danger before us, for, as you know, we may have to fight hard to take the city."

"We can fight! we are ready!" cried the boys.

"Yes, you can," I returned, "and I know you will: mothers are worth fighting for! Only mind, you must all keep together."

"Yes, yes; we'll take care of each other," they answered. "Nobody shall touch one of us but his own mother!"

"You must mind, every one, to do immediately what your officers tell you!"

"We will, we will!—Now we're quite ready! Let us go!"

"Another thing you must not forget," I went on: "when you strike, be sure you make it a downright swingeing blow; when you shoot an arrow, draw it to the head; when you sling a stone, sling it strong and straight."

"That we will!" they cried with jubilant, fearless shout.

"Perhaps you will be hurt!"

"We don't mind that!—Do we, boys?"

"Not a bit!"

"Some of you may very possibly be killed!" I said.

"*I* don't mind being killed!" cried one of the finest of the smaller boys : he rode a beautiful little bull, which galloped and jumped like a horse.

"I don't either! I don't either!" came from all sides.

Then Lona, queen and mother and sister of them all, spoke from her big horse by my side :

"I would give my life," she said, "to have my mother! She might kill me if she liked! I should just kiss her and die!"

"Come along, boys!" cried a girl. "We're going to our mothers!"

A pang went through my heart.—But I could not draw back; it would be moral ruin to the Little Ones!

CHAPTER XXXV

THE LITTLE ONES IN BULIKA

It was early in the morning when we set out, making, between the blue sky and the green grass, a gallant show on the wide plain. We would travel all the morning, and rest the afternoon; then go on at night, rest the next day, and start again in the short twilight. The latter part of our journey we would endeavour so to divide as to arrive at the city with the first of the morning, and be already inside the gates when discovered.

It seemed as if all the inhabitants of the forest would migrate with us. A multitude of birds flew in front, imagining themselves, no doubt, the leading division; great companies of butterflies and other insects played about our heads; and a crowd of four-footed creatures followed us. These last, when night came, left us almost all; but the birds and the butterflies, the wasps and the dragon-flies, went with us to the very gates of the city.

We halted and slept soundly through the afternoon : it was our first real march, but none were tired. In the night we went faster, because it was cold. Many fell asleep on the backs of their beasts, and woke in the morning quite fresh. None tumbled

off. Some rode shaggy, shambling bears, which yet made speed
enough, going as fast as the elephants. Others were mounted on
different kinds of deer, and would have been racing all the way
had I not prevented it. Those atop of the hay on the elephants,
unable to see the animals below them, would keep talking to
them as long as they were awake. Once, when we had halted
to feed, I heard a little fellow, as he drew out the hay to give
him, commune thus with his "darling beast" :

"Nosy dear, I am digging you out of the mountain, and shall
soon get down to you : be patient; I'm a coming! Very soon
now you'll send up your nose to look for me, and then we'll
kiss like good elephants, we will!"

The same night there burst out such a tumult of elephant-
trumpeting, horse-neighing, and child-imitation, ringing far over
the silent levels, that, uncertain how near the city might not be,
I quickly stilled the uproar lest it should give warning of our
approach.

Suddenly, one morning, the sun and the city rose, as it seemed,
together. To the children the walls appeared only a great mass
of rock, but when I told them the inside was full of nests of
stone, I saw apprehension and dislike at once invade their
hearts : for the first time in their lives, I believe—many of them
long little lives—they knew fear. The place looked to them bad :
how were they to find mothers in such a place? But they went
on bravely, for they had confidence in Lona—and in me too,
little as I deserved it.

We rode through the sounding archway. Sure never had such
a drumming of hoofs, such a padding of paws and feet been
heard on its old pavement! The horses started and looked scared
at the echo of their own steps; some halted a moment, some
plunged wildly and wheeled about; but they were soon quieted,
and went on. Some of the Little Ones shivered, and all were
still as death. The three girls held closer the infants they carried.
All except the bears and butterflies manifested fear.

On the countenance of the woman lay a dark anxiety; nor
was I myself unaffected by the general dread, for the whole
army was on my hands and on my conscience : I had brought it
up to the danger whose shadow was now making itself felt! But
I was supported by the thought of the coming kingdom of the
Little Ones, with the bad giants its slaves, and the animals its

loving, obedient friends! Alas, I who dreamed thus, had not myself learned to obey! Untrusting, unfaithful obstinacy had set me at the head of that army of innocents! I was myself but a slave, like any king in the world I had left who does or would do only what pleases him! But Lona rode beside me a child indeed, therefore a free woman—calm, silent, watchful, not a whit afraid!

We were nearly in the heart of the city before any of its inhabitants became aware of our presence. But now windows began to open, and sleepy heads to look out. Every face wore at first a dull stare of wonderless astonishment, which, as soon as the starers perceived the animals, changed to one of consternation. In spite of their fear, however, when they saw that their invaders were almost all children, the women came running into the streets, and the men followed. But for a time all of them kept close to the houses, leaving open the middle of the way, for they durst not approach the animals.

At length a boy, who looked about five years old, and was full of the idea of his mother, spying in the crowd a ,woman whose face attracted him, threw himself upon her from his antelope, and clung about her neck; nor was she slow to return his embrace and kisses. But the hand of a man came over her shoulder, and seized him by the neck. Instantly a girl ran her sharp spear into the fellow's arm. He sent forth a savage howl, and immediately stabbed by two or three more, fled yelling.

"They are just bad giants!" said Lona, her eyes flashing as she drove her horse against one of unusual height who, having stirred up the little manhood in him, stood barring her way with a club. He dared not abide the shock, but slunk aside, and the next moment went down, struck by several stones. Another huge fellow, avoiding my charger, stepped suddenly, with a speech whose rudeness alone was intelligible, between me and the boy who rode behind me. The boy told him to address the king; the giant struck his little horse on the head with a hammer, and he fell. Before the brute could strike again, however, one of the elephants behind laid him prostrate, and trampled on him so that he did not attempt to get up until hundreds of feet had walked over him, and the army was gone by.

But at sight of the women what a dismay clouded the face of Lona! Hardly one of them was even pleasant to look upon! Were her darlings to find mothers among such as these?

Hardly had we halted in the central square, when two girls rode up in anxious haste, with the tidings that two of the boys had been hurried away by some women. We turned at once, and then first discovered that the woman we befriended had disappeared with her baby.

But at the same moment we descried a white leopardess come bounding toward us down a narrow lane that led from the square to the palace. The Little Ones had not forgotten the fight of the two leopardesses in the forest : some of them looked terrified, and their ranks began to waver; but they remembered the order I had just given them, and stood fast.

We stopped to see the result; when suddenly a small boy, called Odu, remarkable for his speed and courage, who had heard me speak of the goodness of the white leopardess, leaped from the back of his bear, which went shambling after him, and ran to meet her. The leopardess, to avoid knocking him down, pulled herself up so suddenly that she went rolling over and over : when she recovered her feet she found the child on her back. Who could doubt the subjugation of a people which saw an urchin of the enemy bestride an animal of which they lived in daily terror? Confident of the effect on the whole army, we rode on.

As we stopped at the house to which our guides led us, we heard a scream; I sprang down, and thundered at the door. My horse came and pushed me away with his nose, turned about, and had begun to batter the door with his heels, when up came little Odu on the leopardess, and at sight of her he stood still, trembling. But she too had heard the cry, and forgetting the child on her back, threw herself at the door; the boy was dashed against it, and fell senseless. Before I could reach him, Lona had him in her arms, and as soon as he came to himself, set him on the back of his bear, which had still followed him.

When the leopardess threw herself the third time against the door, it gave way, and she darted in. We followed, but she had already vanished. We sprang up a stair, and went all over the house, to find no one. Darting down again, we spied a door under the stair, and got into a labyrinth of excavations. We had not gone far, however, when we met the leopardess with the child we sought across her back.

He told us that the woman he took for his mother threw him

into a hole, saying she would give him to the leopardess. But the leopardess was a good one, and took him out.

Following in search of the other boy, we got into the next house more easily, but to find, alas, that we were too late : one of the savages had just killed the little captive! It consoled Lona, however, to learn which he was, for she had been expecting him to grow a bad giant, from which worst of fates death had saved him. The leopardess sprang upon his murderer, took him by the throat, dragged him into the street, and followed Lona with him, like a cat with a great rat in her jaws.

"Let us leave the horrible place," said Lona; "there are no mothers here! This people is not worth delivering."

The leopardess dropped her burden, and charged into the crowd, this way and that, wherever it was thickest. The slaves cried out and ran, tumbling over each other in heaps.

When we got back to the army, we found it as we had left it, standing in order and ready.

But I was far from easy : the princess gave no sign, and what she might be plotting we did not know! Watch and ward must be kept the night through!

The Little Ones were such hardy creatures that they could repose anywhere : we told them to lie down with their animals where they were, and sleep till they were called. In one moment they were down, and in another lapt in the music of their sleep, a sound as of water over grass, or a soft wind among leaves. Their animals slept more lightly, ever on the edge of waking. The bigger boys and girls walked softly hither and thither among the dreaming multitude. All was still; the whole wicked place appeared at rest.

CHAPTER XXXVI

MOTHER AND DAUGHTER

Lona was so disgusted with the people, and especially with the women, that she wished to abandon the place as soon as possible; I, on the contrary, felt very strongly that to do so would be to fail wilfully where success was possible; and, far worse, to weaken the hearts of the Little Ones, and so bring them

into much greater danger. If we retreated, it was certain the
princess would not leave us unassailed! if we encountered her,
the hope of the prophecy went with us! Mother and daughter
must meet : it might be that Lona's loveliness would take Lilith's
heart by storm! if she threatened violence, I should be there
between them! If I found that I had no other power over her, I
was ready, for the sake of my Lona, to strike her pitilessly on the
closed hand! I knew she was doomed : most likely it was decreed
that her doom should now be brought to pass through us!

Still without hint of the relation in which she stood to the
princess, I stated the case to Lona as it appeared to me. At once
she agreed to accompany me to the palace.

From the top of one of its great towers, the princess had, in
the early morning, while the city yet slept, descried the approach
of the army of the Little Ones. The sight awoke in her an over-
mastering terror : she had failed in her endeavour to destroy
them, and they were upon her! The prophecy was about to be
fulfilled!

When she came to herself, she descended to the black hall,
and seated herself in the north focus of the ellipse, under the
opening in the roof.

For she must think! Now what she called *thinking* required
a clear consciousness of herself, not as she was, but as she chose
to believe herself; and to aid her in the realisation of this consciousness, she had suspended, a little way from and above her,
itself invisible in the darkness of the hall, a mirror to receive the
full sunlight reflected from her person. For the resulting vision
of herself in the splendour of her beauty, she sat waiting the
meridional sun.

Many a shadow moved about her in the darkness, but as often
as, with a certain inner eye which she had, she caught sight of
one, she refused to regard it. Close under the mirror stood the
Shadow which attended her walks, but, self-occupied, him she
did not see.

The city was taken; the inhabitants were cowering in terror;
the Little Ones and their strange cavalry were encamped in the
square; the sun shone upon the princess, and for a few minutes
she saw herself glorious. The vision passed, but she sat on. The
night was now come, and darkness clothed and filled the glass,
yet she did not move. A gloom that swarmed with shadows,

wallowed in the palace; the servants shivered and shook, but dared not leave it because of the beasts of the Little Ones; all night long the princess sat motionless : she must see her beauty again! she must try again to think! But courage and will had grown weary of her, and would dwell with her no more!

In the morning we chose twelve of the tallest and bravest of the boys to go with us to the palace. We rode our great horses, and they small horses and elephants.

The princess sat waiting the sun to give her the joy of her own presence. The tide of the light was creeping up the shore of the sky, but until the sun stood overhead, not a ray could enter the black hall.

He rose to our eyes, and swiftly ascended. As we climbed the steep way to the palace, he climbed the dome of its great hall. He looked in at the eye of it—and with sudden radiance the princess flashed upon her own sight. But she sprang to her feet with a cry of despair : alas her whiteness! the spot covered half her side, and was black as the marble around her! She clutched her robe, and fell back in her chair. The Shadow glided out, and she saw him go.

We found the gate open as usual, passed through the paved grove up to the palace door, and entered the vestibule. There in her cage lay the spotted leopardess, apparently asleep or lifeless. The Little Ones paused a moment to look at her. She leaped up rampant against the cage. The horses reared and plunged; the elephants retreated a step. The next instant she fell supine, writhed in quivering spasms, and lay motionless. We rode into the great hall.

The princess yet leaned back in her chair in the shaft of sunlight, when from the stones of the court came to her ears the noise of the horses' hoofs. She started, listened, and shook : never had such sound been heard in her palace! She pressed her hand to her side, and gasped. The trampling came nearer and nearer; it entered the hall itself; moving figures that were not shadows approached her through the darkness!

For us, we saw a splendour, a glorious woman centring the dark. Lona sprang from her horse, and bounded to her. I sprang from mine, and followed Lona.

"Mother! mother!" she cried, and her clear, lovely voice echoed in the dome.

The princess shivered; her face grew almost black with hate; her eyebrows met on her forehead. She rose to her feet, and stood.

"Mother! mother!" cried Lona again, as she leaped on the daïs, and flung her arms around the princess.

An instant more and I should have reached them!—in that instant I saw Lona lifted high, and dashed on the marble floor. Oh, the horrible sound of her fall! At my feet she fell, and lay still. The princess sat down with the smile of a demoness.

I dropped on my knees beside Lona, raised her from the stones, and pressed her to my bosom. With indignant hate I glanced at the princess; she answered me with her sweetest smile. I would have sprung upon her, taken her by the throat, and strangled her, but love of the child was stronger than hate of the mother, and I clasped closer my precious burden. Her arms hung helpless; her blood trickled over my hands, and fell on the floor with soft, slow little plashes.

The horses scented it—mine first, then the small ones. Mine reared, shivering and wild-eyed, went about, and thundered blindly down the dark hall, with the little horses after him. Lona's stood gazing down at his mistress, and trembling all over. The boys flung themselves from their horses' backs, and they, not seeing the black wall before them, dashed themselves, with mine, to pieces against it. The elephants came on to the foot of the daïs, and stopped, wildly trumpeting; the Little Ones sprang upon it, and stood horrified; the princess lay back in her seat, her face that of a corpse, her eyes alone alive, wickedly flaming. She was again withered and wasted to what I found in the wood, and her side was as if a great branding hand had been laid upon it. But Lona saw nothing, and I saw but Lona.

"Mother! mother!" she sighed, and her breathing ceased.

I carried her into the court : the sun shone upon a white face, and the pitiful shadow of a ghostly smile. Her head hung back. She was "dead as earth."

I forgot the Little Ones, forgot the murdering princess, forgot the body in my arms, and wandered away, looking for my Lona. The doors and windows were crowded with brute-faces jeering at me, but not daring to speak, for they saw the white leopardess behind me, hanging her head close at my heel. I spurned her with my foot. She held back a moment, and followed me again.

I reached the square : the little army was gone! Its emptiness roused me. Where were the Little Ones, *her* Little Ones? I had lost her children! I stared helpless about me, staggered to the pillar, and sank upon its base.

But as I sat gazing on the still countenance, it seemed to smile a live momentary smile. I never doubted it an illusion, yet believed what it said : I should yet see her alive! It was not she, it was I who was lost, and she would find me!

I rose to go after the Little Ones, and instinctively sought the gate by which we had entered. I looked around me, but saw nothing of the leopardess.

The street was rapidly filling with a fierce crowd. They saw me encumbered with my dead, but for a time dared not assail me. Ere I reached the gate, however, they had gathered courage. The women began to hustle me; I held on heedless. A man pushed against my sacred burden : with a kick I sent him away howling. But the crowd pressed upon me, and fearing for the dead that was beyond hurt, I clasped my treasure closer, and freed my right arm. That instant, however, a commotion arose in the street behind me; the crowd broke; and through it came the Little Ones I had left in the palace. Ten of them were upon four of the elephants; on the two other elephants lay the princess, bound hand and foot, and quite still, save that her eyes rolled in their ghastly sockets. The two other Little Ones rode behind her on Lona's horse. Every now and then the wise creatures that bore her threw their trunks behind and felt her cords.

I walked on in front, and out of the city. What an end to the hopes with which I entered the evil place! We had captured the bad princess, and lost our all-beloved queen! My life was bare! my heart was empty!

CHAPTER XXXVII

THE SHADOW

A MURMUR OF PLEASURE from my companions roused me : they had caught sight of their fellows in the distance! The two on Lona's horse rode on to join them. They were greeted with a wavering shout—which immediately died away. As we drew

near, the sound of their sobs reached us like the breaking of tiny
billows.

When I came among them, I saw that something dire had
befallen them : on their childish faces was the haggard look left
by some strange terror. No possible grief could have wrought
the change. A few of them came slowly round me, and held out
their arms to take my burden. I yielded it; the tender hopelessness of the smile with which they received it, made my heart
swell with pity in the midst of its own desolation. In vain were
their sobs over their mother-queen; in vain they sought to entice
from her some recognition of their love; in vain they kissed and
fondled her as they bore her away : she would not wake! On
each side one carried an arm, gently stroking it; as many as
could get near, put their arms under her body; those who could
not, crowded around the bearers. On a spot where the grass
grew thicker and softer they laid her down, and there all the
Little Ones gathered sobbing.

Outside the crowd stood the elephants, and I near them, gazing at my Lona over the many little heads between. Those next
me caught sight of the princess, and stared trembling. Odu was
the first to speak.

"I have seen that woman before!" he whispered to his next
neighbour. "It was she who fought the white leopardess, the
night they woke us with their yelling!"

"Silly!" returned his companion. "That was a wild beast, with
spots!"

"Look at her eyes!" insisted Odu. "I know she is a bad
giantess, but she is a wild beast all the same. I know she is the
spotted one!"

The other took a step nearer; Odu drew him back with a sharp
pull.

"Don't look at her!" he cried, shrinking away, yet fascinated
by the hate-filled longing in her eyes. "She would eat you up in
a moment! It was *her* shadow! She is the wicked princess!"

"That cannot be! they said she was beautiful!"

"Indeed it is the princess!" I interposed. "Wickedness has
made her ugly!"

She heard, and what a look was hers!

"It was very wrong of me to run away!" said Odu thoughtfully.

"What made you run away!" I asked. "I expected to find you where I left you!"

He did not reply at once.

"I don't know what made me run," answered another. "I was frightened!"

"It was a man that came down the hill from the palace," said a third.

"How did he frighen you?"

"I don't know."

"He wasn't a man," said Odu; "he was a shadow; he had no thick to him!"

"Tell me more about him."

"He came down the hill very black, walking like a bad giant, but spread flat. He was nothing but blackness. We were frightened the moment we saw him, but we did not run away; we stood and watched him. He came on as if he would walk over us. But before he reached us, he began to spread and spread, and grew bigger and bigger, till at last he was so big that he went out of our sight, and we saw him no more, and then he was upon us!"

"What do you mean by that?"

"He was all black through between us, and we could not see one another; and then he was inside us."

"How did you know he was inside you?"

"He did me quite different. I felt like bad. I was not Odu any more—not the Odu I knew. I wanted to tear Sozo to pieces —not really, but like!"

He turned and hugged Sozo.

"It wasn't me, Sozo," he sobbed. "Really, deep down, it was Odu, loving you always! And Odu came up, and knocked Naughty away. I grew sick, and thought I must kill myself to get out of the black. Then came a horrible laugh that had heard my think, and it set the air trembling about me. And then I suppose I ran away, but I did not know I had run away until I found myself running, fast as could, and all the rest running too. I would have stopped, but I never thought of it until I was out of the gate among the grass. Then I knew that I had run away from a shadow that wanted to be me and wasn't, and that I was the Odu that loved Sozo. It was the shadow that got into me, and hated him from inside me; it was not my own self me!

And now I know that I ought not to have run away! But indeed
I did not quite know what I was doing until it was done! My
legs did it, I think : they grew frightened, and forgot me, and
ran away! Naughty legs! There! and there!"

Thus ended Odu, with a kick to each of his naughty legs.

"What became of the shadow?" I asked.

"I do not know," he answered. "I suppose he went home into
the night where there is no moon."

I fell a wondering where Lona was gone, and dropping on the
grass, took the dead thing in my lap, and whispered in its ear,
"Where are you, Lona? I love you!" But its lips gave no answer.
I kissed them, not quite cold, laid the body down again, and
appointing a guard over it, rose to provide for the safety of
Lona's people during the night.

Before the sun went down, I had set a watch over the princess
outside the camp, and sentinels round it : intending to walk
about it myself all night long, I told the rest of the army to
go to sleep. They threw themselves on the grass and were asleep
in a moment.

When the moon rose I caught a glimpse of something white;
it was the leopardess. She swept silently round the sleeping
camp, and I saw her pass three times between the princess and
the Little Ones. Thereupon I made the watch lie down with
the others, and stretched myself beside the body of Lona.

CHAPTER XXXVIII

TO THE HOUSE OF BITTERNESS

In the morning we set out, and made for the forest as fast
as we could. I rode Lona's horse, and carried her body. I would
take it to her father : he would give it a couch in the chamber
of his dead! or, if he would not, seeing she had not come of
herself, I would watch it in the desert until it mouldered away!
But I believed he would, for surely she had died long ago! Alas,
how bitterly must I not humble myself before him!

To Adam I must take Lilith also. I had no power to make
her repent! I had hardly a right to slay her—much less a right

to let her loose in the world! and surely I scarce merited being made for ever her gaoler!

Again and again, on the way, I offered her food; but she answered only with a look of hungering hate. Her fiery eyes kept rolling to and fro, nor ever closed, I believe, until we reached the other side of the hot stream. After that they never opened until we came to the House of Bitterness.

One evening, as we were camping for the night, I saw a little girl go up to her, and ran to prevent mischief. But ere I could reach them, the child had put something to the lips of the princess, and given a scream of pain.

"Please, king," she whimpered, "suck finger. Bad giantess make hole in it!"

I sucked the tiny finger.

"Well now!" she cried, and a minute after was holding a second fruit to a mouth greedy of other fare. But this time she snatched her hand quickly away, and the fruit fell to the ground. The child's name was Luva.

The next day we crossed the hot stream. Again on their own ground, the Little Ones were jubilant. But their nests were still at a great distance, and that day we went no farther than the ivy-hall, where, because of its grapes, I had resolved to spend the night. When they saw the great clusters, at once they knew them good, rushed upon them, ate eagerly, and in a few minutes were all fast asleep on the green floor and in the forest around the hall. Hoping again to see the dance, and expecting the Little Ones to sleep through it, I had made them leave a wide space in the middle. I lay down among them, with Lona by my side, but did not sleep.

The night came, and suddenly the company was there. I was wondering with myself whether, night after night, they would thus go on dancing to all eternity, and whether I should not one day have to join them because of my stiff-neckedness, when the eyes of the children came open, and they sprang to their feet, wide awake. Immediately every one caught hold of a dancer, and away they went, bounding and skipping. The spectres seemed to see and welcome them: perhaps they knew all about the Little Ones, for they had themselves long been on their way back to childhood! Anyhow, their innocent gambols must, I thought, bring refreshment to weary souls who, their present taken from them and their future dark, had no life save the shadow of their vanished past. Many a merry but never a rude prank did the children play; and if they did at times cause a momentary jar in the rhythm of the dance, the poor spectres, who had nothing to smile withal, at least manifested no annoyance.

Just ere the morning began to break, I started to see the skeleton-princess in the doorway, her eyes open and glowing, the fearful spot black on her side. She stood for a moment, then came gliding in, as if she would join the dance. I sprang to my feet. A cry of repugnant fear broke from the children, and the lights vanished. But the low moon looked in, and I saw them clinging to each other. The ghosts were gone—at least they were no longer visible. The princess too had disappeared. I darted to the spot where I had left her : she lay with her eyes closed, as if she had never moved. I returned to the hall. The Little Ones were already on the floor, composing themselves to sleep.

The next morning, as we started, we spied, a little way from us, two skeletons moving about in a thicket. The Little Ones broke their ranks, and ran to them. I followed; and, although now walking at ease, without splint or ligature, I was able to recognise the pair I had before seen in that neighbourhood. The children at once made friends with them, laying hold of their arms, and stroking the bones of their long fingers; and it was plain the poor creatures took their attentions kindly. The two seemed on excellent terms with each other. Their common deprivation had drawn them together! the loss of everything had been the beginning of a new life to them!

Perceiving that they had gathered handfuls of herbs, and were looking for more—presumably to rub their bones with, for in what other way could nourishment reach their system so rudimentary?—the Little Ones, having keenly examined those they held, gathered of the same sorts, and filled the hands the skeletons held out to receive them. Then they bid them goodbye, promising to come and see them again, and resumed their journey, saying to each other they had not known there were such nice people living in the same forest.

When we came to the nest-village, I remained there a night with them, to see them resettled; for Lona still looked like one just dead, and there seemed no need of haste.

The princess had eaten nothing, and her eyes remained shut : fearing she might die ere we reached the end of our journey, I went to her in the night, and laid my bare arm upon her lips. She bit into it so fiercely that I cried out. How I got away from her I do not know, but I came to myself lying beyond her reach. It was then morning, and immediately I set about our departure.

Choosing twelve Little Ones, not of the biggest and strongest, but of the sweetest and merriest, I mounted them on six elephants, and took two more of the wise *clumsies,* as the children called them, to bear the princess. I still rode Lona's horse, and carried her body wrapt in her cloak before me. As nearly as I could judge I took the direct way, across the left branch of the river-bed, to the House of Bitterness, where I hoped to learn how best to cross the broader and rougher branch, and how to avoid the basin of monsters : I dreaded the former for the elephants, the latter for the children.

I had one terrible night on the way—the third, passed in the desert between the two branches of the dead river.

We had stopped the elephants in a sheltered place, and there let the princess slip down between them, to lie on the sand until the morning. She seemed quite dead, but I did not think she was. I laid myself a little way from her, with the body of Lona by my other side, thus to keep watch at once over the dead and the dangerous. The moon was half-way down the west, a pale, thoughtful moon, mottling the desert with shadows. Of a sudden she was eclipsed, remaining visible, but sending forth no light : a thick, diaphanous film covered her patient beauty, and she looked troubled. The film swept a little aside, and I saw the edge of it against her clearness—the jagged outline of a bat-like wing, torn and hooked. Came a cold wind with a burning sting—and Lilith was upon me. Her hands were still bound, but with her teeth she pulled from my shoulder the cloak Lona made for me, and fixed them in my flesh. I lay as one paralysed.

Already the very life seemed flowing from me into her, when I remembered, and struck her on the hand. She raised her head with a gurgling shriek, and I felt her shiver. I flung her from me, and sprang to my feet.

She was on her knees, and rocked herself to and fro. A second blast of hot-stinging cold enveloped us; the moon shone out clear, and I saw her face—gaunt and ghastly, besmeared with red.

"Down, devil!" I cried.

"Where are you taking me?" she asked, with the voice of a dull echo from a sepulchre.

"To your first husband," I answered.

"He will kill me!" she moaned.

"At least he will take you off my hands!"

"Give me my daughter," she suddenly screamed, grinding her teeth.

"Never! Your doom is upon you at last!"

"Loose my hands for pity's sake!" she groaned. "I am in torture. The cords are sunk in my flesh."

"I dare not. Lie down!" I said.

She threw herself on the ground like a log.

The rest of the night passed in peace, and in the morning she again seemed dead.

Before evening we came in sight of the House of Bitterness, and the next moment one of the elephants came alongside of my horse.

"Please, king, you are not going to that place?" whispered the Little One who rode on his neck.

"Indeed I am! We are going to stay the night there," I answered.

"Oh, please, don't! That must be where the cat-woman lives!"

"If you had ever seen her, you would not call her by that name!"

"Nobody ever sees her : she has lost her face! Her head is back and side all round."

"She hides her face from dull, discontented people!—Who taught you to call her the cat-woman?"

"I heard the bad giants call her so."

"What did they say about her?"

"That she had claws to her toes."

"It is not true. I know the lady. I spent a night at her house."

"But she *may* have claws to her toes! You might see her feet, and her claws be folded up inside their cushions!"

"Then perhaps you think that I have claws to my toes?"

"Oh, no; that can't be! you are good!"

"The giants might have told you so!" I pursued.

"We shouldn't believe them about you!"

"Are the giants good?"

"No; they love lying."

"Then why do you believe them about her? I know the lady is good; she cannot have claws."

"Please how do you know she is good?"

"How do you know I am good?"

I rode on, while he waited for his companions, and told them what I had said.

They hastened after me, and when they came up—

"I would not take you to her house if I did not believe her good," I said.

"We know you would not," they answered.

"If I were to do something that frightened you—what would you say?"

"The beasts frightened us sometimes at first, but they never hurt us!" answered one.

"That was before we knew them!" added another.

"Just so!" I answered. "When you see the woman in that cottage, you will know that she is good. You may wonder at what she does, but she will always be good. I know her better than you know me. She will not hurt you,—or if she does,——"

"Ah, you are not sure about it, king dear! You think she *may* hurt us!"

"I am sure she will never be unkind to you, even if she do hurt you!"

They were silent for a while.

"I'm not afraid of being hurt—a little!—a good deal!" cried Odu. "But I should not like scratches in the dark! The giants say the cat-woman has claw-feet all over her house!"

"I am taking the princess to her," I said.

"Why?"

"Because she is her friend."

"How can she be good then?"

"Little Tumbledown is a friend of the princess," I answered; "so is Luva : I saw them both, more than once, trying to feed her with grapes!"

"Little Tumbledown is good! Luva is very good!"

"That is why they are her friends."

"Will the cat-woman—I mean the woman that isn't the cat-woman, and has no claws to her toes—give her grapes?"

"She is more likely to give her scratches!"

"Why?—You say she is her friend!"

"That is just why.—A friend is one who gives us what we need, and the princess is sorely in need of a terrible scratching."

They were silent again.

"If any of you are afraid," I said, "you may go home; I shall not prevent you. But I cannot take one with me who believes the giants rather than me, or one who will call a good lady the cat-woman!"

"Please, king," said one, "I'm so afraid of being afraid!"

"My boy," I answered, "there is no harm in being afraid. The only harm is in doing what Fear tells you. Fear is not your master! Laugh in his face and he will run away."

"There she is—in the door waiting for us!" cried one, and put his hands over his eyes.

"How ugly she is!" cried another, and did the same.

"You do not see her," I said; "her face is covered!"

"She has no face!" they answered.

"She has a very beautiful face. I saw it once.—It is indeed as beautiful as Lona's!" I added with a sigh.

"Then what makes her hide it?"

"I think I know:—anyhow, she has some good reason for it!"

"I don't like the cat-woman! she is frightful!"

"You cannot like, and you ought not to dislike what you have never seen.—Once more, you must not call her the cat-woman!"

"What are we to call her then, please?"

"Lady Mara!"

"That is a pretty name!" said a girl; "I will call her 'lady Mara'; then perhaps she will show me her beautiful face!"

Mara, drest and muffled in white, was indeed standing in the doorway to receive us.

"At last!" she said. "Lilith's hour has been long on the way, but it is come! Everything comes. Thousands of years have I waited—and not in vain!"

She came to me, took my treasure from my arms, carried it into the house, and returning, took the princess. Lilith shuddered, but made no resistance. The beasts lay down by the door. We followed our hostess, the Little Ones looking very grave. She laid the princess on a rough settle at one side of the room, unbound her, and turned to us.

"Mr. Vane," she said, "and you, Little Ones, I thank you!

This woman would not yield to gentler measures; harder must have their turn. I must do what I can to make her repent!"

The pitiful-hearted Little Ones began to sob sorely.

"Will you hurt her very much, lady Mara?" said the girl I have just mentioned, putting her warm little hand in mine.

"Yes; I am afraid I must; I fear she will make me!" answered Mara. "It would be cruel to hurt her too little. It would have all to be done again, only worse."

"May I stop with her?"

"No, my child. She loves no one, therefore she cannot be *with* any one. There is One who will be with her, but she will not be with Him."

"Will the shadow that came down the hill be with her?"

"The great Shadow will be in her, I fear, but he cannot be *with* her, or with any one. She will know I am beside her, but that will not comfort her."

"Will you scratch her very deep?" asked Odu, going near, and putting his hand in hers. "Please, don't make the red juice come!"

She caught him up, turned her back to the rest of us, drew the muffling down from her face, and held him at arms' length that he might see her.

As if his face had been a mirror, I saw in it what he saw. For one moment he stared, his little mouth open; then a divine wonder arose in his countenance, and swiftly changed to intense delight. For a minute he gazed entranced, then she set him down. Yet a moment he stood looking up at her, lost in contemplation—then ran to us with the face of a prophet that knows a bliss he cannot tell. Mara rearranged her mufflings, and turned to the other children.

"You must eat and drink before you go to sleep," she said; "you have had a long journey!"

She set the bread of her house before them, and a jug of cold water. They had never seen bread before, and this was hard and dry, but they ate it without sign of distaste. They had never seen water before, but they drank without demur, one after the other looking up from the draught with a face of glad astonishment. Then she led away the smallest, and the rest went trooping after her. With her own gentle hands, they told me, she put them to bed on the floor of the garret.

CHAPTER XXXIX

THAT NIGHT

THEIR NIGHT WAS a troubled one, and they brought a strange
report of it into the day. Whether the fear of their sleep came
out into their waking, or their waking fear sank with them into
their dreams, awake or asleep they were never at rest from it.
All night something seemed going on in the house—something
silent, something terrible, something they were not to know.
Never a sound awoke; the darkness was one with the silence,
and the silence was the terror.

Once, a frightful wind filled the house, and shook its inside,
they said, so that it quivered and trembled like a horse shaking
himself; but it was a silent wind that made not even a moan in
their chamber, and passed away like a soundless sob.

They fell asleep. But they woke again with a great start. They
thought the house was filling with water such as they had been
drinking. It came from below, and swelled up until the garret
was full of it to the very roof. But it made no more sound than
the wind, and when it sank away, they fell asleep dry and warm.

The next time they woke, all the air, they said, inside and out,
was full of cats. They swarmed—up and down, along and across,
everywhere about the room. They felt their claws trying to get
through the night-gowns lady Mara had put on them, but they
could not; and in the morning not one of them had a scratch.
Through the dark suddenly, came the only sound they heard the
night long—the far-off howl of the huge great-grandmother-cat
in the desert : she must have been calling her little ones, they
thought, for that instant the cats stopped, and all was still. Once
more they fell fast asleep, and did not wake till the sun was
rising.

Such was the account the children gave of their experiences.
But I was with the veiled woman and the princess all through
the night : something of what took place I saw; much I only
felt; and there was more which eye could not see, and heart only
could in a measure understand.

As soon as Mara left the room with the children, my eyes fell on the white leopardess : I thought we had left her behind us, but there she was, cowering in a corner. Apparently she was in mortal terror of what she might see. A lamp stood on the high chimney-piece, and sometimes the room seemed full of lamp-shadows, sometimes of cloudy forms. The princess lay on the settle by the wall, and seemed never to have moved hand or foot. It was a fearsome waiting.

When Mara returned, she drew the settle with Lilith upon it to the middle of the room, then sat down opposite me, at the other side of the hearth. Between us burned a small fire.

Something terrible was on its way ! The cloudy presences flickered and shook. A silvery creature like a slowworm came crawling out from among them, slowly crossed the clay floor, and crept into the fire. We sat motionless. The something came nearer.

But the hours passed, midnight drew nigh, and there was no change. The night was very still. Not a sound broke the silence, not a rustle from the fire, not a crack from board or beam. Now and again I felt a sort of heave, but whether in the earth or in the air or in the waters under the earth, whether in my own body or in my soul—whether it was anywhere, I could not tell. A dread sense of judgment was upon me. But I was not afraid, for I had ceased to care for aught save the thing that must be done.

Suddenly it was midnight. The muffled woman rose, turned toward the settle, and slowly unwound the long swathes that hid her face : they dropped on the ground, and she stepped over them. The feet of the princess were toward the hearth; Mara went to her head, and turning, stood behind it. Then I saw her face. It was lovely beyond speech—white and sad, heart-and-soul sad, but not unhappy, and I knew it never could be unhappy. Great tears were running down her cheeks; she wiped them away with her robe; her countenance grew very still, and she wept no more. But for the pity in every line of her expression, she would have seemed severe. She laid her hand on the head of the princess—on the hair that grew low on the forehead, and stooping, breathed on the sallow brow. The body shuddered.

"Will you turn away from the wicked things you have been doing so long?" said Mara gently.

The princess did not answer. Mara put the question again, in the same soft, inviting tone.

Still there was no sign of hearing. She spoke the words a third time.

Then the seeming corpse opened its mouth and answered, its words appearing to frame themselves of something else than sound.—I cannot shape the thing further : sounds they were not, yet they were words to me.

"I will not," she said. "I will be myself and not another!"

"Alas, you are another now, not yourself! Will you not be your real self?"

"I will be what I mean myself now."

"If you were restored, would you not make what amends you could for the misery you have caused?"

"I would do after my nature."

"You do not know it : your nature is good, and you do evil!"

"I will do as my Self pleases—as my Self desires."

"You will do as the Shadow, overshadowing your Self inclines you?"

"I will do what I will to do."

"You have killed your daughter, Lilith!"

"I have killed thousands. She is my own!"

"She was never yours as you are another's."

"I am not another's; I am my own, and my daughter is mine."

"Then, alas, your hour is come!"

"I care not. I am what I am; no one can take from me myself!"

"You are not the Self you imagine."

"So long as I feel myself what it pleases me to think myself, I care not. I am content to be to myself what I would be. What I choose to seem to myself makes me what I am. My own thought makes me me; my own thought of myself is me. Another shall not make me!"

"But another has made you, and can compel you to see what you have made yourself. You will not be able much longer to look to yourself anything but what he sees you! You will not much longer have satisfaction in the thought of yourself. At this moment you are aware of the coming change!"

"No one ever made me. I defy that Power to unmake me from a free woman! You are his slave, and I defy you! You may be able to torture me—I do not know, but you shall not compel me to anything against my will!"

"Such a compulsion would be without value. But there is a light that goes deeper than the will, a light that lights up the darkness behind it : that light can change your will, can make it truly yours and not another's—not the Shadow's. Into the created can pour itself the creating will, and so redeem it !"

"That light shall not enter me : I hate it !—Begone, slave !"

"I am no slave, for I love that light, and will with the deeper will which created mine. There is no slave but the creature that wills against its creator. Who is a slave but her who cries, 'I am free,' yet cannot cease to exist !"

"You speak foolishness from a cowering heart ! You imagine me given over to you : I defy you ! I hold myself against you ! What I choose to be, you cannot change. I will not be what you think me—what you say I am !"

"I am sorry : you must suffer !"

"But be free !"

"She alone is free who would make free; she loves not freedom who would enslave : she is herself a slave. Every life, every will, every heart that came within your ken, you have sought to subdue : you are the slave of every slave you have made—such a slave that you do not know it !—See your own self !"

She took her hand from the head of the princess, and went two backward paces from her.

A soundless presence as of roaring flame possessed the house—the same, I presume, that was to the children a silent wind. Involuntarily I turned to the hearth : its fire was a still small moveless glow. But I saw the worm-thing come creeping out, white-hot, vivid as incandescent silver, the live heart of essential fire. Along the floor it crawled toward the settle, going very slow. Yet more slowly it crept up on it, and laid itself, as unwilling to go further, at the feet of the princess. I rose and stole nearer. Mara stood motionless, as one that waits an event foreknown. The shining thing crawled on to a bare bony foot : it showed no suffering, neither was the settle scorched where the worm had lain. Slowly, very slowly, it crept along her robe until it reached her bosom, where it disappeared among the folds.

The face of the princess lay stonily calm, the eyelids closed as over dead eyes; and for some minutes nothing followed. At length, on the dry, parchment-like skin, began to appear drops as of the finest dew : in a moment they were as large as seed-pearls, ran together, and began to pour down in streams. I darted forward to snatch the worm from the poor withered bosom, and crush it with my foot. But Mara, Mother of Sorrow, stepped between, and drew aside the closed edges of the robe: no serpent was there—no searing trail; the creature had passed in by the centre of the black spot, and was piercing through the joints and marrow to the thoughts and intents of the heart. The princess gave one writhing, contorted shudder, and I knew the worm was in her secret chamber.

"She is seeing herself!" said Mara; and laying her hand on my arm, she drew me three paces from the settle.

Of a sudden the princess bent her body upward in an arch, then sprang to the floor, and stood erect. The horror in her face made me tremble lest her eyes should open, and the sight of them overwhelm me. Her bosom heaved and sank, but no breath issued. Her hair hung and dripped; then it stood out from her head and emitted sparks; again hung down, and poured the sweat of her torture on the floor.

I would have thrown my arms about her, but Mara stopped me.

"You cannot go near her," she said. "She is far away from us, afar in the hell of her self-consciousness. The central fire of the universe is radiating into her the knowledge of good and evil, the knowledge of what she is. She sees at last the good she is not, the evil she is. She knows that she is herself the fire in which she is burning, but she does not know that the Light of Life is the heart of that fire. Her torment is that she is what she is. Do not fear for her; she is not forsaken. No gentler way to help her was left. Wait and watch."

It may have been five minutes or five years that she stood thus—I cannot tell; but at last she flung herself on her face.

Mara went to her, and stood looking down upon her. Large tears fell from her eyes on the woman who had never wept, and would not weep.

"Will you change your way?" she said at length.

"Why did he make me such?" gasped Lilith. "I would have made myself—oh, so different! I am glad it was he that made me and not I myself! He alone is to blame for what I am! Never would I have made such a worthless thing! He meant me such that I might know it and be miserable! I will not be made any longer!"

"Unmake yourself, then," said Mara.

"Alas, I cannot! You know it, and mock me! How often have I not agonised to cease, but the tyrant keeps me being! I curse him!—Now let him kill me!"

The words came in jets as from a dying fountain.

"Had he not made you," said Mara, gently and slowly, "you could not even hate him. But he did not make you such. You have made yourself what you are.—Be of better cheer : he can remake you."

"I will not be remade!"

"He will not change you; he will only restore you to what you were."

"I will not be aught of his making."

"Are you not willing to have that set right which you have set wrong?"

She lay silent; her suffering seemed abated.

"If you are willing, put yourself again on the settle."

"I will not," she answered, forcing the words through her clenched teeth.

A wind seemed to wake inside the house, blowing without sound or impact; and a water began to rise that had no lap in its ripples, no sob in its swell. It was cold, but it did not benumb. Unseen and noiseless it came. It smote no sense in me, yet I knew it rising. I saw it lift at last and float her. Gently it bore her, unable to resist, and left rather than laid her on the settle. Then it sank swiftly away.

The strife of thought, accusing and excusing, began afresh, and gathered fierceness. The soul of Lilith lay naked to the torture of pure interpenetrating inward light. She began to moan, and sigh deep sighs, then murmur as holding colloquy with a dividual self : her queendom was no longer whole; it was divided against itself. One moment she would exult as over her worst enemy, and weep; the next she would writhe as in the embrace of a friend whom her soul hated, and laugh like a demon. At length she began what seemed a tale about herself, in a language so strange, and in forms so shadowy, that I could but here and there understand a little. Yet the language seemed the primeval shape of one I knew well, and the forms to belong to dreams which had once been mine, but refused to be recalled. The tale appeared now and then to touch upon things that Adam had read from the disparted manuscript, and often to make allusion to influences and forces—vices too, I could not help suspecting—with which I was unacquainted.

She ceased, and again came the horror in her hair, the sparkling and flowing alternate. I sent a beseeching look to Mara.

"Those, alas, are not the tears of repentance!" she said. "The true tears gather in the eyes. Those are far more bitter, and not so good. Self-loathing is not sorrow. Yet it is good, for it marks a step in the way home, and in the father's arms the prodigal forgets the self he abominates. Once with his father, he is to himself of no more account. It will be so with her."

She went nearer and said,

"Will you restore that which you have wrongfully taken?"

"I have taken nothing," answered the princess, forcing out the words in spite of pain, "that I had not the right to take. My power to take manifested my right."

Mara left her.

Gradually my soul grew aware of an invisible darkness, a something more terrible than aught that had yet made itself felt. A horrible Nothingness, a Negation positive infolded her; the border of its being that was yet no being, touched me, and for one ghastly instant I seemed alone with Death Absolute! It was not the absence of everything I felt, but the presence of Nothing. The princess dashed herself from the settle to the floor with an exceeding great and bitter cry. It was the recoil of Being from Annihilation.

"For pity's sake," she shrieked, "tear my heart out, but let me live!"

With that there fell upon her, and upon us also who watched with her, the perfect calm as of a summer night. Suffering had all but reached the brim of her life's cup, and a hand had emptied it! She raised her head, half rose, and looked around her. A moment more, and she stood erect, with the air of a conqueror: she had won the battle! Dareful she had met her spiritual foes; they had withdrawn defeated! She raised her withered arm above her head, a pæan of unholy triumph in her throat—when suddenly her eyes fixed in a ghastly stare.—What was she seeing?

I looked, and saw: before her, cast from unseen heavenly mirror, stood the reflection of herself, and beside it a form of splendent beauty. She trembled, and sank again on the floor helpless. She knew the one what God had intended her to be, the other what she had made herself.

The rest of the night she lay motionless altogether.

With the gray dawn growing in the room, she rose, turned to Mara, and said, in prideful humility,

"You have conquered. Let me go into the wilderness and bewail myself."

Mara saw that her submission was not feigned, neither was it real. She looked at her a moment, and returned :

"Begin, then, and set right in the place of wrong."

"I know not how," she replied—with the look of one who foresaw and feared the answer.

"Open thy hand, and let that which is in it go."

A fierce refusal seemed to struggle for passage, but she kept it prisoned.

"I cannot," she said. "I have no longer the power. Open it for me."

She held out the offending hand. It was more a paw than a hand. It seemed to me plain that she could not open it.

Mara did not even look at it.

"You must open it yourself," she said quietly.

"I have told you I cannot!"

"You can if you will—not indeed at once, but by persistent effort. What you have done, you do not yet wish undone—do not yet intend to undo!"

"You think so, I dare say," rejoined the princess with a flash of insolence, "but I *know* that I cannot open my hand!"

"I know you better than you know yourself, and I know you can. You have often opened it a little way. Without trouble and pain you cannot open it quite, but you *can* open it. At worst you could beat it open! I pray you, gather your strength, and open it wide."

"I will not try what I know impossible. It would be the part of a fool!"

"Which you have been playing all your life! Oh, you are hard to teach!"

Defiance reappeared on the face of the princess. She turned her back on Mara, saying,

"I know what you have been tormenting me for! You have

not succeeded, nor shall you succeed! You shall yet find me stronger than you think! I will yet be mistress of myself! I am still what I have always known myself—queen of Hell, and mistress of the worlds!"

Then came the most fearful thing of all. I did not know what it was; I knew myself unable to imagine it; I knew only that if it came near me I should die of terror! I now know that it was *Life in Death*—life dead, yet existent; and I knew that Lilith had had glimpses, but only glimpses of it before : it had never been with her until now.

She stood as she had turned. Mara went and sat down by the fire. Fearing to stand alone with the princess, I went also and sat again by the hearth. Something began to depart from me. A sense of cold, yet not what we call cold, crept, not into, but out of my being, and pervaded it. The lamp of life and the eternal fire seemed dying together, and I about to be left with naught but the consciousness that I had been alive. Mercifully, bereavement did not go so far, and my thought went back to Lilith.

Something was taking place in her which we did not know. We knew we did not feel what she felt, but we knew we felt something of the misery it caused her. The thing itself was in her, not in us; its reflex, her misery, reached us, and was again reflected in us : she was in the outer darkness, we present with her who was in it! We were not in the outer darkness; had we been, we could not have been *with* her; we should have been timelessly, spacelessly, absolutely apart. The darkness knows neither the light nor itself; only the light knows itself and the darkness also. None but God hates evil and understands it.

Something was gone from her, which then first, by its absence, she knew to have been with her every moment of her wicked years. The source of life had withdrawn itself; all that was left her of conscious being was the dregs of her dead and corrupted life.

She stood rigid. Mara buried her head in her hands. I gazed on the face of one who knew existence but not love—knew nor life, nor joy, nor good; with my eyes I saw the face of a live death! She knew life only to know that it was dead, and that, in her, death lived. It was not merely that life had ceased in her, but that she was consciously a dead thing. She had killed her life, and was dead—and knew it. She must *death it* for ever and ever! She had tried her hardest to unmake herself, and could

not! she was a dead life! she could not cease! she must *be*!
In her face I saw and read beyond its misery—saw in its dismay
that the dismay behind it was more than it could manifest. It
sent out a livid gloom; the light that was in her was darkness,
and after its kind it shone. She was what God could not have
created. She had usurped beyond her share in self-creation, and
her part had undone His! She saw now what she had made, and
behold, it was not good! She was as a conscious corpse, whose
coffin would never come to pieces, never set her free! Her
bodily eyes stood wide open, as if gazing into the heart of horror
essential—her own indestructible evil. Her right hand also was
now clenched—upon existent Nothing—her inheritance!

But with God all things are possible : He can save even the
rich!

Without change of look, without sign of purpose, Lilith
walked toward Mara. She felt her coming, and rose to meet her.

"I yield," said the princess. "I cannot hold out. I am defeated.
—Not the less, I cannot open my hand."

"Have you tried?"

"I am trying now with all my might."

"I will take you to my father. You have wronged him worst of
the created, therefore he best of the created can help you."

"How can *he* help me?"

"He will forgive you."

"Ah, if he would but help me to cease! Not even that am I
capable of! I have no power over myself; I am a slave! I
acknowledge it. Let me die."

"A slave thou art that shall one day be a child!" answered
Mara.—"Verily, thou shalt die, but not as thou thinkest. Thou
shalt die out of death into life. Now is the Life for, that never
was against thee!"

Like her mother, in whom lay the motherhood of all the
world, Mara put her arms around Lilith, and kissed her on the
forehead. The fiery-cold misery went out of her eyes, and their
fountains filled. She lifted, and bore her to her own bed in a
corner of the room, laid her softly upon it, and closed her eyes
with caressing hands.

Lilith lay and wept. The Lady of Sorrow went to the door and
opened it.

Morn, with the Spring in her arms, waited outside. Softly they

stole in at the opened door, with a gentle wind in the skirts of
their garments. It flowed and flowed about Lilith, rippling the
unknown, upwaking sea of her life eternal; rippling and to ripple
it, until at length she who had been but as a weed cast on the
dry sandy shore to wither, should know herself an inlet of the
everlasting ocean, henceforth to flow into her for ever, and ebb
no more. She answered the morning wind with reviving breath,
and began to listen. For in the skirts of the wind had come the
rain—the soft rain that heals the mown, the many-wounded
grass—soothing it with the sweetness of all music, the hush that
lives between music and silence. It bedewed the desert places
around the cottage, and the sands of Lilith's heart heard it, and
drank it in. When Mara returned to sit by her bed, her tears were
flowing softer than the rain, and soon she was fast asleep.

CHAPTER XL

THE HOUSE OF DEATH

The Mother of Sorrows rose, muffled her face, and went
to call the Little Ones. They slept as if all the night they had
not moved, but the moment she spoke they sprang to their feet,
fresh as if new-made. Merrily down the stair they followed her,
and she brought them where the princess lay, her tears yet
flowing as she slept. Their glad faces grew grave. They looked
from the princess out on the rain, then back at the princess.

"The sky is falling!" said one.

"The white juice is running out of the princess!" cried
another, with an awed look.

"Is it rivers?" asked Odu, gazing at the little streams that
flowed adown her hollow cheeks.

"Yes," answered Mara, "—the most wonderful of all rivers."

"I thought rivers was bigger, and rushed, like a lot of Little
Ones, making loud noises!" he returned, looking at me, from
whom alone he had heard of rivers.

"Look at the rivers of the sky!" said Mara. "See how they
come down to wake up the waters under the earth! Soon will
the rivers be flowing everywhere, merry and loud, like thousands

and thousands of happy children. Oh, how glad they will make you, Little Ones! You have never seen any, and do not know how lovely is the water!"

"That will be the glad of the ground that the princess is grown good," said Odu. "See the glad of the sky!"

"Are the rivers the glad of the princess?" asked Luva. "They are not her juice, for they are not red!"

"They are the juice inside the juice," answered Mara.

Odu put one finger to his eye, looked at it, and shook his head.

"Princess will not bite now!" said Luva.

"No; she will never do that again," replied Mara. "—But now we must take her nearer home."

"Is that a nest?" asked Sozo.

"Yes; a very big nest. But we must take her to another place first."

"What is that?"

"It is the biggest room in all this world.—But I think it is going to be pulled down : it will soon be too full of little nests.— Go and get your clumsies."

"Please are there any cats in it?"

"Not one. The nests are too full of lovely dreams for one cat to get in."

"We shall be ready in a minute," said Odu, and ran out, followed by all except Luva.

Lilith was now awake, and listening with a sad smile.

"But her rivers are running so fast!" said Luva, who stood by her side and seemed unable to take her eyes from her face. "Her robe is all—I don't know what. Clumsies won't like it!"

"They won't mind it," answered Mara. "Those rivers are so clean that they make the whole world clean."

I had fallen asleep by the fire, but for some time had been awake and listening, and now rose.

"It is time to mount, Mr. Vane," said our hostess.

"Tell me, please," I said, "is there not a way by which to avoid the channels and the den of monsters?"

"There is an easy way across the river-bed, which I will show you," she answered; "but you must pass once more through the monsters."

"I fear for the children," I said.

"Fear will not once come nigh them," she rejoined.

We left the cottage. The beasts stood waiting about the door. Odu was already on the neck of one of the two that were to carry the princess. I mounted Lona's horse; Mara brought her body, and gave it me in my arms. When she came out again with the princess, a cry of delight arose from the children : she was no longer muffled! Gazing at her, and entranced with her loveliness, the boys forgot to receive the princess from her; but the elephants took Lilith tenderly with their trunks, one round her body and one round her knees, and, Mara helping, laid her along beween them.

"Why does the princess want to go?" asked a small boy. "She would keep good if she staid here!"

"She wants to go, and she does not want to go : we are helping her," answered Mara. "She will not keep good here."

"What are you helping her to do?" he went on.

"To go where she will get more help—help to open her hand, which has been closed for a thousand years."

"So long? Then she has learned to do without it : why should she open it now?"

"Because it is shut upon something that is not hers."

"Please, lady Mara, may we have some of your very dry bread before we go?" said Luva.

Mara smiled, and brought them four loaves and a great jug of water.

"We will eat as we go," they said. But they drank the water with delight.

"I think," remarked one of them, "it must be elephant-juice! It makes me so strong!"

We set out, the Lady of Sorrow walking with us, more beautiful than the sun, and the white leopardess following her. I thought she meant but to put us in the path across the channels, but I soon found she was going with us all the way. Then I would have dismounted that she might ride, but she would not let me.

"I have no burden to carry," she said. "The children and I will walk together."

It was the loveliest of mornings; the sun shone his brightest, and the wind blew his sweetest, but they did not comfort the desert, for it had no water.

We crossed the channels without difficulty, the children

gamboling about Mara all the way, but did not reach the top of the ridge over the bad burrow until the sun was already in the act of disappearing. Then I made the Little Ones mount their elephants, for the moon might be late, and I could not help some anxiety about them.

The Lady of Sorrow now led the way by my side; the elephants followed—the two that bore the princess in the centre; the leopardess brought up the rear; and just as we reached the frightful margin, the moon looked up and showed the shallow basin lying before us untroubled. Mara stepped into it; not a movement answered her tread or the feet of my horse. But the moment that the elephants carrying the princess touched it, the seemingly solid earth began to heave and boil, and the whole dread brood of the hellish nest was commoved. Monsters uprose on all sides, every neck at full length, every beak and claw outstretched, every mouth agape. Long-billed heads, horribly jawed faces, knotty tentacles innumerable, went out after Lilith. She lay in an agony of fear, nor dared stir a finger. Whether the hideous things even saw the children, I doubt; certainly not one of them touched a child; not one loathly member passed the live rampart of her body-guard, to lay hold of her.

"Little Ones," I cried, "keep your elephants close about the princess. Be brave; they will not touch you."

"What will not touch us? We don't know what to be brave at!" they answered; and I perceived they were unaware of one of the deformities around them.

"Never mind then," I returned; "only keep close."

They were panoplied in their blindness! Incapacity to see was their safety. What they could nowise be aware of, could not hurt them.

But the hideous forms I saw that night! Mara was a few paces in front of me when a solitary, bodiless head bounced on the path between us. The leopardess came rushing under the elephants from behind, and would have seized it, but, with frightful contortions of visage and a loathsome howl, it gave itself a rapid rotatory twist, sprang from her, and buried itself in the ground. The death in my arms assoiling me from fear, I regarded them all unmoved, although never, sure, was elsewhere beheld such a crew accursed!

Mara still went in front of me, and the leopardess now walked close behind her, shivering often, for it was very cold, when suddenly the ground before me to my left began to heave, and a low wave of earth came slinking toward us. It rose higher as it drew near; out of it slouched a dreadful head with fleshy tubes for hair, and opening a great oval mouth, snapped at me. The leopardess sprang, but fell baffled beyond it.

Almost under our feet, shot up the head of an enormous snake, with a lamping wallowing glare in its eyes. Again the leopardess rushed to the attack, but found nothing. At a third monster she darted with like fury, and like failure—then sullenly ceased to heed the phantom-horde. But I understood the peril and hastened the crossing—the rather that the moon was carrying herself strangely. Even as she rose she seemed ready to drop and give up the attempt as hopeless; and since, I saw her sink back once fully her own breadth. The arc she made was very low, and now she had begun to descend rapidly.

We were almost over, when, between us and the border of the basin, arose a long neck, on the top of which, like the blossom of some Stygian lily, sat what seemed the head of a corpse, its mouth half open, and full of canine teeth. I went on; it retreated, then drew aside. The lady stepped on the firm land, but the leopardess between us, roused once more, turned, and flew at the throat of the terror. I remained where I was to see the elephants, with the princess and the children, safe on the bank. Then I turned to look after the leopardess. That moment the moon went down. For an instant I saw the leopardess and the snake-monster convolved in a cloud of dust; then darkness hid them. Trembling with fright, my horse wheeled, and in three bounds overtook the elephants.

As we came up with them, a shapeless jelly dropped on the princess. A white dove dropped immediately on the jelly, stabbing it with its beak. It made a squelching, sucking sound, and fell off. Then I heard the voice of a woman talking with Mara, and I knew the voice.

"I fear she is dead!" said Mara.

"I will send and find her," answered the mother. "But why, Mara, shouldst thou at all fear for her or for any one? Death cannot hurt her who dies doing the work given her to do."

"I shall miss her sorely; she is good and wise. Yet I would not have her live beyond her hour!"

"She has gone down with the wicked; she will rise with the righteous. We shall see her again ere very long."

"Mother," I said, although I did not see her, "we come to you many, but most of us are Little Ones. Will you be able to receive us all?"

"You are welcome every one," she answered. "Sooner or later all will be little ones, for all must sleep in my house! It is well with those that go to sleep young and willing!—My husband is even now preparing her couch for Lilith. She is neither young nor quite willing, but it is well indeed that she is come."

I heard no more. Mother and daughter had gone away together through the dark. But we saw a light in the distance, and toward it we went stumbling over the moor.

Adam stood in the door, holding the candle to guide us, and talking with his wife, who, behind him, laid bread and wine on the table within.

"Happy children," I heard her say, "to have looked already on the face of my daughter! Surely it is the loveliest in the great world!"

When we reached the door, Adam welcomed us almost merrily. He set the candle on the threshold, and going to the elephants, would have taken the princess to carry her in; but she repulsed him, and pushing her elephants asunder, stood erect between them. They walked from beside her, and left her with him who had been her husband—ashamed indeed of her gaunt uncomeliness, but unsubmissive. He stood with a welcome in his eyes that shone through their severity.

"We have long waited for thee, Lilith!" he said.

She returned him no answer.

Eve and her daughter came to the door.

"The mortal foe of my children!" murmured Eve, standing radiant in her beauty.

"Your children are no longer in her danger," said Mara; "she has turned from evil."

"Trust her not hastily, Mara," answered her mother; "she has deceived a multitude!"

"But you will open to her the mirror of the Law of Liberty, mother, that she may go into it, and abide in it! She consents to open her hand and restore: will not the great Father restore her to inheritance with His other children?"

"I do not know Him!" murmured Lilith, in a voice of fear and doubt.

"Therefore it is that thou art miserable," said Adam.

"I will go back whence I came!" she cried, and turned, wringing her hands, to depart.

"That is indeed what I would have thee do, where I would have thee go—to Him from whom thou camest! In thy agony didst thou not cry out for Him?"

"I cried out for Death—to escape Him and thee!"

"Death is even now on his way to lead thee to Him. Thou knowest neither Death nor the Life that dwells in Death! Both befriend thee. I am dead, and would see thee dead, for I live and love thee. Thou art weary and heavy-laden: art thou not ashamed? Is not the being thou hast corrupted become to thee at length an evil thing? Wouldst thou yet live on in disgrace eternal? Cease thou canst not: wilt thou not be restored and *be*?"

She stood silent with bowed head.

"Father," said Mara, "take her in thine arms, and carry her to her couch. There she will open her hand, and die into life."

"I will walk," said the princess.

Adam turned and led the way. The princess walked feebly after him into the cottage.

Then Eve came out to me where I sat with Lona in my bosom. She reached up her arms, took her from me, and carried her in. I dismounted, and the children also. The horse and the elephants stood shivering; Mara patted and stroked them every one; they lay down and fell asleep. She led us into the cottage, and gave the Little Ones of the bread and wine on the table. Adam and Lilith were standing there together, but silent both.

Eve came from the chamber of death, where she had laid Lona down, and offered of the bread and wine to the princess.

"Thy beauty slays me! It is death I would have, not food!" said Lilith, and turned from her.

"This food will help thee to die," answered Eve.

But Lilith would not taste of it.

"If thou wilt nor eat nor drink, Lilith," said Adam, "come and see the place where thou shalt lie in peace."

He led the way through the door of death, and she followed submissive. But when her foot crossed the threshold she drew it back, and pressed her hand to her bosom, struck through with the cold immortal.

A wild blast fell roaring on the roof, and died away in a moan. She stood ghastly with terror.

"It is he!" said her voiceless lips : I read their motion.

"Who, princess!" I whispered.

"The great Shadow," she murmured.

"Here he cannot enter," said Adam. "Here he can hurt no one. Over him also is power given me."

"Are the children in the house?" asked Lilith, and at the word the heart of Eve began to love her.

"He never dared touch a child," she said. "Nor have you either ever hurt a child. Your own daughter you have but sent into the loveliest sleep, for she was already a long time dead when you slew her. And now Death shall be the atonemaker; you shall sleep together."

"Wife," said Adam, "let us first put the children to bed, that she may see them safe!"

He came back to fetch them. As soon as he was gone, the princess knelt to Eve, clasped her knees, and said,

"Beautiful Eve, persuade your husband to kill me : to you he will listen! Indeed I would but cannot open my hand."

"You cannot die without opening it. To kill you would not serve you," answered Eve. "But indeed he cannot! no one can kill you but the Shadow; and whom he kills never knows she is dead, but lives to do his will, and thinks she is doing her own."

"Show me then to my grave; I am so weary I can live no longer. I must go to the Shadow—yet I would not!"

She did not, could not understand!

She struggled to rise, but fell at the feet of Eve. The Mother lifted, and carried her inward.

I followed Adam and Mara and the children into the chamber of death. We passed Eve with Lilith in her arms, and went farther in.

"You shall not go to the Shadow," I heard Eve say, as we passed them. "Even now is his head under my heel!"

The dim light in Adam's hand glimmered on the sleeping faces, and as he went on, the darkness closed over them. The very air seemed dead : was it because none of the sleepers breathed it? Profoundest sleep filled the wide place. It was as if not one had waked since last I was there, for the forms I had then noted lay there still. My father was just as I had left him, save that he seemed yet nearer to a perfect peace. The woman beside him looked younger.

The darkness, the cold, the silence, the still air, the faces of the lovely dead, made the hearts of the children beat softly, but their little tongues would talk—with low, hushed voices.

"What a curious place to sleep in!" said one, "I would rather be in my nest!"

"It is *so* cold!" said another.

"Yes, it is cold," answered our host; "but you will not be cold in your sleep."

"Where are our nests?" asked more than one, looking round and seeing no couch unoccupied.

"Find places, and sleep where you choose," replied Adam.

Instantly they scattered, advancing fearlessly beyond the light, but we still heard their gentle voices, and it was plain they saw where I could not.

"Oh," cried one, "here is such a beautiful lady!—may I sleep beside her? I will creep in quietly, and not wake her."

"Yes, you may," answered the voice of Eve behind us; and we came to the couch while the little fellow was yet creeping slowly and softly under the sheet. He laid his head beside the lady's, looked up at us, and was still. His eyelids fell; he was asleep.

We went a little farther, and there was another who had climbed up on the couch of a woman.

"Mother! mother!" he cried, kneeling over her, his face close to hers. "—She's so cold she can't speak," he said, looking up to us; "but I will soon make her warm!"

He lay down, and pressing close to her, put his little arm over her. In an instant he too was asleep, smiling an absolute content.

We came to a third Little One; it was Luva. She stood on tiptoe, leaning over the edge of a couch.

"My own mother wouldn't have me," she said softly : "will you?"

Receiving no reply, she looked up at Eve. The great mother lifted her to the couch, and she got at once under the snowy covering.

Each of the Little Ones had by this time, except three of the boys, found at least an unobjecting bedfellow, and lay still and white beside a still, white woman. The little orphans had adopted mothers! One tiny girl had chosen a father to sleep with, and that was mine. A boy lay by the side of the beautiful matron with the slow-healing hand. On the middle one of the three couches hitherto unoccupied, lay Lona.

Eve set Lilith down beside it. Adam pointed to the vacant couch on Lona's right hand, and said,

"There, Lilith, is the bed I have prepared for you!"

She glanced at her daughter lying before her like a statue carved in semi-transparent alabaster, and shuddered from head to foot. "How cold it is!" she murmured.

"You will soon begin to find comfort in the cold," answered Adam.

"Promises to the dying are easy!" she said.

"But I know it : I too have slept. I am dead!"

"I believed you dead long ago; but I see you alive!"

"More alive than you know, or are able to understand. I was scarce alive when first you knew me. Now I have slept, and am awake; I am dead, and live indeed!"

"I fear that child," she said, pointing to Lona : "she will rise and terrify me!"

"She is dreaming love to you."

"But the Shadow!" she moaned; "I fear the Shadow! he will be wroth with me!"

"He at sight of whom the horses of heaven start and rear, dares not disturb one dream in this quiet chamber!"

"I shall dream then?"

"You will dream."

"What dreams?"

"That I cannot tell, but none *he* can enter into. When the Shadow comes here, it will be to lie down and sleep also.—His hour will come, and he knows it will."

"How long shall I sleep?"

"You and he will be the last to wake in the morning of the universe."

The princess lay down, drew the sheet over her, stretched herself out straight, and lay still with open eyes.

Adam turned to his daughter. She drew near.

"Lilith," said Mara, "you will not sleep, if you lie there a thousand years, until you have opened your hand, and yielded that which is not yours to give or to withhold."

"I cannot," she answered. "I would if I could, and gladly, for I am weary, and the shadows of death are gathering about me."

"They will gather and gather, but they cannot infold you while yet your hand remains unopened. You may think you are dead, but it will be only a dream; you may think you have come awake, but it will still be only a dream. Open your hand, and you will sleep indeed—then wake indeed."

"I am trying hard, but the fingers have grown together and into the palm."

"I pray you put forth the strength of your will. For the love of life, draw together your forces and break its bonds!"

"I have struggled in vain; I can do no more. I am very weary, and sleep lies heavy upon my lids."

"The moment you open your hand, you will sleep. Open it, and make an end."

A tinge of colour arose in the parchment-like face; the contorted hand trembled with agonised effort, Mara took it, and sought to aid her.

"Hold, Mara!" cried her father. "There is danger!"

The princess turned her eyes upon Eve, beseechingly.

"There was a sword I once saw in your husband's hands," she murmured. "I fled when I saw it. I heard him who bore it say it would divide whatever was not one and indivisible!"

"I have the sword," said Adam. "The angel gave it me when he left the gate."

"Bring it, Adam," pleaded Lilith, "and cut me off this hand that I may sleep."

"I will," he answered.

He gave the candle to Eve, and went. The princess closed her eyes.

In a few minutes Adam returned with an ancient weapon in his hand. The scabbard looked like vellum grown dark with years, but the hilt shone like gold that nothing could tarnish. He drew out the blade. It flashed like a pale blue northern streamer, and the light of it made the princess open her eyes. She saw the sword, shuddered, and held out her hand. Adam took it. The sword gleamed once, there was one little gush of blood, and he laid the severed hand in Mara's lap. Lilith had given one moan, and was already fast asleep. Mara covered the arm with the sheet, and the three turned away.

"Will you not dress the wound?" I said.

"A wound from that sword," answered Adam, "needs no dressing. It is healing and not hurt."

"Poor lady!" I said, "she will wake with but one hand!"

"Where the dead deformity clung," replied Mara, "the true, lovely hand is already growing."

We heard a childish voice behind us, and turned again. The candle in Eve's hand shone on the sleeping face of Lilith, and the waking faces of the three Little Ones, grouped on the other side of her couch.

"How beautiful she is grown!" said one of them.

"Poor princess!" said another; "I will sleep with her. She will not bite any more!"

As he spoke he climbed into her bed, and was immediately fast asleep. Eve covered him with the sheet.

"I will go on her other side," said the third. "She shall have two to kiss when she wakes!"

"And I am left alone!" said the first mournfully.

"I will put you to bed," said Eve.

She gave the candle to her husband, and led the child away.

We turned once more to go back to the cottage. I was very sad, for no one had offered me a place in the house of the dead. Eve joined us as we went, and walked on before with her husband. Mara by my side carried the hand of Lilith in the lap of her robe.

"Ah, you have found her!" we heard Eve say as we stepped into the cottage.

The door stood open; two elephant-trunks came through it out of the night beyond.

"I sent them with the lantern," she went on to her husband, "to look for Mara's leopardess : they have brought her."

I followed Adam to the door, and between us we took the white creature from the elephants, and carried her to the chamber we had just left, the women preceding us, Eve with the light, and Mara still carrying the hand. There we laid the beauty across the feet of the princess, her fore-paws outstretched and her head couching between them.

CHAPTER XLI

I AM SENT

THEN I TURNED and said to Eve,

"Mother, one couch next to Lona is empty : I know I am unworthy, but may I not sleep this night in your chamber with my dead? Will you not pardon both my cowardice and my self-confidence, and take me in? I give me up. I am sick of myself, and would fain sleep the sleep!"

"The couch next to Lona is the one already prepared for you," she answered; "but something waits to be done ere you sleep."

"I am ready," I replied.

"How do you know you can do it?" she asked with a smile.

"Because you require it," I answered. "What is it?"

She turned to Adam :

"Is he forgiven, husband?"

"From my heart."

"Then tell him what he has to do."

Adam turned to his daughter.

"Give me that hand, Mara, my child."

She held it out to him in her lap. He took it tenderly.

"Let us go to the cottage," he said to me; "there I will instruct you."

As we went, again arose a sudden stormful blast, mingled with a great flapping on the roof, but it died away as before in a deep moan.

When the door of the death-chamber was closed behind us, Adam seated himself, and I stood before him.

"You will remember," he said, "how, after leaving my daughter's house, you came to a dry rock, bearing the marks of an ancient cataract; you climbed that rock, and found a sandy desert : go to that rock now, and from its summit walk deep into the desert. But go not many steps ere you lie down, and listen with your head on the sand. If you hear the murmur of water beneath, go a little farther, and listen again. If you still hear the sound, you are in the right direction. Every few yards you must stop, lie down, and hearken. If, listening thus, at any time you hear no sound of water, you are out of the way, and must hearken in every direction until you hear it again. Keeping with the sound, and careful not to retrace your steps, you will soon hear it louder, and the growing sound will lead you to where it is loudest : that is the spot you seek. There dig with the spade I will give you, and dig until you come to moisture : in it lay the hand, cover it to the level of the desert, and come home.— But give good heed, and carry the hand with care. Never lay it down, in what place of seeming safety soever; let nothing touch it; stop nor turn aside for any attempt to bar your way; never look behind you; speak to no one, answer no one, walk straight on.—It is yet dark, and the morning is far distant, but you must set out at once."

He gave me the hand, and brought me a spade.

"This is my gardening spade," he said; "with it I have brought many a lovely thing to the sun."

I took it, and went out into the night.

It was very cold, and pitch-dark. To fall would be a dread thing, and the way I had to go was a difficult one even in the broad sunlight ! But I had not set myself the task, and the minute I started I learned that I was left to no chance : a pale light broke from the ground at every step, and showed me where next to set my foot. Through the heather and the low rocks I walked without once even stumbling. I found the bad burrow quite still; not a wave arose, not a head appeared as I crossed it.

A moon came, and herself showed me the easy way : toward morning I was almost over the dry channels of the first branch of the river-bed, and not far, I judged, from Mara's cottage.

The moon was very low, and the sun not yet up, when I saw before me in the path, here narrowed by rocks, a figure covered from head to foot as with a veil of moonlit mist. I kept on my way as if I saw nothing. The figure threw aside its veil.

"Have you forgotten me already?" said the princess—or what seemed she.

I neither hesitated nor answered; I walked straight on.

"You meant then to leave me in that horrible sepulchre ! Do you not yet understand that where I please to be, there I am? Take my hand : I am alive as you !"

I was on the point of saying, "Give me your left hand,"

but bethought myself, held my peace, and steadily advanced.

"Give me my hand," she suddenly shrieked, "or I will tear you in pieces : you are mine!"

She flung herself upon me. I shuddered, but did not falter. Nothing touched me, and I saw her no more.

With measured tread along the path, filling it for some distance, came a body of armed men. I walked through them—nor know whether they gave way to me, or were bodiless things. But they turned and followed me; I heard and felt their march at my very heels; but I cast no look behind, and the sound of their steps and the clash of their armour died away.

A little farther on, the moon being now close to the horizon and the way in deep shadow, I descried, seated where the path was so narrow that I could not pass her, a woman with muffled face.

"Ah," she said, "you are come at last! I have waited here for you an hour or more! You have done well! Your trial is over. My father sent me to meet you that you might have a little rest on the way. Give me your charge, and lay your head in my lap; I will take good care of both until the sun is well risen. I am not bitterness always, neither to all men!"

Her words were terrible with temptation, for I was very weary. And what more likely to be true! If I were, through slavish obedience to the letter of the command and lack of pure insight, to trample under my feet the very person of the Lady of Sorrow! My heart grew faint at the thought, then beat as if it would burst my bosom.

Nevertheless my will hardened itself against my heart, and my step did not falter. I took my tongue between my teeth lest I should unawares answer, and kept on my way. If Adam had sent her, he could not complain that I would not heed her! Nor would the Lady of Sorrow love me the less that even she had not been able to turn me aside!

Just ere I reached the phantom, she pulled the covering from her face : great indeed was her loveliness, but those were not Mara's eyes! no lie could truly or for long imitate them! I advanced as if the thing were not there, and my foot found empty room.

I had almost reached the other side when a Shadow—I think it was The Shadow, barred my way. He seemed to have a helmet upon his head, but as I drew closer I perceived it was the head itself I saw—so distorted as to bear but a doubtful resemblance to the human. A cold wind smote me, dank and sickening—repulsive as the air of a charnel-house; firmness forsook my joints, and my limbs trembled as if they would drop in a helpless heap. I seemed to pass through him, but I think now that he passed through me : for a moment I was as one of the damned. Then a soft wind like the first breath of a new-born spring greeted me, and before me arose the dawn.

My way now led me past the door of Mara's cottage. It stood wide open, and upon the table I saw a loaf of bread and a pitcher of water. In or around the cottage was neither howl nor wail.

I came to the precipice that testified to the vanished river. I climbed its worn face, and went on into the desert. There at last, after much listening to and fro, I determined the spot where the hidden water was loudest, hung Lilith's hand about my neck, and began to dig. It was a long labour, for I had to make a large hole because of the looseness of the sand; but at length I threw up a damp spadeful. I flung the sexton-tool on the verge, and laid down the hand. A little water was already oozing from under its fingers. I sprang out, and made haste to fill the grave. Then, utterly fatigued, I dropped beside it, and fell asleep.

CHAPTER XLII

I SLEEP THE SLEEP

When I woke, the ground was moist about me, and my track to the grave was growing a quicksand. In its ancient course the river was swelling, and had begun to shove at its burden. Soon it would be roaring down the precipice, and, divided in its fall, rushing with one branch to resubmerge the orchard valley, with the other to drown perhaps the monster horde, and between them to isle the Evil Wood. I set out at once on my return to those who sent me.

When I came to the precipice, I took my way betwixt the branches, for I would pass again by the cottage of Mara, lest she should have returned : I longed to see her once more ere I went to sleep; and now I knew where to cross the channels, even if the river should have overtaken me and filled them. But when I

reached it, the door stood open still; the bread and the water
were still on the table; and deep silence was within and around
it. I stopped and called aloud at the door, but no voice replied,
and I went my way.

A little farther, I came where sat a grayheaded man on the
sand, weeping.

"What ails you, sir?" I asked. "Are you forsaken?"

"I weep," he answered, "because they will not let me die. I
have been to the house of death, and its mistress, notwithstanding
my years, refuses me. Intercede for me, sir, if you know her, I
pray you."

"Nay, sir," I replied, "that I cannot; for she refuses none
whom it is lawful for her to receive."

"How know you this of her? You have never sought death!
you are much too young to desire it!"

"I fear your words may indicate that, were you young again,
neither would you desire it."

"Indeed, young sir, I would not! and certain I am that you
cannot."

"I may not be old enough to desire to die, but I am young
enough to desire to live indeed! Therefore I go now to learn if
she will at length take me in. You wish to die because you do
not care to live : she will not open her door to you, for no one
can die who does not long to live."

"It ill becomes your youth to mock a friendless old man. Pray,
cease your riddles!"

"Did not then the Mother tell you something of the same sort?"

"In truth I believe she did; but I gave little heed to her
excuses."

"Ah, then, sir," I rejoined, "it is but too plain you have not
yet learned to die, and I am heartily grieved for you. Such had
I too been but for the Lady of Sorrow. I am indeed young, but
I have wept many tears; pardon me, therefore, if I presume to
offer counsel :—Go to the Lady of Sorrow, and 'take with both
hands'* what she will give you. Yonder lies her cottage. She is
not in it now, but her door stands open, and there is bread and
water on her table. Go in; sit down; eat of the bread; drink of
the water; and wait there until she appear. Then ask counsel of
her, for she is true, and her wisdom is great."

* William Law.

He fell to weeping afresh, and I left him weeping. What I said, I fear he did not heed. But Mara would find him!

The sun was down, and the moon unrisen, when I reached the abode of the monsters, but it was still as a stone till I passed over. Then I heard a noise of many waters, and a great cry behind me, but I did not turn my head.

Ere I reached the house of death, the cold was bitter and the darkness dense; and the cold and the darkness were one, and entered into my bones together. But the candle of Eve, shining from the window, guided me, and kept both frost and murk from my heart.

The door stood open, and the cottage lay empty. I sat down disconsolate.

And as I sat, there grew in me such a sense of loneliness as never yet in my wanderings had I felt. Thousands were near me, not one was with me! True, it was I who was dead, not they; but, whether by their life or by my death, we were divided! They were alive, but I was not dead enough even to know them alive : doubt *would* come. They were, at best, far from me, and helpers I had none to lay me beside them!

Never before had I known, or truly imagined desolation! In vain I took myself to task, saying the solitude was but a seeming : I was awake, and they slept—that was all! it was only that they lay so still and did not speak! they were with me now, and soon, soon I should be with them!

I dropped Adam's old spade, and the dull sound of its fall on the clay floor seemed reverberated from the chamber beyond : a childish terror seized me; I sat and stared at the coffin-door.— But father Adam, mother Eve, sister Mara would soon come to me, and then—welcome the cold world and the white neighbours! I forgot my fears, lived a little, and loved my dead.

Something did move in the chamber of the dead! There came from it what was *like* a dim, far-off sound, yet was not what I knew as sound. My soul sprang into my ears. Was it a mere thrill of the dead air, too slight to be heard, but quivering in every spiritual sense? I *knew* without hearing, without feeling it!

The something was coming! it drew nearer! In the bosom of my desertion awoke an infant hope. The noiseless thrill reached the coffin-door—became sound, and smote on my ear.

The door began to move—with a low, soft creaking of its

hinges. It was opening! I ceased to listen, and stared expectant.

It opened a little way, and a face came into the opening. It was Lona's. Its eyes were closed, but the face itself was upon me, and seemed to see me. It was white as Eve's, white as Mara's, but did not shine like their faces. She spoke, and her voice was like a sleepy night-wind in the grass.

"Are you coming, king?" it said. "I cannot rest until you are with me, gliding down the river to the great sea, and the beautiful dream-land. The sleepiness is full of lovely things : come and see them."

"Ah, my darling!" I cried. "Had I but known!—I thought you were dead!"

She lay on my bosom—cold as ice frozen to marble. She threw her arms, so white, feebly about me, and sighed—

"Carry me back to my bed, king. I want to sleep."

I bore her to the death-chamber, holding her tight lest she should dissolve out of my arms. Unaware that I saw, I carried her straight to her couch.

"Lay me down," she said, "and cover me from the warm air; it hurts—a little. Your bed is there, next to mine. I shall see you when I wake."

She was already asleep. I threw myself on my couch—blessed as never was man on the eve of his wedding.

"Come, sweet cold," I said, "and still my heart speedily."

But there came instead a glimmer of light in the chamber, and I saw the face of Adam approaching. He had not the candle, yet I saw him. At the side of Lona's couch, he looked down on her with a questioning smile, and then greeted me across it.

"We have been to the top of the hill to hear the waters on their way," he said. "They will be in the den of the monsters to-night.—But why did you not await our return?"

"My child could not sleep," I answered.

"She is fast asleep!" he rejoined.

"Yes, now!" I said; "but she was awake when I laid her down."

"She was asleep all the time!" he insisted. "She was perhaps dreaming about you—and came to you?"

"She did."

"And did you not see that her eyes were closed?"

"Now I think of it, I did."

"If you had looked ere you laid her down, you would have seen her asleep on the couch."

"That would have been terrible!"

"You would only have found that she was no longer in your arms."

"That would have been worse!"

"It is, perhaps, to think of; but to see it would not have troubled you."

"Dear father," I said, "how is it that I am not sleepy? I thought I should go to sleep like the Little Ones the moment I laid my head down!"

"Your hour is not quite come. You must have food ere you sleep."

"Ah, I ought not to have lain down without your leave, for I cannot sleep without your help! I will get up at once!"

But I found my own weight more than I could move.

"There is no need: we will serve you here," he answered. "—You do not feel cold, do you?"

"Not too cold to lie still, but perhaps too cold to eat!"

He came to the side of my couch, bent over me, and breathed on my heart. At once I was warm.

As he left me, I heard a voice, and knew it was the Mother's. She was singing, and her song was sweet and soft and low, and I thought she sat by my bed in the dark; but ere it ceased, her song soared aloft, and seemed to come from the throat of a woman-angel, high above all the region larks, higher than man had ever yet lifted up his heart. I heard every word she sang, but could keep only this:—

"Many a wrong, and its curing song;
Many a road, and many an inn;
Room to roam, but only one home
For all the world to win!"

and I thought I had heard the song before.

Then the three came to my couch together, bringing me bread and wine, and I sat up to partake of it. Adam stood on one side of me, Eve and Mara on the other.

"You are good indeed, father Adam, mother Eve, sister Mara," I said, "to receive me! In my soul I am ashamed and sorry!"

"We knew you would come again!" answered Eve.

"How could you know it?" I returned.

"Because here was I, born to look after my brothers and sisters!" answered Mara with a smile.

"Every creature must one night yield himself and lie down," answered Adam : "he was made for liberty, and must not be left a slave!"

"It will be late, I fear, ere all have lain down!" I said.

"There is no early or late here," he rejoined. "For him the true time then first begins who lays himself down. Men are not coming home fast; women are coming faster. A desert, wide and dreary, parts him who lies down to die from him who lies down to live. The former may well make haste, but here is no haste."

"To our eyes," said Eve, "you were coming all the time : we knew Mara would find you, and you must come!"

"How long is it since my father lay down?" I asked.

"I have told you that years are of no consequence in this house," answered Adam; "we do not heed them. Your father will wake when his morning comes. Your mother, next to whom you are lying,—"

"Ah, then, it *is* my mother!" I exclaimed.

"Yes—she with the wounded hand," he assented; "—she will be up and away long ere your morning is ripe."

"I am sorry."

"Rather be glad."

"It must be a sight for God Himself to see such a woman come awake!"

"It is indeed a sight for God, a sight that makes her Maker glad! He sees of the travail of His soul, and is satisfied!—Look at her once more, and sleep."

He let the rays of his candle fall on her beautiful face.

"She looks much younger!" I said.

"She *is* much younger," he replied. "Even Lilith already begins to look younger!"

I lay down, blissfully drowsy.

"But when you see your mother again," he continued, "you will not at first know her. She will go on steadily growing younger until she reaches the perfection of her womanhood—a splendour beyond foresight. Then she will open her eyes, behold on one side her husband, on the other her son—and rise and leave them to go to a father and a brother more to her than they."

I heard as one in a dream. I was very cold, but already the

cold caused me no suffering. I felt them put on me the white garment of the dead. Then I forgot everything. The night about me was pale with sleeping faces, but I was asleep also, nor knew that I slept.

CHAPTER XLIII

THE DREAMS THAT CAME

I GREW AWARE OF existence, aware also of the profound, the infinite cold. I was intensely blessed—more blessed, I know, than my heart, imagining, can now recall. I could not think of warmth with the least suggestion of pleasure. I knew that I had enjoyed it, but could not remember how. The cold had soothed every care, dissolved every pain, comforted every sorrow. *Comforted?* Nay; sorrow was swallowed up in the life drawing nigh to restore every good and lovely thing a hundredfold! I lay at peace, full of the quietest expectation, breathing the damp odours of Earth's bountiful bosom, aware of the souls of primroses, daisies and snowdrops, patiently waiting in it for the Spring.

How convey the delight of that frozen, yet conscious sleep! I had no more to stand up! had only to lie stretched out and still! How cold I was, words cannot tell; yet I grew colder and colder —and welcomed the cold yet more and more. I grew continuously less conscious of myself, continuously more conscious of bliss, unimaginable yet felt. I had neither made it nor prayed for it : it was mine in virtue of existence; and existence was mine in virtue of a Will that dwelt in mine.

Then the dreams began to arrive—and came crowding.—I lay naked on a snowy peak. The white mist heaved below me like a billowy sea. The cold moon was in the air with me, and above the moon and me the colder sky, in which the moon and I dwelt. I was Adam, waiting for God to breathe into my nostrils the breath of life.—I was not Adam, but a child in the bosom of a mother white with radiant whiteness. I was a youth on a white horse, leaping from cloud to cloud of a blue heaven, hasting calmly to some blessed goal. For centuries I dreamed— or was it chiliads? or only one long night?—But why ask? for time had nothing to do with me; I was in the land of thought—

farther in, higher up than the seven dimensions, the ten senses :
I think I was where I am—in the heart of God.—I dreamed
away dim cycles in the centre of a melting glacier, the spectral
moon drawing nearer and nearer, the wind and the welter of a
torrent growing in my ears. I lay and heard them : the wind and
the water and the moon sang a peaceful waiting for a redemption drawing nigh. I dreamed cycles, I say, but, for aught I knew
or can tell, they were the solemn, æonian march of a second,
pregnant with eternity.

Then, of a sudden, but not once troubling my conscious bliss,
all the wrongs I had ever done, from far beyond my earthly
memory down to the present moment, were with me. Fully in
every wrong lived the conscious I, confessing, abjuring, lamenting the dead, making atonement with each person I had injured,
hurt, or offended. Every human soul to which I had caused
a troubled thought, was now grown unspeakably dear to me, and
I humbled myself before it, agonising to cast from between us
the clinging offence. I wept at the feet of the mother whose
commands I had slighted; with bitter shame I confessed to my
father that I had told him two lies, and long forgotten them :
now for long had remembered them, and kept them in memory
to crush at last at his feet. I was the eager slave of all whom I
had thus or anyhow wronged. Countless services I devised to
render them ! For this one I would build such a house as had
never grown from the ground ! for that one I would train such
horses as had never yet been seen in any world ! For a third I
would make such a garden as had never bloomed, haunted with
still pools, and alive with running waters ! I would write songs to
make hearts swell, and tales to make them glow ! I would turn
the forces of the world into such channels of invention as to make
them laugh with the joy of wonder ! Love possessed me ! Love
was my life ! Love was to me, as to him that made me, all in all !

Suddenly I found myself in a solid blackness, upon which the
ghost of light that dwells in the caverns of the eyes could not
cast one fancied glimmer. But my heart, which feared nothing
and hoped infinitely, was full of peace. I lay imagining what the
light would be when it came, and what new creation it would
bring with it—when, suddenly, without conscious volition, I sat
up and stared about me.

The moon was looking in at the lowest, horizontal, crypt-like windows of the death-chamber, her long light slanting, I thought, across the fallen, but still ripening sheaves of the harvest of the great husbandman.—But no; that harvest was gone! Gathered in, or swept away by chaotic storm, not a sacred sheaf was there! My dead were gone! I was alone!—In desolation dread lay depths yet deeper than I had hitherto known!—Had there never been any ripening dead? Had I but dreamed them and their loveliness? Why then these walls? why the empty couches? No; they were all up! they were all abroad in the new eternal day, and had forgotten me! They had left me behind, and alone! Tenfold more terrible was the tomb its inhabitants away! The quiet ones had made me quiet with their presence—had pervaded my mind with their blissful peace; now I had no friend, and my lovers were far from me! A moment I sat and stared horror-stricken. I had been alone with the moon on a mountain top in the sky; now I was alone with her in a huge cenotaph : she too was staring about, seeking her dead with ghastly gaze! I sprang to my feet, and staggered from the fearful place.

The cottage was empty. I ran out into the night.

No moon was there! Even as I left the chamber, a cloudy rampart had risen and covered her. But a broad shimmer came from far over the heath, mingled with a ghostly murmuring music, as if the moon were raining a light that plashed as it fell. I ran stumbling across the moor, and found a lovely lake, margined with reeds and rushes : the moon behind the cloud was gazing upon the monsters' den, full of clearest, brightest water, and very still.—But the musical murmur went on, filling the quiet air, and drawing me after it.

I walked round the border of the little mere, and climbed the range of hills. What a sight rose to my eyes! The whole expanse where, with hot, aching feet, I had crossed and recrossed the deep-scorched channels and ravines of the dry river-bed, was alive with streams, with torrents, with still pools—"a river deep and wide!" How the moon flashed on the water! how the water answered the moon with flashes of its own—white flashes breaking everywhere from its rock-encountered flow! And a great jubilant song arose from its bosom, the song of new-born liberty. I stood a moment gazing, and my heart also began to exult : my life was not all a failure! I had helped to set this river free!— My dead were not lost! I had but to go after and find them! I would follow and follow until I came whither they had gone! Our meeting might be thousands of years away, but at last—*at last* I should hold them! Wherefore else did the floods clap their hands?

I hurried down the hill: my pilgrimage was begun! In what direction to turn my steps I knew not, but I must go and go till I found my living dead! A torrent ran swift and wide at the foot of the range: I rushed in, it laid no hold upon me; I waded through it. The next I sprang across; the third I swam; the next I waded again.

I stopped to gaze on the wondrous loveliness of the ceaseless flash and flow, and to hearken to the multitudinous broken music. Every now and then some incipient air would seem about to draw itself clear of the dulcet confusion, only to merge again in the consorted roar. At moments the world of waters would invade as if to overwhelm me—not with the force of its seaward rush, or the shouting of its liberated throng, but with the greatness of the silence wandering into sound.

As I stood lost in delight, a hand was laid on my shoulder. I turned, and saw a man in the prime of strength, beautiful as if fresh from the heart of the glad creator, young like him who cannot grow old. I looked: it was Adam. He stood large and grand, clothed in a white robe, with the moon in his hair.

"Father," I cried, "where is she? Where are the dead? Is the great resurrection come and gone? The terror of my loneliness was upon me; I could not sleep without my dead; I ran from the desolate chamber.—Whither shall I go to find them?"

"You mistake, my son," he answered, in a voice whose very breath was consolation. "You are still in the chamber of death, still upon your couch, asleep and dreaming, with the dead around you."

"Alas! when I but dream how am I to know it? The dream best dreamed is the likest to the waking truth!"

"When you are quite dead, you will dream no false dream. The soul that is true can generate nothing that is not true, neither can the false enter it."

"But, sir," I faltered, "how am I to distinguish betwixt the true and the false where both alike seem real?"

"Do you not understand?" he returned, with a smile that might have slain all the sorrows of all his children. "You *cannot* perfectly distinguish between the true and the false while you are not yet quite dead; neither indeed will you when you are quite dead—that is, quite alive, for then the false will never present itself. At this moment, believe me, you are on your bed in the house of death."

"I am trying hard to believe you, father. I do indeed believe you, although I can neither see nor feel the truth of what you say."

"You are not to blame that you cannot. And because even in a dream you believe me, I will help you.—Put forth your left hand open, and close it gently : it will clasp the hand of your Lona, who lies asleep where you lie dreaming you are awake."

I put forth my hand : it closed on the hand of Lona, firm and soft and deathless.

"But, father," I cried, "she is warm!"

"Your hand is as warm to hers. Cold is a thing unknown in our country. Neither she nor you are yet in the fields of home, but each to each is alive and warm and healthful."

Then my heart was glad. But immediately supervened a sharp-stinging doubt.

"Father," I said, "forgive me, but how am I to know surely that this also is not a part of the lovely dream in which I am now walking with thyself?"

"Thou doubtest because thou lovest the truth. Some would willingly believe life but a phantasm, if only it might for ever afford them a world of pleasant dreams : thou art not of such! Be content for a while not to know surely. The hour will come, and that ere long, when, being true, thou shalt behold the very truth, and doubt will be for ever dead. Scarce, then, wilt thou be able to recall the features of the phantom. Thou wilt then know that which thou canst not now dream. Thou hast not yet looked the Truth in the face, hast as yet at best but seen him through a cloud. That which thou seest not, and never didst see save in a glass darkly—that which, indeed, never can be known save by its innate splendour shining straight into pure eyes—that thou canst not but doubt, and art blameless in doubting until thou seest it face to face, when thou wilt no longer be able to doubt it. But to him who has once seen even a shadow only of the truth, and, even but hoping he has seen it when it is present no longer, tries to obey it—to him the real vision, the Truth himself, will come, and depart no more, but abide with him for ever."

"I think I see, father," I said; "I think I understand."

"Then remember, and recall. Trials yet await thee, heavy, of a nature thou knowest not now. Remember the things thou hast seen. Truly thou knowest not those things, but thou knowest what they have seemed, what they have meant to thee! Remember also the things thou shalt yet see. Truth is all in all; and the truth of things lies, at once hid and revealed, in their seeming."

"How can that be, father?" I said, and raised my eyes with the question; for I had been listening with downbent head, aware of nothing but the voice of Adam.

He was gone; in my ears was nought but the sounding silence of the swift-flowing waters. I stretched forth my hands to find him, but no answering touch met their seeking. I was alone— alone in the land of dreams! To myself I seemed wide awake, but I believed I was in a dream, because he had told me so.

Even in a dream, however, the dreamer must do something! he cannot sit down and refuse to stir until the dream grow weary of him and depart: I took up my wandering, and went on.

Many channels I crossed, and came to a wider space of rock; there, dreaming I was weary, I laid myself down, and longed to be awake.

I was about to rise and resume my journey, when I discovered that I lay beside a pit in the rock, whose mouth was like that of a grave. It was deep and dark; I could see no bottom.

Now in the dreams of my childhood I had found that a fall invariably woke me, and would, therefore, when desiring to discontinue a dream, seek some eminence whence to cast myself down that I might wake : with one glance at the peaceful heavens, and one at the rushing waters, I rolled myself over the edge of the pit.

For a moment consciousness left me. When it returned, I stood in the garret of my own house, in the little wooden chamber of the cowl and the mirror.

Unspeakable despair, hopelessness blank and dreary, invaded me with the knowledge : between me and my Lona lay an abyss impassable ! stretched a distance no chain could measure ! Space and Time and Mode of Being, as with walls of adamant unscalable, impenetrable, shut me in from that gulf ! True, it might yet be in my power to pass again through the door of light, and journey back to the chamber of the dead; and if so, I was parted from that chamber only by a wide heath, and by the pale, starry night betwixt me and the sun, which alone could open for me the mirror-door, and was now far away on the other side of the world! but an immeasurably wider gulf sank between us in this—that she was asleep and I was awake! that I was no longer worthy to share with her that sleep, and could no longer hope to awake from it with her! For truly I was much to blame: I had fled from my dream! The dream was not of my making, any more than was my life: I ought to have seen it to the end! and in fleeing from it, I had left the holy sleep itself behind me! —I would go back to Adam, tell him the truth, and bow to his decree!

I crept to my chamber, threw myself on my bed, and passed a dreamless night.

I rose, and listlessly sought the library. On the way I met no one; the house seemed dead. I sat down with a book to await the noontide: not a sentence could I understand! The mutilated manuscript offered itself from the masked door: the sight of it sickened me; what to me was the princess with her devilry!

I rose and looked out of a window. It was a brilliant morning. With a great rush the fountain shot high, and fell roaring back. The sun sat in its feathery top. Not a bird sang, not a creature was to be seen. Raven nor librarian came near me. The world was dead about me. I took another book, sat down again, and went on waiting.

Noon was near. I went up the stairs to the dumb, shadowy roof. I closed behind me the door into the wooden chamber, and turned to open the door out of a dreary world.

I left the chamber with a heart of stone. Do what I might, all was fruitless. I pulled the chains; adjusted and re-adjusted the hood; arranged and re-arranged the mirrors; no result followed. I waited and waited to give the vision time; it would not come; the mirror stood blank; nothing lay in its dim old depth but the mirror opposite and my haggard face.

I went back to the library. There the books were hateful to me—for I had once loved them.

That night I lay awake from down-lying to uprising, and the next day renewed my endeavours with the mystic door. But all was yet in vain. How the hours went I cannot think. No one came nigh me; not a sound from the house below entered my ears. Not once did I feel weary—only desolate, drearily desolate.

I passed a second sleepless night. In the morning I went for the last time to the chamber in the roof, and for the last time sought an open door : there was none. My heart died within me. I had lost my Lona !

Was she anywhere? had she ever been, save in the mouldering cells of my brain? "I must die one day," I thought, "and then, straight from my death-bed, I will set out to find her ! If she is not, I will go to the Father and say—'Even thou canst not help me : let me cease, I pray thee !' "

CHAPTER XLIV

THE WAKING

THE FOURTH NIGHT I seemed to fall asleep, and that night woke indeed. I opened my eyes and knew, although all was dark around me, that I lay in the house of death, and that every moment since there I fell asleep I had been dreaming, and now first was awake. "At last !" I said to my heart, and it leaped for joy. I turned my eyes; Lona stood by my couch, waiting for me ! I had never lost her !—only for a little time lost the sight of her ! Truly I needed not have lamented her so sorely !

It was dark, as I say, but I saw her : *she* was not dark ! Her eyes shone with the radiance of the Mother's, and the same light issued from her face—nor from her face only, for her death-dress, filled with the light of her body now tenfold awake in the power of its resurrection, was white as snow and glistering. She fell asleep a girl; she awoke a woman, ripe with the loveliness of the life essential. I folded her in my arms, and knew that I lived indeed.

"I woke first !" she said, with a wondering smile.

"You did, my love, and woke me !"

"I only looked at you and waited," she answered.

The candle came floating toward us through the dark, and in a few moments Adam and Eve and Mara were with us. They greeted us with a quiet good-morning and a smile : they were used to such wakings !

"I hope you have had a pleasant darkness !" said the Mother.

"Not very," I answered, "but the waking from it is heavenly."

"It is but begun," she rejoined; "you are hardly yet awake!"

"He is at least clothed-upon with Death, which is the radiant garment of Life," said Adam.

He embraced Lona his child, put an arm around me, looked a moment or two inquiringly at the princess, and patted the head of the leopardess.

"I think we shall meet you two again before long," he said, looking first at Lona, then at me.

"Have we to die again?" I asked.

"No," he answered, with a smile like the Mother's; "you have died into life, and will die no more; you have only to keep dead. Once dying as we die here, all the dying is over. Now you have only to live, and that you must, with all your blessed might. The more you live, the stronger you become to live."

"But shall I not grow weary with living so strong?" I said. "What if I cease to live with all my might?"

"It needs but the will, and the strength is there!" said the Mother. "Pure life has no weakness to grow weary withal. *The* Life keeps generating ours.—Those who will not die, die many times, die constantly, keep dying deeper, never have done dying; here all is upwardness and love and gladness."

She ceased with a smile and a look that seemed to say, "We are mother and son; we understand each other! Between us no farewell is possible."

Mara kissed me on the forehead, and said, gayly,

"I told you, brother, all would be well!—When next you would comfort, say, 'What will be well, is even now well.' "

She gave a little sigh, and I thought it meant, "But they will not believe you!"

"—You know me now!" she ended, with a smile like her mother's.

"I know you!" I answered: "you are the voice that cried in the wilderness before ever the Baptist came! you are the shepherd whose wolves hunt the wandering sheep home ere the shadow rise and the night grow dark!"

"My work will one day be over," she said, "and then I shall be glad with the gladness of the great shepherd who sent me."

"All the night long the morning is at hand," said Adam.

"What is that flapping of wings I hear?" I asked.

"The Shadow is hovering," replied Adam : "there is one here whom he counts his own! But ours once, never more can she be his!"

I turned to look on the faces of my father and mother, and kiss them ere we went : their couches were empty save of the Little Ones who had with love's boldness appropriated their hospitality! For an instant that awful dream of desolation overshadowed me, and I turned aside.

"What is it, my heart?" said Lona.

"Their empty places frightened me," I answered.

"They are up and away long ago," said Adam. "They kissed you ere they went, and whispered, 'Come soon.'"

"And I neither to feel nor hear them!" I murmured.

"How could you—far away in your dreary old house! You thought the dreadful place had you once more! Now go and find them.—Your parents, my child," he added, turning to Lona, "must come and find you!"

The hour of our departure was at hand. Lona went to the couch of the mother who had slain her, and kissed her tenderly —then laid herself in her father's arms.

"That kiss will draw her homeward, my Lona!" said Adam.

"Who were her parents?" asked Lona.

"My father," answered Adam, "is her father also."

She turned and laid her hand in mine.

I kneeled and humbly thanked the three for helping me to die. Lona knelt beside me, and they all breathed upon us.

"Hark! I hear the sun," said Adam.

I listened : he was coming with the rush as of a thousand times ten thousand far-off wings, with the roar of a molten and flaming world millions upon millions of miles away. His approach was a crescendo chord of a hundred harmonies.

The three looked at each other and smiled, and that smile went floating heavenward a three-petaled flower, the family's morning thanksgiving. From their mouths and their faces it spread over their bodies and shone through their garments. Ere I could say, "Lo, they change!" Adam and Eve stood before me the angels of the resurrection, and Mara was the Magdalene with them at the sepulchre. The countenance of Adam was like lightning, and Eve held a napkin that flung flakes of splendour about the place.

A wind began to moan in pulsing gusts.

"You hear his wings now!" said Adam; and I knew he did not mean the wings of the morning.

"It is the great Shadow stirring to depart," he went on. "Wretched creature, he has himself within him, and cannot rest!"

"But is there not in him something deeper yet?" I asked.

"Without a substance," he answered, "a shadow cannot be— yea, or without a light behind the substance!"

He listened for a moment, then called out, with a glad smile,

"Hark to the golden cock! Silent and motionless for millions of years has he stood on the clock of the universe; now at last he is flapping his wings! now will he begin to crow! and at intervals will men hear him until the dawn of the day eternal."

I listened. Far away—as in the heart of an æonian silence, I heard the clear jubilant outcry of the golden throat. It hurled defiance at death and the dark; sang infinite hope, and coming calm. It was the "expectation of the creature" finding at last a voice; the cry of a chaos that would be a kingdom!

Then I heard a great flapping.

"The black bat is flown!" said Mara.

"Amen, golden cock, bird of God!" cried Adam, and the words rang through the house of silence, and went up into the airy regions.

At his *Amen*—like doves arising on wings of silver from among the potsherds, up sprang the Little Ones to their knees on their beds, calling aloud,

"Crow! crow again, golden cock!"—as if they had both seen and heard him in their dreams.

Then each turned and looked at the sleeping bed-fellow, gazed a moment with loving eyes, kissed the silent companion of the night, and sprang from the couch. The Little Ones who had lain down beside my father and mother gazed blank and sad for a moment at their empty places, then slid slowly to the floor. There they fell each into the other's arms, as if then first, each by the other's eyes, assured they were alive and awake. Suddenly spying Lona, they came running, radiant with bliss, to embrace her. Odu, catching sight of the leopardess on the feet of the princess, bounded to her next, and throwing an arm over the great sleeping head, fondled and kissed it.

"Wake up, wake up, darling!" he cried; "it is time to wake!"

The leopardess did not move.

"She has slept herself cold!" he said to Mara, with an upcast look of appealing consternation.

"She is waiting for the princess to wake, my child," said Mara.

Odu looked at the princess, and saw beside her, still asleep, two of his companions. He flew at them.

"Wake up! wake up!" he cried, and pushed and pulled, now this one, now that.

But soon he began to look troubled, and turned to me with misty eyes.

"They will not wake!" he said. "And why are they so cold?"

"They too are waiting for the princess," I answered.

He stretched across, and laid his hand on her face.

"She is cold too! What is it?" he cried—and looked round in wondering dismay.

Adam went to him.

"Her wake is not ripe yet," he said : "she is busy forgetting. When she has forgotten enough to remember enough, then she will soon be ripe, and wake."

"And remember?"

"Yes—but not too much at once though."

"But the golden cock has crown!" argued the child, and fell again upon his companions.

"Peter! Peter! Crispy!" he cried. "Wake up, Peter! wake up, Crispy! We are all awake but you two! The gold cock has crown *so* loud! The sun is awake and coming! Oh, why *won't* you wake?"

But Peter would not wake, neither would Crispy, and Odu wept outright at last.

"Let them sleep, darling!" said Adam. "You would not like the princess to wake and find nobody? They are quite happy. So is the leopardess."

He was comforted, and wiped his eyes as if he had been all his life used to weeping and wiping, though now first he had tears wherewith to weep—soon to be wiped altogether away.

We followed Eve to the cottage. There she offered us neither bread nor wine, but stood radiantly desiring our departure. So, with never a word of farewell, we went out. The horse and the elephants were at the door, waiting for us. We were too happy to mount them, and they followed us.

CHAPTER XLV

THE JOURNEY HOME

It had ceased to be dark; we walked in a dim twilight, breathing through the dimness the breath of the spring. A wondrous change had passed upon the world—or was it not rather that a change more marvellous had taken place in us? Without light enough in the sky or the air to reveal anything, every heather-bush, every small shrub, every blade of grass was perfectly visible—either by light that went out from it, as fire from the bush Moses saw in the desert, or by light that went out of our eyes. Nothing cast a shadow; all things interchanged a little light. Every growing thing showed me, by its shape and colour, its indwelling idea—the informing thought, that is, which was its being, and sent it out. My bare feet seemed to love every plant they trod upon. The world and my being, its life and mine, were one. The microcosm and macrocosm were at length atoned, at length in harmony! I lived in everything; everything entered and lived in me. To be aware of a thing, was to know its life at once and mine, to know whence we came, and where we were at home—was to know that we are all what we are, because Another is what he is! Sense after sense, hitherto asleep, awoke in me—sense after sense indescribable, because no correspondent words, no likenesses or imaginations exist, wherewithal to describe them. Full indeed—yet ever expanding, ever making room to receive—was the conscious being where things kept entering by so many open doors! When a little breeze brushing a bush of heather set its purple bells a ringing, I was myself in the joy of the bells, myself in the joy of the breeze to which responded their sweet *tin-tinning*,* myself in the joy of the sense, and of the soul that received all the joys together. To everything glad I lent the hall of my being wherein to revel. I was a peaceful ocean upon which the ground-swell of a living joy was continually lifting new waves; yet was the joy ever the same joy, the

---

* Tin tin sonando con si dolce nota
  Che 'l ben disposto spirto d' amor turge. *Del Paradiso*, x. 142.

eternal joy, with tens of thousands of changing forms. Life was a cosmic holiday.

Now I knew that life and truth were one; that life mere and pure is in itself bliss; that where being is not bliss, it is not life, but life-in-death. Every inspiration of the dark wind that blew where it listed, went out a sigh of thanksgiving. At last I was! I lived, and nothing could touch my life! My darling walked beside me, and we were on our way home to the Father!

So much was ours ere ever the first sun rose upon our freedom : what must not the eternal day bring with it!

We came to the fearful hollow where once had wallowed the monsters of the earth : it was indeed, as I had beheld it in my dream, a lovely lake. I gazed into its pellucid depths. A whirlpool had swept out the soil in which the abortions burrowed, and at the bottom lay visible the whole horrid brood : a dim greenish light pervaded the crystalline water, and revealed every hideous form beneath it. Coiled in spires, folded in layers, knotted on themselves, or "extended long and large," they weltered in motionless heaps—shapes more fantastic in ghoulish, blasting dismay, than ever wine-sodden brain of exhausted poet fevered into misbeing. He who dived in the swirling Maelstrom saw none to compare with them in horror; tentacular convolutions, tumid bulges, glaring orbs of sepian deformity, would have looked to him innocence beside such incarnations of hatefulness —every head the wicked flower that, bursting from an abominable stalk, perfected its evil significance.

Not one of them moved as we passed. But they were not dead. So long as exist men and women of unwholesome mind, that lake will still be peopled with loathsomenesses.

But hark the herald of the sun, the auroral wind, softly trumpeting his approach! The master-minister of the human tabernacle is at hand! Heaping before his prow a huge ripple-fretted wave of crimson and gold, he rushes aloft, as if new launched from the urging hand of his maker into the upper sea —pauses, and looks down on the world. White-raving storm of molten metals, he is but a coal from the altar of the Father's never-ending sacrifice to his children. See every little flower straighten its stalk, lift up its neck, and with outstretched head stand expectant : something more than the sun, greater than the light, is coming, is coming—none the less surely coming that it is long upon the road! What matters to-day, or to-morrow, or ten thousand years to Life himself, to Love himself! He is coming, is coming, and the necks of all humanity are stretched out to see him come! Every morning will they thus outstretch themselves, every evening will they droop and wait—until he comes.—Is this but an air-drawn vision? When he comes, will he indeed find them watching thus?

It was a glorious resurrection-morning. The night had been spent in preparing it!

The children went gamboling before, and the beasts came after us. Fluttering butterflies, darting dragon-flies hovered or shot hither and thither about our heads, a cloud of colours and flashes, now descending upon us like a snow-storm of rainbow flakes, now rising into the humid air like a rolling vapour of embodied odours. It was a summer-day more like itself, that is, more ideal, than ever man that had not died found summer-day in any world. I walked on the new earth, under the new heaven, and found them the same as the old, save that now they opened their minds to me, and I saw into them. Now, the soul of everything I met came out to greet me and make friends with me, telling me we came from the same, and meant the same. I was going to him, they said, with whom they always were, and whom they always meant; they were, they said, lightnings that took shape as they flashed from him to his. The dark rocks drank like sponges the rays that showered upon them; the great world soaked up the light, and sent out the living. Two joy-fires were Lona and I. Earth breathed heavenward her sweet-savoured smoke; we breathed homeward our longing desires. For thanksgiving, our very consciousness was that.

We came to the channels, once so dry and wearyful: they ran and flashed and foamed with living water that shouted in its gladness! Far as the eye could see, all was a rushing, roaring, dashing river of water made vocal by its rocks.

We did not cross it, but "walked in glory and in joy" up its right bank, until we reached the great cataract at the foot of the sandy desert, where, roaring and swirling and dropping sheer, the river divided into its two branches. There we climbed the height—and found no desert: through grassy plains, between grassy banks, flowed the deep, wide, silent river full to the brim.

Then first to the Little Ones was revealed the glory of God in the limpid flow of water. Instinctively they plunged and swam, and the beasts followed them.

The desert rejoiced and blossomed as the rose. Wide forests had sprung up, their whole undergrowth flowering shrubs peopled with song-birds. Every thicket gave birth to a rivulet, and every rivulet to its water-song.

The place of the buried hand gave no sign. Beyond and still beyond, the river came in full volume from afar. Up and up we went, now along grassy margin, and now through forest of gracious trees. The grass grew sweeter and its flowers more lovely and various as we went; the trees grew larger, and the wind fuller of messages.

We came at length to a forest whose trees were greater, grander, and more beautiful than any we had yet seen. Their live pillars upheaved a thick embowed roof, betwixt whose leaves and blossoms hardly a sunbeam filtered. Into the rafters of this aerial vault the children climbed, and through them went scrambling and leaping in a land of bloom, shouting to the unseen elephants below, and hearing them trumpet their replies. The conversations between them Lona understood while I but guessed at them blunderingly. The Little Ones chased the squirrels, and the squirrels, frolicking, drew them on—always at length allowing themselves to be caught and petted. Often would some bird, lovely in plumage and form, light upon one of them, sing a song of what was coming, and fly away. Not one monkey of any sort could they see.

CHAPTER XLVI

THE CITY

LONA AND I, WHO walked below, heard at last a great shout overhead, and in a moment or two the Little Ones began to come dropping down from the foliage with the news that, climbing to the top of a tree yet taller than the rest, they had descried, far across the plain, a curious something on the side of a solitary mountain—which mountain, they said, rose and rose, until the sky gathered thick to keep it down, and knocked its top off.

"It may be a city," they said, "but it is not at all like Bulika."

I went up to look, and saw a great city, ascending into blue clouds, where I could not distinguish mountain from sky and cloud, or rocks from dwellings. Cloud and mountain and sky, palace and precipice mingled in a seeming chaos of broken shadow and shine.

I descended, the Little Ones came with me, and together we sped on faster. They grew yet merrier as they went, leading the way, and never looking behind them. The river grew lovelier and lovelier, until I knew that never before had I seen real water. Nothing in this world is more than *like* it.

By and by we could from the plain see the city among the blue clouds. But other clouds were gathering around a lofty tower— or was it a rock?—that stood above the city, nearer the crest of the mountain. Gray, and dark gray, and purple, they writhed in confused, contrariant motions, and tossed up a vaporous foam, while spots in them gyrated like whirlpools. At length issued a dazzling flash, which seemed for a moment to play about the Little Ones in front of us. Blinding darkness followed, but through it we heard their voices, low with delight.

"Did you see?"

"I saw."

"What did you see?"

"The beautifullest man."

"I heard him speak!"

"I didn't : what did he say?"

Here answered the smallest and most childish of the voices— that of Luva :—

"He said, ' 'Ou's all mine's, 'ickle ones : come along ! ' "

I had seen the lightning, but heard no words; Lona saw and heard with the children. A second flash came, and my eyes, though not my ears, were opened. The great quivering light was compact of angel-faces. They lamped themselves visible, and vanished.

A third flash came; its substance and radiance were human.

"I see my mother !" I cried.

"I see lots o' mothers !" said Luva.

Once more the cloud flashed—all kinds of creatures—horses

and elephants, lions and dogs—oh, such beasts! And such birds!
—great birds whose wings gleamed singly every colour gathered
in sunset or rainbow! little birds whose feathers sparkled as with
all the precious stones of the hoarding earth!—silvery cranes;
red flamingoes; opal pigeons; peacocks gorgeous in gold and
green and blue; jewelly humming birds!—great-winged butterflies; lithe-volumed creeping things—all in one heavenly flash!

"I see that serpents grow birds here, as caterpillars used to
grow butterflies!" remarked Lona.

"I saw my white pony, that died when I was a child.—I
needn't have been so sorry; I should just have waited!" I said.

Thunder, clap or roll, there had been none. And now came
a sweet rain, filling the atmosphere with a caressing coolness.
We breathed deep, and stepped out with stronger strides. The
falling drops flashed the colours of all the waked up gems of the
earth, and a mighty rainbow spanned the city.

The blue clouds gathered thicker; the rain fell in torrents;
the children exulted and ran; it was all we could do to keep
them in sight.

With silent, radiant roll, the river swept onward, filling to the
margin its smooth, soft, yielding channel. For, instead of rock or
shingle or sand, it flowed over grass in which grew primroses and
daisies, crocuses and narcissi, pimpernels and anemones, a starry
multitude, large and bright through the brilliant water. The river
had gathered no turbid cloudiness from the rain, not even a
tinge of yellow or brown; the delicate mass shone with the pale
berylline gleam that ascended from its deep, dainty bed.

Drawing nearer to the mountain, we saw that the river came
from its very peak, and rushed in full volume through the main
street of the city. It descended to the gate by a stair of deep
and wide steps, mingled of porphyry and serpentine, which continued to the foot of the mountain. There arriving we found
shallower steps on both banks, leading up to the gate, and along
the ascending street. Without the briefest halt, the Little Ones
ran straight up the stair to the gate, which stood open.

Outside, on the landing, sat the portress, a woman-angel of
dark visage, leaning her shadowed brow on her idle hand. The
children rushed upon her, covering her with caresses, and ere she
understood, they had taken heaven by surprise, and were already
in the city, still mounting the stair by the side of the descending

torrent. A great angel, attended by a company of shining ones, came down to meet and receive them, but merrily evading them all, up still they ran. In merry dance, however, a group of woman-angels descended upon them, and in a moment they were fettered in heavenly arms. The radiants carried them away, and I saw them no more.

"Ah!" said the mighty angel, continuing his descent to meet us who were now almost at the gate and within hearing of his word, "this is well! these are soldiers to take heaven itself by storm!—I hear of a horde of black bats on the frontiers : these will make short work with such!"

Seeing the horse and the elephants clambering up behind us— "Take those animals to the royal stables," he added; "there tend them; then turn them into the king's forest."

"Welcome home!" he said to us, bending low with the sweetest smile.

Immediately he turned and led the way higher. The scales of his armour flashed like flakes of lightning.

Thought cannot form itself to tell what I felt, thus received by the officers of heaven.* All I wanted and knew not, must be on its way to me!

We stood for a moment at the gate whence issued roaring the radiant river. I know not whence came the stones that fashioned it, but among them I saw the prototypes of all the gems I had loved on earth—far more beautiful than they, for these were living stones—such in which I saw, not the intent alone, but the intender too; not the idea alone, but the imbodier present, the operant outsender : nothing in this kingdom was dead; nothing was mere; nothing only a thing.

We went up through the city and passed out. There was no wall on the upper side, but a huge pile of broken rocks, upsloping like the moraine of an eternal glacier; and through the openings between the rocks, the river came billowing out. On their top I could dimly discern what seemed three or four great steps of a stair, disappearing in a cloud white as snow; and above the steps I saw, but with my mind's eye only, as it were a grand old chair, the throne of the Ancient of Days. Over and under and between those steps issued, plenteously, unceasingly new-born, the river of the water of life.

* Oma' vedrai di sì fatti uficiali.—*Del Purgatorio*, ii. 30.

The great angel could guide us no farther : those rocks we must ascend alone!

My heart beating with hope and desire, I held faster the hand of my Lona, and we began to climb; but soon we let each other go, to use hands as well as feet in the toilsome ascent of the huge stones. At length we drew near the cloud, which hung down the steps like the borders of a garment, passed through the fringe, and entered the deep folds. A hand, warm and strong, laid hold of mine, and drew me to a little door with a golden lock. The door opened; the hand let mine go, and pushed me gently through. I turned quickly, and saw the board of a large book in the act of closing behind me. I stood alone in my library.

CHAPTER XLVII

THE "ENDLESS ENDING"

As yet I have not found Lona, but Mara is much with me. She has taught me many things, and is teaching me more.

Can it be that that last waking also was in the dream? that I am still in the chamber of death, asleep and dreaming, not yet ripe enough to wake? Or can it be that I did not go to sleep outright and heartily, and so have come awake too soon? If that waking was itself but a dream, surely it was a dream of a better waking yet to come, and I have not been the sport of a false vision! Such a dream must have yet lovelier truth at the heart of its dreaming!

In moments of doubt I cry,

"Could God Himself create such lovely things as I dreamed?"

"Whence then came thy dream?" answers Hope.

"Out of my dark self, into the light of my consciousness."

"But whence first into thy dark self?" rejoins Hope.

"My brain was its mother, and the fever in my blood its father."

"Say rather," suggests Hope, "thy brain was the violin whence it issued, and the fever in thy blood the bow that drew it forth.— But who made the violin? and who guided the bow across its strings? Say rather, again—who set the song birds each on its bough in the tree of life, and startled each in its order from its perch? Whence came the fantasia? and whence the life that danced thereto? Didst *thou* say, in the dark of thy own unconscious self, 'Let beauty be; let truth seem!' and straightway beauty was, and truth but seemed?"

Man dreams and desires; God broods and wills and quickens.

When a man dreams his own dream, he is the sport of his dream; when Another gives it him, that Other is able to fulfil it.

I have never again sought the mirror. The hand sent me back : I will not go out again by that door! "All the days of my appointed time will I wait till my change come."

Now and then, when I look round on my books, they seem to waver as if a wind rippled their solid mass, and another world were about to break through. Sometimes when I am abroad, a like thing takes place; the heavens and the earth, the trees and the grass appear for a moment to shake as if about to pass away; then, lo, they have settled again into the old familiar face! At times I seem to hear whisperings around me, as if some that loved me were talking of me; but when I would distinguish the words, they cease, and all is very still. I know not whether these things rise in my brain, or enter it from without. I do not seek them; they come, and I let them go.

Strange dim memories, which will not abide identification, often, through misty windows of the past, look out upon me in the broad daylight, but I never dream now. It may be, notwithstanding, that, when most awake, I am only dreaming the more! But when I wake at last into that life which, as a mother her child, carries this life in its bosom, I shall know that I wake, and shall doubt no more.

I wait; asleep or awake, I wait.

Novalis says, "Our life is no dream, but it should and will perhaps become one."